POISON AND OPIUM

毒とアヘン

ACT II:

TALISMANS OF SIN

ALYSSA LAUSENG

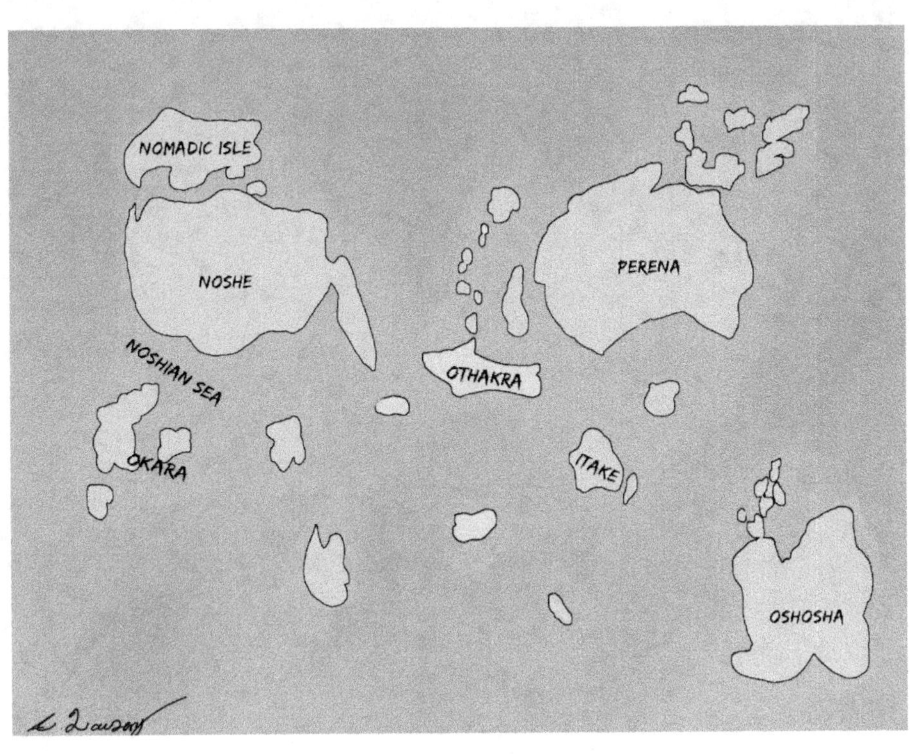

NOMADIC ISLE
NOSHE
NOSHIAN SEA
OKARA
OTHAKRA
PERENA
ITAKE
OSHOSHA

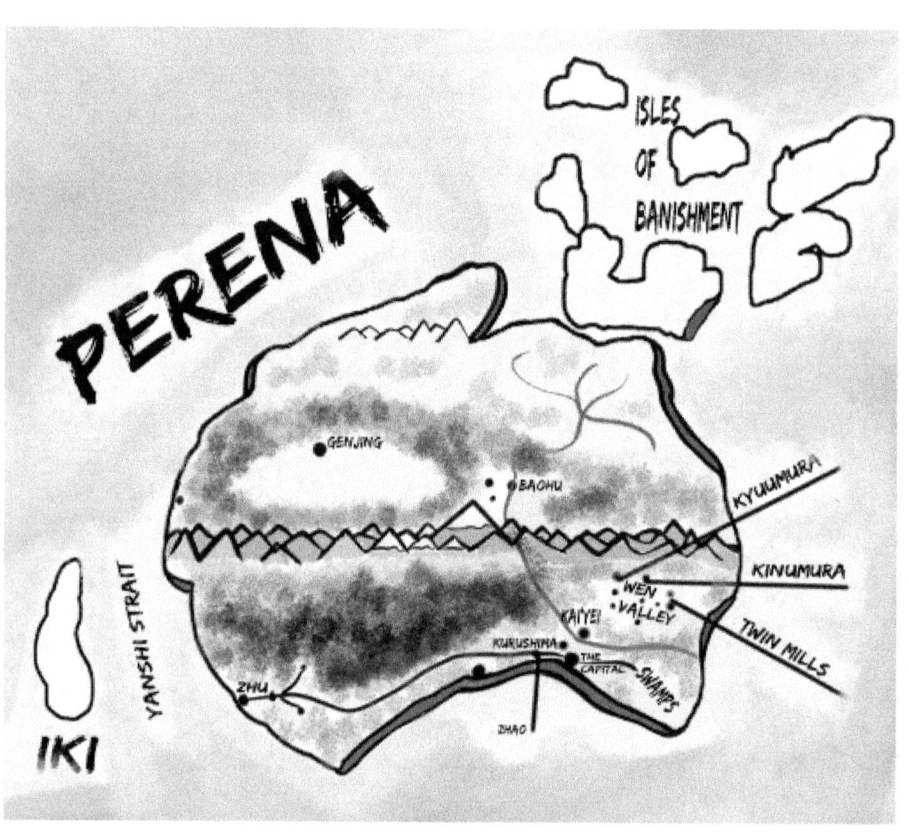
PERENA
ISLES OF BANISHMENT
GENJING
BAOHU
KYUUMURA
KINUMURA
WEN VALLEY
KAIYEI
TWIN MILLS
KURUSHIMA
THE CAPITAL
SWAMPS
YANSHI STRAIT
ZHU
ZHAO
IKI

This book contains material that may make readers uncomfortable. This list is to give everyone a broad idea of what they can expect to find, but not necessarily comprehensive. Let's dive in:

Violence (stabbing, fighting, hitting)
Imprisonment
Blood
Murder
Death
Suicide
Underage drinking
Underage smoking
Drug use
Self-harm
One (1) nonconsensual kiss
Brief mention of CSA

CONTENTS

WHAT A FUCKING DISASTER.

Within a spinning blur of seconds, a simple retrieval mission had become infinitely more complex, and Obito's thoughts kept circling back to the same conclusion: this was a fucking disaster. Whatever Master Yujin sent him and Daisuke to bring back from Zhu was clearly not a simple artifact as they'd been led to believe, and on top of it being stolen from their possession with humiliating ease, his partner was missing. That was dangerous enough for any young onmitsu in this situation, but a multitude of factors stacked against Daisuke meant they were racing an invisible clock to reunite. However, hours of hunting through Perena's most prominent slave port hadn't shown Obito even a single trace of his friend, leaving his anxieties to fester the longer he looked.

He glanced toward the sun, now an orange sphere nestled low in a pink sky and wrapped in a sheen of haze against distant, heavy purple clouds—wintry weather would come early this year. The skies also told him he'd have no choice but to abandon his search soon, as trying to find Daisuke in the dark wasn't going to yield different results.

The pair had previously designated the inn where they were staying as a place to meet should they become separated; reluctant as he was, Obito eventually convinced himself it'd be wise to return to this point. Although he doubted his luck would change much, it was a better plan than aimlessly wandering Zhu's streets.

Unfortunately, it also looked like his best option, as asking anything of the public sector seemed pointless. The average citizen rarely took note of differences between each Northern Nomad they encountered, and one never knew where certain parts of society's underbelly lurked in a crowd, namely the slave hunters who had an undeniable presence in the city. Obito *thought* he'd understood why Daisuke was so ill at ease throughout their westward travels from the Capital, and had tried not to be dismissive of his friend's many, valid concerns about staying in Zhu. Being faced with reality felt so much worse than anything he could've imagined. Now that he had to entertain possibilities of where his companion could've gone, abject horror wrapped around him as worry relentlessly squeezed at his insides.

"Gods be damned," he cursed between gritted teeth as he pulled his fingers through his dark hair, trying to suppress his renewed agitation—letting panic win wouldn't help.

He chose to keep the few remaining fragments of his rationality in check by retracing his steps one last time. When he arrived at his final stop, a fresh wave of disappointment sank his heart into the pit of his stomach like a stone. He helplessly stared at the potter's demolished home as he had hours before; it still lay in a smoldering heap of glowing embers, debris, and rubble from the strange black flames which consumed it earlier. Crowds that gathered to mourn or speculate didn't look as if they planned to disperse anytime soon, but Daisuke wasn't among them, nor was he nearby from what Obito could see.

He'd at least managed to recover his tanto from the alley where they'd encountered the cloaked figures, but it was one success while so many other things had gone wrong. With his partner missing during the largest slave auction day on the continent, two civilians senselessly and brutally killed, and the focus of their assignment stolen, calling the whole operation an abysmal failure didn't seem to lend the gravity of the situation any justice.

He turned away from the destroyed home to return to the inn as nighttime shadows fully consumed the city. Originally, he and Daisuke had planned to rush home with the strange artifact—he supposed that, even though the situation had changed, he still should've been making those preparations. According to onmitsu protocol, should an operative become separated from his teammate in a highly dangerous situation, they needed to seek reinforcements from other spies straightaway. As far as Obito knew, the Capital was his closest hope. He ruled against going back as soon as the thought crossed his mind—no amount of incompetence or unwillingness from the local infantry would make abandoning his friend an option. By the time he returned home and relayed what little information he had, Daisuke could be miles away or worse before anyone investigated his whereabouts. Even if Master Yujin showed immense concern and sent out teams right away, there was no guarantee anyone could find him by then.

Speaking of the Intelligence Master, Obito knew he didn't have a chance of processing events on his own. He *needed* Daisuke to corroborate his story—both for his sanity's sake and preserving his good reputation with Master Yujin.

The innkeeper's head swiveled around at the jingle of a bell strung to the door when Obito entered the main hall; the tray he held over his head, loaded with foaming tankards of brown ale and delicate sake cups alike, wobbled slightly at the abrupt stop. Obito instinctively tensed, prepared to help the man catch anything that might fall, which thankfully wasn't necessary in the end. The innkeeper gracefully swerved around some tunelessly singing drunks, then dropped off the order before tucking the tray under his arm and marching toward Obito, who had frozen place after accidentally meeting his demanding eyes.

Without a word, he made a subtle motion for Obito to follow him as he passed by, but didn't otherwise acknowledge his younger counterpart until he'd safely slipped behind the counter.

He spoke in a low voice once Obito joined him, "Now, I know there's supposed to be two of you. What happened to your little friend?"

"We...got separated."

Obito hadn't wavered in his previous assessment about not knowing who to trust, but Hayate hadn't shown him or Daisuke an ounce of ill will over the last two weeks; he was aware that one never went anywhere without the other. Moreover, he understood *why*. Obito decided he'd adjust accordingly and leave judgement for what the next few passes in their conversation revealed.

The innkeeper's face set into a stern expression, underlined with a bit of worry he couldn't disguise. "Awfully dangerous for a Northern Nomadic boy to get lost in these parts, you know. Not to mention, probably one of the worst nights for it to happen."

"I'm aware, believe it or not," Obito replied, unable to keep the defensive edge out of his tone as his shoulders reflexively stiffened.

"Easy, easy, I'm not your enemy." Hayate's eyes shifted toward something on his left.

Obito's gaze subconsciously trailed and landed on an ink painting of a higanbana tucked away on a sidewall. By the time he finished absorbing the sight of the spider lily and looked back, Hayate was already busy with another patron, discussing room rates while pumping more of the sour-smelling ale from a tap.

"We both already know where you need to go looking. After all, it's easiest to eliminate the most obvious suspect, first." Hayate leaned forward on his elbow when he was able to continue their discussion. "But, listen, don't let this higanbana get your hopes up. His Highness has greatly limited what I'm allowed to do, and Senator Hajime knows my face—you won't be able to get near his estate if I'm involved."

"It sounds like you have issues with the Senator."

"Where to begin? The man *loathes* me. When I first took Zhu as my post, I kept a close watch over Senator Hajime on Yu—*Master* Yujin's behalf. Local politics and all. Killed a few of his guards, freed dozens of his slaves over time—I...I suppose those are stories for another day, though. Anyway, since His Highness has my neck in a noose nowadays, I'm not as...*able* to get mixed up with the Senator's business." Hayate's face had gone from pride, to amusement, to quiet regret as he spoke.

"Willing," you mean. Obito clenched his jaw to keep the thought from escaping. While he didn't believe it to be wrong, and wasn't against saying it aloud, this wasn't the time to discuss it. His personal feelings aside, he understood why anyone would hesitate to bring themselves under the Emperor's scrutiny—all the gods couldn't help him or Daisuke when Akuwara learned of what happened here. He looked up when Hayate straightened again.

"More to the point," the innkeeper continued, "Your face isn't known. And if you find someone at the barracks who's willing to help, you might be able to get somewhere; like onmitsu, the patrol units here tend to work in pairs. Maybe someone will want to swap with you for a day."

"Are any of the captains worth my time?"

"You would hope. I'm afraid they're nice and snug in the Senator's pocket."

Irritated, Obito rolled his eyes. He thought through their conversation for a moment, then turned toward the rest of the main room, where his eyes subconsciously landed on a city map Hayate nailed to the far wall. Since Okaran products—namely slaves—were among the primary goods Zhu and its surrounding villages provided the rest of Perena, he already held doubts that anyone at the infantry outpost would help. Not many would be willing to pit their livelihoods or reputations against Senator Hajime's influence in the first place; the handful of people who *might* was a number which would fall further when they learned the request was on a

Northern Nomadic person's behalf. It was a grim, infuriating reality, but a wider problem to face in the future.

"I'm sorry I personally can't do more to get involved, but as the senior onmitsu here, I *can* give you full permission to act as you see fit."

Obito barely spared Hayate a glance. "I plan to."

"Fuck," Daisuke moaned as he opened his eyes to the warm glow of a lantern. His head throbbed at the gentle intrusion of light as his surroundings slowly came into focus. The ground beneath him was cold and hard, and he stared at a stone wall as he lay on his side.

He jerked upright at the sudden realization that he wasn't at the inn with Obito, though he instantly regretted it. Not only did his headache worsen, but he had to clutch his right side to calm a sudden jab of pain—he must've landed on his tanto. He could never let Master Yujin know he'd finally learned to keep it at the back of his belt the hard way.

Another surge of panic swelled in his chest when he noted his weapon's absence. He couldn't feel his dagger anywhere on him, and despite how it made his head spin, he quickly looked at the rest of the cramped room. He seemed to be trapped in a cell of sorts. He lurched to his feet and stumbled toward the iron bars, but something heavy on his wrists and arms kept him from moving too far, which was when he finally realized he'd been chained to the cell's back wall. He groaned and gripped the wall beside him for support instead as the pain radiating from his hip to his ribs flared from all the unwanted activity. Broken bits of glass were also digging into his side, a little above the sore spot. An area of sopping wetness on his uniform clung to his skin, which meant the vials he'd stored there had shattered from some sort of impact. They weren't filled with deadly tinctures, thankfully, but the liquids made his fresh cuts burn and itch. He winced at the added weight on his arms when he moved them to assess things. What little was left of the bottles slipped from loops he'd sewn into his uniform when he opened his black gi and shitagi to confirm. He swore under his breath, shook out bigger pieces along with nearly invisible fragments, then braced himself against the cold, stone wall, and brushed his free hand along his side to scrape away anything left. He carefully avoided the large red and purple bruise the tanto left behind.

Everything was still a blurry mess in his mind. A sentient shadow—he couldn't think of another way to describe it—had wrapped around him, rendered him immobile, and ripped him away from Obito as if he'd been sucked into a violent whirlwind. It also took the box containing the stupid artifact they'd retrieved from the potter's house moments beforehand. Evidently, he'd lost consciousness at some point during the chaos. It didn't fill in all the gaps in his memory, or explain how he'd ended up in this situation, but he figured that would come later.

As if on cue, a sudden, visceral image of his father screaming at him while hitting him burst before his eyes; he blinked it away before the memory sank its claws into his psyche. What happened after the shadow grabbed him returned with pervasive clarity. It pulled him under a shroud of intense, dark melancholy that challenged his will to live as it showed him more than he could bear of similar incidents from his life. Every shade of humanity's ugliness he'd experienced since childhood, all the deep heartache and immense anger left behind by parents who never showed affection or mercy—the gloom forced him to feel every ounce of pain he hid beneath a stubborn and fiery surface until it left him breathless. Then, just as unexpectedly as it began, everything went black, and he'd awoken here.

Unfortunately, he griped, grunting in discomfort as he made himself stand straight so he could take in his surroundings again. Across from him was a small bench where his tanto rested. Above it was a much more menacing sight. Iron hooks held several pairs of shackles and leather collars, which meant he wasn't being detained in a holding cell at the military barracks. He'd been taken by a slaver. Whoever this person was, they obviously weren't inexperienced in owning—or capturing—slaves. Normally, this observation wouldn't narrow his list of suspects in a city like Zhu, but his mind was already on Senator Hajime. The Senator notoriously caught any unfortunate Northern Nomad he or the bastards he employed encountered, whether they were free or already owned—Daisuke gagged at the word—by someone else. Something about the setup was too sophisticated to lead him anywhere else. From what he knew, few others in this city had the wealth or influence for it, either. Other nobles or otherwise rich families purchased their slaves from the Senator and auctions—no need to spend time or money on things like cells.

Daisuke wasn't left to speculate much longer. Voices drifted nearer to the heavy oak door from a passage on the other side—a man and a woman were arguing in hushed, tense tones as they approached the room. He quickly kicked the glass shards under the few patches of hay scattered around to insulate the floor—*Quite literally, barely even a pot to piss in,* Daisuke thought—and turned to tidy his formals, a short-sleeved all-black uniform he and Obito had both worn for meeting the potter to give themselves an official air. He hoped for a similar result here, though in seeming less disheveled rather than more dignified. Surely, if his appearance thoroughly reflected his military background, the Senator would realize his mistake and release him. In an ideal world, these fatigues would be all the indication needed; since he knew this life was far from it, he prepared to advocate for himself.

He'd just finished adjusting his uniform when a middle-aged couple entered the room, which was also when their argument ended. The graying Giahatian man dressed in elegant green robes carried a ring of keys in his right fist. Deep-set frown lines marked the corners of his mouth; looking at his sour countenance, Daisuke didn't have to dwell on how they'd gotten that way. His gaze went to the noblewoman who stood behind him. Soft, pink rouge on her cheeks complimented the dark green shadow on her eyelids, bringing a deceptive warmth and elegance to her snow-white face. The accompaniment of delicate, silver ornaments in her immaculately styled hair made her look like an Empress—judging by the way she held herself, she seemed to believe she was one. Daisuke wondered how many children's souls she'd eaten for such an appearance.

"Is this the stray they told us about? What a scrawny little thing," she commented dispassionately from behind a dark red folding fan.

Not nearly enough, apparently. Daisuke decided with a grimace.

Senator Hajime—Daisuke thought the man's identity was obvious, unless proven otherwise—glared at his wife. "I don't want another damn house slave taking up food and space. I'll be taking this one the Kurasaki estate tomorrow."

"I'd rather keep him for entertainment. The other ladies will like this one—he's almost as pretty as a girl."

"Frivolous reasons such as those are precisely why women shouldn't be involved in these decisions."

She rolled her eyes, but the Senator was too busy ramming a key into the cell's lock to notice. Metal hinges on the door softly creaked as he stepped inside with Daisuke; the man made sure he carried himself as proudly and intimidatingly as possible, hoping to break his captive's willpower with ease—a damn near laughable assumption in any other situation. Daisuke's eyes narrowed into a defiant glower the longer Senator Hajime sized him up, though his bravery flagged a bit when the man came closer again. His heart leapt into his throat when the Senator reached for him.

"Keep your fucking hands off me, old man!" Daisuke hurriedly stumbled back, chains rattling with his movements until he felt hard rock behind his shoulders.

The noble eyed him with pure disgust and finished crossing the room, which was when Daisuke noticed the handle of a whip poking out of his belt. He didn't need to see the rest of the curled lash to know this man wasn't about to show kindness or listen to pleas for freedom. Still, it didn't stop Daisuke from spitting at him.

"One of those types, I see," the Senator emotionlessly responded before backhanding him, as if it were a subconscious reaction to disobedience. Daisuke felt a distantly familiar jolt of fright as he reeled from the blow; a bitter sense of powerlessness welled in his gut as his memory simultaneously touched dozens of similar moments from his past. "But it's no matter. I've sorted out plenty of slaves in my time—three days without food or water is about all it takes. I don't *usually* need to drag them to the post."

The whip's handle ominously called for Daisuke's attention again as the Senator took out a cloth to clean the spittle from the bridge of his nose; he understood the threat in no uncertain terms, and suspected this was the one time he'd escape such punishment. He swallowed hard.

"Does this mean you've changed your mind, my Lord?" the woman asked, a self-satisfied smirk pulling at her lips.

Senator Hajime merely glanced at her in annoyance as he took a pipe from the inner folds of his shirt. "Woman—"

"Y-you can't do this to me," Daisuke interrupted; gods, this was worse than a nightmare. The Senator looked up from lighting his pipe when he added, "I am a free Imperial citizen enlisted with the military. If you let me go now, I'll pretend we never met, and you never face charges for treason."

"What a nasty little charlatan. You dare defame our honored military?" Hajime's eyes narrowed. He took a long drag off the pipe, then leaned close and blew the smoke in Daisuke's face. As he coughed and waved it away, the Senator unexpectedly grabbed him by the throat and squeezed. "Three days is a long time, boy. No matter how much you lie or fight me, you will learn your place."

Daisuke grabbed the Senator's wrist and made sure his fingernails dug into the man's skin. "F-fuck you."

Hajime released him with a shove. "Chizuru, you've involved yourself. Take responsibility for this thing."

"Of course, my love."

Shock numbed Daisuke's mind as he touched his throat, though his anger quickly revived when the Senator turned away, preparing to leave.

"He always gives me the interesting ones, doesn't he?" Chizuru mused once her husband was gone, fluttering her fan. The air between them changed the second her clever eyes locked on Daisuke again. After another moment, she beckoned for him to come closer, addressing him slowly and emphatically, "Do you have a name?"

Great, she thinks I'm *the stupid one, here.* He clenched his fists, then took a couple of hesitant steps toward her; the Senator was still close enough to call back at a moment's notice, and he wasn't about to push his luck any further.

"My name is Daisuke," he answered shortly, knowing he wouldn't have much time to speak. "Please listen. I—"

"Not a terrible name."

"Thank you?"

"I suppose I don't mind it enough to change it."

Daisuke's jaw fell open in disbelief. Lady Chizuru closed her fan, red-painted lips pursed as she reached toward him. He flinched when her hand brushed his cheek, then froze altogether when she gently gripped his left earlobe, just above his earrings. Her thumb carefully traced over the two smooth black studs, as if she were mesmerized by the piercings.

"I've noticed your kind wearing a few variations of these. Do the earrings have meaning?"

Daisuke pulled away from her unwanted touch with no resistance, then stepped back a few paces for good measure, feeling exceptionally violated. "They acknowledge one's personhood—their body and spirit."

"So, you *do* know. It's an interesting and rather amusing belief, isn't it? Now, then, be a good boy and give them to me."

"...What?" The request was no less than a slap to his face; like all Northern Nomads with their traditional piercings, he'd had these four earrings since infancy. His grandmother had done them herself.

"You just admitted those earrings give you the idea that you are an entity belonging to yourself. None of my slaves should be convinced of such nonsense. In your case, especially, it can only lead to problems, which would be entirely irresponsible on my part." Lady Chizuru's dark lashes lowered as she smoothed the white and gold kimono she wore; a wicked smirk cracked her regal demeanor. "I'll let you out of those nasty, heavy chains if you do."

Daisuke gave no response beyond a derisive snort.

"Come, come, give them over. I don't want to use force, and I'm sure you would like more comfort in this dank little cell—it's going to be quite hard to sleep now that you aren't incapacitated."

As onmitsu, Daisuke was uncomfortably aware that, sometimes, surrender was a calculated matter; cooperating with her now might save him a bit of agony later. Plus, while he loathed admitting it, and doing so made the taste of bile rise in the back of his throat, she was right—the restraints *were* heavy and painful on his wrists. He was achy enough everywhere else to make any small amount of relief tempting.

Although his heart lurched and his hands shook, his fingers uneasily went toward his right ear first.

Chizuru triumphantly bounced the studs in her palm as if they were a set of dice after he handed all four to her, then looked at him with another smug little smirk, though she didn't speak again until after she fulfilled her end of the bargain. The chains dropped to his sides with heavy *clangs* against the floor. "Seems you *can* be reasoned with after all, but that makes me curious. You must be somewhere between thirteen and fifteen, which means you're practically full-grown, yet, you severely lack even the most basic manners. Your previous master couldn't have possibly been so neglectful."

"Previous ma—" He'd been mostly ignoring her, rubbing his wrists to relieve the discomfort, so it took Daisuke a moment to fully process what she'd said. When he finally did, his temper sparked and crackled like fire. He glared at her, much to her entertainment—what a toad. "Lady, I'm no one's slave, and you need to let me go."

"I beg to differ." She pressed the bamboo sides of her folding fan into her powder-white cheek, grinning widely.

"There is a *tattoo* on my arm, you *fucking hag*." He tugged at his right sleeve, which covered the onmitsu higanbana tattoo, for emphasis. "*Clearly*, I am not property."

Lady Chizuru, however, didn't so much as glance at it. Instead, her face went rigid with unspeakable fury. Daisuke recognized his mistake the second the words flew off his tongue, but trapped as he was, he could do little more than stare as he awaited her reaction. Whether from her or someone else, he knew to expect pain. That, at least, he hadn't forgotten.

The noblewoman acted with the speed of a serpent, knuckles turning white as her grip constricted around the fan and she drew her arm back to strike. No amount of anticipation on Daisuke's part helped lessen the impact of hard, flat bamboo on his cheekbone. He cried out involuntarily, though it stopped short when she struck him again. She hit him in the face twice more, before his self-preservation instincts took over, and he remembered to fight back. He targeted the fan and awkwardly caught it between his wrists; they struggled against one another for a moment, but in the end, Daisuke disarmed her and sent her weapon—along with his earrings—clattering across the floor.

His gaze defiantly settled on her once more, desperate not to show how much she'd hurt him or the slight quiver that repressing the pain sent through his body. He'd done the same many times during beatings from his father, as it'd piss Honda off just enough to make him leave, and hoped for the same result now.

When Lady Chizuru elegantly bent to retrieve the fan, he felt he was already beginning to pick apart her puzzle; none of this was a resounding victory in his mind, but at least he'd keep his earrings and a bit of his dignity. Daisuke swallowed to soothe a dry patch forming at the back of his throat.

"I believe that's all for tonight," she announced, tucking away a lock of dark hair which had fallen from its carefully pinned position during their altercation. She smirked. "Perhaps, if you behave less ferally in front of the ladies I'm having around tomorrow, I can convince my husband to give you a little sip of water."

Daisuke snorted again, then glowered at the wall to his left. "As if I trust you."

"Frankly, I don't give a damn if you do, but I suppose it *is* a decision you can still make for yourself, isn't it? However, you would do well to consider how you'd like to be housebroken—that is, by our will or your own. Will you continue to be a stubborn devil? You must be thirsty after tonight's events."

Daisuke subconsciously swallowed another time. She was trying to figure him out, too, and having far more fun with it; a smug grin tugged at her lips when she noticed his throat bob at the mere suggestion of water. He had to let cold logic take over and formulate a plan, as letting his temper run loose clearly wasn't getting him anywhere. His gaze swept over Chizuru and the room once more; she still hadn't pinned her hair correctly again, and he spotted something gleaming in the lantern light on the floor near the cell door. Without a proper assessment of guards or the estate's layout, overpowering the noblewoman was more of a risk than quietly breaking himself out—for now, he'd let her believe she'd won. He made his shoulders slump forward in defeat.

"Fiery ones like you are my favorite to break—it's all the enjoyment I can find around here," Lady Chizuru told him as she stepped out of the cell and locked it once more.

Daisuke leaned against a wall and scowled at her as she placed the key ring on a hook. "What a sad life you must live."

Her steps faltered, but she pointedly ignored him as she went toward the exit. "Remember, you'll be a good little pet for me tomorrow if you want your drink."

Once she was gone, Daisuke stiffly gathered the four scattered earrings and retrieved the hairpin she'd lost during their confrontation. Although he could hardly say he'd come out on top, he still grinned at the thin but sturdy metal pin before his gaze went to the door again.

We'll see about that, won't we? Stupid fucking hag.

INVOLVING THE ONMITSU IN their endeavors was rarely a proud moment for any assassin or footsoldier. In turn, no onmitsu willingly admitted to asking the other two branches for help, nor were they generally fond of the idea. The rightly given reputation both factions had for being bumbling brutes meant it was wiser to avoid needing their assistance altogether when possible. So, when Obito conceded defeat and settled on going to the barracks the following morning, it was only after mentally working through several scenarios he'd drawn up in the last few hours; he'd been awake since long before dawn and no closer to a better solution. Sometimes, surrender included acknowledging one's own limitations. He couldn't take more failure or afford to lose any chances he'd have at finding Daisuke.

He knew not to expect much, due to the inherent distaste for cooperation among the three military branches. Emperor Akuwara saw little reason to curb the issue unless something spun out of control; at that point, all individuals involved suffered major, very public consequences that made Obito wince just to think about. While the Intelligence Master generally punished the onmitsu himself, His Highness was known to personally deal with the team in question if he believed the situation called for it. Obito once again shuddered at the thought of what might happen to him and Daisuke once they returned to the Capital empty-handed, but didn't allow himself to dwell on it for long; without his partner, there was no sense even imagining he'd go home.

When he arrived at the barracks, Hayate's words came to mind once more; rather than wasting his time talking with ranked personnel, he'd have better luck picking off someone lower on the chain of command. Someone with little to no status had more freedom to move about as he pleased, and—hopefully—hadn't been bought by the Senator, but he'd still need a way of speaking with them privately to ask for their help. He glanced at a

13

sign reading "West Barracks" arching over the main entrance as he walked past, then went around back toward the training yard.

The wall surrounding the yard was made of stone, but an iron gate toward the back provided a way to peek inside. When Obito peered through the bars, he found a Perenin soldier who looked to be around seventeen or eighteen, wielding a spear as he moved through a form with ease. The morning sun cast a warm glow on his dark skin and threaded bluish streaks through his neatly tied black hair. Although Obito was sure it wouldn't end well, after spending some time watching the soldier practice, he gently pushed on the unlocked gate. It opened quietly, then slammed with a reverberating *clang* once he slipped through; he froze when the other boy cried out and rounded on him, knuckles white as his fingers clenched around the spear's shaft.

"H-halt! By Imperial order!" He aimed the deadly tip of his shaking weapon at Obito's throat, trying to appear as though the intrusion hadn't nearly sent his soul to the heavens. He crossed some of the space between them, spear still held high and black eyes narrowed. "Citizens are not permitted on barracks grounds. If you need something, go around to the front entrance and request to speak with one of the captains."

Obito put his hands up to show he didn't intend to draw the tanto at his belt, then also stepped forward to close the gap more. "I'm not a private citizen, so surely this isn't an offense."

The other boy blinked, then slowly began lowering his weapon. "You sound like you're from the Capital. Did one of the Generals send you?"

"I'm not infantry, either." Onmitsu protocol stated that one shouldn't boldly declare himself as such, even when among the military ranks, which Obito thought was entirely sensible. He gave the soldier a chance to examine his uniform, though annoyance crawled forward when the other boy dug his spear's blunt end into the partially frosted earth. While it signaled some semblance of amicability, the grin now occupying the soldier's face suggested this exchange might thoroughly test his already limited patience.

"Onmitsu? Really?" The soldier scratched at some patchy stubble on his right cheek while he thought. "Well, this *is* a pleasant surprise. You must be desperate if you're lurking around here."

"Don't rub it in." Obito rolled his eyes.

"Name's Junpei Ikimori, junior training captain. What honor do you owe me for helping you?"

"Obito." He chose to make a point of not acknowledging the rest of Junpei's nonsense. The unimpressed arch of his eyebrows, coupled with his deadpan reply, made the soldier's self-assurance noticeably shrink. "My partner went missing last night, and since I believe Senator Hajime is holding him, I need—"

"Hold on—what makes you think the Senator has anything to do with it? Knowing you sneaks, he could be hiding anywhere."

"Unless you know of another onmitsu being detained *here*, it's a perfectly logical assumption."

Junpei tilted his head to one side. "Look, I know the Senator doesn't have the cleanest reputation in Zhu when it comes to the locals or the politicians, but he's a bit busy to get involved with random kidnappings. I highly doubt he has anything to do with your friend's alleged disappearance. That'd be treason."

"I'm aware, but—"

"I mean, unless your friend was a slaveborn or some—"

"He *is* Northern Nomadic."

"...Fuck. Well...what else did you expect? Don't you know how stupid it was to bring a slaveborn *here*, of all cities? You two should've gone up to Baohu or something if you wanted to be left alone."

Obito reined in his temper as much as he could manage with a deep breath. "Master Yujin sent us, but that's hardly your concern *or* the point. Can you help me find Daisuke or not?"

"Daisuke? As in Akahana?"

"Great." Obito pinched the skin between his brows. "You know each other."

"Know him? Hell, I was in basic with that little silk-spinner for a bit before I transferred into the main infantry. I never thought they'd put him with *intelligence*." Junpei laughed.

Obito's fists clenched until his nails dug into his palms, but he miraculously calmed himself. "Just as I'm sure he wouldn't be surprised to find *you* stationed in Zhu."

Junpei's jaw fell open as if he intended to say something else, but in the end, a retort never came. Instead, he started for a weapon rack not far from where he stood to set his spear in its designated place, gaze occasionally darting over his shoulder to look at Obito. When he returned, he seemed to have recovered slightly from whatever effect those words had—it could've been Obito's imagination, but Junpei almost seemed embarrassed. Finally, the soldier came back to his senses and crossed his arms with a frown.

"I'm not sure what you think I can do. My old man always says, 'silk-spinners should stay where silk-spinners belong.' And frankly, who gives a fuck if Senator Hajime has one more? *If* he's even there in the first place."

"This is my teammate and my friend you keep insulting," Obito warned; naturally, it went ignored.

Junpei spread his hands, gesturing with every word as if he were arguing with himself. "I, I mean, sure, I might not *hate* Daisuke, but I'm sure as hell not about to risk a spot like *junior* training captain to help him. He should've stayed in the Capital if this was going to be such an issue. Why didn't the Intelligence Master use his *intelligence* to send someone else with you?"

Obito crossed his arms this time. "Are you being stupid on purpose?"

The soldier did the same again. "Well, what in all the gods' names would you have us—and *me,* for that matter—do? I'm only a soldier posted here, not an officer or general with actual authority. I'm not here to go against Senator Hajime or my superiors, and *you* sure as hell don't have the authority to give me orders."

"This is a fellow soldier's life." Obito was too busy holding back his rising temper to point out the error in Junpei's last statement, though it flared again when the soldier scoffed at him.

"No, this is a slave who tried to be something he never should've played at in the first place. I think we both know he had no business leaving the plantations."

Obito's anger finally boiled over. His fist landed on Junpei's cheekbone before he fully realized he'd swung for the older boy. They stared at each other in shock; clouds formed in front of them as the air filled with the sounds of their breath. Left with the echoes of his own words and a throbbing red mark, Junpei stayed quiet for a long moment, then slowly dropped his gaze. Stunned by how he'd reacted, Obito also didn't speak for a few minutes, until he flexed his aching fingers and remembered how little time he had to dither around with a belligerent idiot.

"I'll ask one more time. Can you help me?"

Junpei sighed, then softly replied, "Listen, I think you're way out of line for going after the Senator, but...you're obviously desperate. Give me proof, and I'll do whatever you need. Just don't punch me anymore."

"I won't promise that—you'll probably deserve it again." Still fuming, Obito silently studied Junpei for another moment, then just as wordlessly turned on his heel without bowing and took his leave.

"H-hold on!" the soldier called just as he passed through the wretchedly noisy gate, interrupting a rapid recalculation of plans. "Where are you going?"

Obito rolled his eyes and slowed his strides enough to give the other boy time to catch him, though he didn't stop entirely. He waited until they were across the street from the barracks before answering, "To Senator Hajime's estate."

"*Still*? Why? Just what are you planning?"

"We're going to conduct a wellness check and residential search."

"'We?' What makes you think—"

Obito finally paused and glanced at their surroundings, which made Junpei do the same; the other boy's face blanched when he realized how far from the barracks he'd wandered, as he no doubt understood he was as good as an accomplice if he went much further. Obito gave him a moment to grapple with whether he wanted to continue before he kept walking. Junpei was on his heels again in seconds, though he soon appeared at his side to shoot him a suspicious glare. Obito couldn't keep a small smirk off his face—curiosity was a hell of a thing.

Junpei snorted when he noticed his companion's amusement at his expense. "Don't act like you won or whatever. There's no way in all of Kuro's Hells that I'd let you do this alone, anyway—you'll offend the Senator."

"I promise I don't care about how the Senator feels."

"Exactly." Junpei made a frustrated noise, likely not realizing he'd presented a decent argument, then went quiet for another spell before he asked, "What makes you think we'll even be able to get inside?"

"It shouldn't be too difficult. Someone reported a suspicious character sneaking into the Senator's house."

"When did that happen?"

Obito sighed. "You need to keep up if you're coming along."

Daisuke slowly cracked one eye open; he'd spent most of the night and early morning in a lotus position on the cell floor, his focus bouncing between meditation and any slight noise that reached his ears. Between these instances, he tried to keep himself busy either with exercises like the push-ups General Aki—and his own loose tongue—taught him to hate, or by picking the cell's lock with Lady Chizuru's forgotten hairpin. He couldn't quite angle his arm correctly for the right amount of leverage to spring himself. Sleep occasionally came when he was too exhausted to keep upright, but never lasted long.

Not sleeping's probably for the best, he thought as he retrieved the pin from the back of his belt and went for the lock again. He yawned. *What a night.*

Whenever Daisuke did manage to drift off, his dreams brought him back to the alley where he and Obito were attacked. Long shadows would wriggle like snakes on the ground as they ran from an unseen enemy, until he inevitably tripped over the small wooden box which once carried the artifact he and his partner were meant to take home with them. If not inside that nightmare, he'd find himself in the cave burrowed deep into the unknown mountainside, where seven jade dragon statues awaited him. The one on the far left from the center still glowed brightly, while a dim ball of light emanated from the forehead of the one on the far right. As for the largest statue in the middle, it seemed as though the cracks in its structure had grown longer and deeper than the last time he'd visited the hidden shrine—if that's what it even was. It was the only thing Daisuke could think of calling it. He'd visited these dragons regularly in his sleep for three years, but still couldn't make sense of what they were trying to tell him.

His heart fluttered with excitement when the lock made a noise, but after yanking on the bars, the door still didn't budge. He huffed as his shoulders slumped in disappointment; he assumed this would've been much easier.

I should ask Obito if he knows how to do this. His heart sank just after it'd settled again, no matter how he tried to fight off the thought that he might not reunite with his friend as he hoped. Although he believed Obito *would* look for him—it'd be an insult to their friendship to think otherwise—he doubted those efforts would yield much success. A slower sigh escaped him as he fiddled with the lower stud in his left ear; at least losing the earrings was issue he'd been able to fix.

I fucking hate this city.

Daisuke looked up when he heard movement in the corridor be-yond where he was imprisoned. His heart jumped into his throat when he tried to dislodge the pin and discovered it was stuck in the keyhole; thankfully, it only took a few desperate tugs before it came free, and he'd narrowly resumed his lotus position in time. He nervously eyed the hairpin as the door opened—he'd been forced to abandon it where it fell just outside the cell.

Lady Chizuru stepped over the threshold following the creak of metal hinges and greeted him with a wicked smile once she smoothed out her deep purple skirts. "You're looking well this morning."

Daisuke rested his chin on his hand and mirrored her expression. "How I wish I could say the same for you, curmudgeonly swamp hag."

Lady Chizuru glowered, then indignantly turned her back to him and examined the rows of shackles and collars on the rack opposite his cell. His temper simmered as he watched her; before it could boil over, his eyes drifted toward his tanto, still taunting him from the bench. While tempting, he once again dismissed the idea of overpowering her once the door opened—even if he did injure her enough to grab his dagger and get away, he wasn't in the best shape to outrun guards or fight his way to freedom.

Never mind the mess it'd cause when word got back to the Capital. Daisuke shuddered. Emperor Akuwara and Senator Hajime had about as close of a friendship as one could get in politics, so it wouldn't take long to figure out which slaveborn attacked the Senator's wife. He and Obito were in enough trouble already.

Chizuru straightened her shoulders again when she faced him with her selection, her hurt expression unable to hide how his words had af-fected her. A strange, unexpected sense of guilt planted itself in his heart, though it hardly lasted the span of a second. She stuck her arm between the bars, holding out a collar. Daisuke firmly reminded himself to control the impulse to smack it out of her hand, though he couldn't suppress the revulsion creeping into his face. As if the shadows in his dreams had left traces of their melancholy behind, his mind flashed through the last time he'd been forced to wear a collar, and his throat tightened. The greasy smell of fried duck, the metallic taste of a nobleman's blood in his mouth, and the blistering agony of a cane striking his bare back rushed at him, then just as quickly receded into his subconscious once more. He shook himself to stay present.

"Come, now. I want you to look somewhat proper while you serve my guests today. You will wear it."

"I will not."

"You insolent—!" Her knuckles turned white from how hard she gripped the collar—Daisuke leaned back a little further to ensure she couldn't hit him with it. She collected herself. "I won't open this door until you do."

"Fine by me." He grinned when fury sparked in her eyes again. "*You're* the one who wants me out, lady. I'm quite content minding my own business in here."

"Would a conversation with my husband perhaps change your mind? He's been eager to test out the new whip he bought the other day."

A chill danced along his spine. While he thought it was clear the Senator held Lady Chizuru in high contempt—and received the same from her—Daisuke didn't doubt the man would enthusiastically take all his hatred out on his newest captive's back. He winced. Growing up on Grandmaster Norio's plantations, he'd seen whippings more times than he cared to count. Images of raw and bleeding flesh, spiderwebs of gnarled scars, and sadistic glee on the faces of those who held the lash abruptly invaded his vision. He could do without firsthand experience.

"Fuck's sake. *Fine*, you dried-out toad." Scowling, Daisuke stiffly got to his feet and approached the door. He didn't take the collar.

"Get it out while you can," the noblewoman warned as she casually dropped it into his hand. "If your attitude and mouth are still this foul once my guests arrive, I won't hesitate to beat you senseless in front of everyone and then send you to my husband for more. You'll do well to remember how *he* wanted to sell you straightaway—*I* advocated for you to stay and even offered you water. You'll need to earn the privilege back now."

Daisuke had nearly managed to push aside his dry mouth and hunger until she mentioned the former—he hadn't fulfilled either need since early the previous day, hours before he and Obito left the inn to retrieve the artifact. With several threats now stacked against him, he shakily brought the collar closer to his throat, mentally repeating that all he had to do was stay calm and let her believe she'd won for now. He could kick his makeshift lock-pick back into the cell either when he left or was brought back.

His breath hitched at the uncomfortable squeeze of leather against his jugular.

"Are we really doing this?" Junpei grimaced, then looked away from the heavy oak doors and white plaster wall guarding Senator Hajime's property.

He and Obito had just completed a third, seemingly normal, patrol of the street in front of the Senator's home. Given the slave auctions held during the harvest moon festival which had just taken place, an extra patrol unit or two in affluent areas was hardly out of place. Despite going unnoticed, Junpei was still hesitant to fully commit and get his hands dirty with their plan. He'd all but begged Obito to search elsewhere.

"You're overthinking things," Obito finally told him, brows furrowing at how absurd the complaint sounded coming from him. "Besides, watching the house from across the street like this is more suspicious than anything we're about to do."

"You *do* realize how many guards this man has working for him, right? How do you plan on us fighting all of them off?"

"You aren't serious, are you? That'd be suicide. I didn't plan to fight at all if we could avoid it."

"Typical onmitsu," Junpei muttered under his breath as he ran a hand through his dark hair; a few more strands of his previously immaculate bun fell out of place. "You're sure this is a smart move?"

"No, but we're doing it anyway."

"All the gods help me."

"I'm not sure what you expect them to do in this situation." Obito ignored Junpei's annoyed, sidelong glare and started toward the Senator's property.

A guardsman armed with a spear stood on each side of the entrance, though their weapons seemed rather useless, as neither man looked particularly engaged with his duties. Observation with each pass by the Senator's grand estate suggested the guards spent most of their time conversing with each other rather than paying attention to their surroundings—one even stood with his back to the road while he talked. He'd since settled, but Junpei had made several, baffled comments on it, which turned into a wonderful tirade Obito hated to interrupt when he needed to capture his focus.

"Look at this," one guard muttered to his counterpart as they approached. He leaned against the door. "Infantry dogs. What d'you two want?"

That made "little sneaks" sound like a compliment, Obito thought. Granted, he and Daisuke were too old now to be referred to as such by assassins or footsoldiers, but he'd heard the nickname given to young onmitsu plenty of times before. He glanced at Junpei, who clearly wasn't willing to speak first.

"We're here to conduct a residential welfare check," Obito explained, the lie flowing off his tongue more naturally than he expected.

The guard spit out a thick, dark wad of tobacco into the brass planter beside him; apprehension lined his features, despite the aggressive look in his eyes. "What're you on about, boy?"

"A concerned citizen said they noticed a shady-looking person trying to sneak into the Senator's house."

"Did ya ever think they might've been lyin'? We ain't noticed a damn thing all mornin'."

"Better to know for certain, isn't it? It could mean your heads if you don't at least let us look." Of course, the last part was wild speculation on Obito's part, but given the way worry creased each guard's brow, he assumed he hadn't been too far from the truth. While he didn't imagine many people enjoyed having their belongings stolen, men like Senator Hajime thought it to be exceptionally personal, and would often go to great lengths to blame and punish their staff for "letting" it happen. He'd met a few of these unpleasant types when he still had a seat at his father's table.

"We're here to help," Junpei said, tone surprisingly sincere—maybe he thought they were. Whether it was to clear the Senator's name or to protect the man from the team of onmitsu, perhaps even he didn't know.

"...Wait here. I'll inform the Senator," the second guard finally spoke after glancing at his counterpart.

He disappeared behind the heavy doors, leaving Junpei and Obito with little else to do besides awkwardly avoid eye contact with the one remaining, who was now leaning against the wall while keeping a suspicious scowl on the pair. Thankfully, he'd given up on questions, granting them the relief of silence, but the air became incredibly tense the longer they waited. Obito tried to act as if he didn't notice Junpei nervously picking at the skin around one of his fingernails; he didn't need his own anxieties raised any higher.

When the other guard eventually returned, he peered around the door timidly at first, looking pale and slightly shaken. Obito imagined the Senator hadn't taken kindly to an interruption; he likely didn't hesitate to demonstrate as much, either. The guard cleared his throat as he slinked out, trying to maintain a straight posture.

"The Senator will receive you now. Right this way."

Junpei elbowed Obito to ensure he also bowed in thanks out of propriety—had they been anywhere else, Obito might've told him off for it—before they followed. They stayed on the guard's heels as he led them down a white cobblestone path lined by neatly trimmed cedar hedges; no one spoke as they approached a man standing at the top of a flight of stone stairs with long, polished railings carved from cypress. The Giahatian man awaiting them had streaks of gray at his temples and in his brows, which knitted together as they joined him, making no secret of how much displeasure he took in greeting the soldiers. He crossed his arms inside the wide sleeves of his yellow and green robes, lifting his chin when his guard knelt before him.

"Hikari's sake, not now," the man chastised, nudging the guard with his foot. He ignored the fumbled apology he received as his dark eyes turned on Obito and Junpei. "I am told suspicious activity around the estate was reported to your unit."

"Th-that's correct, sir," Junpei replied.

The man, who Obito easily guessed was Senator Hajime, heaved a sigh laden with the burden of being inconvenienced. "Very well, then. I suppose it *is* your job. But, I *will* be speaking with your commanding officers about ensuring that only *experienced* soldiers are on this patrol route from now on."

"Of course, Senator. You have my captain's permission to command as you believe to be fit."

The guard who'd led the pair scowled at them, not giving Obito a chance to make a face at the exchange. "You two better not take long. Lady Chizuru is entertaining guests and won't take kindly to an interruption."

The man faltered, as if abruptly remembering his place—someone's personal guard held no rank over an official infantryman, nor did he have any business speaking on his employer's behalf if the man was present. From the corner of his eye, Obito saw Junpei tense, and could only try to maintain an air of indifference.

"That's quite enough." Senator Hajime flicked his sleeves, which gave his words an edge of finality; Obito reminded himself not to flinch, as his father's mannerisms weren't much different when someone—usually Obito—pissed him off. It often served as a last warning not to tread further. "Let's get this over with. You will not make a scene, and I expect a prompt arrest and exit should you find anything."

"Of course, Senator." He rolled his eyes as soon as Senator Hajime turned to open the manor's main doors.

The Senator's home was orderly and suffocating, much like the man's presence. A worried knot began to form in Obito's stomach when they stepped into the main foyer, as self-doubt crept toward his previous convictions about where Daisuke had gone, but he forced it away. If he was wrong, that would be the end of his intrusion here, and he'd look elsewhere. He had no other choice. Yet another guard awaited them on this side, giving weight to what Junpei had previously mentioned about the number of men working for the Senator. Frankly, Obito wasn't sure if he was more impressed or disgusted by it.

Senator Hajime curtly nodded at the man as he led Obito and Junpei past. The two wordlessly trailed behind, occasionally making a show of stopping the small group to check a closet or nook. Eventually, they came to a set of double doors painted with cranes and fanning bamboo leaves; muffled chatter and laughter came from within the room. The Senator's face set into an even more stern expression as he looked down at the pair before gripping the shining, deep brown handles.

"If I hear about so much as a *hint* of disrespect, I will personally address your commanding officers *after* I've handled you miscreants myself. Am I understood?"

Junpei cringed—the threat only applied to him...for now. "Yes, Senator."

The doors slid aside, blasting Obito's senses with a heavy, nearly nauseating wave of various perfumes, sickeningly sweet sticky buns, and floral tea.

"Chizuru, my dear," Senator Hajime said, making every woman's head turn. Although he'd addressed her with warm words, it didn't carry into his voice, and he continued scowling at the pair beside him rather than sparing his wife a glance. "These young men say they're with the infantry—they won't be long, but please allow them a few moments to search the room. I'll be in my study should you need me."

Obito barely remembered to bow to the Senator, as his eyes were already busy scanning the room. He froze when they fell on the familiar figure of a raven-haired boy dressed in what looked to be the black onmitsu formals, who turned toward them when the door slid shut once more.

His chest tightened at the sight of a worn leather collar latched around Daisuke's throat.

"YOU FOUND ME," DAISUKE muttered, dumbfounded. He shook his head, then locked eyes with Obito as the ghost of a devilish grin graced his lips. "Gods be damned! So, you've finally caught me, have you? Infantry bilge rats!"

"What the f—?"

"That's right," Obito quickly cut Junpei off and stepped forward as if he were about to lunge for Daisuke. "Now come quietly. You've disturbed these people long enough."

Daisuke schooled his expression as the women present began exchanging concerned murmurs, then shifted his gaze to his left, wordlessly indicating a half-ajar door that could've easily been mistaken for part of the wall—a servant's passage, their easiest escape route. Obito barely tilted his head in a nod. Their silent conversation was interrupted when one of the women, presumably the lady of the house, cleared her throat. She rose from her seat, then indignantly marched up to Obito and Junpei. Lady Chizuru gave them a tight smile, though it wasn't long before irritation subtly snarled the corners of her mouth.

She bowed, though the gesture could hardly be called welcoming or courteous. "I do apologize, soldiers, but I believe you're mistaken. This boy is one of our slaves."

"I understand there might be some confusion, miss, but this one's a fugitive of the law," Obito stated calmly, hoping he sounded convincing as he tried to slow his racing heart.

Lady Chizuru coolly raised her eyebrows, red lips pursed as she tried to determine the legitimacy of his claim. "You don't say. Then I suppose you won't mind an inquiry about the charges."

Faced with the proof he'd asked for, and finally shaken from his doubts, Junpei didn't hesitate to insert himself this time—whether or not he wanted to admit it, Obito was impressed. "He's a crook and wanted for several violent murders. Why, he could be staking out his next chance to strike as we speak."

Stop while you're ahead, idiot. Obito's good opinion plummeted as he fought the urge to roll his eyes. Calling Daisuke a thief would've been plenty to get Lady Chizuru to cooperate; the more serious the accusation, the less believable their story sounded. He braced himself.

"This boy? A murderer?" The noblewoman chuckled, but her arrogant countenance slipped into concern; she looked as if her complexion had gone sallow beneath the layer of white paint on her skin. Obito watched her tensely. "Is that why a dagger was found on him?"

"Y-yes, that's right. We'll be taking him into custody, now." Junpei's eyes widened when he scanned the room again and realized Daisuke had snuck away in the mounting confusion. "He...he's gone."

Junpei *likely* hadn't meant to incite hysteria, but after inelegantly announcing that an alleged, malicious criminal had vanished without a trace, a few of the women shrieked, and several more scrambled to their feet in fright. The ensuing rush to clear the room worked to their advantage, but Obito knew better than to assume they had time before someone brought in the Senator's personal guard to investigate—he could already hear the lady of the house crying out for them from down the hallway.

He grabbed Junpei's uniform by the sleeve to redirect him and jogged across the room, where the board used to cover the servant's passage had fallen flat on the floor and left the entrance exposed. He urged Junpei through first so he could cover their tracks. The passage was tight, so Obito guarded their back as they ran up a steep flight of rickety stairs to the next landing. The dimly-lit, dusty passage widened a bit to accommodate an upward twist in the staircase, and the ceiling was also a little higher because of it, but there still wasn't much room. They paused to listen for any indication they'd been followed, but all they heard was confused, indistinct shouting coming from the tearoom they'd just fled—they were still safe for now. At Obito's feet, he noticed a collar had been haphazardly taken off and tossed aside. Junpei looked at him, but all his questions were answered before he could open his mouth.

"Obito, catch me," Daisuke's dry voice hissed from above them.

Obito's attention automatically went toward his friend's call. Daisuke had wedged himself against the ceiling, sprawled out and clinging to the corner with his hands and feet like a lanky spider. He wasn't *that* far off the ground, but it seemed like getting himself up there to hide had taken quite a bit of effort, and softening his landing was smarter than allowing him to hit the floor at full force. Obito didn't think twice about doing as he'd been asked. As soon as Daisuke saw his opening, he twisted his body around a bit, then let himself fall into his partner's arms.

It felt as if time stopped when their eyes met as Obito gently lowered him to the ground once more, and for a moment, neither could tear himself away from the other. Dozens of unspoken questions along with their equally silent answers buzzed in the air around them until, reminding the pair of his presence, Junpei cleared his throat.

Still partially wrapped in his arms, Daisuke jumped back against Obito when his eyes fell on the solider. Although he rarely mentioned it these days, he hadn't forgotten a second of the older boy's hateful behavior from when they were in basic infantry together. "What the hell is *he* doing here?!"

"He's helping. I'll explain later." Obito pulled Daisuke off, embarrassed that he'd let himself get so caught up in emotions he couldn't quite place. Relief was one thing, but didn't fully describe what he'd felt, nor did it explain why his heart was still beating so fast.

Annoyed with how easily he'd been cast aside, Junpei crossed his arms and glared at them. Although he looked ready to make some sort of snide comment, he started for the stairs and said, "Come on, then. Let's keep moving."

"There's a window in the hallway above us." Daisuke gritted his teeth and rubbed his forehead as he and Obito followed; his headache had intensified over the course of the morning. "The hag had me up there earlier. We should be able to jump down from it."

Junpei crouched beside the panel leading into the upstairs hall, slid it open a crack, then looked at Daisuke from over his shoulder. "Are you *trying* to make sure we all break our legs?"

"It shouldn't be a problem if you land right. You'd know that if you were smarter."

"Who are you calling stupid? *You* don't even know where we'd fall."

"Anywhere is better than in *here,* idiot."

"Enough." Obito maneuvered around Daisuke and nudged Junpei out of the way so he could peek into the hallway.

After taking his time to survey the corridor, listening intently to the clamor from the floors below, he signaled for the other two to remain quiet, then slipped through the passage's entrance. Daisuke almost sighed with relief when he and Junpei joined his partner, and they started for the window he'd previously mentioned. As he should've guessed, though, whatever god he'd pissed off most recently couldn't let him get away so easily. He turned when voices and heavy footfalls trampled up the formal staircase at the opposite end of the hall. Time snapped forward again, as if the servant's passage existed in some sort of bubble. He didn't know why, but Daisuke nervously reached backward, pawing at the air for his partner's arm, sleeve, *something* ensuring he was still there.

"Obito..." His fingers clenched when he gripped the front of his friend's uniform, heart pounding so hard it hurt.

"I'm behind you. Let's go." Obito pushed Daisuke forward, unfreezing him.

Junpei rushed toward the window, opening it so carelessly he nearly tore off the paper screen and its bamboo frame. The inviting scent of cool fresh air crept in as he poised himself to make the leap, then jumped down into the gardens below. A few choice curses rose into the air following his descent to accompany the sound of crashing leaves and snapping twigs, but after Obito checked to see whether he'd been injured, he ushered Daisuke to his side as the thundering of footsteps grew louder. Daisuke's stomach dropped when he saw how far it was, but upon remembering how he'd escaped the plantations on Okara, his bravery surged, and down he went.

He landed with surprising softness in the bushes and quickly stumbled out so Obito could join him on the ground. Once he'd oriented himself, he caught Junpei's dark eyes on him, though neither said anything until Obito was with them again. Junpei held a finger to his lips and firmly pointed toward the complex's outer wall less than ten feet from them before guiding the group there.

Daisuke stared up at the top of it, groaned, then rubbed his face. "This is embarrassing, but...I think I need a lift."

"Then make one." Junpei huffed, began climbing, and disappeared from sight once more.

"What's with him?" Daisuke asked as Obito knelt to give him a boost. It was one thing for the soldier to treat *him* that way, but he'd never really known Junpei to snap at anyone else in such a manner.

"He's been stuck with me all day. Ready?"

"That's what *I'm* supposed to say." Daisuke laughed, the sound somewhat hollow, then stepped into the foothold Obito made from his cupped hands.

Obito kept a watchful eye on their surroundings until his partner was most of the way up, then followed him to the other side. As soon as all three touched down on the side street, they sprinted for the main road until Daisuke suddenly stopped in his tracks, nearly causing the other two to trip over him.

"Fuck." He turned. "My tanto—it's still inside."

Junpei rolled his eyes and grabbed him by the collar when he tried to step forward. "Don't even think about it. Just get a new one when you get back to the Capital."

Long past his limits of how much disrespect he could tolerate, Daisuke bristled at the other boy's grip, especially when an instinctive attempt to free himself failed. He rounded on him with a nasty scowl. "What? No slur to go with telling me what to do this time?"

Junpei was genuinely surprised. "What kind of fucking attitude is that?!"

"'*Attitude*?!' What? You want me to bow down to you instead? Who the *fuck* do you think—"

"Knock it off, both of you," Obito interrupted, deftly hooking Junpei's wrist to remove his hand from Daisuke's uniform as he walked by. "We don't have time for this."

Daisuke glanced at the large homes and immaculate streets surrounding them. Any sign of disruptive behavior in an upscale district like this would draw unwanted attention; they needed to put as much distance between themselves and Senator Hajime's property before someone caught up to them.

I hate it when he's right. He crossed his arms as he watched his partner continue onward, though he dropped them when he realized Junpei had done the same. They glared at each other one more time, then settled for stalking behind Obito in sullen silence.

TENSE QUIET PERMEATED THE air on the walk back to the inn once Daisuke and Obito parted ways with Junpei, who had stormed off while muttering some nonsense to himself about the "shameless onmitsu," as if the day's ordeal had driven him thoroughly mad. Daisuke normally would've relentlessly teased and laughed at the soldier for his ramblings, his emotions were so scattered between anger and anguish, but he couldn't summon that part of himself just yet. Although the dreams of dragons and shadows often rattled him, nothing compared to living his worst nightmare—ever since he'd fled his home on Okara, the fear that he'd fall into the hands of people like Senator Hajime floated somewhere in his subconscious.

Except... Daisuke peeked at Obito. Whenever the scenario clawed its way forward to poison his daydreams, no one was there to help him. His dry throat prickled with discomfort as it closed around another swelling emotion.

Sensing the way curious eyes studied him intently, Obito turned to his friend.

They slowed to a stop under the shade of a fiery red maple when their gazes met, though neither said a word at first. Obito knew better than to insult Daisuke's pride by treating him as a fragile person—it was hardly the case, anyway—but surely there was *something* he could say to reassure him. In the face of everything, any gesture seemed useless.

To his surprise, Daisuke rushed into his arms the second he saw an opening, holding tight. Pushing through a wave of awkward embarrassment and a whole slew of other things he couldn't think about right now, Obito hesitantly did the same.

"Do you want to talk about it?" he finally worked up the courage to ask, trying to ignore how hot his face felt despite the chilly early autumn air.

Daisuke shook his head, but didn't let go; he worried he'd be a teary-eyed mess if he tried to speak or pull away before he was ready. He buried his face, and it wasn't for another long moment before he managed on a strained voice, "You came for me, and now it's over—that's all that matters."

Obito brought Daisuke through a gate at the rear of the inn's courtyard and led him to the privacy of an empty kitchen, where they were joined by Hayate soon after; he or one of his staff must've been on the lookout for them. The senior onmitsu set to work right away once he lowered Daisuke onto a bench beside a table and sent Obito off to get his partner food and water. He asked plenty of questions and listened to the answers patiently, careful with his touch as he gently looked over bruises and red marks. Daisuke thought Hayate's voice felt far away, as if his head had been plunged underwater. Twin tendrils of sudden, irrational anger and resentment curled around the sense he was being pitied while the innkeeper finished his examination, though he also couldn't deny how badly he needed gentleness. Even if it *were* only pity, he didn't see how pushing away the person who offered it would preserve the dignity he'd already lost over the last two days. A phantom sensation of the leather collar against his throat prickled under his skin.

"You'll be right," Hayate said when Obito returned with a bowl of rice and a cup of water, voice quiet and warm. "But you need a decent meal and plenty of rest, so I'm pulling rank and grounding the both of you for the rest of the day. I'll come by to check on you two later, but for now, I should get to the barracks so that soldier you mentioned doesn't hear it from his useless captains."

"Are you sure you should go?" Obito asked.

Hayate smiled a bit as he opened the door. "Realistically, I should be ashamed of myself for letting you two handle things to this point; I hope you can forgive me for being a coward. I need to remind them—and myself—why I *shouldn't* be on their doorstep. Now, then, behave. I'll be back after a while."

Obito set down the items in his hands and took a seat on the bench opposite his partner once the innkeeper left, though neither could find their words this time, so Daisuke settled for digging into his offerings. He made sure not to eat or drink too quickly, as making himself sick and unable to enjoy either didn't sound like a pleasant way to celebrate being free again. After several minutes of eating in silence, he realized exactly how uncertain things still seemed between them—perhaps he'd gotten a little too caught up in his emotions earlier when he'd hugged Obito. His partner wasn't much of one for being touched, which Daisuke knew, and admittedly danced on his boundaries with it far too much.

He meant to ask about it, but somehow, a different question clumsily tumbled out of his mouth when Obito came back with more water. "Hayate's with intelligence, then?"

Obito nodded. "It's probably why Master Yujin usually has onmitsu stay here when he sends them this way."

Although it was one of the answers Daisuke needed, it still wasn't where he'd meant to take their conversation, and he wanted to try again.

He mentally cursed when he swerved away from his intended question yet another time. "How the hell did you get Junpei Ikimori, of all the people, to go along with you?"

"We just talked."

"You bullied him into it, didn't you?" Daisuke laughed when Obito averted his eyes, as if looking away would help him avoid giving an answer—gods, it felt good to genuinely laugh again after the last couple of days. "You did! I can't believe you were *that* mean to someone, and I had to miss it."

Knowing he had little in the way of defending himself, Obito rolled his eyes and didn't comment, though the ghost of an amused smile on his lips didn't escape Daisuke's notice. He chuckled a little more as he placed his cup on the table again, then sighed.

"Like Hayate said, I'll be right, and soon. When can we leave this shithole city?"

DAISUKE AND OBITO MADE one final stop in Zhu before backtracking across town to the road home. Burrowed in their cloaks and already carrying their travel packs, they brought three sticks of incense each to the ashen remains of Rin and Gero's house under the cover of early dawn; night had barely lifted enough to move about the back streets without lantern light, and they had a little time before the first signs of life began moving about the city. Since news of the strange fire and the couple's subsequent demise had quickly spread to Hayate's inn, he'd offered to come with them and pay his respects, as well, though Obito suspected he had other reasons he hadn't mentioned.

He glanced over his shoulder at Hayate, who had walked behind them in chilling silence since they stepped foot off his property. Realistically, he'd taken it upon himself to escort them to where the house once stood and then out of the city, unwilling to take further chances with all the trouble they'd caused. Between the three of them, there was little doubt the barracks and Senator's house had spent the remainder of the previous

33

day in an uproar; the senior onmitsu had advised them to clear out of Zhu as early as possible. Hayate didn't breathe a word of what happened when he visited the barracks, but *had* briefly mentioned it'd be wise for Junpei to do the same if he were able. That was plenty to encourage both boys to keep their curiosity contained and not ask for further details.

The three knelt on the cold ground near the blackened remnants of the potter's home and stuck the incense into a soft spot of soil in front of them; charred beams and half-melted, unidentifiable objects were now mere silhouettes against the weak daylight. Although neither Daisuke nor Obito prayed, they remained perfectly still and quiet as thin, pale wisps of smoke rose toward the sky. It was only right to offer something to the innocent souls tangled in the crosshairs of whatever truth surrounded the artifact.

Daisuke glanced at Obito when the last flicker of ember on the incense died as a breeze carried the ashes away—they had a lot to discuss on the way home.

"I can manage the infantry captains and Senator Hajime from here," Hayate insisted once everyone got to their feet. "But I'm afraid it's past time for you two to go."

"What are you planning?" Daisuke asked as he shouldered his bag again.

"I think it's time for me to fall into some old habits again." A sly inflection crept into the innkeeper's voice. "It's been a while since I've visited the Senator's place—if he willingly held one Imperial soldier, who's to say there aren't more on his property? I won't know until I investigate, and the captains can't afford to be wrong by refusing to help me search. Thanks to you boys, I have a bit of leverage and control. More than I've had in years."

Hayate sent them off shortly after, promising to send a report to Master Yujin as soon as he was able, though they all understood it wouldn't arrive before they did. Daisuke and Obito stepped onto the road home under the first signs of sunlight, at last ready to leave Zhu after two months away from the Capital; it would be just over another month before they saw home again if their travels went well. Hayate had ordered the guards normally stationed at the city's entrance to stand down until the boys went through, which meant they could at least begin their journey in much-needed peace.

"I think we've learned an important lesson while we've been here," Daisuke announced as they walked through the city's unattended arch, barely containing the urge to sprint down the road. Obito gave him a look that was at once quizzical and skeptical. "We're too nice."

Obito's expression didn't change. "Have either of us ever been accused of that?"

"No, but I'm pretty sure we deserve to be worse."

"I hate it when you have a point."

"I know. You'll get over it."

Obito didn't respond again as they passed under the low branches of a yellow birch, but Daisuke noticed when a small smirk crossed his friend's lips.

They briefly stopped for supplies in the village of Kagechi; once through the little town, they were several miles out from Zhu, which was when Daisuke felt the last of his gloom fall away. He'd taken care of the bulk of it the previous night when an unexpected surge of tears descended on him during a bath. In turn, he finally felt ready to talk about some of what they'd been through; the most logical place to start was none other than the moment they'd become separated. An image of the three heavily cloaked figures who cornered them flashed across his vision, as did the way the wooden box reacted when called by the one he imagined was at the head of the group. It had thrashed around in his clutches before shadows billowed out from it—whatever was inside clearly wasn't *just* an obscure artifact.

Daisuke tapped Obito's shoulder to get his attention. "To be clear, we both saw the same thing in that alley, right?"

"We did. Unfortunately," Obito slowly confirmed. Waving those events off as a vivid hallucination they'd somehow shared would've been easier, but didn't explain anything that happened, and would've painfully undermined what Daisuke had gone through with Senator Hajime. Whether he liked it or not, the whole ordeal was undeniable, and now they were left to speculate on it.

"What do you think was in the box that made those people want it so badly?"

"Don't you remember? Master Yujin told us during the briefing before we left." Obito sighed when Daisuke gave him a blank look. "Because of all the hysteria Senator Hajime started raising about it thanks to the rumors he heard, Emperor Akuwara believes it's an Okami relic."

"But *you* don't, do you?" Daisuke tilted his head.

"I'll admit, I don't know much about the Okami, but blaming them for what happened to Rin and Gero doesn't seem...well, it's not right, and it sure as hell isn't accurate. Since Senator Hajime is a terrible person, I think it's more likely he went along with whatever His Highness decided was true to get a team to Zhu as fast as possible."

"I think you're right. The Okami might not *want* Giahatian advancement on their lands, but if they went around handing out cursed objects like festival sweets, I'm sure we would've heard about it before now. And it doesn't make sense for them to let one fall into a citizen's hands in the middle of a ceasefire."

"Which we might be able to point out to Master Yujin, but I doubt we'll get any further with it unless we can provide an alternative to investigate. Even so, I think it's safe to eliminate them as the artifact's source." Obito's eyes rolled skyward. "We'll be researching for months when we get home if Master Yujin doesn't skin us alive first."

Daisuke had long held a strong sense that everything they'd learned about the Okami wasn't true, and knowing his partner felt the same eased some self-doubt about the matter. The more he'd analyzed scholarly writings about Othakra's wolf-Shifters, the harder his misgivings toward the Empire's narrative had become to dismiss—one scholar in particular, Makoto Higurashi, sounded quite fond of them in his essays describing their culture, though his work was becoming increasingly difficult to find. Daisuke wanted to ramble more on the subject, but determined it was a different matter best saved for another time, and brought their conversation back to his original point.

"Didn't Rin tell us she got it from her sister?"

Obito nodded again.

"...She said her sister's name was Misame, right?"

"You remember that, but not what Master Yujin said?"

"Well, I *did* dream about a woman with her name getting murdered." Daisuke left it there, knowing his partner understood the implications behind his statement—a Northern Nomad's dreams might be vague and strange, but rarely wrong in what they depicted. He let the soft crunch of fallen leaves under their boots fill the air for a while before he spoke again. "Do you think Misame knew what she was getting her sister into?"

"We don't even know what *we've* gotten into at this point. I think right now, we should focus on where Misame would've gotten the artifact in the first place, and why someone would've tracked it down to steal it."

Although Daisuke could point to several other things they hadn't included in their analysis thus far, he knew they'd have plenty of time to discuss and chase down those answers on the way home, so he turned his thoughts elsewhere. His eyes swept across the landscape before and all around him. It all seemed more vivid and beautiful than he'd previously noticed. Colorful leaves rustling in the wind as a few strays landed in scattered piles along the Eastbound Road, mountains looming in the distance, the bright sun, a clear blue sky, and the person beside him. An easy smile warmed Daisuke's face. Even if a punishment inevitably awaited him and Obito in the Capital, *this* nightmare had ended.

AT LEAST THREE WEEKS had passed since Lady Shadow and Haruki absconded from Zhu with Saigai's talisman in their possession. Although they'd encountered two members of Imperial forces and caused a massive disturbance with the unpredictable power of Kanashimi's shadows, the widow leading Zandaka's cult couldn't help but praise their efforts.

After many stops to rest their hardworking carthorse, Lady Shadow finally felt they'd placed enough space between themselves and that dirty city—moreover, they were at last a safe distance away from Perena's denser southern populations. With help from Kanashimi and Haruki, she performed nightly meditations around Saigai's talisman to keep the demon calm until they returned to the mountaintop recesses where her followers awaited them. The Demon of Disaster was plenty agitated at the beginning of their journey, but now, the dragon lying dormant within the stone talisman didn't seem interested in further destruction. Even back at the potter's house, Saigai hadn't been particularly aggressive about escaping his confines. While Lady Shadow was tempted to blame the other humans involved for upsetting his spiritual energy, Kanashimi had soothed her worries after examining the talisman themself. Something as simple as a vengeful prayer or careless curse uttered within the potter's house could've created these inconsistencies, but wouldn't totally suppress or destroy his true might.

"Lady Shadow?" Haruki cautiously asked from the driver's seat as she encouraged their horse to pull off to the side of the road for a little reprieve. A light snow fell around them and muffled the steady, pounding hoofbeats moving through the few inches accumulated on the ground.

Once the nag obeyed the command to stop, Lady Shadow removed her hood and turned in her seat to eye Haruki, who seemed too nervous to face her. Lady Shadow continued to study her wordlessly, then sighed—she couldn't imagine where the girl's thoughts were, but she was glad that

Haruki finally found her voice. She'd spent the last few days of their journey looking positively sick with worry.

"Something's been troubling you, my dear. Let's hear it." She tried her best to replicate a motherly tone, despite how likely it was to fall flat; Lady Shadow never bore children during her marriage, and they were an extremely scarce sight within the confines of the abandoned spa where her following resided. Not that Haruki, a former trainee of the hitokiri masters, had come to expect such a thing from the widowed matron, but unnecessary harshness wouldn't win her any favors with the women she led—especially not Haruki, whose timidness stemmed from doubt in her intelligence and being raised by atrociously abusive brutes. Fainthearted as the girl could seem, Lady Shadow had a habit of keeping a close watch on her katana, whether or not its master was close enough to wield it. At some point, she'd become aware that it wasn't unlike how one might scrutinize a feral animal they'd let inside, ever fearful of its natural instincts taking over once more.

Haruki's fists clenched as she dug her gloved fingers into the fabric of her trousers—although rarely vulgar, she wasn't always careful or articulate when she spoke. "The onmitsu we took Saigai's talisman from...what do you think happened to them?"

The dowager looked away as she weighed the possibilities. While she highly doubted either of the young spies suffered a fatality when she used Kanashimi's shadows to separate them, she also recognized her control over those abilities was quite weak. She didn't know her own strength when commanding them. She couldn't determine if the onmitsu met their demise with any certainty unless someone went looking for them, which came with another uncomfortable idea—if the boys *were* still alive, they couldn't be allowed to relay what they'd seen to Imperial Intelligence. If they'd survived like she assumed, they were already forcing her hand.

Finally, she looked forward again. "We'll be in Mizutake soon. We can rest there for the night and discuss this more once we've settled."

"You're sure you want to stay directly in the village, my Lady?"

"Yes. The inn might be a little underkept, but judging by the clouds, the weather won't stay on our side much longer. It's best if we have a secure shelter tonight."

Though hesitant, Haruki eventually nodded, then urged their horse into motion once more.

Lady Shadow had previously made a point of avoiding any inns or villages peppered along this mountain to prevent locals from becoming familiar with her, or the paths that she or any of her followers took. On this trip, Haruki had unobtrusively slipped into the markets for supplies as needed. However, Kanashimi had indicated after completing the previous evening's meditations that Saigai wouldn't remain complacent for much longer. The Demon King's favored disciples were unpredictable in half-awake states; the nightly ritual of soothing their sibling's spirit took a toll on the Demon of Grief, which made their contributing spiritual energy weaker. The road through Mizutake, a small village surrounded by stalks of bamboo near a crystal clear, trickling mountain stream, was a shortcut on their journey home. Even if they spent the night there, their trip would end several days sooner than if they took the usual, lesser-known road around it. Since winter was already upon the mountains, as expected, snowstorms and squalls might also arrive at any minute—purposely dawdling on the back roads could easily mean peril for travelers.

The tiny inn was located near the village's square. As predicted, it hadn't seen the best care over the years, as it had likely welcomed few visitors, but Lady Shadow found the accommodations acceptable. Rundown wasn't the same as dirty. It helped that the owner was an amicable gentleman, who even let her get away with some flirtatious back-and-forth in exchange for putting up the horse at no additional charge. She ordered liquor and food to be delivered to the room she and Haruki settled in; while she awaited their items, her thoughts went back to the onmitsu they'd run into previously.

Those young men likely didn't understand what they'd been sent to retrieve from the traitor Misame's sister. Senator Hajime firmly believed Saigai's talisman was actually an Okami relic due to the way it had "haunted" the couple whose possession it had fallen into, assuming it was cursed with a grudge toward any Giahatian or Perenin who touched it. Lady Shadow learned as much when she stopped the messenger running from Rin's to the inn where the onmitsu had taken up their lodgings. If the bumbling fool of a Senator thought it to be the truth, there was little chance the Emperor thought differently—Zhu's chattier, well-connected locals said the two had communicated frequently about the matter.

"Have you shown any of our other Healers how to make our voices change?" Lady Shadow asked Haruki once their meals arrived and they were alone again.

"I have, my Lady. Out of the three, Emi is probably the most proficient so far."

Lady Shadow pursed her lips in thought. Before they'd discovered the talismans containing Tatakai and Saigai the first time, Haruki had learned from an elderly woman, one of Lady Shadow's first strays along with the girl, and Misame, whose betrayal still tasted bitter on her tongue. By now, Haruki far surpassed her mentor. Since she also had strong combat skills, she spent her days teaching others who were interested or capable when not acting as Lady Shadow's personal guard. The matron wasn't sure how those women would fare without Haruki for a few more months, but it seemed she had no other choice.

"We'll use the Giahatio's tactics against it, then."

"My Lady?"

Lady Shadow squared her shoulders and lifted her cup, swirling it around once; the gingery fragrance of the clear liquor filled her senses and gave off a pleasant warmth. "I want you to infiltrate the Palace, Haruki. If you happen to run into our little friends or the General who has the Talisman of Tatakai, do as you want with them—our sole concerns are retrieving the Demon of War and making sure those intelligence flies are unable to report us."

Haruki gulped as the meaning behind the matron's words s.

"You'll leave in the morning," Lady Shadow continued as if she hadn't seen the apprehension in her eyes. "Use your Healing abilities to either hide amongst infirmary staff or slip in with the maids. Either way, you should have total access to most of the Palace's wings and barracks, and have ample opportunity to search for those onmitsu and the talisman."

After a moment, the worry faded from her face, and Haruki took a deep breath before nodding. "Yes, my Lady."

HARUKI LEFT AT THE earliest light, taking a sack of provisions and their trusted map with her as she disappeared into the long shadows of a forested path. If Lady Shadow's calculations were right, it would provide the most direct route to the Capital from Mizutake. Although Haruki had proven herself to be a capable girl, she still clutched the necklace holding Kanashimi's talisman while she watched her go, inexplicably worried for her safety both during travel and when she arrived at her destination. She hadn't set foot in the Capital since the last time she'd visited to corner Lord Hideo and interrogate him over the whereabouts of Tatakai's talisman; though she preferred staying out of the city, something told her she couldn't avoid more trips in the coming years. After all, Emperor Akuwara still planted his pompous ass on the throne she wished to claim in Zandaka's stead.

Rather than mire her thoughts in the Emperor's despicable affairs—prostitutes, favoritism, heavy taxes on anyone he singled out on a whim—she decided to prepare herself for the remaining journey ahead. After tethering her horse to a tree on the north side of the village, she ventured toward the small market area where shops and stalls were just beginning to open for the day. It was a charming little square, intermingled with quaint homes, which appeared sturdy enough for the mountain winters despite their size. The vendors she interacted with as she picked out provisions of salted meats, dried fruits, and plain rice crackers were pleasant and jovial. For the first time in what felt like ages, Lady Shadow allowed herself to get wrapped up in the simple pleasure of it. Before the failed revolution that took away her husband, this was how she spent many afternoons, and she reveled in the familiarity. She'd nearly forgotten how peaceful life could be outside of her grander schemes.

She was even about to ignore the distinct sound of shattered pottery, until a harsh expletive erupted from a man's voice.

Then he followed it up with, "Natsumi, you useless bitch!"

Lady Shadow's head jerked in the direction from where she'd heard his bellowing. The same second her eyes landed on the giant, boorish beast of a man, she watched him slap the woman at his side before he grabbed her by the wide sleeves of her pale blue outer robe and continued screaming at her.

She shuddered as fiery heat rolled across her skin—no matter the cause, this would *not* stand in her presence. Lady Shadow quickly excused herself from the vendor she was speaking with and picked up her already full satchel before wedging herself between two buildings. She used a sharpened pin from her hair to prick her finger and smear the tiny bead of blood across the talisman's surface. She clutched her pendant and quietly called for the demon who lay within, and in a blink, Kanashimi's beautiful, jade green figure appeared before her, the dragon's white hair and layered robes flowing in every direction.

Lady Shadow didn't waste time on needless greetings. "Kanashimi, are you only able to use my grief for your powers? Or does it include another's, as well?"

"Now that I am bound to you, Priestess, your grief is both a source and a conduit to the resentment that controls my shadows. Should you wish it, it's much the same for those I have no connection to...if their emotions are strong enough."

"Hers?"

The dragon demon lifted their snout and flicked out their tongue as if testing the air for what they sought. Their few seconds to think felt as though it took ages, with the woman's helpless sobs filling Lady Shadow's ears as the shouting grew louder, and the poor soul's husband violently shook her. Kanashimi growled low in their throat and, as if the two were joined on a string, lifted their arm along with Lady Shadow's. She staggered from the heavy, unexpected wave of emotion pressing on her chest. Just when she realized it belonged to the other woman, a blast of darkness burst forth from the shadow priestess's open palm, engulfing the man and the house. Before Lady Shadow could figure out how to control the sheer force of angered sorrow from within the woman's heart, she heard the deafening boom of a crack forming in the earth.

However, the woman's grief was far from expended. As she collapsed to her knees in a terrified, weeping heap, Kanashimi pulled even more from her; a flicker of panic Lady Shadow sensed through their connection told her they hadn't meant to draw further on her emotions, as if they were unable to stop themselves, like a starving parasite feasting on a bountiful host. The shadows swirled in a mass before the woman, until Kanashimi closed their fist, along with the Priestess's. Once released, the shadows fanned in all directions and sped like wailing, furious spirits throughout the village, erupting when they collided with anything solid. They destroyed everything in their path; snow melted beneath where they raced.

Just as well. The Shadow Priestess told herself when she felt the weight of resentment lift; she took a moment to appraise Kanashimi's handiwork as she fought to catch her breath. *Mizutake is so damn small, there isn't a single chance that no one knew he treated her like this—they've all stood there and pretended it didn't exist.*

"Priestess," Kanashimi said from beside her, interrupting her thoughts—they sounded dazed. "I...I am exhausted. That human's emotions were stronger than I expected, and it's been tasking to keep my brother in place until we return to the shrine—please, allow me to rest."

"Of course. Thank you."

Lady Shadow bowed to Kanashimi, then dangled the chain attached to the talisman between them. The dragon demon levitated their long, serpentine body in front of it and bowed to her in return before they disappeared in a plume of darkness that pulled itself into the stone's surface once more; the emblem of them and their name glowed red, then disappeared again. So long as Kanashimi remained loyal to her, recalling them when needed would always be the simple part, though she much preferred leaving them the dignity to excuse themselves.

She ran to the woman who still cowered inside the shallow crater she'd inadvertently made in the frosty street. At the sound of her boots crunching the thin layer of snow, their eyes met, but she remained frozen in place even as Lady Shadow drew nearer.

"Such amazing power," the woman whispered in awe.

"Natsumi, right?" Lady Shadow knelt in front of her and extended her hand. "I merely borrowed it from you for the moment. I hope you don't mind."

The woman's eyes widened, and she slowly surveyed the desecrated village. "Then...*I* did all this?"

"You carried immense sadness and resentment." Lady Shadow carefully guided her to her feet and tucked a lock of medium brown hair behind her ear. For a moment, this enchanting stranger's innocent eyes and fairer Giahatian complexion reminded her of another she'd known when she was younger, and she added tenderly as if speaking to her, "May those things no longer burden you."

"Then, I'm...I-I'm free? I'm free. Gods, I'm *free*." Natsumi scanned her surroundings again; either the shock hadn't yet worn away, or she truly felt no remorse. She swallowed, trembling slightly as she eased away from Lady Shadow's grasp. "B-but, w-where will I go now?"

"Do you have family you wish to see? I can help you reach them."

Natsumi shook her head.

Lady Shadow rarely wasted opportunities to collect society's strays, but her intent was much softer than normal when she asked, "Then...what if you joined me? I'm returning home after a long journey to Zhu. I could use the company while my handmaid attends to other matters, and I know *my* family would love to meet you."

The woman's eyes shifted to her decimated home, then went to the mess of charred, demolished buildings nearby, as well as the large circle of melted snow surrounding them. "W-what about your husband? Won't he disapprove? He...he won't take me as a concubine, will he?"

Since Lady Shadow knew her bearing and sense of style often gave off the impression that she belonged to a high-ranking noble family, this wasn't an overtly rude thing to ask, though married men outside of those in the royal family rarely had concubines in addition to their wives. Outright affairs were much more popular these days. Rather than taking offense to the question, she mutely shook her head, tone gentle when she spoke again.

"My husband was no such man. He was unfairly executed by the military several years ago, but even if he were still alive, he wouldn't have thought twice about us taking you in."

Natsumi was silent for a long while before she said, "I was never meant to be here, or end up like this. My father...he forced my marriage because he didn't like the attention I gave other women."

"Is that more resentment I detect? You'll fit in so perfectly with my family." Lady Shadow smiled at her and, feeling unusually timid, chose to change the subject. "My horse is hitched on the north side of the village's outskirts. Shall we?"

She extended her hand to Natsumi once more. When her new companion took it, her light skin flushed a soft red, a familiar emotion which had been dormant for ages fluttered in Lady Shadow's chest.

"My Lady," Natsumi piped up after another moment, once they'd retrieved the discarded sack of goods previously bought. "What should I call you?"

Lady Shadow hummed; she hadn't used her given name in years. Though it'd feel strange to say aloud, something about the young woman beside her made her hesitant to state otherwise. "Kagura is my birth name. Use it sparingly, and please keep it between us."

THE HIGH PRIESTESS FROZE at the sight of her reflection in the clear pool. Two of the rubies in her headpiece had turned into odd-looking stones of marbled obsidian and green jade; another seemed to have the faintest traces of the same, though it stayed just out of focus. Trembling, she brought the first two fingers of her right hand to the hexagonal gold plate resting against her forehead, though she already knew it was a futile effort; no pulsation of spiritual energy would be strong enough to cleanse the stones and change them back to their former appearance.

What she saw staring back at her was an irrefutable, dark omen—the visions she'd had of roaring dragons rising high into Perena's skies and a mountain village laid to waste couldn't be dismissed as only nightmares. She stood from where she'd knelt beside the reflection pool to care for its eternal water lilies and went to the altar on the far side of the temple's main sanctuary, thoughts buzzing incessantly as she went. This body was not strong enough to confront Zandaka or his demons again; although immortal, Hikari wouldn't stand a chance at defending herself should they come for her. If she so much as tried, she would merely share the same fate as Kuro—sealed away by the dragons in the belly of a forgotten mountain cave.

She lit incense on the altar and clutched her hands together, trying to calm her spirit. The priests would insist upon more dedication to prayer and meditation if they sensed her agitated state, though only one of those things would serve her well. The prayers chanted by the priesthood and passed through the generations were designed by Zandaka's curse to contain her within this human form and immensely limit what she could do with her spiritual powers. In addition to the way his demons had taken away the sources of her might, it essentially ensured the seal upon her never grew weak enough to be broken.

Telling the priests about her misgivings or visions would be of little help, anyway. Putting righteous—rather, *self*-righteous—men in positions of power over her had been a mistake from the beginning, though not a choice she'd had any agency in making. The details of what had transpired between Zandaka sealing her and when she'd awoken in this human vessel were still unclear centuries later; not a soul besides the Demon King and Kuro would know, and they'd sealed themselves away on the same day, mere moments after the Between Realm's lord commanded his demons to drain her. In any case, the priests who were meant to serve under her would only try to soothe her worries or convince her they were baseless concerns.

The High Priestess closed her eyes and inhaled the pine-infused scent of the incense. The smell brought her to a snowy mountain pass, where she'd previously witnessed the decimation of a village during her morning meditations. She hadn't *seen* the exact cause of so much destruction, but the traces of grief and resentment left behind like a shadow confirmed what she feared—one of Zandaka's demons, a spirit who had stolen a portion of her power, bore responsibility. Perhaps worse, there were remnants of a human's energies which overlapped with the demon's. The High Priestess was certain that whoever had summoned the demon had also uncovered another of the beasts' hidden talismans. It was like a suffocating, eerie sense she couldn't shake, confirmed by the strange transformation of the rubies on her headpiece.

As she envisioned this flattened village once again, an idea came to her. She needed time and space to fortify what little spiritual power she had at her disposal, especially if she was still expected to give traditional blessings on solstice night during the Winter Festival. It'd be so much easier without the priests circling her with constant questions or doubts, and to be free of their prayers; unfortunately, ones uttered in other temples across the land would still keep her true power subdued. As holy men, though, they couldn't ignore the souls who had perished in the sudden disaster. They needed proper rites in order to proceed to the afterlife, lest they wander the grounds as ghosts or malicious spirits for the rest of eternity.

The High Priestess opened her eyes again, the undeniable tug of a smirk at the corner of her mouth. By the time the sun rose the following day, she would be alone in the Palace Temple. Her consort of priests would be on their way to bless the now cursed grounds of Mizutake, and she could remain locked in her chambers, deep in isolated meditation.

Neither Zandaka nor his demons posed a great threat as of yet—not with only two of those horrid creatures gaining awareness of the mortal realm once more. For now, the most she could do was prepare. She was certain that, if she meditated and concentrated her spiritual power enough, she could find a way to stop the uprising of the demons of the Between Realm.

Hikari's confidence slipped when she turned to leave the main sanctuary, as she realized how little she could truly do in this body, from the Temple's confines.

DAISUKE AND OBITO WERE miserably exhausted by the time they arrived in the Capital. When nighttime descended, so did a storm of rain mixed with icy pellets, accompanied by whipping winds that cut right to one's bones. Even Daisuke's game of annoying his friend with pleas to be carried hadn't gone on for long after they passed through Zhao, the city's closest neighbor. Instead, they huddled close as they trudged through dark streets, guided toward the Palace by what few lanterns could still brave the weather.

An empty, eerie silence greeted them once they closed the door to a side entrance they'd found, though mounted torches on the Palace's inner walls burned brightly. Daisuke shivered, but tried to dismiss his unease. They'd spent the last couple of months surrounded by a constant stream of noise, whether it was at Hayate's inn, chatting with fellow travelers on the road, or rustling from within the forest at night. It'd been a while since he'd experienced true, deep quiet. He couldn't tell if he'd missed it or not.

They continued toward their rooms with few words exchanged between them; what little was said mainly centered around the relief of being home after a long journey. They'd pushed themselves hard over the last few days for this reason, and because the decent weather looked like it might turn for the worse. The unfortunate side effect was how horribly leaden every step felt, especially with all the stairs going up to the onmitsu dormitories.

When Obito reached the top of the staircase that opened into the commons area, he froze. Daisuke did the same when he came to his friend's side and found two of their seniors waiting near the fireplace. One wore a velvety black patch over his right eye and waved them closer.

"You're finally back." Raku smiled at them pleasantly before the two teams traded a bow. He looked as exhausted as they did. A dark, half-moon shape had formed under the eye not covered by the patch. "Now we can report to Master Yujin and go to bed."

Daisuke's brows furrowed. "Were you waiting for us?"

"The last four nights." Jido, Raku's partner, explained; while he usually sounded stern, there was rarely any fire behind it, and this time was no different. "Master Yujin thought you'd be arriving soon and wanted confirmation when you returned."

Raku glanced at Jido, and together, they wordlessly agreed they'd fulfilled their duties to the Intelligence Master. "We'll let Master Yujin know you've arrived, but you're still expected to report to him tomorrow. I recommend doing yourselves a favor by not making him wait too long."

"I see, the *real* reason he's made you two stand around like this." Daisuke laughed, though it lacked his typical liveliness—Obito didn't even have enough of it to scold him for what he said.

Raku didn't seem to mind either way. Instead, he gently chided, "Maybe you'll make better time during your next assignment."

The four onmitsu bowed to one another again, and soon Raku and Jido disappeared down the stairway Daisuke and Obito had just ascended. More silence filled the space they left behind, interrupted only by wind whistling through the drafty walls and an occasional crackle from the glowing coals in the fireplace; not even a cough or quiet conversation came from the hall where their rooms were, nor was there any sign of movement between the shadows and firelight of the torches. Unable to stand how uneasy it made him feel, Daisuke looked over at Obito. He'd recently found a hilarious new way of getting under his friend's skin and thought it was the perfect way to break up the tension in the air.

He grinned and casually tossed his bag onto one of the tables the onmitsu used either for studying or playing low-stakes games with one another. "I'm leaving this here and going for a bath. You're joining me, right?"

Obito's shoulders stiffened. "Why would I do that?"

Gets him every time, Daisuke thought as his smile turned a little more wicked. He quickly schooled his expression before he flicked his hair and nonchalantly stated, "Let's not pretend it's anything new. We've been living together the last few months—"

"—That's terribly misleading—"

"—So I know *I* have nothing to hide. Don't act like you do, either."

Obito's face burned as a small wave of anxiety rose up along with a twinge of shame, but he didn't have the energy—or words—to argue. He knew from many nights of waiting until after everyone else had gone to bed that they'd be lucky to pull enough water for a single bath this late, never mind two. Outside of that, he didn't have a good reason to decline, as they were in desperate need of one before they could even think about collapsing into their beds. Daisuke enjoyed teasing, but he *was* fully aware of the reasons Obito preferred not to bathe with others, although those weren't the source of his reservations this time.

One night, around the halfway point of their journey, he realized that, instead of looking at the blank page in his journal, he was staring at his friend's slumbering form; Daisuke tended to use his gi and shitagi as extra blankets rather than sleeping with either on. Already distracted by a stray thought, Obito's eyes had fallen upon the stark contrast of his partner's bright red higanbana tattoo against his pale skin when he rolled onto his back and stretched halfway out of the covers. His gaze shifted when Daisuke did, bringing his attention to faded scarring on his shoulder. He pretended that was the real reason behind what was happening, and why his gaze lingered, though he knew better—he knew *himself* better. He wasn't sure what came over him, but when he finally snapped out of this unwelcome trance, overwhelming guilt followed. After firmly telling himself that it—accidental or not—wasn't acceptable, he'd closed his book and pulled the covers over his friend's slender shoulders. He assumed that'd be the end of it and had done his best to ensure it the rest of the way home.

"Fine," Obito finally said, trying to find the tone he used when he didn't want to admit Daisuke was right.

Seeming not to notice his nerves or the narrow miss in his inflection, the little menace beamed and grabbed him by the wrist to lead the way.

As expected, the darkened Palace halls were wrapped in a shadowy blanket of sleepy silence as the pair made their way to the men's bath chambers, only interrupted by interspersed whispers of conversation from guards who patrolled the corridors. Although one unit paused to observe them as they walked by, no one bothered them—Daisuke couldn't help the sigh of relief that came once they made it past the pair without incident. He'd nearly forgotten how much freedom to wander the onmitsu uniform alone allowed him, even at night, and how much he'd come to rely on that passive permission over the last few years.

Several large pools for bathing were carved into the rugged stone floor and molded with smooth obsidian, while regular wooden washtubs for clothing were piled off to the side of the room. The bath chamber itself was empty, which meant they had no shortage of choices from the full supply of towels, washcloths, and soaps regularly stocked by the Palace staff. Still slightly out of sorts and extremely nervous about the idea, Obito took a wooden bath token from where it hung on the wall, hand shaking ever so slightly as he dropped it into a slot near the pool Daisuke chose. Within minutes, hot water pumped into the bath, and they climbed in one after the other. The token would be brought back by whoever cleaned the bathing area to be used again later.

"See? We got in together, and nothing bad happened," Daisuke teased, his voice echoing softly against the high ceilings and fully bringing Obito back into the present. They'd taken one of the vacant baths on the far wall in case they were unexpectedly joined by others, but so far, the extra precaution hadn't seemed necessary. "You know, I'm actually a little disappointed. Here I thought the world would come to a catastrophic end."

Obito rinsed the soap off his face and glared at his friend, who stood on the opposite side of the pool in waist-deep water, feigning innocence and scrubbing weeks of travel from his hair as if he hadn't said anything. "I'm going to drown you."

A WARM, ORANGE GLOW bathed the room in light with the ignition of an oil lamp dangling from a hook in the stone wall. Now thawed from the weather and clean after a bath, Daisuke was thrilled to at last hide away in his room for the first time in nearly four months. He carelessly tossed the pack he'd retrieved from the commons onto the floor and took a moment to simply enjoy the quiet and safety he hadn't experienced in so long.

Once he basked in the silence long enough, he dug around in his dresser for sleep clothes and discarded his current uniform set in a basket at the foot of his bed, which was when he noticed the gritty feeling under his bare feet. It didn't take long for Daisuke's eyes to rake over traces of pink powder sparkling on the floor as the lamplight caught it, or for him to follow the trail to the top-right drawer of his desk, which looked out of place, as if it'd been broken when someone pulled too hard and then haphazardly closed again. The measuring spoon which held the irritating powder and copper coil he'd used as a spring were tossed aside on the floor near his desk, ripped out from the drawer in anger.

His mind went blank with disbelief.

He'd originally set the trap as a prank on himself and expected to pay for his own paranoia when they got back from Zhu, scrubbing powder from his eyes while Obito laughed at him for it. It certainly would've been better luck than this—what happened was undeniable. Someone had, at some point, gone after something in there. Disgust wrapped around his insides as he pulled on the drawer, careful with the way it stuck, and peered in at his poisons journal. Unsurprisingly, whoever had dared to violate his privacy in such a way hadn't even had the decency to take care of the little book or put it back neatly—it was flipped over the wrong way and crooked, with bends at the corners and frays in the black silk cord he tied around it.

He pulled out the drawer a bit further, barely relieved when he saw the other items had been spared the same mishandling. His fingers gently brushed the surface of the old charm General Aki had given him, though he didn't remove it from where it rested in a wrapping of white silk cloth, and he bit his lip when he saw the helix earring still sitting nearby; the pink and green finch feathers and the pink, blue, and green beads on the little gold hoop didn't show any signs of the abuse his journal had suffered. Although most traditions were stupid in his mind, he *was* quite proud of his earrings. After having them taken away by Lady Chizuru, no matter how temporarily, he didn't think he'd be able to take it in stride if he'd lost this Northern Nomadic rite of passage to adulthood, not in addition to everything else he'd just found. Unable to absorb the scene or untangle his thoughts regarding the journal's apparent theft and return, he listlessly stared a bit longer, then sighed and shut the drawer again.

Daisuke didn't see the need to put up many firm boundaries, other than a request for his classmates to not enter his room without his permission. As it was the one place he had that wasn't communal in some way, much like everyone else, he felt it was an easy rule to honor—impossibly, infuriatingly simple. Why would anyone go out of their way to ignore it? Who, among all his peers, disrespected him enough to do this?

He rubbed his face and groaned, frustrated beyond what his vocabulary could properly explain right then, before going to the oil lamp mounted on the wall and extinguishing the light.

Daisuke flopped onto his back as a wave of exhaustion pushed him to the bed. He cursed after minutes trudged by and his heavy eyelids still refused to close; his eyes burned as he continued staring at a ceiling swallowed in blackness. It was like reliving his first night in the onmitsu dormitories all over again—lonely, afraid, uncertain. This was nowhere near the experience he'd expected to have after so much time away. Despite the chain latch locking the door, this space no longer felt like it was his, or all too private. Instead, an all-consuming, empty silence threatened to enclose him. A far cry from nights filled with chirping crickets at the end of summer or the rattle of dry leaves and stripped tree branches knocking together as they swayed in autumn winds. He'd almost forgotten how much he hated sleeping alone.

He flung the covers back and hauled himself upward once more.

Obito opened his door not long after Daisuke landed a flurry of knocks against it, looking a bit out of sorts, as if all the racket had pulled him from a deep sleep. In the morning, Daisuke would lament missing this opportunity to tease him about it.

When his mind finally caught up with what was going on, Obito muttered under his breath and rubbed his face. "What are you doing?"

Suddenly unable to look at him, Daisuke hugged himself and leaned against the doorframe. "You remember that trap I set before we left? Something—or, I guess, *someone*—tripped it. I think they took my poisons journal. Anyway, I don't really feel safe, and...and I...I can't sleep."

"But I *can*, so hurry up if you're coming in."

It took Daisuke a second to register what Obito meant, as he'd stepped away from the door soon after giving his equally short response, but left it wide open for him to follow. When he poked his head into the pitch-black room, dull light from the torch in the hall showed his friend taking a folded quilt from the bottom drawer of his dresser; everyone else had a similar one for intensely cold winter nights. Daisuke couldn't place why, but the calmness he couldn't find on his own flooded his chest as he stepped inside, then closed them in for the night.

"What are we going to tell Master Yujin?" Daisuke asked as he and Obito approached the Intelligence Master's office the next day. They'd awoken around midmorning and hurried through getting ready, anxious to speak with their superior and unwilling to test his patience. Now that they drew closer, their steps had slowed a bit as a newfound twinge of fear accompanied their nerves.

"I don't see much of reason to lie," Obito said after a moment of struggling to reach a conclusive answer. He hadn't been able to think clearly ever since he woke up with Daisuke draped halfway across him. He cleared his throat, hoping it'd help collect the scattered bits of his mind. "We'll only make things worse for ourselves if we try. Since we don't have the box or artifact anymore, Master Yujin will probably want to hear Hayate's side of things, too."

"Good thing he's sending a report, I guess. But...he can only confirm what happened with Senator Hajime if we include that, right?"

"Right. Now figure out how to explain what happened to Rin and Gero, the box, and you."

"...Well—"

"In a way that makes sense and doesn't make us look like we're lying." The corners of Obito's mouth subconsciously ticked upward as he watched his friend mentally grapple with a solution fitting the criteria he'd laid out. When an exasperated "fuck" escaped the little pest on a sigh, he knew he'd won. "The truth sounds wild enough, don't you think?"

"You have no idea how badly I want to disagree with you right now."

"I know. You'll get over it."

Daisuke playfully scowled at him as he leaned against the doorframe and gestured. "After you, then."

"You just want to make sure you're out of Master Yujin's reach."

"You're damn right."

Master Yujin's muffled voice came from the other side of the door not long after Obito knocked. Spines stiff with fear, they traded a look with one another before he wordlessly removed the last barrier between them and their fates. Daisuke's fingers dug into his shoulders as they entered, apparently using him as a human shield of sorts—he'd get back at him for it later. Somehow.

They found Master Yujin standing in front of his desk with his hands behind his back, ready to receive them and the mysterious artifact that had caused so much trouble. Obito peeled Daisuke's hands off, and they nervously bowed to the Intelligence Master, who inclined his head in turn. The older man's face had been warm enough at first, but upon recognizing their halting movements, a more familiar austerity swept over him.

He cleared his throat, adopting a more neutral expression. "Good to see you back, boys. Are your reports ready?"

"We still need time to finish," Obito told him, willfully neglecting the fact that neither had thought to write a single sentence yet.

Although the answer was unsurprising, Yujin wasn't exactly satisfied when he heard it. Emperor Akuwara had pestered him nonstop the entire time they'd been away, demanding to know when they'd return and further demonstrating his paranoia over the matter with each inquiry. However, since he didn't have the flexibility in his schedule to chain them to a desk and loom over them like a threatening cloud while they worked, he elected to extend their deadline.

"You have until tomorrow evening. If I am not here when you're ready to hand them in, you will put them under the door. I don't want to track you down for these—is that clear?"

"Yes, sir," they agreed in unison.

Daisuke let out a silent breath of relief. Obito at least had the foresight to make quick notes of things throughout the assignment, such as where they stopped and for how long to prove they weren't slacking off, but he hadn't even started on his yet.

"Very well. Now, where is the artifact?" Yujin raised his eyebrows when Daisuke and Obito reflexively looked at one another, as if both hoped his partner could think fast enough to start talking and supply an explanation. In that minute exchange, the Intelligence Master realized it was just as he'd dreaded—something had gone horribly awry. He let them squirm a bit before prompting again, "Boys? The artifact?"

"We *had* it," Daisuke began, wincing a bit harder as each hesitant word left his mouth. "Everything went fine at first, but then...these strange things started happening before we left the potter's house. Something dark was there—like a presence. We all felt it. They all but kicked us out to make us leave with the artifact that much faster. After that, though..."

"After that...?" Yujin coaxed when the black-haired boy paused to wring his hands together, letting a fraction of impatience show.

"W-we were ambushed by three people wearing cloaks. Their faces were covered, too. One of them used some...magic, or—or something, we don't exactly know yet—to take the artifact, then separated us."

Yujin had studied Obito's face the entire time Daisuke spoke, searching for any slight reaction that might suggest his partner was lying, but the boy's expression never changed. A creeping, uneasy sense warned the Intelligence Master this wasn't some tall tale, and that he shouldn't doubt his young agents. Twisting the truth was a necessity to survive and thrive in their profession; while both boys were plenty capable of it, Master Yujin didn't see the sense in why they *would* at present. Emperor Akuwara would choke on his own blood from rage when he learned they'd come home empty-handed. Nothing could quell that, which further added to the sense of dread seeping into Yujin's bones. Daisuke wasn't just trying to keep Obito or himself out of trouble.

He pinched the bridge of his nose and sighed. "How did you return home together, then?"

"Obito and some dumbass infantry grunt saved me from Senator Hajime."

Yujin blinked slowly, then lowered his head into his palms as he felt the first nagging signs of a headache. He'd have more in-depth explanations once he finally got his hands on their reports—which was also when he could scrutinize them for inconsistencies—but it didn't lessen his frustrations. He'd advised His Highness not to send them. He'd stated, in no uncertain terms, why having a Northern Nomad on this assignment was a potential for disaster. While he wasn't sure he believed the allegation of the thieves using magic, its existence in the world was undeniable when it came to the abilities of Healers and the Okami. If nothing else, Yujin was prepared to admit there was more of it than he knew about. He wanted a small hint of evidence before placing any weight on this incident—he felt that was plenty reasonable.

In any case, getting past him was the easy part, whether Daisuke and Obito realized it or not. Once Emperor Akuwara heard they failed to retrieve the artifact, only the gods could say if he'd have the patience to read their reports and find out why. Even if he *did*, those accounts wouldn't guarantee either of them immunity from some sort of disciplinary action. He doubted his plan to double their patrol duties and other menial work would do much to assuage His Highness—it certainly wouldn't help the Emperor vent his inevitable fit of fury.

Luckily for the boys, acknowledging Akuwara's temper put Yujin in a rather generous mood. "You will keep every word of what happened in Zhu between the three of us until I hear from Hayate. In the meantime, you two will dedicate all your free time to researching this incident. I also want you to visit the High Priestess once you've turned in your reports to tell her about this."

Daisuke's brows furrowed after he and Obito looked at one another for a third time. "So...you *do* believe us?"

"Yes. While I'm not sure what that says about my sanity, it makes even less sense to me that you'd lie, especially since the whole of your story involves a high-ranking official like Senator Hajime."

The pair remained quiet for a little while, steadily chiseling away at Yujin's composure; it was never easy for him to guess at what either one thought at any given point. They didn't look particularly relieved—not that he blamed them, knowing what lay ahead—but each boy's posture seemed to relax ever so slightly. Finally, Obito nudged Daisuke, and they bowed.

"Thank you, sir," Obito said as they both straightened again.

Yujin curtly inclined his head, formally dismissing them.

"I ALREADY HATE THIS," Daisuke complained later that evening as he shuffled through a stack of notes from Obito's journal.

They sat alone at one of the long tables set in an alcove just off the Palace kitchens. While other staff, maids, and courtesans ate in their own sectioned-off areas, guards and onmitsu took their meals here, which meant it sometimes became awfully crowded and noisy. Normally, the absence of others buzzing about gave it an uncanny sense of being *too* empty. However, aside from an occasional interruption of clanging pots and pans coming from the scullery, this time Daisuke found more peace than anything else in the quiet. His nerves still felt frayed from the stress of traveling, and he hadn't quite gotten over the events in Zhu.

Obito glanced at him, taking his attention away from the small mound of tobacco and papers in front of him—with the promise of being allowed to keep a few, he'd agreed to roll some cigarettes for an older classmate who'd recently broken his thumb while sparring. "It'll be easy if you focus. All you need to do is compare my notes with anything different you might've noticed—we'll *both* need to state as much—and, of course, decide how much detail you want to include about your time at the Senator's estate."

"I'd rather forget about it, honestly. How did you get so good at that, by the way?"

"My mother smokes, but you knew that—stay on topic. It doesn't help you to say nothing."

"You're really trying to protect me, aren't you?" Daisuke half-muttered as he leaned forward on his elbow, careful not to smudge the ink on his friend's papers. He sighed. Although he'd been reluctant to talk about Zhu, there was one thing he hadn't said yet; it was desperately overdue. "I guess I shouldn't be surprised. I don't thank you enough for how much you save my ass."

Silence fell when they paused to look at one another. Obito was lost for words. He hadn't expected Daisuke to say those things, nor was he sure he'd wanted him to; it didn't seem right to accept. Fortunately, he didn't need to struggle with it for long, as footsteps echoing against the stone floors caught his attention. The light shade of pink coloring Daisuke's cheeks just as quickly drained, and he hurriedly placed the papers facedown over the materials between them.

"I heard you were finally back." Mika smiled broadly and clapped Daisuke on the shoulder in an enthusiastic greeting, but his cheerfulness didn't seem entirely genuine; an almost nervous edge had crept into his voice, which instantly made the target of his attempted charm suspicious. "A bunch of us were going to go out for a bit tonight since we're off duty. You should come with us. It'll be more fun than hanging around here with...*certain* others, and you can tell us all about the mission."

Even when purposefully and pointedly ignoring him, Mika still managed to insult his cousin. It wasn't the only reason Daisuke thought he should decline, though; the excuse left him more on instinct than by conscious choice. "I would, but Master Yujin wanted us to work on our reports. Isn't that right, Obito?"

Obito froze in place when Daisuke's gaze locked onto him from across the table, wordlessly pleading for any imaginable reason to stay behind. After a brief, nearly imperceptible round of them silently debating whether he'd play along, he irritably rolled his eyes. The little pest always won somehow. He cleared his throat and straightened his posture, doing his best to look pissed at the mere idea of being abandoned.

"I don't mind if you go, Daisuke," he said slowly, secretly enjoying the look of wide-eyed panic as it hit his partner's face. "But you know how much I hate doing your work for you. I'll be very upset if I end up finishing your half of the report by myself because you aren't back on time, and Master Yujin *will* know about it."

Sensing a hint of seriousness behind the act, Daisuke swallowed, then sheepishly peered up at Mika. "Can't have that, now, can I? I guess we have our answer."

"Guess so," Mika snarled. His hazel eyes went to Obito, irate, though his gaze was never returned. "Lighten up, you fuck."

"That couldn't have gone better," Daisuke sarcastically grumbled as he watched Mika's gloomy figure storm away, then turned back to his friend. "Thanks—I guess—for lying for me."

Obito raised an eyebrow. "Who's lying?"

Daisuke blinked. He laughed nervously when Obito expressionlessly handed him the notes once more, then went back to rolling cigarettes.

HEAVY GREY CLOUDS EASILY drifted through the skies over the Capital and Palace grounds, carrying bitterly cold winds and large wet snowflakes common to the first few snowfalls of early winter. A small alcove arched over a side entrance to the Palace protected Daisuke and Obito from the inclement weather, though it wouldn't last long once they finished smoking. With their reports turned in and awaiting the Intelligence Master's review, their next task was seeking an audience with the High Priestess at the Palace Temple. There wasn't much choice in the matter, but over the two days since they'd first made the plan to go, Obito couldn't shake the sense they'd be wasting their time.

He glanced at Daisuke after snuffing out his cigarette on the sole of his boot, then tossed it into a nearby brazier, where it sizzled before it sank in a pool of half-frozen water to settle among others left by those who had previously done the same. Neither boy was entirely welcome in the Temple, a fact they hadn't been brave enough to remind Master Yujin about when he gave the order, especially since he'd likely forgotten in his urgency to head off the Emperor's notorious temper with answers. Daisuke and Obito agreed they'd rather skirt around His Highness for as long as possible and deal with the minor inconvenience of annoying, self-important priests.

Their low opinions of clergymen weren't totally unfounded. Around a century ago, the priesthood began slinging the word "heathenism" at enslaved Northern Nomads who clung to their ancestral beliefs, which gradually led to outright banning them from entering any of Hikari's Temples. No one was entirely sure what had incited the campaign—whether it came from the throne, slavers, or the clergy itself—but since the High Priestess in those times never refuted the claims, people took it as Hikari's will and judgement. Today's priests were generally a bit too enthusiastic in their efforts to enforce it.

Obito's reasons were far less overt, but ever-present. What his uncle did would've been enough without adding how rarely his family entertained religious ideals. While Daisuke knew about those first two reasons, a third had recently placed itself alongside them. The Temple might try to say it was due to his sexuality, but in truth, that was the least of it; really, it had more to do with the "heathen" these budding affections were toward. Not that any of it mattered. He was determined to keep it to himself for as long as he could manage, as accepting it and confronting it were entirely separate things—he barely had a grasp on the first part.

"Did you get lost again?" Daisuke teased, snapping him out of his thoughts.

He forced himself not to wince at the question—it was a matter of time before a certain little pest figured everything out on his own...if he hadn't already. Obito squared his shoulders and pulled up the hood of his cloak. "Never mind. Let's get this over with."

Brows furrowed, Daisuke tilted his head. His eyes never fully pulled away from Obito's face as he also put out his cigarette in the brazier beside him. Something was obviously on his mind, but he didn't try pressing the subject; unless he could finesse his inquiries just right in the meantime, he wouldn't get an answer until his friend felt like giving one. It was simply Obito's way sometimes. Once he followed suit and put up his hood, and they began their trek across the grounds to the Palace Temple, there wasn't much room for a conversation, anyway.

A sheet of ice glazed the grass and walkways while gusting, biting winds easily cut through to the bone; it was a slow, miserable walk that kept them huddled close together and burrowed as deeply into their cloaks as possible. Daisuke hoped they'd encounter a priest who felt merciful enough to bring them out of the elements when they arrived, but he knew the Temple's history with Northern Nomads better than he cared to admit—even if he ignored it, he hadn't the slightest clue what to expect out of its occupants.

He turned to Obito when they neared the Temple, hopeful for some guidance. "What do we even do if we're allowed inside?"

"I just turned fifteen and I've been to a temple twice in my life. Do what you will with that information."

Daisuke opened his mouth to comment, but his attention diverted when he paused to study one of several flowerbeds marked for twilight petunias. These fussy medicinal flowers first bloomed in the middle of spring, with soft violet petals and deep blue centers, and surrounded the

Temple grounds. Although they were widely known as the High Priestess's favorite, the beds looked as though they hadn't been tended to since the last growth budded at the end of summer; spindly, wilted stems lay beneath a layer of half-melted snow in hard-packed soil, tangled with overgrown dead weeds.

"What are you thinking?" Obito asked, startling him into releasing the plant he'd subconsciously taken into his hand.

"I'm not sure." Daisuke's eyes swept over the nearest beds, each in similar conditions. He stifled the disconcerting feeling creeping into his chest, then started toward the Temple's stairs once more. "It just feels like something's off."

Obito glanced at the brittle brown plants when he passed by to follow his partner. The High Priestess usually tended to the botanical arrangements on the Temple grounds and prepared them for the harsh Perenin winters—with neither done, his friend's observation was correct, though he also couldn't place what might be wrong.

Daisuke stopped at the base of the Temple's steps to stare up at the door, brows knitted slightly while his gaze flicked between the pagodas near it and black Imperial flags billowing in the winds. He sighed and pulled down his hood; flecks of white instantly dotted his raven hair. "Look, I know *I* can't go in there—let's not act like the priests or High Priestess will care if it's for something that might be important—so...how should we work this?"

"You really think you get to stay out here and wait?"

"Wouldn't it be better? With the law being what it is..."

"There's ways around it."

"Obito." Daisuke grinned, batting his eyelashes in a way he knew would make his friend's shoulders tense. "Are you suggesting we sneak into the Palace Temple?"

"Well, I didn't *exactly* say—"

"It's so underhanded, it almost sounds like one of *my* ideas. I can't believe it. Fine, you've convinced me. Let's do it."

Obito pinched the bridge of his nose. "I'm throwing you in a snowbank when we're done."

"You're so mean," Daisuke snickered, trailing behind Obito as they ascended the Temple's icy stairs.

At first, Obito thought the weather had partially frozen the door when he tugged on it and it didn't budge. However, upon a second try without a change in luck, he could only stare at it in confusion. Even in the middle of the night, these doors should've been open—all temples were meant to be safe havens no matter the time of day. Nothing less was expected of the altar where the Emperor himself made offerings and prayed. He sighed. At least Daisuke was already willing to go along with this; were it not for the flags providing them with some cover, he might've suggested returning at night or trying something different altogether.

"You're in luck, looks like we *are* sneaking in."

As predicted, Daisuke's eyes sparkled with mischief. He glanced around at the options available, then pointed at a small, rectangular window just off to the side of the doors, over where one flagpole was anchored to the outer wall. He blew on his hands and vigorously rubbed his palms together. "Think you can help me get up there?"

"Only if you can balance on the pole, but it might be slick. Maybe we should—"

"It'll be fine."

"Daisuke..."

"Just stay under me so you can catch me if I fall. Ready?"

Obito nodded, and once they were in position under the window, Daisuke climbed onto his shoulders. They'd gotten better at this since their first attempt a few years back, when they infiltrated the Ivory Snake, an expensive inn tucked away in the nobility district. Unlike their first endeavor, this time came with far less swearing and tumbling; Obito now knew how to distribute his weight better to accommodate the addition of Daisuke's, so they didn't so much as wobble when his partner reached for the flagpole. His fingers slipped at first when he tried pulling himself up, but held firm with a second attempt. Obito took a couple of steps back to avoid getting kicked in the face, watching warily as Daisuke made it onto the pole, then, using the wall and window's outer ledge for support, got to his feet. The window itself popped open with ease, and moments later, Daisuke soundlessly disappeared through it.

Admittedly, it was an impressive feat, but also quite dangerous—it wouldn't take much for Daisuke to injure himself if either of them fucked up even in drier conditions, so Obito generally tried to find other methods during these types of excursions. Unfortunately, he couldn't see many alternatives this time. If the main door into the Temple was locked, there was little chance the rear entrance on the ground floor would yield different results. Either way, he was certain that breaking into the Palace Temple like a couple of common thieves bordered on blasphemy; the idea probably shouldn't have amused him as much as it did.

The world came into focus again when he heard the bar on the other side slide with a light metallic grind, and soon after, Daisuke pulled open one of the heavy doors.

"Nothing to it." The little pest grinned.

Obito shook his head and stepped forward, but hesitated when the toes of his boots touched the threshold. Unsure why he bothered with the propriety, he bowed before he stepped into the Temple. Curious, Daisuke tilted his head, shrugged, then turned to face the room and copied his actions. Once they closed the heavy double doors behind them, they were free to examine their surroundings again.

A long, obsidian altar sat against the wall opposite the entrance, holding rows of red candles and ornate incense burners, all surrounding a large, golden statue of the Mother Goddess, Hikari. Intricately decorated offering boxes sat on the floor on each end of the altar, near a small pool with water lilies floating on the surface, all of which lay in front of deep red cushions on the floor for kneeling during prayer services. A painting of Perena's mountain range stretched the length of the wall, with the tallest peak, called Hikari's Landing, at the center behind the statue. It was about as stuffy as Daisuke had expected, yet not a single priest tended to the altar or wandered the room, and while lanterns provided them with light, both the candles and incense burners looked as though they hadn't been lit in quite some time. The whole place seemed to be filled with a jarring, uncomfortable silence.

"It's...quiet in here," Daisuke whispered, eyes warily darting between each end of the large main sanctuary hall.

"It *was*," Obito corrected, earning an elbow to his upper arm. Despite his comment, he couldn't disagree with Daisuke's assessment—it seemed entirely unoccupied. It remained as such as they descended the stairs to the levels below. The main sanctuary where they'd entered was on the top floor, but with how few people were allowed to come pray at the Palace Temple to begin with, Obito hadn't expected to find the High Priestess there.

Still, she should've been *somewhere* in the halls or rooms of the first floor they explored, though all they came across were the bunks where the priesthood slept, along with their kitchen and dining area. When they reached the lower floor, although the scent of pine incense lingered heavily in the air, nothing more than a row of clay pots on pedestals greeted them. Although they were quite aware they were trespassing, something about the air down here made it seem as though they were especially unwelcome.

Obito paused to examine the pots, inexplicably drawn to the symbol painted on each one. Three right-facing swirls—tomoe, he believed they were called—surrounded by a thick circle with a flame-like pattern that pointed in each cardinal direction. He felt hands on his shoulders as Daisuke cautiously peered around him to see what had his attention.

"Excuse me."

Daisuke nearly leapt onto Obito's back at the unexpected voice from behind them. When they turned, a woman with long black hair, adorned in layers of red, white, and gold robes carefully embroidered with silver peonies was stepping out of one of the side rooms. She stared at them for another moment, then approached as she tucked a string of dark purple beads and pieces of rose quartz away in the red sash belt at her waist.

"You shouldn't be here," the woman said coldly, black eyes icily fixated on them.

"I know, I know, laws and all, but—"

"Forget the laws," she muttered tersely. She held up a hand to keep Daisuke silent, bewildering Obito and possibly all the gods when it worked. "This humble priestess is supposed to be in isolation to fortify my spiritual energy before the winter solstice. The Temple is closed while the priests are away. If you must pray or make an offering, please use one of the other temples in the city."

"Is that why the gardens look so miserable?"

Obito was about to ask why the priests were absent, but now it was his turn to elbow Daisuke, though with a little more force than what his friend previously used on him. Their personal feelings about religion didn't matter when addressing the High Priestess of Hikari.

The woman's even steps faltered, and her eyes narrowed. There was a hint of contempt in her voice when she said, "You are onmitsu. Does the Intelligence Master require something of this humble priestess?"

Still massaging the spot where he'd been nudged, Daisuke glared at Obito—who pretended he didn't notice—before saying, "No, but he did send us to speak with you."

"You have questions for my humble self?" The High Priestess's gaze swept over them when Obito traded a look with Daisuke, and they both nodded. She sighed, as if her next suggestion both exhausted and bored her. "Very well. What do you wish to know?"

"We were recently in Zhu and had an...odd encounter," Obito began, waiting for her signal to continue. "Someone who called themselves the Priestess of Shadows cornered us after we retrieved an unknown artifact from a potter and his wife, then made off with it. We were hoping you could tell us more about it."

The High Priestess swallowed, her mouth forming into a worried line. She struggled to keep her voice even when she said, "That is indeed strange, though I am afraid that is precious little to work with."

Daisuke added, "This other priestess also seemed like she could manipulate shadows. It's how she took the box containing the artifact from us—she also called out the names Kanashimi and Saigai."

"...You speak the names of figures who appeared in legends and stories in ancient times," the High Priestess said stiffly. She indignantly lifted her chin, then turned away. "Similarly, the use of shadow magic has not been seen in centuries—anyone who practiced it in the old ages would no longer be alive. The gods themselves *guaranteed* it would not be passed to new generations."

"But, we saw—"

"I would think the young men enlisted with Imperial Intelligence would have far more important things to do than chase bedtime stories. You would be better off searching for your answers in the Royal Library if that is how you wish to spend your time."

The gold, hexagonal-shaped plate dangling from the High Priestess's headpiece jingled delicately when she turned to look at them once more, scorn flashing in her eyes anew. This time, Obito took note of the unmistakable gleam of a gem resting at each point—four rubies, and two that were marbled black and green. She quickly turned away when she realized he saw them, as if ashamed, and took several steps in the opposite direction. Just as his eyes narrowed with suspicion, from his periphery, he noticed Daisuke mirroring his expression for the same reason.

"You're *sure* you can't tell us anything?" Obito pressed. "Not even about this so-called Priestess of Shadows?"

"No," the High Priestess answered curtly, frigidly glaring at them from over her shoulder. "You both need to leave now. This humble one has entertained your nonsense questions and tolerated this intrusion long enough."

"Hardly. It sounds more like you're hiding something from us."

"Daisuke," Obito hissed, warning him.

"I—"

"What? If anyone knows anything about this, it *should* be her."

Fear abruptly broke through the harsh countenance in the woman's eyes, as if Daisuke's words struck a nerve. The High Priestess somehow closed the gap between them with a single step, grabbed them each by an arm, linked them together, and shoved them backward with a burst of power neither expected from her. However, instead of stumbling through a wall or screen like they'd braced themselves for, when they looked around, they were outside once more. Obito shivered at the sudden influx of winter air jabbing at his skin. Daisuke blinked as he checked their surroundings, his head on a swivel, though he didn't take his arm away from Obito's. Not only was the way she'd cast them out abrupt and strange, but also familiar—chillingly so. At least they'd been allowed to stay together this time.

"What isn't she telling us?" Daisuke quietly wondered once they'd regained their bearings.

Ignoring his racing heart, Obito freed himself and started their walk back toward the Palace, trying to process everything as quickly as he could force it. "Hard to say, but we won't get anywhere with her right now. Come on—we should still tell Master Yujin *something* so he knows we weren't just wasting time this morning."

"Now you're suggesting a lie?" Daisuke teased as he fell into step beside him, grinning like a sly little demon.

"Not a lie," Obito answered. "We just won't tell him everything."

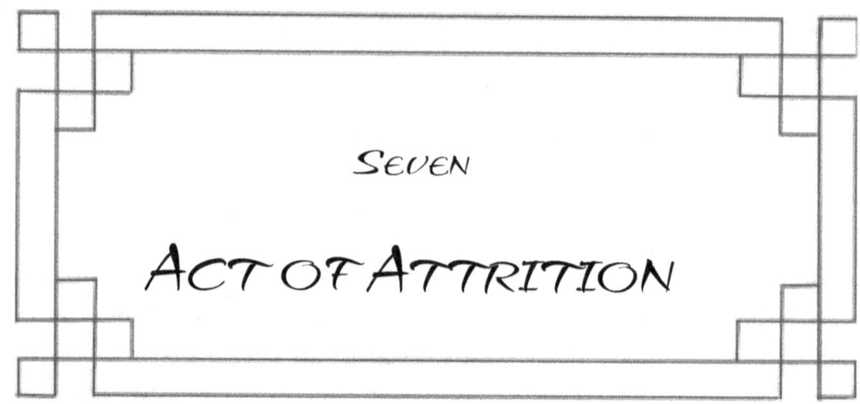

MASTER YUJIN'S OFFICE WAS empty when they arrived to report on the morning's events, which furthered the sense of defeat that had started to settle in on the way back from the Temple. Daisuke never could've guessed the High Priestess would be so difficult to work with—not to mention, a bit on the ill-tempered side.

Foiled for now, Obito suggested they go back to their rooms, make sure their cloaks had a place to dry properly, and then prepare to join their classmates for any remaining morning lessons. Although Daisuke would've much preferred going back to bed, for some stupid reason, he went along with his partner's plan instead—and kicked himself when the words left his mouth. Now that he'd agreed, Obito wouldn't give him a second chance to get out of it.

"You tricked me," Daisuke whined playfully.

Obito couldn't help the small smirk on his lips. "Even if we pretended that's what happened, would it kill you to be a responsible student?"

"I mean...it might. We don't know that it *won't*."

"It hasn't yet. You'll be fine."

They'd only made it as far as the old arrow slats from their rooms when an interruption halted them, bringing Daisuke's endless inner moaning about how he was his own worst enemy to a stop, as well.

"Obito, Daisuke," Master Yujin's voice called from down the corridor, making them jump as they turned to face him. The Intelligence Master wore a grim expression, which gave them both pause, but it wasn't long before Obito gathered enough courage to go toward their superior. He didn't greet them beyond the initial call of their names when they drew near; instead, he turned on his heel with a curt, "Follow me."

Daisuke shot Obito a confused look; it wasn't often the Intelligence Master appeared in this part of the Palace to begin with. The subtle hints of worry flashing in his friend's eyes were hardly a reassuring sight as they obeyed Master Yujin's order. For a long portion of their walk through the Palace, the one noise filling the air between the three was the steady sound of boots tromping against the stone floor. Obito and Daisuke kept glancing at one another as they trailed their superior, though neither knew the right questions to ask, nor if they were in a position to speak.

"Master Yujin," Daisuke began when he couldn't take it anymore. He traded another nervous look with Obito, who silently urged him to continue. "We spoke with the High Priestess, sir. Well, sort of—mostly. She didn't seem to know what we experienced, either, but—sir, please, this is killing me. What's going on?"

Master Yujin let out a long, slow sigh. "Never mind the Priestess for now. I met with His Highness this morning while you two were at the Temple. As you might've expected, he isn't impressed with your reports."

They stayed on Master Yujin's heels down a short flight of stairs before Obito stated, "Because of his connection to Senator Hajime, he wants to handle this himself."

"Correct." The Intelligence Master spared them a glance over his shoulder. "He doesn't believe a word of what either of you wrote and doesn't trust me to...deal with you properly—I suppose that's one way to put it. So, while I won't be delivering your punishment, I *will* be present. I suggest you do yourselves a favor and be men about it."

"What does that mean?"

"Daisuke," Master Yujin muttered his name out of reflexive exasperation more than the intent to answer.

The rest of their journey carried on in the same heavy silence as it before, until they reached a room where two men awaited the group, one with graying dark brown hair and the other nearly bald with a long, elegantly groomed beard. Judging by the multiple layers and materials of their uniforms, they were members of the Emperor's personal guard; they didn't even bow to Master Yujin when the three stiffly greeted each other. Only the guards and an incense burner were present—not even the usual décor of Imperial flags graced the walls. Before Master Yujin could offer further instruction to his pupils, Daisuke and Obito were grabbed and dragged to the center of the room, then pushed to their knees without a care for how hard they'd land.

Too stunned to think, Daisuke's eyes went to the glazed porcelain incense burner at the front of the room, carved to look like a pair of hands cupping something. He barely heard when they were ordered to remove their shirts and just as numbly obeyed.

"You will kneel here and reflect on your grievous errors," the man with graying hair pulled into a tight bun explained as he knelt beside the incense burner. "Think hard, boys. Once this burns down, we'll be back to deliver your *real* punishment."

The Emperor's other guard also took out a stick of incense, and once ready, the two were simultaneously lit. With the threatening speech already out of the way, they wordlessly started for the door with one of the sticks still in their possession. Master Yujin hesitated, dipped his head, then followed them on soundless feet. Silence filled the room as their steps disappeared down the corridor.

"Does 'reflecting' mean we can't talk?" Daisuke whispered once they were gone.

"Good question," Obito answered. "Think about it for a bit and tell me what you come up with."

Got it. Daisuke tensely eyed the burner and tried for several minutes to let his mind go blank, as he didn't want to think about what awaited them afterward—branding, dismemberment, and lashings were all possibilities running through his mind. He shivered, and eventually, his gaze wandered toward his friend.

He'd expected a harsh punishment; Emperor Akuwara wouldn't have it any other way. The highest authority in the land couldn't have a slaveborn making him look like the rabid fanatic Daisuke suspected he might be. He just assumed, from the beginning, he'd go through it alone; he didn't predict Obito getting dragged this far down with him. In fact, much to his embarrassment, he realized he hadn't taken the possibility seriously until now. A stray, intrusive thought told him it was *because* of him that Obito was also in this terrible predicament. His fists clenched as the subconscious, nervous grip on his trousers tightened; from the cool air against his bare skin to the fact that he'd gotten someone else into trouble and a subsequent punishment with him, it was impossible to avoid thoughts of his childhood on the plantations. Hell, even down to the chance of a bareback beating—both Honda and Grandmaster Norio fervently implemented those.

Guilty by association, or whatever the fuck they'd say—if Obito had been with anyone else, nothing more would've come of this whole thing.

The muted rustle of fabric against stone batted his thoughts away when it reached his ears, saving him from voicing them to his partner and from becoming too entangled with them. He glanced to his left, finding Obito's forest-green eyes already on him and wordlessly asking the same question about who could be approaching this time, though neither had an answer.

A boy of about seven or eight years old entered the room; his black robes with gold and green accents dragged along the floor, which were the main source of any noise he made as he came into view before them. Although small, a red lotus painted on his forehead starkly stood against his skin, which was much fairer than the average Perenin's or Giahatian's, just like the Emperor's. Moreover, his forehead marking could only belong to one person in the Palace—when Akuwara abdicated the throne, it'd be replaced by the silver Imperial circlet.

Prince Akuko's expressionless obsidian eyes studied them for a while, never wavering in the slightest. Unease gripped Daisuke's insides, but not just because of the Prince's unsettling quiet. He should've been around Kulako's age, and being forced to face the disparity between the lives each boy led made resentment bubble in his veins, though it wasn't solely aimed at the royal family. Most of it was directed at himself. He'd kept it out of his mind for a while, now, but Daisuke didn't know if he'd ever forgive himself for abandoning his little brother, still living as a slave, still suffering their father's hatred for their existence.

"Father says you both deserve to be punished," the Crown Prince finally said, shattering the dome of self-loathing threatening to encase him. The boy's thin, delicate brows furrowed, then relaxed, almost too quickly to be considered a change. "He believes I should watch, that way I will know what to do when the decision is mine to make."

Daisuke dared a glance at Obito, and though their eyes met, neither found himself brave enough to speak. Had these words come from any other child, they would've been entirely laughable.

"Strangely," Akuko continued. "I believe Father is mostly wrong—Father believes this will be the end of the matter, while I do not, and neither does Master Yujin. If it *were* my decision, this would be a *warning* not to fail again."

Obito's stomach knotted.

"I do wonder how this will make you act in the future, but for now, I will watch as Father wants." The Prince smiled, though the expression held no light or warmth, nor did it seem like a natural thing for his features to do. To further mock them and their situation, he folded his arms into his sleeves, bowed, and then left.

"That boy's one of Kuro's devils, I swear," Daisuke muttered once he was sure the Prince wouldn't turn around, chills still prickling at his skin.

Despite everything, Obito couldn't help but smirk, and unknowingly released the guilt erratically buzzing around in his partner's head. "I don't think insulting one of the gods is going to improve things for us."

The incense faintly hissed as the last bits of ash remaining on the stick fell into the burner's tray; Daisuke swallowed. Right on cue, two clomping sets of boots, accompanied by the measured, soft swish of silk against stone flooring, approached from the corridor. Daisuke and Obito traded a final glance as the Emperor and his guards drew nearer—one last apology, one more unspoken reassurance, and wryly wishing one another good luck. At the very least, they'd live.

They flinched in unison when two hollow *bangs* of bamboo poles reverberated against the floor. Forced as it sounded, Master Yujin's familiar voice commanded, "Backs straight and eyes forward for His Highness, Emperor Akuwara, and Crown Prince Akuko."

Daisuke instinctively more than voluntarily looked toward the presence he sensed in the doorway, where the Emperor's towering figure steadily came into view, trailed by the Prince, who preceded the Intelligence Master. Both royals held their heads high, arms tucked into their wide sleeves as they walked toward the center of the wall with an even, imposing gait. When he reached the center of the wall, Emperor Akuwara elegantly turned to the two onmitsu kneeling before him while his guards shut the heavy door, then took their places behind the boys, barely noticed. Obito and Daisuke had only seen the Emperor from a distance, so they weren't prepared to feel so unnerved when this close to the man; they barely dared to breathe. Meanwhile, Akuko found a spot several paces back from his father, revealing nothing that would've hinted at his earlier appearance, and Master Yujin took his place beside the Emperor.

"I see no reason to waste time on a lengthy preamble," Emperor Akuwara began once he was certain all eyes were on him, his voice grave. "As I said when I spoke with Master Yujin this morning, there are no words to express how deeply disappointed I am in you both for failing such a disgustingly simple mission. However, there are consequences to failures in our ranks, and your lies will not be accepted or tolerated—be eternally grateful I have not found it necessary to charge you with treason for either of these egregious errors. By my grace and Hikari's, may you learn your lesson once we are through here."

The bamboo poles struck the ground twice more. Master Yujin's subtle wince didn't go unnoticed by his younger subordinates, but still, he nodded at the older pair behind them. Daisuke closed his eyes and braced himself. Lie, tell the truth, it hadn't mattered in his previous life when someone's definition of justice demanded fulfillment; apparently, it made no difference now, either.

He lost count of how many times the bamboo pole hit him across his back, but he tried to follow Obito's example of enduring the punishment in as much silence as he could manage. In a strangely Giahatian way, it was an act of defiance now that more overt options were no longer available, though it looked as if his partner's nails were about to tear through his trousers from how hard he was gripping them. One strike came down so hard, the metallic taste of blood invaded Daisuke's mouth upon impact—still, nothing louder than the most tightly restrained grunts escaped his throat. Occasionally, his vision blurred from the overlapping sensations of pain before it settled again, landing on Master Yujin's guilt-stricken face for a fraction of a second.

As much as he tried to keep himself together, with every strike and each wave of agony that went through his muscles down to his bones, Daisuke's anger grew until the weight of a thousand shouted curses sat on his tongue. Rather than let them loose, he clenched his jaw so hard he thought his teeth might crack. *Fuck this! Fuck, fuck, fuck! How many fucking times do I have to put up with this in my fucking life?!*

Just when he thought he couldn't hold on any longer, the final swing struck his back, and the punishment was over.

"Bow to His Highness, you ungrateful dogs," one of the guards spat. Daisuke thought he could *feel* the unspoken rage emanating from his partner, but when he looked out of the corner of his eye, he saw Obito's hands spread in front of him, and his forehead touched the floor. He begrudgingly bit his tongue and did the same—gods, it hurt to move, but kowtowing like this when instructed was better than inviting further suffering.

"May you both remember today, and why this had to happen, for years to come." Emperor Akuwara had remained expressionless until now; a tiny yet incredibly smug smile touched his lips, and the calm in his voice dripped with chilling satisfaction. His head tilted toward his Intelligence Master, whose stoic face looked to have gone slightly pale. "And may *you* remember this as well, Intelligence Master."

The Emperor took another long look at them, basking in their shared misery, then departed with a swirl of his robes, trailed closely by his two guards, the Prince, and Master Yujin.

Obito waited until he was sure everyone was gone, then stiffly nudged Daisuke. His back throbbed and needles of pain jabbed into his legs from how long he'd knelt in place, but he managed to pull himself upright and stand somewhat properly. Although Daisuke desperately wanted to know if it looked as bad as it felt, he spared Obito what little dignity he could at this point by not allowing his gaze to wander while they dressed once more. When ready, the pair cautiously crept from the room, wary of being seen by their classmates in this sorry state, before they began a slow, half-stumbling trudge toward the infirmary. Never one to stay quiet for long, Daisuke launched into a tirade about the injustice of it all as they went onward, ignoring curious glances he received from passersby. Although Obito thought it was better to let Daisuke vent, part of him wished he had the energy to shut him up.

Since Daisuke's rant easily ensured he could be heard from down the corridor, a young woman wearing a Palace Healer's plain blue dress and white outer robe had already risen to greet them from behind the main desk before they fully entered the room. Her bright, placating smile wavered when her large brown eyes settled on them; after a long pause, she scrambled to find her cheery demeanor, though her smile was awkward and uncertain when it returned.

"M-may I help you?"

"Bruising medicine, please," Obito told her.

"Bruises?" She blinked, confused. "Wouldn't you rather I just heal them?"

Wouldn't that piss off Akuwara? Daisuke mused before he insisted, "Just the medicine, miss."

"Are you sure? It wouldn't take but a m—"

"Haruki," an older Healer scolded her from where she'd come to browse nearby shelves of brown medicine jars. She sternly shook her head. "Those are the ones the guards told us about earlier."

Haruki hesitated, then smiled at them apologetically before handing over a small jar of medicine. Daisuke said nothing about the faint defensive wounds on her wrist when her sleeve fell back slightly, but the way Obito faltered before taking the jar told him enough. She directed them to an available cot in the far corner, where they sat together to treat each other's wounds. The other Healers and medics in the ward clearly understood they were to be ignored, and did so with undeniable intent. Daisuke shuddered at the cold familiarity of it as he stripped off his gi and shitagi once again; his father also never let anyone—not even his mother—interact with him or Kulako once he was through with them. That unspoken but keenly felt layer of humiliation kept the sting of being punished from fading too quickly.

Obito muttered something at the sight of Daisuke's back, but he didn't quite catch it; he decided he didn't want to know how it looked, anyway. Instead, he braced himself and kept his gaze trained on the Healer who originally spoke to them, trailing her as she stocked medicines, towels, and wiped various surfaces. Once, she looked back at them with a calculating look, then hurriedly turned around again when she saw he was watching. He couldn't place exactly what he found so odd about her behavior, only that it felt unsettling.

Daisuke's thoughts abruptly came to a halt when cool salve touched one of the furiously inflamed and broken welts blooming on his skin. The sensation was soon replaced by one more akin to thousands of flesh-eating fire ants burrowing into his injuries; he clamped his jaw shut to keep from making too much noise. The medicine would ease some of the inflammation and prevent an infection in any open sores, but it wasn't meant to relieve the pain. He nearly thanked the unfeeling heavens when Obito eventually stopped, and they traded places.

Daisuke paused when he sat behind Obito apply the ointment to his back—with his fingers hovering just above, he realized how hot to the touch each deep red, blistering mark was, how many overlapped, and how angry they looked even against his partner's dark skin. The sight cut off any quips he might've made, and the same rage from before roiled through his veins, though it just as quickly evaporated—he knew Obito wouldn't take this in stride, either.

"Death to this fucking Empire," he subconsciously muttered.

"What?"

"N-nothing." He snapped back to reality at his partner's question. After he finished gently rubbing the medicine into Obito's welts, he decided to change the subject; he could *feel* the way his partner's thoughts lingered on his first comment. "It's too bad they don't have any red poppy ointment. It smells way better than this stuff and would've helped more with the inflammation—hell, we wouldn't even be feeling half as miserable as we are right now."

"That's one good reason why they don't have it. Besides, aren't red poppies the ones that won't grow on Perena?"

"They'll grow, they're just...finnicky, and that's an understatement." Daisuke snickered, knowing Obito wouldn't believe him or the old story the next part came from. "Ancient oracle's curse."

Even so, he caught the faint hint of a smile on his partner's face. Satisfied with his reaction, he reached into his discarded shitagi to retrieve a small pouch of white leaf and shook it a few times to redirect Obito's attention. He'd already planned on sneaking off with it once afternoon lectures wrapped up, but now his harmless mischief felt twice as vindicated. Obito glanced between him and the pouch, then sighed as if immensely disappointed in himself. Daisuke's curiosity turned into a round of laughter when his partner took the familiar white leaf pipe from his belt.

DAISUKE LOOKED UP FROM his book, suddenly aware of how deafeningly quiet the corridor outside his room had been all morning. Not even the occasional bout of laughter had echoed down the hall from the commons area. Aside from the poisons copying Master Yujin assigned him and Obito, he'd spent the last few days doing as little as he could get away with while he recovered from Emperor Akuwara's beating, which meant holing up in his room during the majority of his free time. He kept his door slightly ajar whenever he lounged on his bed to keep himself from feeling *too* isolated. Since the general noises of his classmates and when to expect them had grown familiar, the air became entirely too somber with their absence. His focus always broke the second he noticed it.

Guess that means it's time to bother Obito. Come to think of it...have I seen him at all today? He wondered as he rested the book on his stomach and shifted his gaze toward the ceiling. *My attention span isn't so bad that I'd forget if I did...right?*

He was sure he hadn't been across the hall to annoy him yet. Although Daisuke hadn't taken a break from pestering him, he felt that Obito had also—quite understandably—become more withdrawn over the week. Crinkled old pages rustled as he shifted a bit and closed the book he'd stuffed under his bed months ago, before he and Obito even knew they were being sent to Zhu. A random section he'd flipped to when he first pulled it off the library shelf had piqued his curiosity by mentioning demonic mythology, a taboo topic most people wouldn't discuss, no matter their religious beliefs. Distasteful, forbidden, whatever—the subject was especially relevant now, but all he'd read so far was the exhausting tale of a wandering priest who wanted to know if such creatures existed as told by the texts of his time. Daisuke was beginning to doubt either of them would receive an answer by the end of these esoteric ramblings.

They'd call me a madman if I went off and wrote driveling nonsense like this. He chuckled to himself and set the book aside on the mattress. He sat up, stretched his arms past his toes while ignoring how his back still ached at the movement, then slid off the bed to find his boots.

He darted across the hall and knocked on Obito's door. Curiously, he didn't receive a response, not even when he tried a second time and called his partner's name. He knew his friend's habits well, which meant he wouldn't be sleeping, but he couldn't remember if he'd said anything about going out today. Since the idea of barging in uninvited made him too uncomfortable to even try, Daisuke decided to look elsewhere.

As he suspected, there wasn't another soul in sight when he passed through the dormitory's main area, as most everyone was busy with training, assignments, patrols, or classes by now. He found a few of his other off-duty classmates huddled at one of the long tables outside the kitchen, but none seemed in the mood for conversation, as they were hunched over an intense match of weiqi; the two currently playing wore deep frowns, fully concentrated on the board and its smooth black and white pieces. Since he wasn't much of one for the game and didn't want to deal with the consequences of interrupting, he concluded he should move along without saying a word.

He tried to slip by the kitchen staff unnoticed for some rice balls he saw on a large island in the center, though this plan was soon foiled. The cook who was preparing vegetables to put in a large pot of miso soup recognized him for taking care of a large rat several months ago—Daisuke had named it Squeaks before poisoning it—and insisted he take more out of gratitude. Bewildered but unable to decline such a polite offer, he left the kitchen again carrying a cloth bundle that could barely contain the onigiri he'd been given.

He aimlessly meandered as he ate two of the rice balls, trying to figure out where else to look for Obito that wasn't as obvious as the library. Since he wasn't after his partner for anything urgent or an important reason, he thought he might as well use it as a way to entertain himself; if nothing else, it gave him an excuse to roam and stretch his legs. He paused when he came upon a group of first-year onmitsu in one of the corridors, and a sense of warmth gently brushed his heart; it wasn't long ago that he and Obito could've been among that cluster. The four boys were bent over a scroll, whispering in frustrated tones, though they all froze and stood at attention when Daisuke came closer.

He laughed at them. "At ease, at ease. Hungry?"

They each gave him a wary look at first, but when he held out his bounty of extra food, they visibly relaxed and passed the cloth holding the onigiri around to one another until it was empty. As they did, Daisuke peeked at the scroll they were fretting over; it was a poison sheet. Specifically, one of the ones he and Obito had to pen and copy for classes that week. At least their hard work and suffering were doing *some* good. As the group of four ate, he asked about his partner's whereabouts and described him. Although three looked helplessly lost—they must've been painfully misguided about the definition of male beauty—the tallest of them lit up at the opportunity to give him information.

"I think I saw him going toward the memorial hall earlier," the boy said.

"You're sure?" Daisuke tilted his head. It'd be an unusual place to find him, but it was his best bet before bundling up and making the trek to Aunt Kiko's house. He smiled when his younger counterpart nodded, looking quite proud of himself for being able to help. "I guess I'll be off, then. By the way, don't stress yourselves out about that poison. It's pretty useless and overly complicated compared to some of the others. Come to me sometime, and I can help you make a better substitute."

The boys stared; whether it was shock, curiosity, or outright horror at the idea of defying Master Yujin, Daisuke thought all were valid reactions. He laughed again and thanked them, slightly taken aback when they gave him a quick bow as he left.

The pleasant scent of sandalwood filled his senses when he entered the memorial hall, then made his way toward the small altar at the back, where he also found Obito kneeling before a shiny black tablet. Thousands of similar plaques lined the walls, all belonging to previous onmitsu who were killed in action. Daisuke had once heard that Master Yujin's living quarters had an altar dedicated to those who had preceded him as Intelligence Master.

"Surprised to find you here," he said softly as he came to Obito's side. Obito briefly met his gaze, but didn't show any other signs of responding. Daisuke read the name painted in gold lettering on the little obsidian plaque propped up on the altar, then solemnly knelt beside his partner.

Although he'd never known Obito to participate in these sorts of ceremonies, he recognized this as a simpler variant of the several that existed within Giahatian beliefs, involving a stick of incense, a dearly departed one's memorial tablet, and a bit of time reflecting in quiet. He wasn't sure what had compelled Obito to kneel before Itsuki, his former partner, but guessed his mind wasn't entirely on the other boy; a glance at his friend revealed nothing more than the usual, far-off expression he wore when deep in thought. Rather than pester him for answers, Daisuke also placed an incense in the burner, bowed to the obsidian slate, and sat with his friend in silence while another thin wisp of smoke joined the one already climbing toward the ceiling.

Eventually, Obito's eyes went upward, following the last trails of incense smoke as they curled around the rafters and dissipated. Daisuke tilted his head at his friend's pensive expression. His curiosity grew tenfold when Obito took a deep breath, then wordlessly got up and began wiping down Itsuki's memorial tablet with a cloth; his face still hadn't changed when he hung it on the wall once more.

"Something's on your mind," Daisuke said as he shook the ash from the incense burner into a bin.

"That's part of why I came here." Obito took the burner from his hands to place it on its designated shelf near the altar, which was slightly out of reach for the shorter boy. "It's a conversation I overheard when Itsuki and I went to Zhao the first time. I thought I'd remember the details better if I...sat with him for a bit today."

"Does that mean you're ready to tell me about it?"

"I think so—it's been bothering me for a few years." Obito's forest-green eyes finally settled on Daisuke for a long moment. "There's something bothering you, too."

He blinked; he hadn't even been aware of it until now. "How did you know?"

Obito wasn't in the mood to explain how his friend wasn't nearly as good at hiding his emotions as he assumed of himself, at least not when they were around each other, and shrugged instead. Whether it was due to impulse, trust, or a strange combination of both, this nonverbal response was all it took for his partner to begin explaining himself.

"It's the whole thing in Zhu—and the fact that the High Priestess clearly knows something about what happened and what we're dealing with, but won't say a word about it." Daisuke jumped a bit when he heard voices in the corridor outside. After a moment of thought, he said, "Come back to my room with me. We'll have some privacy there."

He perched on his bed while Obito took a seat on the floor once they arrived in his room and shut the door. He listened intently as his friend recounted a brief but tense spat between him and Itsuki, dissolved by the latter's naturally easy demeanor; even so, this had separated them when they first arrived in Zhao those three years ago. While Obito waited for Itsuki to return, his uncle had also made an appearance and drove him into hiding for the duration of the conversation—just hearing Giichi's name set Daisuke's teeth on edge. What he wouldn't give to enact *some* justice for the painful secret Obito guarded so close to his heart, all because of that man.

"He met with someone else, but I couldn't make out anything about them. Now that I think about it, they were dressed similarly to the people who attacked us in the alley." Obito paused, and Daisuke sat forward with anticipation. "Either way, this person indicated Giichi had a part in following orders from someone they called Zandaka's Servant. Apparently, whoever that is wants to dismantle the Empire because they're upset about Prince Akuko being named Emperor Akuwara's heir."

"Hikari's sake, this succession shit again? Isn't there a good chunk of the nobility who feels the same way?"

Obito nodded. "My uncle being no exception, or Lord Hideo, who was also in on whatever this part of the plan was."

Daisuke had been gazing at a wrinkle in his bedding, but his eyes snapped to Obito when he heard the other nobleman's name. He slid off the bed and went to his desk, mind racing as he began rummaging around in the top drawer, thankful he'd discarded the makeshift trap and cleaned up any signs of harming himself with the scalpel. He tried not to look at his beaten-up poisons journal as he placed it on the desk's surface; he could hardly stand the sight of it now, but also couldn't bear to leave it unattended for long periods of time. Despite how rarely he'd thought about it before, he didn't go far without it lately unless it was under Obito's attentive watch. Maybe he *was* overreacting, but Daisuke didn't care. He'd take absolute pleasure in the pettiest revenge when he found out who was responsible for breaking his trust.

"That reminds me." He cleared his throat, hoping it'd dispel his other thoughts and keep him focused, though he paused again when he uncovered the helix earring. "There's something I haven't told anyone, either. A couple weeks before General Aki brought me to Master Yujin, one of the General's old friends came around the barracks. I was...voluntarily cleaning—"

"—Scrubbing the floors because you can't keep your mouth shut—"

"Same difference at some point, isn't it?"

"At least you're self-aware."

Daisuke snickered and absentmindedly passed the small hoop of colorful beads and dyed finch feathers into Obito's hand, knowing it'd be safe. "Anyway, Lord Horseshit—I mean, *Hideo*—was the visitor. He dropped something when he was trying to recruit General Aki into whatever he's messing with and said it was a good luck charm, or something like that. But the General's too smart for him, so naturally, he didn't buy it. He *did* keep the charm, though. Since General Aki didn't want anything to do with it after Horsesh—*Hideo* left, he gave it to me."

He pulled the enfolded pendant from its hiding place and set it on the desk beside the poisons journal, heart inexplicably fluttering when he sensed Obito peering at it from over his shoulder. He mentally shook himself to keep out whatever was going on in his mind, then peeled back the covering he'd kept the charm in for all this time. He'd forgotten how disappointingly plain it looked...and how badly it needed a thorough cleaning.

"That's embarrassing," he grumbled to himself, then picked it up and turned to his teammate. "This is what he tried pawning off on the General. I try not to think about it being in here."

Obito took it from his friend's outstretched hand to study it more closely; it didn't look like much on the surface, but something he couldn't logically explain warned him not to underestimate it—like something ancient and powerful resided within, although believing as much sounded like utter nonsense. He didn't dare mention those things to Daisuke and moved their conversation along instead. "I wonder if this is what Giichi was talking about, then—the person he met with asked if Hideo had the talisman he was supposed to deliver to General Aki."

"A talisman?" Daisuke blinked, blankly taking the charm when Obito gave it back. "Hideo's visit to the General would've been *months* after Giichi's meeting with that person in Zhao, but I guess if your ultimate plan is to overthrow the crown, it's smart to move slow sometimes."

"From the sounds of it, we'll have to track Lord Hideo down at some point. I *do* think that, whatever this is, it's connected to the artifact taken from us in Zhu. I'm just not sure how yet."

"For what it's worth, I think you're right. I almost forgot because of everything else, but I had a dream while we were in Zhu. The shadows used by that 'priestess' and the artifact's box were in it. This talisman, if that's what it really is, showed up, too."

"Then that probably means Zandaka's Servant and the Priestess of Shadows are also connected to each other somehow."

"They might even *be* the same person—wait, I'm getting ahead of myself, aren't I?"

"Hard to say. We won't know until we do some research into the solid information we already have, then we can start asking more questions."

"Right, stick with what we know first...not that it's much. Gods, what a fucking mess we've found ourselves in." Daisuke tiredly rubbed his face. After moment, he cautiously asked Obito, "Don't get me wrong, I'm glad you told *me* about all that, but why didn't you say anything to Master Yujin back then?"

"Pissed off nobles are hardly news to Master Yujin." Obito looked away. Judging by the expression in Daisuke's eyes, he could tell it wasn't the whole answer; he wouldn't necessarily press for more information, but he *would* wait for it. In hindsight, Obito knew his reasoning sounded ridiculous, and while he *had* only been twelve at the time, he couldn't help the twinge of embarrassment he felt for it. "And this was only about a year after everything...*else* happened at home. Since no one believed me about Giichi then..."

"Why would you expect anyone to believe you about something else at that point, either, right?" Daisuke had to rein in the sympathetic look he wanted to give his friend before it slipped past his guard. While they loved sharing thoughts and ideas with one another, the things they were ashamed of didn't always come out as naturally. He changed the direction of their conversation instead. "Time to hit the books?"

Immensely relieved by the change in subject, Obito agreed, and they put everything away once more, except for the poisons journal. For the sake of his friend's sanity, Obito took it across the hall and put it in his desk for safe storage—even if someone was brave enough to break into his room to look for it, he could only think of one person who dared, which would easily implicate them as the culprit in stealing it from Daisuke. Really, this person made a perfect suspect—bold enough to try, but stupid enough to not see it as a trap.

Obito had to hope his intuition was wrong this time.

THEY DIDN'T MAKE IT to the library after setting out as they'd intended—in fact, *several* hours passed between their decision to go and when they finally settled into the nook Obito usually sought. Daisuke's innocent—as much as it could be—inquiry about a cigarette turned into a search for the onmitsu who originally let Obito keep a few in exchange for rolling them, which became accompanying him on trip to the commissary in the furthest infantry barracks. After listening to him do far too much joking and chatting with every familiar person along the way, they finally had their somewhat legally purchased tobacco and papers. Once the cigarettes were rolled, smoked, and Daisuke *finally* remembered they were supposed to be in the library, evening had fallen.

How does he get me to go along with these things? Obito wondered as he set a few potentially useful books on their table. He leaned forward on his elbows and rubbed his temples, pushing away the fuzzy outline of an answer lingering in the back of his mind.

Noticing the irritability in his demeanor, Daisuke sheepishly grinned at him as he added more books to the pile. "Sorry."

"You aren't."

"W-well...these books look helpful, don't they?" Daisuke ran his thumb along their pages and pointed at each one. "This one's supposed to be about ancient talismans, this one has incense rituals, that one—"

"Sounds like you have a lot to get started on." Obito rolled his eyes when he dared to peek into the one about incense, then instantly closed it again. "This one is about *fertility* rituals and prayers. Are you even taking this seriously?"

"Of course! What makes you think I'm not?"

"I don't believe you." Obito glared at him without any true anger behind the expression, and Daisuke's jaw dropped in false hurt.

"I don't believe *this!* My own teammate and friend—why, I'm *wounded*, Obito."

Unable to keep it going, Daisuke's theatrics fell apart with a cackle. Obito rolled his eyes again, a hint of an exasperated smile touching the corners of his mouth as his friend plopped into the open spot across from him.

They studied in silence, with little sound between them other than the rustling of old pages or occasional, soft brushstrokes on paper as they made what few notes they could, trying to discern what might be helpful from utter nonsense. Obito tried to concentrate on the words in front of him, but his mind kept wandering to another nagging idea—the woman whose death Daisuke had brought up multiple times now, Misame. He tapped on the open book as he tried to dismiss his theory, but when he looked up at Daisuke again, he knew he couldn't keep it to himself. However, when he opened his mouth to speak, he caught movement on the other side of the shelf behind his friend; a long white ribbon that starkly contrasted its wearer's dark hair and the oak shelving they stood behind. Unsure if his instincts were right, he tried to return to his reading, but his nerves were on edge. Whoever it was had appeared so soundlessly, he didn't trust his senses to pick up on when or if they left. When he raised his eyes again and found them in the same position, he pulled a piece of parchment from the center of the desk and dipped his brush into the inkwell, which drew Daisuke's attention.

He wrote a simple, *"We're being watched."*

"What's this?" Those violet eyes flashed with intrigue as his brows furrowed. He turned the paper toward himself before he took the brush from his friend's grip. He looked up at Obito after reading. "Wait, I pass you notes in class all the time and you ignore them. How is this fair?"

Obito rolled his eyes. "You're so annoying. Just...tell me what you think."

Obtuse as he was acting, during this brief exchange, Daisuke began their second, unspoken conversation. *"Behind me?"*

"Did you hear?"

"No. Should we leave?"

"Slowly."

"Well, if you *really* like this girl, *obviously* you should just tell her." Daisuke waved his hand over the parchment a few times to help the ink dry faster, then folded it neatly and tucked it inside the book he'd opened. When he looked up again, he couldn't help but cackle at the way his friend seemed torn between telling him off or leaving without him. Had he accidentally struck a nerve?

Later, he told himself. He knew better than to poke at the subject too much. Besides, he wouldn't get anywhere with it right now, not with a more pressing question looming over their heads. Instead, he helped Obito pack their things, lamenting the need to abandon a disappointingly short research session.

Obito didn't pause to check their surroundings again until they were near the onmitsu dormitories. Daisuke leaned against one of the old arrow slats, enjoying a cool blast of air against his back as he waited for his friend to explain what he'd seen in the library—so far, it seemed they hadn't been followed.

"Healers in the infirmary wear white ribbons, right?" Obito asked. The onmitsu, hitokiri, footsoldiers, and guards all had similarities between their uniforms to create some intentional confusion so special forces weren't easily identified. That wasn't the case for people like medics and Healers.

Daisuke nodded. "As far as I've seen. But Healers usually aren't as stealthy as one of us. They don't need to be."

"They're mostly women, too. It's not unheard of, but men almost never have their abilities."

"Which means it's a *really* good place for someone with bad intentions to hide, but that also means it'll take a while to root her out—you *did* only notice her because you were lucky enough to look up and see her at just the right moment."

"Maybe not. I'm sure we both remember that Healer who helped us last week." He couldn't recall her name to save his life, and since Daisuke didn't offer it, it seemed he had the same issue. There was little else they could do besides trying to catch her in the act, which likely wouldn't happen now that they knew their library nook was compromised. Obito stayed silent for a moment until he changed subjects. "There's something else I wanted to bring up, but I don't know how much it helps."

Daisuke perked up, undeniably interested, so Obito continued.

"I think the Shadow Priestess killed Misame, or had her killed. She probably felt Misame betrayed her, which is why she tracked down her sister, Rin, for the artifact. If Rin's account is anything to go by, Misame would've arrived in Zhu well after that cloaked person met with my uncle."

"I wonder if the cloaked person *was* Misame, then. We know she worked for Zandaka's Servant, which means she might've worked for the

Shadow Priestess, too. It could also be why she wouldn't tell Rin what was going on." Daisuke paused. "This might be a stretch, but given that Healer's defensive wounds, I don't think she should be taken lightly."

"I'd hardly call it a stretch. She's obviously had some sort of training, and might report to the Shadow Priestess or the Servant."

"Maybe they sent her after us for finding out too much—wait. That's hardly fair. We barely know *anything*."

"The Emperor just took his eyes off us, so we shouldn't start anything with the Healer consort yet. For now, let's be more careful about where we are when we talk about this."

Daisuke shamelessly grinned. "My room's always open for you."

"Stop that." Obito pinched the bridge of his nose.

They jumped when distant footsteps echoed in the corridor, then continued toward the dormitories, hoping to outpace whoever it was making steady strides in their direction. Whether it was the Healer, a guard, or someone even less dangerous, they weren't in the mood for talking to outsiders.

HARUKI TOOK A DEEP breath when the two onmitsu absconded from the library without warning; she was certain she'd been noticed, and thought it too risky to pursue them right away. Truthfully, she wasn't sure if she should try at all. While they were no doubt quite green, they weren't exactly lacking in martial ability or training. She wasn't discounting her own capabilities, but it made the prospect of drawing a dagger—let alone her katana—on them in this tight setting tricky. On top of that, the Palace was constantly bustling with activity; empty corridors seemed to rarely stay quiet for long, especially for one in the Royal Healer's consort. She was still considered a new arrival to the Healers who worked at the Palace infirmary, but she'd already learned that as soon as someone recognized the white ribbon, white outer jacket with blue trims, and blue dress she wore, any time she'd carved out for herself was bound to end abruptly.

Really, Haruki didn't mind. She enjoyed feeling as though she was doing something genuinely good, without the accompanying shadow of her matron's underhanded scheming, which only ever made her temples ache. While guilt frequently awoke her from a dead sleep, drenched in sweat, and she often felt as though she had abandoned Lady Shadow simply by not being at her side, life here was gentler in many ways.

Which was why she didn't know if she could bring herself to spill blood from the two onmitsu Lady Shadow targeted.

Although she knew anything they might learn about the dragon demons or the cult would greatly threaten her lady's mission, Haruki couldn't help but question if it *should* be compromised. After all, forcing the entire nation to bend to her whims and those of the Demon King didn't sound as particularly loving as she'd been told over the last several years, nor did it feel like an alternative to the tyranny of the Imperial throne. The Palace and the Capital itself were so full of vibrant and diverse life, something Haruki was beginning to feel Lady Shadow had hidden herself away from for far too long. If only she'd step back into the fold...

Strange as it might've been, Haruki thought those two spies represented a broader aspect of life outside the confines of the abandoned spa—although they were also trained for a militant existence, they appeared to enjoy life far more than anyone she knew under Lady Shadow's care. She felt more compelled to help than harm them. It was part of why she'd insisted on healing their wounds several days ago when they'd stiffly ambled into the infirmary during her shift, though she knew she shouldn't have, even before the other Healer scolded her for trying. The entire time she'd listened to them tease each other and watched them study just now, her uncertainty in her mission deepened. By the time she realized the Giahatian boy had seen her, she didn't move to avoid rousing his suspicions further, but she'd had no fight inside her.

She needed more room to decide when or if she wanted to deal with them; her inner world felt like such a mess these days. She shuddered when she remembered what had happened to Misame when Lady Shadow accused her of betrayal. Misame had always treated Haruki as a younger sister, and while she'd never say as much to Lady Shadow, she'd felt an immense, quiet anger since her execution.

A letter should settle things for now...

Deciding to grant herself the space she couldn't expect Lady Shadow to give, Haruki made her way toward the royal librarian's desk for stationery.

Even though her heart pinched at the idea of sending a messenger to the mountains, one disappearing up there in the middle of winter wouldn't draw the Intelligence Master's attention.

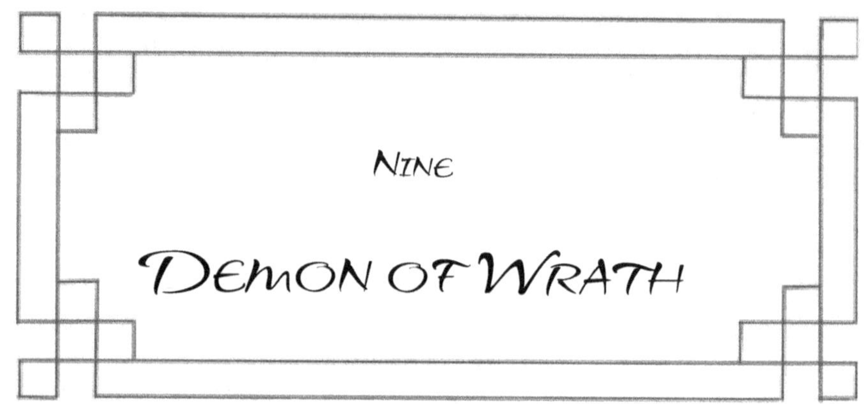

"KAGURA?" DESPITE THE FAMILIARITY of using her given name, Natsumi sounded hesitant, which brought the cult matron's attention to her new lover. She was holding one of the expertly-crafted jars Misame had brought back from Zhu right before admitting to her treachery—Lady Shadow had forgotten about them. "Are you saving this for something? I...I found several in that closet down the hall when I went looking for a broom."

Lady Shadow let the gauzy floor-length curtain drop from her grasp as she turned to Natsumi, heart stuttering from hearing her name. She watched the younger woman for a moment, then crossed the darkened room to where she nervously stood at the threshold. She held out her hands to take the heavy ceramic vase, expressionless when it was given over without question. Lady Shadow turned it a few times, dispassionately examining it, then carefully set it down on the floor before tucking her arms into her kimono sleeves. Natsumi flinched, which was when Lady Shadow realized the overwrought silence she'd allowed to permeate the air. She forced a small smile to ease Natsumi's worries.

"I once asked one of my subordinates to retrieve these from Zhu. They were meant to hold very special treasures, but I've since changed my mind—I don't believe hiding them away is the answer anymore."

"Treasures?"

Lady Shadow's smile turned genuine as she twisted the pendant around her neck, where Kanashimi had remained sleeping inside their talisman ever since she'd asked for their power in Mizutake; keeping their brother's spirit calm and unleashing the fury of their shadows had proved more taxing on the demon than Lady Shadow expected. Truthfully, the nightly sacraments of keeping Saigai soothed were draining for her, as well, though she tried not to let it show.

"The power that fended off your beast of a husband belonged to an ancient demon. They have siblings, who we're working to excavate from hidden places across Perena. If I were to put their talismans, such as the one on my necklace, inside those vases and paint a sealing symbol upon them, I would severely weaken our greatest allies. It doesn't seem fair, does it?"

Lady Shadow hadn't divulged the cult's deepest intentions to Natsumi yet. As far as the young woman was concerned, this place was merely a haven for women and their children—she wasn't entirely wrong for thinking in such a manner, but the Priestess of Shadows knew she would eventually need to ask more of her following. Now armed with two demons of the Between Realm, and with one steadily feeding her power while only asking for blood and loyalty, she felt she was at last in a better position to make those demands. Those who didn't want to pursue further action against the Giahatio, despite how it'd ruined their lives, would be welcome to leave at such a point. If they did not desire vengeance, they were too weak to serve the Demon King Zandaka.

However, it was still a long way off—months or years, perhaps, but far enough that she didn't intend to let it slip anytime soon.

Visibly uncomfortable and desperate to change the subject, Natsumi reached into her sleeve to retrieve a roll of parchment. "You also received a letter, my Lady."

"Natsumi, please, I don't need you to call me—" Lady Shadow's eyes narrowed, as there were very few individuals who knew where their sanctuary was located. "From whom? Is the messenger still here?"

"I-I didn't get the name of the sender, but I know you want this place to remain private, so I sent him off to the springs and gave him a room for the night. Please, forgive me." Natsumi held out the letter with both hands.

Too intrigued to keep worrying about the messenger, Lady Shadow took it from her, brows furrowed. She recognized Haruki's handwriting the second she unfurled the rolled-up parchment and read through the letter eagerly, hoping to see news of two slain onmitsu.

"That foolish, idiot girl," she snarled when no such thing appeared on the page, though a whimper from Natsumi brought her back from the brink of rage. She hurried to mend things, delicately cupping her chin. "Not you, my love. The one who sent this to me—for one, she knows better than to use outsiders for communications. For another, she sent me nothing but utter disappointment. You did everything right. I will personally take care of the messenger later. While he's sleeping, perhaps."

Natsumi's eyes widened, though resolve soon overtook her features. "Let me, my Lady."

Although a proud smile curled her lips, Lady Shadow pretended she didn't hear and kept reading the letter; she didn't want Natsumi to dirty her dainty hands if it wasn't necessary. Despite her agitation with the method and lack of real progress, Haruki had at least delivered good news; the report stated she had successfully infiltrated the Palace as a Healer in the royal infirmary, and that while she couldn't be certain yet, she believed she found the two onmitsu from Zhu. While Lady Shadow wished she wouldn't be so cautious and deal with the suspects in the most straightforward manner possible, she understood rashness could compromise Haruki's mission. If those dogs from the Palace got hold of her, she'd become a victim of Emperor Akuwara's torment, or his illegitimate brat's—Lady Shadow didn't want to think of what she'd need to do if such things came into fruition. For now, she sighed and folded the letter, placing it in her belt before donning a long, black jacket.

"Kagura?" Natsumi gently broke into her thoughts; she'd barely noticed what she was doing.

"Never mind the letter for now. I'm going to the garden near the old shrine," she explained, trying to make herself sound just as warm. "I'd be delighted if you joined me. I need you to see these beautiful deities for what they are."

Natsumi hesitated, then took her own cloak from the peg beside where Kagura's usually hung before following her into the wintry afternoon.

Sunlight reflected brightly off high snowbanks. An easy breeze slithered through the bare branches of the few deciduous trees surrounding the frozen pool that lay beside the footpath to the shrine where Kanashimi had first awakened; the wind carried the scent of pine, cedar, and impending snowfall. Not many were allowed back here, as it was known as Lady Shadow's special place to meditate and pray to Zandaka; more typically, she came to have private conversations with Kanashimi.

When she and her following first found this place, the shrine looked ready to fall apart; its altar was made of little more than rotted wood, with no place for incense or offerings, and its floor and walls each had at least a few holes or cracks. Although this was no longer a place to pray to Hikari, Lady Shadow had decided she couldn't allow the demons of the Between

Realm to greet the modern age in such shameful, dilapidated conditions, and had since worked to restore the small shrine. Given that it was to further their cause of summoning the Demon King, when she—posing as the Servant of Zandaka—petitioned her noble benefactors for the money and supplies, they'd each sent a generous donation.

Lady Shadow left the shrine's door open to allow in the crisp winter air and leave room for the guests she anticipated. Despite their exhaustion, Kanashimi was adamant about being present for their brother's first summoning—it was too simple of a request for Lady Shadow to deny. Besides, once the Demon of Disaster reawakened, and no longer required careful rituals to keep his seal in place, they could all have a long, well-deserved rest.

The Priestess of Shadows smiled to herself. *But, first...*

Desperate to learn all she could about her new lover's life, Natsumi watched with rapt attention as Lady Shadow popped Kanashimi's talisman out of its bail on her necklace. Curiosity held her in a chokehold when the older woman set the stone upon the altar, so Natsumi's voice died in her throat when she saw the gleam of a dagger's blade. She bit her lip when Kagura pierced her own fingertip and squeezed out a crimson bead of blood, which was then smeared across the talisman's surface. A flash of bright white light forced her to shield her eyes from whatever happened next, but something like a sixth sense—or morbid curiosity—made her peek through her fingers. Her jaw dropped when a massive jade-green dragon wound through the shrine's door and climbed into the air above her.

Entirely too pleased with Natsumi's reaction and seeing Kanashimi again, Lady Shadow was still smiling as she stepped out of the shrine once more; Natsumi noticed the way she watched the dragon with familiarity and adoration. It circled the garden a few times before coming to rest upon a boulder near the shrine.

"Feeling better?" Kagura asked the beast as if it were an old friend. Natsumi was certain the creature seemed smaller, now—almost human in size.

"I am, Shadow Priestess," it replied in a rich voice that sounded neither male nor female, scaring Natsumi out of her skin. She couldn't stop the whimper that escaped her, which brought the demon's piercing golden eyes onto her. "Who is this?"

"This is Natsumi, the young woman we rescued in Mizutake."

"K-Kagura," Natsumi choked out. "W-what...what *is* that?"

The thing looked positively offended—if that were even possible—but rather than react, it waved its clawed hand to make a black folding fan appear in a cloud of billowing darkness, which it waved several times in front of its snout.

Lady Shadow blinked, confused, though she supposed her partner was having the most natural reaction to meeting a demon of the Between Realm. Perhaps her calmness was the true outlier in this scenario. She held out a hand for the demon to take, as if she were introducing a woman of high noble birth. "Natsumi, this is Kanashimi, the Demon of Grief. Between their power, mine, and yours, we were able to flatten Mizutake and free you from your husband. Please, don't fear them. They won't hurt you."

A thin puff of smoke came from Kanashimi's nostrils, like a quiet, derisive snort, but they remained silent as they studied Natsumi. In turn, the young woman helplessly stared back at the ancient creature. She could feel their power thrumming in the air; quiet, barely restrained, unmistakable. Uncertain, she bowed to Kanashimi, who appeared entirely unimpressed by the gesture. They closed their fan with a sharp snap, and it disappeared in the same fashion as it had been conjured.

"Kanashimi," Lady Shadow called the demon's attention. "Are you ready for me to summon Saigai?"

The dragon's gaze lingered on Natsumi, barely shifting toward Lady Shadow when they spoke again. "Get rid of her. My brother's temper is unpredictable—though quite fond of human souls in the Between Realm, that was long ago, before Hikari poisoned us."

Natsumi wanted to make an impression of bravery, and hoped she didn't seem too eager to flee despite her terror. She pressed her lips into a thin line before stating, "Kagura, I'll bring you some tea and onigiri. You've mentioned these rituals can be quite hard on you, and you've looked so tired these last few days. Allow me to make it a bit easier."

Lady Shadow's heart sank a little as she watched Natsumi retreat toward the inn, though she tried not to let it show. She squared her shoulders and, with a nod of approval from Kanashimi, went back into the shrine. She fished the Talisman of Saigai, Demon of Disaster, from a special pocket stitched into her outer jacket and placed it on the shining mahogany altar beside his sibling's. She stared back at her reflection in the polished wood, then took a deep breath and pierced her finger once more.

"Saigai, Demon of Disasters and Strife who wields Hikari's wrath, the Priestess of Shadows summons thee."

Black mist arose from the talisman while her blood simultaneously drained from its surface. Wind wound through Lady Shadow's loose hair, and the same excitement she'd felt upon first meeting Kanashimi coursed through her veins. A ball of green light shot past her and settled over the frozen pond, then violently split apart in an eruption of flame and smoke. When it cleared, a dragon even larger than Kanashimi was left in its wake, hovering above the icy, slate-colored waters.

Saigai was dressed in the same layers of white, purple, and gold robes as Kanashimi, with a similar outer jacket to match, though subtle flame patterns could be spotted on his under the sunlight. A long white beard matched the hair flowing from the demon's head, which was kept in a neat half-bun with ornate, golden pins, giving him a more regal appearance than any emperor could ever hope to have—certainly surpassing Akuwara. Like Kanashimi, black streaks came down from the corners of Saigai's eyes, though the shape soon morphed into something different, like a misty black splotch around each eye. Lady Shadow wasn't sure if the markings symbolized anything, but she was in just as much awe of this beautiful divine creature as she was with his sibling. Gold shimmered above his long white brows, forming into a headpiece with a hexagonal-shaped center, which boasted six gleaming rubies at each point. His eyes slowly opened, revealing blank yellow irises against black sclera.

"Who dares to awaken me?" the demon demanded. His deep voice rumbled so powerfully, as if barely constraining a deep rage, it seemed to shake the ground.

"The Priestess of Shadows, Demon King Zandaka's willing servant. Welcome, Master Saigai."

With a fierce growl, his unfocused eyes turned onto Lady Shadow. The dragon demon pulled back, looking like a snake ready to strike. Narrow slits split his irises as pupils finally appeared when he lunged forward, though he didn't slow until he heard a more familiar call.

"My brother!"

"Kanashimi?" Saigai halted, then lowered himself toward the pool's solid surface as his sibling went to him, flowing white locks trailing like a cloud of smoke. The two twisted around each other as if in a dance, and his anger palpably dissipated. "This human summoned you, as well? Then what of the others?"

"The Shadow Priestess is still searching for them. Do you remember what happened to us?"

"Not...quite." Saigai's golden eyes turned pensive, as if sifting through centuries of forgotten memories; Kanashimi was visibly disappointed. "What I *can* recall, is that upon being sealed in that human vessel, Hikari's wrath was so great it would have threatened the very life she created—unfathomable disasters would have besieged the world. As such, I absorbed her fury, but also her ability to *cause* those disasters."

"What about the humans who unwittingly kept your talisman?" Kanashimi pressed.

"Their voices greatly irritated me," Saigai casually admitted. "I believe I scared them into silence a few times—it was effective. Otherwise, they wouldn't give me enough peace to continue meditating. I couldn't sleep for quite some time."

"I have fantastic news, then," Kanashimi explained, a satisfied smirk at the corner of their mouth. "We killed them. Together, with the Shadow Priestess, you and I ended them for keeping you imprisoned."

The Demon of Wrath's eyes widened, as if he hadn't expected or wanted to hear such an answer. "Why do I not remember this?"

"If I may, you were still half-awake, and in the hands of other thieves at the moment," Lady Shadow offered, unflinching when Saigai's scowl turned to her. "Those thieves were working for the Emperor, who is a pillar of greed and torment. I wish to rid the world of such a scourge, which is why I need you and your siblings—without any of you, I am powerless and cannot summon Zandaka."

"Summon Zandaka?"

"That is correct. It's necessary for a new order, free of Imperial tyranny. Without the King, you, or your siblings, I do not wield enough power."

"It is a foolish endeavor, no matter your reasons." Saigai glared at her. "You cannot possibly believe that, even with all six of us, you would convince His Highness to kneel to your desires."

"He has spoken to her," Kanashimi murmured, "Just as he spoke to us. 'Grief is a shadow of resentment, disasters are the fire of divine fury—to Kanashimi and Saigai, I entrust these powers of the Goddess.'"

"A fire I will not use lightly, no matter how many times you utter that part of His Highness's unjust curse at me," the other dragon demon warned with a growl that rolled like thunder across the skies. "I may have absorbed Hikari's wrath, and her ability to cause disasters which would permanently alter landscapes, but I will not wield it unless need-ed—and especially not at *your* will, human."

Lady Shadow merely smiled at Saigai. "I have no intention to bend you to my desires. I simply wished to free you from your bonds."

"By binding me to *your* blood?" The dragon's maw opened to re-veal long, white fangs as his glowing body dipped toward Lady Shadow.

"Saigai," Kanashimi called to him. "It truly was the only way."

"I would rather remain in that wretched half-awake state for eter-nity than be forced to pledge any loyalty to one of *these* creatures."

"I will not ask for that," Lady Shadow told him, quiet but firm. The demon's yellow eyes narrowed once more as he scanned her features for any hint of deceit. "*Because* of my bond with Kanashimi, they are strong, and able to come and go as they please from their talisman. I want the same for you. As I told Kanashimi, should you allow it, I would devote myself entirely to you and Demon King Zandaka."

Kanashimi raised a long eyebrow, but remained silent. The expres-sion briefly etched into their features went unnoticed by their broth-er, but not Lady Shadow—she couldn't quite identify what flashed through the demon's countenance, but it resembled incredulity, which she tried to ignore. She couldn't place why anything like doubt had appeared on Kanashimi's face; it was more or less an identical speech to the one she'd given them upon their awakening. Surely, her companion understood the necessity in placating Saigai and keeping his temper under control.

Moving past whatever had occurred to them, they turned to their brother. "Once you have regained some strength, I will explain further, but the Shadow Priestess tends not to make a habit of summoning us when we aren't needed. As she said, I am mostly free to leave my talisman as I wish. Today, she summoned me with her blood because I was resting—tomorrow, I will come visit this garden of my own volition to meditate. However, if we wish to break our curse, we must all be summoned forth from our talismans."

Saigai's brows knitted together while he listened to his sibling. Thankfully, after a moment to consider their words, it seemed like a sufficient explanation, as he drifted low to the ground. Soon, he came toward the shrine, near the altar where his talisman still lay.

"If that is true, then I will retire for now. You have given me much information to consider," he said, eyes narrowing into slits as they settled on Lady Shadow once more. "But know this, human. I will not trust you until I see you've made good on your promises with my siblings."

Kanashimi had made a similar proclamation upon their first meeting, and their bond had flourished naturally since. The Priestess of Shadows did not pursue or call out to the demon as he disappeared into his talisman in another flourish of flame and smoke. Instead, a satisfied smirk tugged at the corner of her lips at the thought of it; getting Saigai, the Demon of Disaster and Wrath, to trust her would be a challenge with immense reward.

"That other mortal has your real name," Kanashimi stated quietly once the snow-covered garden was empty again, peering at their reflection in the glaze of clear ice on the pool. "I don't believe you've given such a name to anyone else, Priestess."

An inexplicable wave of fear and guilt surged into Lady Shadow's chest, though it quickly dispersed once more. "You mean the name 'Kagura'? As I told her, it's a name I haven't used in years, one I've barely thought about since the Giahatio executed my late husband. No one else was around to call me by it after his death. She was vulnerable and terrified—I had to do *something* to make her feel safe with me."

"Then what shall *I* call you? I now know of at least three names, two of which are titles."

Lady Shadow hesitated. In the books she'd used to learn how to summon the demons, there were plenty of tales cautioning against directly giving beings from the Between Realm one's true name; if Kanashimi knew, they'd likely tell Saigai. Whether it was a spirit such as those of Zandaka's disciples or a lost soul wandering the mortal plane, the openness of offering one's name potentially invited all sorts of curses and chaos. On the other hand, to give Natsumi her true name without doing the same for Kanashimi implied she trusted one over the other—as things currently stood, she wasn't sure that was correct. Before now, she thought she'd had implicit faith in the demon, though a horrifying twinge of doubt made itself known in the pit of her stomach.

"Whichever you prefer, I will answer to," she finally answered vaguely.

"Is that so?"

Lady Shadow swallowed, unable to place the reason behind her pounding heart. "Yes."

Kanashimi's thoughtful expression returned. Rather than announcing which they would use from then on, they merely dipped their head and summoned their fan, sweeping it across their body and leaving behind a cloud of wispy shadow. The shadows billowed out, then engulfed them. All signs of the demon's presence dissipated into thin air, leaving the space beside Lady Shadow empty and cold in the frigid mountain winter. Shivering, the Priestess of Shadows pulled her cloak closer. She didn't—rather, she *couldn't*—move again until she heard Natsumi's footsteps crunching in the snow behind her.

Dreams rarely left Daisuke alone for long.

The talisman—if one could call it that—he'd kept in his desk now sat in the center of his floor, bathed in blood and surrounded by thrashing tendrils of black shadow. Although the sight of so much of the deep red ooze sickened him even in this dream-state, he couldn't resist reaching through the wall of dark energy. The hazy black mist pulled apart like a curtain, and his trembling fingers grazed the talisman's grubby surface; the blood and darkness evaporated when he made contact. The same eerie, jade green glow of the seven dragon statues he'd seen in his dreams for the last three years flooded his room. However, when he looked around for them, he instead found the white wolf spirit who helped him flee Okara staring back at him with pensive golden eyes. She said nothing when she brushed past him, and he followed as if she pulled him along on a string.

His mouth fell slightly open in awe when he turned to see the thin, forested trail he now stood upon; with nowhere else to go, he began to make his way up the steep path. The further he went, the lush greenery turned drier, sickly and brittle, until only bare branches and bushes scraped his arms. Occasionally, crimson flecks on them gleamed in the dying sunlight.

Haunting silence stifled the air as Daisuke walked along with no sign of the white wolf or other forest life; he couldn't even hear his own breath or heartbeat despite the steady uphill climb. Eventually, the trail widened, and he stepped into a cold, foggy meadow. Although it appeared empty at first, he jumped when he noticed a silhouette standing a mere foot or so away from him. A pale, bloody hand holding the hilt of a katana was the last thing he saw before the dream ended.

He groaned and rubbed his face when his eyes opened, pushing away the strands of damp hair sticking to his forehead. The real world steadily trickled into view once more, dispelling the strange dream that haunted him for the fourth night in a row. Other than needing to learn more about the talisman, he couldn't glean any useful information from it, and now he wasn't sure if he was more frustrated or annoyed by it.

Panic suddenly surged through his body after another moment of lying awake—he should've been in Master Yujin's office by now.

Master Yujin looked up from an unfurled scroll on his desk when Daisuke rushed over the threshold to his office, hair still loose and breathless since he'd run all the way from the dormitories. The Intelligence Master's lips pressed together in a tight, thin line before he heaved an exasperated sigh; Daisuke decided to save himself some face and give what little respect he could by turning around to tie his hair into its usual ponytail. A small courtesy when in front of a higher rank that he'd learned during his infantry days; he figured any goodwill he could earn from Master Yujin was worthwhile.

Doesn't he know how inhumane getting up this early is? I was supposed to be off-duty today. Daisuke internally sulked while he tied the hair ribbon, knowing his superior wasn't interested in hearing any of it. Just as he was about to fumble out a half-hearted apology when he spun back around, his eyes fell on a polished, ivory skull sitting in one of the upper corners of Master Yujin's desk. The sight stole any words he might've had right from his mouth. It looked human, but the large canine fangs in place of normal incisors in the upper jaw, with smaller ones in the lower, piqued his curiosity.

Accidentally casting aside propriety for questions, he asked, "Master Yujin, what...what is that?"

"An Okami skull," Master Yujin answered solemnly as he set the scroll aside. He seemed to be doing everything he could to avoid it, including turning himself slightly away from it. "Emperor Akuwara's latest example of what it means to 'know your enemy,' I suppose."

"Fucking gods," Daisuke blurted, willing away gruesome mental images of how the now-nameless Shifter must've become a casualty of the Emperor's rabid hatred. He shook his head before he got himself into trouble with further commentary. "What did you need me for, sir? Jido didn't give any details last night when he said you wanted me here this morning."

"I'm going to Kurushima to collect their enlistment sheets so I can start preparing my commanding officers for their new charges in the springtime," Master Yujin explained. "Normally, this would be handled by a team of older onmitsu, but His Highness has highly encouraged me to start looking for an apprentice—*your* future Master of Intelligence. Unfortunately for both of us, that means I need to make a personal appearance, and you happened to be available to come along today."

Daisuke grimaced, trying to shove away the image of the blood-stained hand from his dream. "Who the hell wants to go to that death pit?"

"Very few, but onmitsu who are already on thin ice generally don't complain much." Yujin stared at him pointedly while rising from his seat.

A warm blush crept into Daisuke's face as his gaze drifted toward the skull again, though pity soon overwhelmed his heart and forced his eyes elsewhere. It felt like those empty, cavernous sockets could see straight into his soul somehow.

"Let's be on our way—it's a long walk."

APPEARANCES WERE AN IMPORTANT aspect of Giahatian life, exceptionally so within the nobility and military, where how appropriately one postured determined how seriously they would be taken in any given situation. As such, Daisuke understood his presence was merely a formality—the Intelligence Master ought to be accompanied by at least one subordinate at a time like this, though two would've served him better. Had he not already signed off on Obito training with Raku and Jido, Master Yujin would've brought him along as well. Still, Daisuke couldn't help his annoyance at being dragged across five miles of rough terrain once they left the Capital's outskirts. Trudging through blowing snow didn't help, either.

Unlike the onmitsu and footsoldiers, Kurushima's "students" were purposefully isolated from the rest of the population; it was necessary for the institution's perpetuation. Not only would the public become outraged if it weren't—Daisuke suspected not for wholesome reasons, given how most ignored slavery—but if future hitokiri roamed outside its walls during their internment, they risked developing that pesky thing called empathy, which could prevent them from mindlessly murdering on command. Also different to the other military branches, Kurushima enlisted its members extremely young—boys had to be at least eleven to join the infantry, whereas the assassins raised in this cesspit were just seven years old when conscripted. Some were kidnapped, others sold, and more still freely offered. No matter their origins, the hitokiri masters taught them from the first day that violence—and their capacity for it—wasn't merely survival, but service to the Empire. They trained from dawn to dusk with few days for rest, and punishments were delivered swiftly, often with the most brutal means suiting the situation. Death was weakness.

Daisuke shuddered as they closed the gap between the game trail and a massive black iron gate fixed to high stone walls which allowed no chance for escape. He swallowed when they came to a stop, glancing at Master Yujin for guidance, though the Intelligence Master kept his indifferent gaze forward while men from guard towers shouted orders to grant him entrance. The screech of metal gears made Daisuke's stomach flip as the doors slowly parted. He tried to urge his body into motion when the Intelligence Master pressed onward, but his legs wouldn't budge—everything inside him warned him not to set foot on Kurushima's grounds.

Rather than make a fool out of Master Yujin, he forced himself to move, and was on his superior's heels in seconds. He squared his shoulders and adopted a similar stony appearance despite how his tangled nerves twisted themselves into knots. A man in a black gi with purple and gold strips along the lapels greeted them on the other side—if that's what his discerning sneer could be considered. His purple cloth belt and black outer robe swirled around black trousers and boots in the wind.

"State your business, Intelligence Master," the man said.

"Master Sheng," Master Yujin replied coolly, dropping all pretense of his usual politeness; Daisuke had to hold in a snicker at the way Sheng faltered. "It's time for me to collect your numbers. His Highness would also like me to consider taking an apprentice from the group graduating in spring. Hikari help you, I'd better not be disappointed by what I see."

"Hoji!" Sheng bellowed after a pause, nearly sending Daisuke's soul to the goddess.

Soon, a man wearing a uniform with identical embellishments came to his side, looking even more foul-tempered than his counterpart. However, his arrogant posturing didn't last long; Hoji hurried to bow the second he realized he stood before the Intelligence Master.

"How may we help you today, Master Yujin?"

Daisuke rolled his eyes when the pair decided to be insufferable by making Master Yujin explain himself once more, his gaze then wandering around Kurushima's inner complex; onmitsu or not, he didn't dare let his tongue get the best of him here. Rows of long buildings stood in the distance, past the silhouettes of trainees milling about and ongoing combat drills. There didn't seem to be a tree or decorative thing in sight. If hopelessness was meant to be ingrained into Kurushima's aesthetic, the master assassins who ran the place had certainly achieved as much, though perhaps they deserved to feel that way. Active-duty hitokiri got to live in the Capital—and occasionally beyond—once they graduated from here, whereas masters and instructors were forced to return and live within these walls again after tasting freedom for an undetermined number of years. To Daisuke, it seemed more like undue cruelty rather than a promotion. He couldn't imagine how it felt to live it.

Gods, this place is bleak. He shivered again at a sense of barrenness burrowing into his chest when his eyes found the whipping posts not far behind Sheng and Hoji—he tried not to look at the young man currently being subjected to discipline there. His lungs constricted.

Master Yujin's simple command by way of calling his name reclaimed his focus—neither Hoji nor Sheng were anywhere to be found, which hopefully meant they'd gone to find their enlistment book. Meanwhile, the two onmitsu were passed off to yet another hitokiri master of slightly lower rank, who was charged with bringing them to a bridge suspended between observation towers while they waited. This man didn't seem as belligerent as the other two, but Daisuke hardly found him likeable, given how he was trying to placate Master Yujin's visibly thin patience with the promise of letting him witness a demonstration as a "treat."

Ohagi from Shiba's is a treat. Not whatever the hell he's talking about, Daisuke thought as they stepped onto the bridge; it softly creaked under their weight, as well as accumulated ice and snow. He peered over the ropes and iron for only a second at the grounds, where an instructor paired together boys ranging from ages eight to twelve. The nervous gaggle stood near rings marked by twine and posts with bright red flags.

Since Master Yujin's mood seemed to improve the longer he conversed with their current escort, Daisuke felt it was safe for him to pay attention to something else. He didn't want to bear witness to what he feared was about to take place below them, anyway.

"Is...is that a Northern Nomadic lad in that ring?"

Daisuke's head jerked in Master Yujin's direction at the softly-spoken question; had he dared to wander further away, he might've been fortunate enough to miss it entirely. As if pulled by the will of the universe rather than his own, he padded toward the two men, dread like an anchor in his gut. He knew what happened to slaveborns who were sold to Kurushima—any brought into this hellish pit almost inevitably became live bait for the bigger and stronger Perenin or Giahatian boys. So far, there wasn't a single record of one of his own people surviving until the graduation ceremony.

"Sure is," the hitokiri master replied indifferently. "Boy's father handed 'im over fer seven silvers—cheap trade fer live bait, I guess, but now we can't seem to get rid of 'im."

Daisuke's chest tightened as he silently went to Master Yujin's side and leaned over the metal railing for a better look. His heart plummeted into his stomach when he peeked at the two boys standing on opposite sides of the ring marked with wooden stakes below.

"No." Although he wanted to scream, Daisuke's voice was barely a choked whisper. He froze, despite his instinctive desperation to dash down the stairs, scoop the boy into his arms, and run like hell. *No, not Kulako, not Kulako, not—*

Daisuke's eyes widened with horror. No matter how many times he tried to tell himself it wasn't, nothing would've allowed him to sink into such deep denial. It looked as though they'd removed his earrings, but the bright red hair, controlled expression which seemed too stoic and cold for such a young face, and perhaps most damningly, the fire of Honda's anger burrowed deep in those violet eyes, all indisputably belonged to his little brother.

"W-what are they doing?" he muttered to himself in disbelief as an instructor ordered the two to bow to him, and then to one another, unwillingly affixed to the scene below. He gripped the railing so hard his knuckles turned stark white when he saw the flash of a blade in Kulako's left hand—a panicked scan of the other boy, whom Daisuke had barely noticed, revealed he also brandished a weapon.

Daisuke's violently trembling hands involuntarily covered his mouth when the instructor gave them the order to begin. The anger in Kulako's eyes changed to pure hatred, and in a flash, he'd lunged at the other boy who'd barely had a chance to raise his dagger. A half-formed cry to stop his brother became lodged in Daisuke's throat when the blade sank into the opponent's abdomen with a loud, sickening squelch; a trickle of blood spilled onto Kulako's hand, running down to his wrist in crimson rivulets. The hand from the dream flashed through Daisuke's mind again.

"Daisuke...?" Master Yujin cautiously laid a hand on his shoulder and shook him gently. "Daisuke?"

Desperate to control his emotions and violently churning stomach, he didn't look at the Intelligence Master when he asked through clenched teeth, "May I wait for you outside, sir?"

Master Yujin glanced at the aftermath of what had just taken place in the ring, then briefly inclined his head. As soon as he had permission to take his leave, Daisuke quickly descended the steps from the observation decks and sprinted from Kurushima's grounds, fleeing before his brother would ever have a chance to know he was there.

DAISUKE TIPTOED DOWN GRAY stone stairs leading to the beach, feet crunching snow and ice beneath them as he avoided a slip by carefully descending each step, guided by nothing other than the golden hues of a setting sun sinking low in the sky. In the summer, few sounds reached these lower boardwalks other than those of the steady ocean breeze and black waves rolling into a glittering, misty white froth seconds before breaking on wet sand; in winter's silence, it felt abandoned—empty as the promises he'd made to his little brother about finding a safe home one day.

He didn't know if he wanted to scream, cry, or walk onto the ice floes piling on the beach and wait for whatever fate befell him there. He tossed the ideas around halfheartedly as he kept marching toward an unknown point in the distance. All the while, self-loathing balled itself up in his chest, and the temptation to take the scalpel from his drawer and release it taunted him, steadily growing in timbre as it crashed against his willpower like the waves on the sand. He didn't want the stinging pain, the blood, or more scars on his skin—but the suggestion that he'd be released from these ugly, tumbling emotions was tantalizing.

Daisuke stopped and his gaze turned to the black sea beneath a leaden sky. Above all, he didn't want to feel this wretched guilt anymore. It was all he'd been able to think about during the wordless walk back from Kurushima.

He'd meant to retreat to his room, but instead found himself at the doorway of one of the indoor training halls on the Palace's ground floor, standing beside Jido, who watched whatever conversation was taking place between Obito and Raku in his usual manner of stern quiet. The older onmitsu acknowledged Daisuke with a nod while they waited for their respective partners to finish, but otherwise let him be. He sighed with relief. He didn't want to imagine what might've happened if he were stuck with someone as talkative—or irritating—as Mika.

Daisuke waited until their conversation looked like it was nearly over, then soundlessly slipped into the room as to not obstruct any further instruction from Raku. He squinted at the weapon in Obito's hand; his eyebrows raised slightly when he realized it was a kyoketsu-shoge, a dagger attached to a chain on one end with a ball-shaped counterweight on the other. Not all onmitsu knew how to wield one. Apparently, the two older agents had acquired permission to start training some of their younger counterparts.

Obito's forearms were littered with circular bruises from the thing, and the straw training targets on posts in the center of the room looked as if they'd seen enough for one day. Daisuke chuckled half-heartedly at the sight, then sat down heavily against the wall and pulled his knees to his chest, staring at the wooden beams high above him until Raku dismissed himself. He sensed more than he saw when Obito crouched in front of him.

"What do they even feed them at Kurushima?" he asked after swallowing the pressure in his throat, trying to keep his emotions at bay.

"Worm soup."

That got Daisuke's attention. His head whipped toward his partner. "Really?"

Obito offered him a small smile, but he could easily tell something wasn't right. "No?"

"Are...are you sure?"

"Suddenly not as sure as I was," he admitted quietly. "What brought this up?"

Daisuke chewed his lip and was silent for a long time as he struggled to find the right words. Finally, he mumbled, "I had to go there with Master Yujin today. They have my brother."

Obito knelt and moved in closer. Daisuke had kept his emotions restrained with the thinnest, most frayed thread all afternoon; as much as he resented this vulnerability, he couldn't deny he felt safe when he leaned into Obito's shoulder. As expected, he broke seconds later.

Still, his pride was a hellishly tenacious thing. He sat up again and hurried to scrub away the tears welling in his eyes.

"I failed him," he said quietly, voice trembling.

"You didn't," Obito told him just as softly, the conviction in his statement as strong as ever.

Daisuke thought he could've somehow pulled himself together if his friend had simply agreed with him. However, since he couldn't remember the last time Obito lied to him about...*anything*, he had to trust it was sincere. As soon as the words reached his ears, a sob wracked his body, and he buried his face in Obito's shoulder, clinging to his friend for dear life.

THE ARRIVAL OF THE Winter Festival did wonders for Daisuke's mental state. Perhaps it was the colorful celebrations, the music and other arts performances, but something about it at last interrupted the self-hatred he'd been wallowing in since the visit to Kurushima. For better or worse, it also meant he felt up to finding mischief for the first time in a couple of weeks by the time solstice night came; since Obito was dragged into a patrol at the last minute, there was no voice of reason to talk him out of it, either.

He absentmindedly hummed a familiar dizi tune as he scoured the kitchen pantries, searching for salt to load into a pouch just to see how it reacted with a tincture he'd haphazardly thrown together in his room earlier that day. A small jug of wine sitting in his peripherals made him pause. It was the same cherry blossom-infused wine sold in the Capital's markets during the Spring Festival every year; someone must've left it out either for themselves or by accident after finding it. As it was out of season now, no one would dare serve it to the Emperor or his small gathering of nobles for the feast he hosted in the Palace on solstice night.

Daisuke picked up the potent liquor for the sole purpose of scowling at it. He'd tried it several months back—it hadn't been a great experience.

"Why does it always seem like you're up to something whenever I find you?" Mika's voice came from across the room.

Thankfully, Daisuke had enough self-control over being startled to set the wine on a shelf before he dropped it, then turned to his friend, who wore a teasing grin as he leaned against the doorframe. He did his best to shoot him an answering smirk, though he recognized how his throat tightened around his nerves. "Such accusations. Why do you *think* I'm always up to something when you find me?"

"Experience."

That's fair, Daisuke conceded internally, reluctant to verbally do the same. He stiffened against the pantry when he realized Mika was coming closer.

"Are you seriously planning on spending the last night of the festival cooped up inside?" the other boy asked once he was an arm's length away, taking their conversation in a rather unexpected direction. "You've spent the whole thing indoors, and that's not like you."

"That's not true. I've been out here and there."

Mika hesitated, not looking him in the eye when he finally said, "I'm worried about you."

Brows now furrowed, Daisuke once again had to ask, "...Why?"

Mika's guilt-ridden expression offered little explanation; Daisuke didn't have the mental or emotional capacity to analyze it just yet. Besides, he knew he'd made it a bit too easy for his classmates to sense something wasn't right lately. Some had carefully asked him about his sudden lack of spirit—a few even went to Obito, who naturally refused to answer—but he'd mostly been able to put them at ease with a vague excuse and a wave of the hand. While he guessed that Master Yujin had put things together, his partner was the lone soul who *knew* what he'd seen at Kurushima, and he didn't want to bring it up to anyone else. Moreover, he didn't *trust* the information with others.

"Look, I'm fine. I've just been busy," he tried to assure Mika with the same thing he'd told everyone else.

"Come out with me, then," Mika said as he looped his arm around Daisuke's and pulled, not giving him a chance to decline the invitation while forcing him to abandon the salt pouch. "You've been working too much, and Obito made you spend all of this year's Spring Festival copying from a boring old text."

Daisuke didn't have the heart to tell him that version of events wasn't the full truth—especially the part about the Spring Festival. Rather than do responsible things like studying or training, that was when he'd snagged a jug of the cherry blossom wine from the kitchens and drank too much of it in one night. He awoke on his floor the following day, wretchedly ill with the room still spinning and the half-empty jug beside him. While Obito—rightfully, he supposed—had showed no sympathy for his suffering afterwards, he'd lied flawlessly on Daisuke's behalf when Mika invited him to join the festivities.

What I wouldn't give for that excuse now. Daisuke rolled his eyes. He didn't outright dislike the other boy, but lately, his instincts warned him to be wary. Their friendship already stood on tenuous ground because of Mika's commitment to misinterpreting nearly everything his cousin said or did, and being shamelessly nasty about it. With his guard and suspicions already high, spending time with him was becoming increasingly complex without the convenient distractions of being in a group. Really, Daisuke wasn't sure if he ever *did* enjoy spending time alone with Mika.

Daisuke carefully extracted his arm while his friend was talking about a girl he'd met working in the infirmary earlier in the day. He knew better than to assume he'd be free, though; Mika couldn't handle it when he *politely* rejected his company. Imagining what might happen if he randomly disappeared—or was caught trying to sneak away—was enough to make Daisuke feel guilty for even entertaining the idea.

To Mika's credit, he knew Daisuke liked seeing the acrobat performances, and announced his plan to take him there shortly after they left the Palace. Enjoying the fresh wintry air, they briefly stopped to inspect the wares at a jewelry stand. Daisuke bought a sleek, black resin bracelet, though what really caught his attention was its dark green neighbor—it gleamed under the lanternlight much like Obito's eyes, and a strange warmth engulfed his insides at the sight. Of course, since he couldn't *tell* Mika that, he'd made a rushed but satisfying decision on something else to purchase. He feigned obliviousness to endure the confused look the other boy gave him as he put it on. The pair moved on quickly afterward, but didn't speak again until Mika awkwardly pointed out a stall selling fresh steamed buns, and Daisuke remembered he hadn't eaten yet today.

They arrived at the area reserved for the acrobat troupe in the main square outside the Palace gates just as the routine began. Perhaps a little too smug, Daisuke smiled a when he saw a basket between where Kiko and her life companion, Retsuko, stood during performances—a cloth lay atop the basket, sporting the same purple peonies as the one which covered the sweet buns he knew Obito had delivered earlier that day. The sight soothed him, maybe because they'd picked them out together in the morning.

Of course, whatever part of the universe he'd pissed off through mere existence could never allow the feeling to last long. When he was about halfway through eating his bao filled to the brim with seasoned vegetables and tofu, he noticed his friend ignoring his own food and squinting into the crowd at a nearby tea shop.

"I think that's my old man," Mika said. He smiled brightly and waved his arm. "It is! You should meet him—hang on. Father! Over here!"

Gods, why me? Daisuke whined to whatever spirit would listen when Mika successfully flagged down his father. He'd been so full of fire and fury the first time he met the man, more than happy to leave him with a terrible impression of himself, but that was done with the belief they'd never see each other again. Between what Giichi did to Obito and how he viewed Northern Nomads as lesser beings, they weren't bound to be on good terms anytime soon. Daisuke stuffed the last bite of the steamed bun into his mouth to keep any commentary to himself, not looking at the blustering nobleman once he joined them.

"Convenient that you saw me. I've been looking for you to talk about the poi—" Giichi hesitated, as if he hadn't noticed the other boy standing beside his son at first; Daisuke pretended he didn't see him until the man said, "And who do we have here?"

"This is my friend, Daisuke," Mika enthusiastically introduced him as he pushed the shorter boy forward slightly.

Daisuke let a pointedly unimpressed glance sweep over the nobleman, then coolly greeted, "Lord Tanaka."

Giichi scowled at him before sharply inclining his head—apparently, he hadn't forgotten how their first meeting went, either. Since Mika seemed unaware of their animosity toward one another, Daisuke decided he shouldn't waste what little remained of his good mood on explanations that wouldn't matter to his friend.

"Mika, do you think we could talk privately for a few minutes?" Giichi shot another glare at Daisuke and shouldered his way between the pair, ignoring the offended noise that came from the shorter boy. "I know it's solstice night, but it's a family matter."

A prickle of unease passed through the group. Mika's gaze darted between his father and his friend, hesitant to dismiss either.

Eager to escape, Daisuke chose to spare him the discomfort and plastered a bright smile onto his face. "This is actually pretty good timing—I saw some girls getting their nails painted at a stall over that way. I want to see if they have any colors I like before they close up for the fireworks. See you in a bit?"

"Sure. I'll come find you." Mika looked so dumbfounded by his plan, Daisuke nearly burst into laughter, but he kept his composure as the other boy nodded in agreement.

Daisuke spun on his heel and made his way toward the stall he'd indicated, heaving a sigh of relief as he disappeared further into the crowds. However, it seemed that no matter how much distance he put between himself and Giichi, he could still feel those harsh hazel eyes on his back. His skin was still crawling by the time he reached his destination.

He paused to look over his shoulder once he was out of sight. As he did, he couldn't help but wonder, *Was he about to say "poison"?*

GIICHI WATCHED THE RETREATING boy's back as he weaseled through the crowd, gaze firmly trained until the scrawny little thing disappeared amongst the flock. Then he turned to his son, who appeared flabbergasted, likely at the ridiculous proclamation of a man engaging in an almost exclusively feminine activity; at least *that* much had remained sensible about him.

Some things, however, clearly didn't. "I have to say, Mika, I'm surprised. Friends with a slaveborn? Never mind one like...*that*. Are we emulating the Nakamuras, now?"

Mika jolted as if he'd been jabbed in the ribs with something sharp. His downcast eyes couldn't hide his embarrassment even in the shadows between overhanging lanterns. Picking at the skin around his thumb, he mumbled, "He's not so bad…"

"I suppose it can't always be helped these days." Giichi shook his head dismissively and waved his hand; his two ruby rings gleamed under the light. "If His Highness is willing to allow a whore's bastard to inherit the throne, it's no surprise he'd let a dirty silk-spinner into the elite order of onmitsu."

"Father…have you been drinking?"

Giichi laughed uproariously—he supposed he *had* used more inelegant language than he usually would without the assistance of alcohol, but the mere sight of that silk-spinner boy dressed in military fatigues incensed his disgust. Wherever he'd come from, Master Yujin should have considered his attempt to enlist an insult and dishonor of the highest degree to his ranks; there was no logical reason he hadn't been cast aside without a second thought. Most onmitsu were the youngest sons of noblemen or wealthy merchants; they shouldn't be forced to work alongside one so far beneath them. In a sane world, the boy would've been in servitude to those families, thus sparing their fourth or fifth sons the same social ridicule. Giichi held back a menacing smile when he thought of how other nobles might react if they also knew, then forced his attention back to his own child.

"What did you need, father? Is something wrong? You said it was a family matter."

Giichi collected himself. "Not quite—truthfully, I only said as much in hopes of politely scaring off your friend."

Mika was noticeably confused, so Giichi gestured for him to follow him to a quieter place he'd noticed while hunting for his son through the obnoxious festival cluster. The area he'd spotted was slightly too far away from the main events in the square to be a convenient resting place, which meant he could lead Mika to it without feeling the need to be wary. Once they came to one of the stone benches surrounding the base of a peach tree which bloomed with lovely pink and white flowers in the spring, he sat beside Mika, watching the festivities with his son from a distance for a while before speaking again.

"Do you remember the book you borrowed for me a few months ago?" Of course, he was referring to a journal he'd convinced his son to steal from one of his friends with a higher aptitude for poisons and medicines. "Your friend who penned those tinctures has quite a creative mind. I'd like to meet him someday."

"You just did," Mika timidly confessed.

"You don't say." Giichi couldn't stop another smile filled with vicious glee spreading across his lips. What luck—if things went wrong, he had the perfect scapegoat obliviously waiting to take the blame. "Believe it or not, I found a few other things in there that I plan to use."

"B-but...but you said you needed it to find medicine for Mother."

"She was never sick, as far as I know. She's moved home with your uncle, and your brother has the estates—I haven't heard from her in months. I do apologize for misleading you, but surely you understand I had no choice. The organization I'm working with demands absolute secrecy."

Mika's eyes went wide as his expression flashed between bewilderment and distress. His voice closed around his throat even as he struggled to find the right words, until he finally squeaked out, "Organization?"

"You know how I feel about our current royals and noble families the Emperor favors. You also know I'm not alone in this. Now that we've found a way to join forces, we can work on our ultimate goal to end this humiliating regime before it passes onto the next generation."

The boy shook his head, baffled.

"Since I've found the proper resources, one of your friend's poisons is going to propel us to our next step, now. Your mother and older brother might be lost causes in this, but I couldn't have gotten this far without help from my favorite child." Giichi smiled gently this time and patted him on the shoulder. "I'll need you again soon. I've no doubt the onmitsu will eventually find something out, and when such a time comes..."

Mika swallowed.

"Would you stop bothering the cat?" Obito irritably huffed at Daisuke, who sat near him on the tatami floor in Aunt Kiko's personal library with an opened book in his lap. It was a cozy room on the house's second floor, which had once been used for extra guest space, but as Aunt Kiko gradually saw fewer of those in recent years, she eventually found a new purpose for it. Since they'd had little luck in the Royal Library and he knew about her eclectic collection of books, Obito thought she might have something that could give them some direction. Daisuke rarely turned down a chance to visit Aunt Kiko, so he readily agreed to come along, though keeping him focused was another undertaking altogether.

Snickering, the little pest looked up from the bookmark ribbon he was dangling in the face of a brown tabby with unimpressed green eyes. Although the cat was clearly annoyed by Daisuke's presence, it didn't seem too thrilled about the idea of simply *moving* away from him, and apparently chose to endure his antics instead. Somehow, Obito could relate.

"What? We have something better to do?" Daisuke asked.

Obito rolled his eyes, absentmindedly petting his aunt's other cat, a sleek black menace, when it nudged him with its head and hopped onto his lap. "We're supposed to be researching."

"I was waiting for my nails to dry—kill a man for getting distracted."

"Keep it up, and I might." Obito begrudgingly looked at the fresh coat of paint Daisuke was trying to show off. "Black again?"

"I think it suits me," he answered with a proud, sly grin.

"It does look nice."

Daisuke felt like his mind stopped working for a second. He shook his head to clear it, laughed, then jiggled his new, solid black bracelet around his right wrist before going back to the pages he'd been ignoring. His studious silence lasted even less time than usual, however, as an interested hum came from his throat as it normally did when something piqued his curiosity. "Obito, look at this."

He flipped the book over and held it out so his partner could see better.

Obito squinted at the drawing on the page. "...Isn't that the symbol we saw in the Palace Temple? The tomoe?"

"I think it is, too, but this is a book about warding off evil or whatever. Why would it be on the jars in the Temple?"

"Probably because of the Kurushima graduations," Aunt Kiko's voice drifted in from the doorway, startling everyone in the room; Obito wasn't sure if he was happier to have avoided a cat's claws or his partner's nails digging into his leg from the fright. His aunt smiled apologetically, warmth touching her emerald-green eyes. "Sorry, but you two were having such a fascinating conversation, I didn't want to interrupt."

"You recognize this symbol, though?" Daisuke scooted closer to Obito and got up on his knees to face Aunt Kiko better as she strode toward them, half-melted snowflakes still in her intricately-styled dark hair. Winter was dwindling, but true spring weather wouldn't begin warming the earth for another couple of weeks. Tired of being cooped up, she'd gone to visit her long-term partner, Retsuko, and asked them to leave the library door open while she was out for the day.

Aunt Kiko nodded. "It's a sealing and cleansing symbol. You see, those who die during the Kurushima and Genjing graduations aren't considered...fit, I suppose, by the Emperor for proper funeral rites. Instead—at least the ones from Kurushima; I don't know enough about Genjing's practices—they're buried in a mass grave in a far corner of the Palace's grounds, but because their bodies aren't burned, their spirits and souls are left to wander the area. So, the High Priestess is tasked with taking one of those jars with that symbol on it to collect them before they turn into resentful energy. Once the souls are sealed in the jar, they'll eventually begin the reincarnation cycle."

Daisuke shuddered in revulsion and a chill ran down his spine as he tried not to think if the same might happen to his brother one day. Instead, he pushed the conversation forward. "Resentful energy?"

"Energy left behind by the departed."

"What does it do?"

Imagine if he had this sort of enthusiasm for Master Yujin's lectures. Obito shook his head, trying to look at anything besides the sparkle of intrigue in his friend's eyes. He wasn't about to be hard on him for it, anyway.

Ever since Daisuke had gone to Kurushima with Master Yujin, any mention of the place made a tremor pass through him, and horrible thoughts followed. Obito couldn't stop where his friend's mind would inevitably go when it was brought up, nor could he shield him from Kurushima's existence, so he much preferred the few instances when Daisuke's attention was successfully redirected.

"There's a few theories," Aunt Kiko hummed, bringing his own wandering thoughts back to the present; since the Nakamura family didn't take religion seriously, she could approach this more lightheartedly than most would. "Some believe leaving the energy around makes it easier for your heart to succumb to evil, others think it makes summoning demons and devils easier. My personal favorite is the idea it'll attach to someone and slowly make it so that their soul becomes too fractured to reincarnate."

She gently took the book from Daisuke and brought it close to her eyes, squinting as she studied the symbol. After a moment, she turned it around once more and pointed to the center so she could explain.

"It's been a while since I've even looked at this—my parents made us go to the Temple at least once a month for good appearances, but they died when I was about the same age as you two, and I haven't been since. Anyway, one thing I do remember is this. These three right-facing tomoe, or mitsudomoe, in the center represent the three realms of the afterlife: Hikari's heavens, Kuro's hells, and the Between Realm. The circle is the barrier between them and human life, and the flames on the compass points symbolize the four base elements of nature."

Daisuke frowned at the page, though surprise quickly overtook his features when she handed the book back to him.

"Keep it—from what you told me earlier, you two might need it."

Daisuke shot Obito a shameless, roguish grin when he glared at him—sure, it broke protocol, but since they weren't getting far with their own research, he recruited outside help. He was sure he'd be forgiven in a few minutes...or hours, depending on his friend's mood. "What? She asked."

Trying to ignore the way his heart skipped a beat, Obito sighed; he should've expected his partner to speak to his aunt without restraint when he'd left them alone to make tea earlier. While he enjoyed listening to their chatter, they talked constantly when together, and the way they erratically bounced between topics made it hard for him to keep up. The same had happened today, which was when he'd decided to take a break for his own sanity. Resigned, he made a mental note to pay more attention to their conspiring in the future, but didn't press the issue. Besides, he didn't exactly deserve to be annoyed—what he was about to suggest to Daisuke wasn't much different. They couldn't do everything on their own.

"Fine," he conceded as he stood. "We'll keep the book. But it might be time to admit we should talk to General Aki."

"We haven't gotten anywhere else trying to hunt people and names down, so why not?"

"You didn't even try to argue. Are you sick?"

"Don't be mean—you know how much I like General Aki."

A clever gleam flashed through Aunt Kiko's eyes when she watched Obito help Daisuke to his feet, but she stayed quiet about whatever occurred to her. Instead, she said, "Before you two go, Daisuke, Retsuko gave me something to pass on to you."

"A bill?" Daisuke tilted his head. Due to the amount of work he and Obito had been trying to trudge through all winter, he'd fallen behind in his lessons from the acrobat matron. He'd still been practicing during combat training, but he hadn't had time to show her his progress; he worried it nullified their deal.

"Nothing of the sort, don't worry." Aunt Kiko chuckled and took out a small, pink cloth pouch from her obi. "She found some red poppy seeds for a real bargain a few days ago. When I told her you boys were here today, she gave them to me to pass on to you—we both think they're better off in your hands."

For being such tiny seeds, the package they came in seemed immensely heavy. Daisuke nervously looked at Obito, but his eyes were back on the pouch within seconds. *I've grown a few plants and flowers for our poisons, but I don't know if I have enough experience for these.*

As if sensing his concerns, she added, "Come back in the spring after I've started my garden, and I'll help if I can. Retsuko said she'd take a jar or two of the ointment as thanks, anyway."

Daisuke grinned. "I knew she had a price."

YUJIN KEPT HIS EYES affixed to a painting on the far wall of the Emperor's study while His Highness read through the letter he'd handed over moments before. Senator Ming had disappeared from Fukainuma, a village in the center of Perena's southeastern swamplands, where most of the nation's rice was produced. This note came from a concerned relative who had not heard back from the senator about attending the celebration of a nephew's birth, but Yujin tried to remain focused on the precise, careful brushstrokes of a cherry blossom branch in the foreground. In the background, gray mountains stood tall and stoic, stark against the soft pink petals before it. Something about this painting gave him immense comfort when delivering negative or stressful news to Emperor Akuwara.

"How do you intend to handle this?" His Highness asked as he set the scroll on his desk, rubbing a spot on his temple just below where the Imperial silver circlet rested. In a highly unusual instance that seemed to surprise them both, they'd agreed that the Senator was much too young and healthy to have died; he hadn't even fathered his first child yet. Moreover, no one else in his jurisdiction had mentioned his passing, nor was there any notable spread of disease to raise concerns.

Yujin's stomach churned as relief and anxiety danced around one another. For once, he was sympathetic to Akuwara's frustration; in addition to usual matters, this letter was on the heels of another pressing issue, having arrived a few days after a report about an assassin who had apparently disappeared into thin air. It wasn't an uncommon happening—sometimes the hitokiri found better opportunities as a nobleman's personal guard or simply died due to various causes on the return trip from assignments, but nonetheless, they had to be tracked down and dealt with accordingly.

"Because the assassin reportedly disappeared around Nishinuma—only an hour or so down the road from Fukainuma—I will assemble a small squadron of onmitsu to investigate both villages. Ideally, they'll return either with the assassin in chains or his head in a sack, and the Senator's whereabouts will be uncovered in the meantime."

"Resolve it quickly," the Emperor conceded after a moment, disinterested, although not in his usual manner. "Dismissed."

The ball of tension sitting heavily between his shoulders eased slightly when Yujin bowed and took his leave. He couldn't remember the last time a briefing had gone so seamlessly; His Highness must still be distracted by whatever action he planned to take against Senator Hajime. Naturally, it wasn't in retaliation to capturing an Imperial intelligence operative and intending to auction him off as a common slave, but rather because of Hayate's report of how deep corruption ran through the military base in Zhu. In a rare case of Akuwara's paranoia paying off, he'd chosen to threaten the Senator with certain sanctions, though he hadn't been transparent regarding those plans. Either way, it stemmed from an inherent distrust of being able to control his infantry should the time come; the Senator's personal interests could *not* override Imperial command. Given recent events, Zhu's military was undeniably compromised, and the Senator could not be trusted to uphold the throne's standards. Yujin surmised this was the closest Akuwara felt to true betrayal in quite some time.

In any case, it wasn't the Intelligence Master's concern just yet—His Highness had made as much exceedingly clear. Yujin wasn't sure if he should feel relieved or worried regarding the Emperor's tight lips about the situation, but settled on the thought that he'd prod about it in a few weeks if Akuwara kept his silence, and happily let it slip from his mind for now.

He paused when he came to a window overlooking one of the Palace's inner courtyards—finding a team to send to the southern swamps was his top priority, and so far, all he really knew was that he'd be sending Raku and Jido. Both were among his first and most fit choices to replace him as Intelligence Master—while accepting some traditions should be broken—before Emperor Akuwara forced him to change plans by insisting on someone from Kurushima. With any luck, the brutish young man he'd selected would prove himself incompetent within weeks, and His Highness would be forced to capitulate.

Yujin shook his head and forced himself to concentrate once again. Raku and Jido were obvious choices for both this mission and his other plans, but he couldn't send them alone. He decided to add Mika and Shinta to the roster; in plain terms, it was because he felt they needed more experience, although they wouldn't be happy since they'd just returned from escorting a group of merchants to Imasu the previous day. Two more onmitsu should fill out the numbers nicely, so long as they were analytical and adaptive enough to keep up with Raku and Jido.

With a pained sigh, he begrudgingly selected his last team—given that he had the report from Hayate to clear their names, he'd kept them grounded long enough.

"CAN WE STOP FOR food first?" Daisuke asked as they took to the Capital's streets from the nobility quarter; it was the quickest way to the basic infantry barracks from Aunt Kiko's home. "I'm starving."

Obito furrowed his brows. "I thought you ate before we went to Aunt Kiko's."

"I'm a growing boy, Obito, I can't help it."

"'Growing,'" he scoffed. "You haven't grown since we got back from Zhu."

"I *have,* just not as much as *you.*" Daisuke snickered.

Obito paused to assess what his friend said. He'd always been a bit taller than Daisuke, but now that he took the time to notice, the gap had increased considerably. Desperate not to let his gaze linger, he turned his eyes toward the nearby shops again. Daisuke was all too aware of how pretty he was, and how many people agreed with him on that front—men and women alike. He didn't want to be lumped with the lot.

Not that they're wrong, but—wait, what the hell am I thinking?

"Are *you* sick?" Daisuke teased, snapping him out of his short-lived dilemma by being less than an inch away. "Your face turned a bit red all of a sudden."

"Quiet." He irritably pushed the cackling little pest back. "I was thinking."

"About?"

"Have you figured out who stole your poisons journal yet?"

Obviously, that wasn't true, but it was clearly an effective distraction, as Daisuke's expression became pensive. Although it added yet another item to their frustratingly long list of unanswered questions, Obito felt it was the most solvable, but his partner hadn't been terribly keen on devoting much time to it. While he understood why Daisuke would want to avoid it altogether, it wasn't a tenable strategy. Whoever did it *should* face some form of accountability.

"I think I have an idea of who might've *wanted* to do it, I just can't imagine *why.*"

Obito had a feeling they suspected the same person, but since he'd finally convinced him to talk about it, he wanted to keep his partner going. "You can't think of anything that would make them want to take it?"

Daisuke sighed. "That's sort of the problem, isn't it? No one would have a reason to do it *except* to be a massive prick and get on my bad side. It's kind of useless. No different than what you saw the last time I showed you what I was working on. Most of the stuff in there is theoretical nonsense—*I* don't even know how effective any of it is since it's all based off derivatives from other poisons I've made. So, unless you're an idiot like—wait, isn't that Masaki?"

Through the overlapping chatter of people on the street, Daisuke heard the younger onmitsu calling their names, and quickly rooted him out among the crowd. Once the younger boy realized they'd noticed him, he waved enthusiastically to flag them down as he and his partner, Yuki, pushed past people to get closer. Both boys nearly fell into Obito once they'd wriggled their way through, ignoring plenty of outraged comments from pedestrians.

"We finally found you two." Masaki beamed, looking as proud as he had when he'd helped Daisuke locate Obito several months back.

"We thought Master Yujin was going to have our heads soon," Yuki added, though he sounded genuinely nervous. He shrank a bit behind his partner once the two older onmitsu turned away from each other to face them and wouldn't look at either directly; he was a shy boy, but seemed to be particularly afraid of drawing Obito's attention. Daisuke made a mental note to tease his partner about it later.

Masaki's enthusiasm dimmed slightly as his face turned serious, as if his partner's comment reminded him of their mission. "He said he needs you to report to his office."

Obito traded a concerned, if not confused, glance with Daisuke before turning to the other pair again; he was quite certain they'd been staying out of trouble lately. "Did he happen to say why?"

Yuki shook his head, then waved for them to follow him and his partner back toward the Palace.

"Fuck," Daisuke whined, voicing Obito's thoughts, until a mischievous little snicker made him regret siding with him. "Just as well, I guess. We probably wouldn't be able to see the General without sending a messenger first, anyway."

Obito stopped. "You knew that the whole time, but decided not to mention it?"

"What? It's not every day you forget something that I don't. I had to run with it." Daisuke grinned, earning Obito's elbow in his upper arm. The two younger onmitsu ignored the resulting yelp, sighing at him in exasperation as they kept walking ahead.

"WHAT'S TAKING MIKA SO long?" Jido impatiently crossed his arms and leaned on Raku, who had already resigned himself to resting against the wall.

Allegedly, a Senator who presided over the small villages in the eastern swamps hadn't returned correspondence in weeks, which was highly unusual. Around the same time, an assassin named Yin—whom Daisuke and Obito had the misfortune of knowing—had also gone missing while on assignment in the area. Concerned about the circumstances, Master Yujin decisively organized a team of six onmitsu for the job, briefed them the previous evening, and ordered them to move out at dawn with Raku and Jido at the helm. The pair making up the lead team were more than a couple of pretty Perenin faces; having just entered their twenties, they were the eldest and the most experienced of the group, and their capabilities had earned Master Yujin's utmost confidence. Seniority aside, the decision to put them in charge came without argument.

Even so, the party couldn't leave until Mika joined his five teammates, and they'd been waiting for at least an hour in the alcove of an entrance which led to the rear Palace grounds. Cold wind and snow regularly blasted their faces despite the shelter; only Daisuke remained mostly unaffected by it at this point.

Shinta adjusted his glasses, looked at the irritable faces of those surrounding him, then frowned. He wasn't happy about being expected to take accountability for his partner. "He said he had to check in with his father before we left."

Raku furrowed his brows, the expression in his one visible brown eye lined with apprehension. "That's a bit odd. He's hardly a child who needs permission...did he say why?"

"No, but he should be here any minute." Shinta added under his breath, "I hope."

"Why didn't he take care of this last night after we were briefed?" Jido pressed, rolling his eyes when Shinta helplessly shrugged in response.

Daisuke and Obito exchanged a glance, but stayed quiet; despite what they knew about Giichi and Mika, it wasn't inherently suspicious information, just...*strange*. Of course, it was entirely plausible that Mika made these plans before being dragged into another assignment—he and Shinta *had* returned from one only a day or two prior—but something told Daisuke to hold onto his misgivings. Obito would be doing the same, though whether he'd ever speak on it remained a mystery for now. The known contention between him and his cousin often made him hesitate to openly express judgement against Mika. However, given the multitude of examples he could pull from memory, he knew something wasn't right about the sudden closeness Giichi was fostering with his youngest son. His uncle was never this interested in any of his children.

The group spoke no further and huddled around a blazing brazier for warmth as the sun climbed higher into the sky. Fortunately for Mika, he came sprinting toward them just before midmorning, tumbling over rapid, profuse apologies and nearly his own feet in the process.

"I'm so sorry," he said one final time once he joined them, bowing to Jido and Raku with cupped hands between heaving breaths. If he'd met Giichi in the nobility quarter, he'd run quite the distance.

Raku sighed and tugged on his eyepatch to adjust it, purposefully ignoring the face his partner made at the action. "Never mind—let's get going."

The continuous, soft crunch of hardpacked snow underfoot became monotonous and familiar as Raku led the way eastward with Jido close to his side; a few paces behind, Mika and Shinta each guarded a flank of the formation, while Obito and Daisuke stayed at the back. After the lengthy delay, Raku kept them moving at brisk, relentless pace, which limited conversations.

Within two days, he brought them to the edge of the forests surrounding the Capital by early evening. Thick evergreens parted and opened to vast lands of long brown grasses and frosty cattails swaying in the breeze;

the terrain dipped lower, and the road narrowed to barely fit the ox carts which often traveled it. A group of passing locals headed toward the Capital warned them to be mindful of the width to avoid a stumble into chilly, swampy waters.

Because Raku had pushed them to cover so much ground, Daisuke was already tired before they began the next several miles of their trek through the swamp. He glanced at heavy gray clouds that had followed them all day; the air became bitingly cold as they darkened the sky, and now he could detect the faint, indescribable scent of impending snowfall. Their leader must've noticed as well, as he swiftly spun on his heel and raised a hand to get everyone's attention—a storm could be unpredictable in these lowlands, so caution was wise.

"We risk getting lost in a snowstorm if we stay on the road much longer," he announced once all eyes were on him. "There's a village up ahead—Master Yujin expected we might need to stop at an inn, so he made an allowance for it."

That beats the hell out of camping again. Daisuke hoped he didn't look nearly as relieved as he felt. While it'd kept them dry and warm, they'd all been uncomfortably wedged under one tent the last couple of nights.

"I just don't know if it'll be enough to pay for six rooms and food." Raku winced when he realized everyone was still listening to him.

Jido snorted. "Don't be ridiculous. Since I doubt this place has a big enough room for all of us, we'll just divide into our usual teams for the night and pay for three instead. That should cut costs sufficiently if we need a place to stay in Fukainuma or on the way back."

Finally given the opportunity, Shinta asked, "Raku, do you think all six of us are going to be...well, *necessary* for this?"

Raku pursed his lips as if unsure how to answer, then said, "As Master Yujin told us, this has the potential to be very dangerous if we are dealing with a hitokiri with new loyalties. I doubt he *wants* to be brought back to the Capital to be publicly tortured and executed—who can blame him? But, because of that, we can expect him to put up a violent fight no matter what, and those chances will double if he's also the reason Senator Ming went missing. This is mostly about strength in numbers, and while Daisuke and Obito also have a little experience, Master Yujin thinks both of your teams could use the training."

"I'm not sure you can call what we have 'experience,'" Obito muttered.

"We have experience, too, remember?" Mika quickly argued, drowning out Obito's remark; Shinta mouthed a curse to the heavens and buried his face in his hands. "We just got back from escorting a caravan of merchants to Imasu."

"My mistake, then." Raku smiled politely, then turned to keep the group moving toward the village. Jido fluidly fell into step with him as he passed by, and Shinta followed. Mika, however, paused long enough to coldly eye Obito from over his shoulder. His lips slipped into a smug smirk, and he took a couple of steps toward them, leaning in so he could keep his voice low.

"Want to know something else?" he taunted. "*We* didn't fuck it up, either."

Apparently feeling quite satisfied with his quip, he shot them another spiteful look before rejoining the others, as if nothing had happened. Daisuke's fists clenched—Mika really was too comfortable with mocking Obito in front of him. Just as he was about to lunge forward to chase him down and attack, he felt a tug on the back of his belt.

"He's not worth it." Obito let go of him again.

Daisuke scowled at Mika, then glanced at the thin sheet of ice glazing the wetlands on each side of the road. "Are you sure we can't just drown him?"

Obito sighed. "Stop it—you know the swamp isn't deep enough here, anyway."

"We'll tie him up and bury him under the ice. It should be frozen over again by morning."

"We'd still have too many witnesses."

"You're taking all the fun out of this."

"Don't get mad at me if you can't outsmart the simple facts."

"Obito, Daisuke!" Jido suddenly shouted from the front of the formation, making them jump. "Quit lagging!"

The inn Raku brought them to was a small, pleasantly cozy establishment not far from the village's eastern entrance. Despite the owner telling Raku that he hadn't seen such a large party in weeks, he was quick and efficient in making sure he had enough space for everyone. Once bags were set down and beds were made for the night, the group reconvened around a table in the inn's main room for a light but satisfying dinner. Warm candlelight, a hot meal, and a roaring fire at the hearth thawed them while they ate.

Daisuke's eyes went to everyone seated around the table when he finished the last of his fish and rice. To his left, Shinta and Mika were arguing over something he didn't care to know about, while on his right, Jido explained the political machinations of a rich merchant's family drama to Obito, who looked horrendously bored despite listening intently. Raku was being held hostage in a more general conversation with the innkeeper while simultaneously trying to monitor the other four, which meant he probably wasn't paying attention to his fifth charge—not due to a lack of effort, either.

I hope Master Yujin gives him a promotion or something after this. Daisuke shook his head and chuckled, an amused smirk tugging at the corner of his mouth. When he felt the opportunity was right, he slipped away, unnoticed even by the handful of other patrons he passed.

Outside, he found a spot around the building's corner, perfect for watching whatever he could see from the veranda in peace. Daisuke tilted his face toward the cold air and breathed it in slowly, reveling in the muted sound of fluffy snowflakes, and how peacefully quiet the world became amid snowfall. Wind chimes danced in the breeze, and his mind went delightfully blank as he leaned against the wall. Nothing about talismans, shadows, magic, or failures entered his thoughts for the first time in months while he gazed at the sunset through distant trees. It'd been a long winter.

He didn't turn the corner to look, but he thought he recognized the pattern of long, sure strides as contrastingly soft footfalls landed against the deck. After a moment, he heard the hissing strike of a match, and the pungent aroma of burning white leaf curled around the building, piquing his interest.

"Obito?" Although he couldn't see his partner, a teasing grin still worked its way onto his lips. "Are you smoking white leaf without me? I'm wounded."

"You pest." The silver pipe appeared at the corner first. "I thought you went upstairs."

"Please. You know it's too early for me to go to bed."

Daisuke took a couple of steps to his left to make room for Obito when his partner joined him on his side. Exhausted from their travels, neither said a word while they smoked together and watched a few stragglers rushing through the weather as nighttime enveloped the village. Even if they *could've* found a better pastime, Daisuke hadn't realized how much he needed the simple ease of being alone in comfortable quiet with Obito. Not long after the last of the white leaf burned down and the smell dissipated a little, they each lit a cigarette with the intent of turning in for the night once they were finished. However, Daisuke's mind never stayed quiet for long.

His brows furrowed as he took the last drag off his cigarette. "That's right, you asked me if I had any journal-thief suspects before we got dragged into this mission."

"I did." As much as Obito wanted to pick on his friend's attention span, they hadn't had time to resume their conversation since being accosted for the briefing.

"Here's a hint: I left the journal under your bed before we left because it was safer there than it'd be with us."

"What else have you hidden under my bed?"

"Wildly unimportant, but—"

The reverberation of boots against planks stopped their conversation.

Daisuke put a finger to his lips and crept toward the building's edge, pinning his friend—who instantly went rigid—to the wall when he snaked around him for a better view. "Mika's coming. Looks like Shinta's with him, too."

"Daisuke—" Obito cleared his throat, which made him realize how close they were and the pained expression he wore. "—please get off me."

A devilish, irresistible idea crashed into his mind as he shot his partner a mischievous grin. Forest green eyes locked onto him in a way that was at once infuriated and suspicious, to the point Daisuke could barely contain his laughter. It really had been too long since he properly teased Obito—as far as he was concerned, this was overdue.

"No time," he whispered, latching onto Obito's shirt and pulling himself closer, taking secret and immense delight in the scent of his skin.

Before his partner had time to protest or otherwise react, their heads turned toward the sound of Shinta groaning and the distinct noise of a bottle being uncorked. The light of a lantern glowed against their surroundings, and Obito tried to flatten himself further against the wall to avoid detection; Daisuke—poorly—pushed down the smugness building in his chest.

"How did you even get your hands on that?"

Mika chuckled, followed by the creak of weak boards as both sat down heavily on the dry veranda. "It's just the red wine they keep on hand in the

Palace, so it's not hard to find by any means. Are you drinking with me or not?"

"...Fine, but save some for our next stop, too. We can't afford to be useless while we're with Raku and Jido—they won't hold back when they report to Master Yujin, you know."

"You worry too much."

"No, *you* don't worry enough. How are we supposed to get better pay or assignments if they think we're deadweights?"

"Shut up." Mika spat. Daisuke and Obito grimaced on Shinta's behalf. "It's not like we're the other two."

"What does that even mean?"

"That they couldn't even bring a stupid fucking rock back from—you know what? Never mind. I don't want to talk about them, anyway."

Mika knowing vague details about their failed mission to Zhu was hardly a surprise; according to Daisuke, he'd been in the infirmary sometime after they were disciplined by the Emperor, and rumors spread like wildfire in certain corners of the Palace. Obito was sure a line could be drawn between his cousin's words and the guards who had inflicted the punishment. Daisuke's grip tightened.

Feeling quite dejected, Shinta sighed and dropped the subject, followed by a spell of tense quiet, during which the only sound came from liquid sloshing back and forth in the bottle they passed between themselves. By then, Obito evidently reached his limit of how much unwanted physical contact he could stand. He carefully pried Daisuke's hands away, his expression in the near darkness still managing to firmly say they should keep quiet, and his eyes darted toward the left. Daisuke nodded, reluctantly freed himself from Obito's gentle grasp, then wordlessly led them toward the other end of the walkway.

RAKU AND JIDO PAID no mind to complaints the following morning when they roused their subordinates to leave the inn, although even the two older onmitsu seemed to be as stiff and sore as anyone else would've been after covering so much ground in such a short time. Last night's snow had turned into freezing rain by dawn, but it didn't deter the group. Sunrise broke over the horizon when they set foot on the road once more, where tall wooden posts with bright red flags tied to the top marked their way to Fukainuma, the largest of the three main towns in the swamplands. Once they finished their investigation there, they would move onto Nishinuma, a little further to the east. Despite the previous night's snowfall, the air felt warmer and more humid this morning than it had yesterday; it wouldn't be much longer before springtime visited the land again.

Daisuke walked near Obito's side at the back of the formation in sullen silence, apparently still pissed about getting dragged out of bed so early. As far as Obito was concerned, it was his partner's own fault he'd had to take the phrase so literally while packing their things. Neither of the two leading this mission had much patience for antics; it wouldn't do them any good to push boundaries unnecessarily with the dire matter they faced. Plus, there was a certain—and admittedly mean-spirited—satisfaction in the idea that Daisuke hadn't completely gotten away with his nonsense from last night.

Even so, the little menace never stayed quiet for long. By midmorning, he'd become so bored, he looked like he might burst. Obito almost felt guilty for finding it as amusing as he did, but watching Daisuke struggle with his willful pride and unyielding need for chatter was easy entertainment. Especially when stubbornness began losing.

A loud, frustrated groan suddenly left his lips, making Obito jump. He just barely remembered to lower his voice when he asked, "Why the hell would an assassin like Yin run away just to hide in a low-populated area like these swamps, anyway?"

"I can't believe you held out that long," Obito commented dryly.

Despite his tone, he was relieved someone else finally mentioned it; he'd expected his partner to have doubts mirroring his own, but they hadn't been given much of a chance to discuss whatever they were. Raku had made it exceedingly clear during the first leg of their journey that he didn't think anyone in the group should speculate on the situation before they knew more. While Obito disagreed with the method, he saw the wisdom in it; Raku couldn't stop them each from having their preconceived notions, but he *could* prevent them from spreading those to each other and further skewing facts that may appear.

"Whatever." Daisuke huffed. "You know I'm right."

"But no thoughts on the missing Senator?"

"A wild conspiracy, actually. Interested?"

"You know I am."

"I think it's all related. I think Yin kidnapped or coerced Senator Ming into going along with some scheme of his, and they're both hiding out in Nishinuma."

Obito looked at his feet while he worked through how Daisuke's theory stacked against his own. "I don't think it's that wild. It wouldn't surprise me if we found out there's some resource or financial thing for Yin to get out of this—it's how he operates. If I remember right, he wouldn't help Haruto with the black lotus poison because he couldn't offer either one."

Yet, somehow, Itsuki still ended up paying the ultimate price for that assassin's ambitions. Now neither of them were alive. Obito was surprised when Yin's name initially came up as part of this investigation. He thought the assassin would keep his head down after coming so close to incurring the Intelligence Master's wrath along with Haruto, and barely escaping with his own life as a result. Whatever had tempted him to come out of hiding after all this time must've promised significant gains.

"Given those things," he continued. "I'm willing to bet someone paid him well for whatever we're walking into."

Daisuke grinned. "Are you gambling?"

"I've told you, I don't gamble. I just know when I'm right."

Fukainuma was a small village still surrounded by a defensive wall built during the Perenin Empire. It was sometime around noon when the group approached the town's old arch, wood rotting in some places while its faded red paint peeled in others; Obito couldn't explain it, but the sight filled him with a sense of dread. Worse, Daisuke seemed to share it, judging by his expression when they exchanged a glance through the dwindling rain before following the forward march of the other four. However, as they stepped under the arch, a more prevalent, nagging sense of unease permeated the air like a thick fog. This time, the whole group paused to look at one another first, then their surroundings.

Although it was now melting here as well, it looked as though snow hadn't been cleared from Fukainuma's streets in weeks, and there wasn't a soul in sight. None of the merchant stalls appeared to have been in use for just as long; the elements had stripped paint or broken shutters on some homes and shops, too. On a warm day nearing the end of a long winter, even a town of this size should've been buzzing with activity.

"This is...odd," Raku muttered, brows knit as he tried to work through what he was seeing. "It's like it's been abandoned."

Jido had stepped several paces away from everyone else, and now abruptly stopped. They all went rigid in response. He paused to think, then turned to his partner. "Take Shinta and Mika to investigate the town, and I'll take Daisuke and Obito to check on Senator Ming. We'll meet at the mansion in an hour—that should give us all plenty of time."

Mika opened his mouth to protest when Raku nodded in agreement, but Shinta sharply elbowed him in the chest. Daisuke started to cackle and soon found himself suffering the same unfair fate from Obito. Thankfully, neither of the senior onmitsu seemed to notice—nobody was in the mood to be scolded.

"Be smart and stay safe," Raku warned, eye firmly on Jido even when he added, "*All* of you."

The manor's heavy doors creaked as Jido and Obito pushed them open while Daisuke kept watch over an empty courtyard at the group's otherwise unguarded back. A faint, musty odor infiltrated the air when they cautiously stepped over the threshold and into the dark main hall, unpleasantly seizing their collective anxieties and whirling it into a heavy cloud over their heads.

Jido quietly instructed them to investigate the home's east wing while he took the west. Despite the importance of Perena's rice industry, a Senator in an area such as Fukainuma often didn't have the same level of wealth as one in charge of grand cities like Zhu or Baohu, so there wasn't nearly as much space to search through as one might expect. Truthfully, calling the place a "mansion" was rather generous.

And not a slave collar in sight. Miraculous, Daisuke thought to himself as he and Obito began their part of the work.

They opted to equally divide the rooms they were put in charge of searching. Obito found nothing of note in the first few rooms he explored, only dust and the same eerie emptiness which was present throughout the rest of the village, but it quickly changed when he came upon what must've been Senator Ming's study. A putrid smell, like rotting food, came from a basket sitting in the center of a large desk; it grew stronger when he approached it. He placed a hand over his mouth and nose before bending to take a closer look at the contents. Orange snowberries—the key ingredient used in one of Daisuke's experimental poisons, blackwater. If he remembered correctly, they also gave the tincture its distinct color and most of its side effects. The majority had turned into moldy, decomposed mush, but the few that hadn't were unfortunately undeniable. These snowberries grew year-round in most of Perena's swampy lowlands, were inedible and, while not fatally so, toxic to humans if ingested.

Most people would just avoid these, and Daisuke's the only one who should know about the blackwater poison. But... Obito's unease returned tenfold as he turned this unexpected puzzle piece over in his mind. Assuming the berries had been gathered for one of his friend's experiments might've been a massive leap in logic, but at the same time, it somehow made the most sense. He couldn't imagine another reason for anyone to harvest the berries. He'd also personally seen the damage done to Daisuke's desk drawer and journal when his friend first asked him to help investigate. Although he didn't mention it, he'd also found half of a strange, greasy-looking print on one of the pages when he'd flipped through the poisons journal to check it for missing sections. While Daisuke was frequently carefree about many things, the notes he kept regarding subjects that piqued his interest weren't among them. The poison journal's condition was always immaculate. Along with a few others, blackwater's name was purposely misleading—why, not even his partner seemed to know—so he wouldn't be surprised if that was what had drawn someone to it.

"Obito," Daisuke whispered from the doorway, nearly sending his soul to the heavens.

"Did you find something?" Obito asked, trying to cover how badly he'd been startled.

"I think so, but what did *you* find?" Upon noting the odor wafting through the room and his friend's expression, Daisuke pushed himself off the frame and came to his side. His face paled as his eyes widened with horror when he peered into the basket. "A-are those...?"

Obito nodded slowly. "What are the odds that somebody copied blackwater out of your journal after they stole it?"

"...Gods." Daisuke chewed on his thumbnail, not giving a second thought to ruining the coat of black polish he'd been so proud of days earlier, then gripped his hair. "Fuck—gods, fuck. This is bad, Obito. *Really* bad—I...I could be killed for this."

"It's just a hunch. We don't have any proof it's what those are being used for."

"Orange snowberries are useless medicinally *unless* you're making a poison. This basket is *plenty* of proof, and we both know it. Gods be damned, I'm so fucked."

"Daisuke." Obito resisted the urge to grab him by the shoulders. The firmness in his voice brought Daisuke's gaze back from somewhere beyond the dusty sunbeam trying to peek through the window. "We'll figure it out. If the berries can grow around here, that means they're probably also in Nishinuma—where Yin is."

Daisuke swallowed and blinked; as if it'd helped his mind function properly again, his brows furrowed as they often did when he was thinking about something. "You're assuming the two are related, then? Maybe those are the resource Yin wanted, but because of Nishinuma's small population, he took everyone who was here, too. But who put him up to this? *He* didn't steal blackwater's recipe out of my journal...Mika did."

Obito wasn't entirely surprised to hear his cousin's name leave Daisuke's mouth. Although he hoped they were wrong, the brief flash of a rueful look in his friend's eyes told him exactly how much thought he'd given this, as did a slightly sick feeling forming in the pit of his stomach. Whatever Mika had dragged himself into, it couldn't be good. Sure, they hadn't been close in years, but the imprinted memory from childhood and how things used to be often left Obito wondering if he should try talking some sense into him these days. However, an instant recall of how he couldn't seem to get near Mika without his presence alone intensifying the other boy's anger—or jealousy, or possessiveness, or whatever he might've felt on a given day—always made him reconsider.

Before he could ask further questions, his partner shook his head and started toward the door again, waving for him to follow. Obito's feet were moving before he fully realized it.

"Yin told us he's good at poisons, and that other assassins would pay him to make them if they couldn't," Daisuke mused as they crossed the hall. "But, for some reason, he decided he needed to include the Senator and his people in making blackwater, which means Yin would've had to *make* Senator Ming cooperate."

Daisuke opened the door to a large bedroom with a vanity, two wardrobes, and a large round window on one side, while the other was lined with bookshelves. Obito was too caught up in his partner's deductions to interrupt, so he silently moved with him when he padded over to the bed and stooped over the left side. Although it went unmentioned, both felt as though a strange energy lingered nearby; Obito tried dismissing it as the general unease he'd been grappling with since they set foot in Fukainuma.

"I think the lady of the house is dead," Daisuke said as he pulled back the sheets, revealing the grisly sight of russet stains near the pillow on one side of the mattress, marring otherwise pristine white bedding—whoever had once rested there couldn't have possibly survived losing so much blood.

Still, Obito had to ask, "What makes you think it was her and not Senator Ming?"

"Did you smell that when I moved the blankets? Other than the blood, I mean. It's plum blossom perfume."

"And how would you know?"

"There's a group of women who like to talk to me whenever we're on morning patrols—you're usually too far ahead of me by the time we're near their brothel to notice them, but I promise they're nice. You should stick around sometime. Anyway, the plum blossom perfume's been popular this year, so they all wear it. It's *heavy*."

"I almost hate to say it—"

"—What? Come on, that was—"

"—I know. I was about to say it's a solid observation, and I think you're right." Obito held back a laugh when Daisuke glared at him. "Killing her would've given Yin plenty of leverage to make Senator Ming go along with any of his demands. Speaking of, you mentioned the other assassins paying Yin to make their poisons, which means someone would've had to pay him to make the blackwater."

"For what, though?" Daisuke's expressive eyes widened slightly with anticipation as he leaned toward his partner a little more.

Obito nearly forgot what he was about to say. He mentally shook himself and forced away the wave of strange yet familiar feelings which threatened to come forward—he wasn't sure how much longer he'd be able to keep them back.

"There you two are. I've been calling—" Jido froze when his eyes fell on the bed.

RAKU ADJUSTED HIS EYEPATCH as if it'd been obscuring the view in his good eye once Daisuke and Obito finished describing their findings, though the sight before them needed little explanation. He leaned toward the bloodstained sheets as Jido, who'd demanded they stay put while he fetched his partner, scowled at the sight from further back. When Raku continued messing with his eyepatch, as seemed to be his nervous habit, Jido intervened and pulled his hands away from his face. His surprisingly gentle touch and the other's soft smile made their younger counterparts blush and avert their gazes.

"Our group didn't find any signs of violence anywhere else in the village—at least, not like this. A struggle here and there, sure, but not murder," Raku commented, as if to himself. His brows furrowed as he paused to think again. "The snowberries still don't make sense, but I do think Yin used the mistress as leverage for Senator Ming's cooperation, as you two stated."

"Hard to confirm what happened to her without a body," Jido added before letting a slow, frustrated exhale escape through his nose. "But I think it's outright stupid to deny what we're looking at."

Raku didn't speak for another moment. "Let's go find Mika and Shinta. They should be back from the additional perimeter check I sent them to do."

Obito didn't move right away when the team of older onmitsu left the room, and neither did Daisuke. They shared a long, worried look loaded with even more questions than the ones they'd already answered. While they'd neglected to mention their theory behind Yin's actions, and how the snowberries might've connected things, they figured more would come to light in Nishinuma—hopefully without implicating Daisuke. By now, they both understood that someone wealthy, who somehow knew both Mika and Yin, was pulling the strings behind the scenes. Obito had his suspicions already, and thought it was safe to assume he and Daisuke believed Giichi had a heavy hand in this.

When Daisuke eventually stepped toward the threshold, a deep sorrow settled onto his shoulders like an immense weight. Without understanding why, he looked backwards at the bed, then turned to his partner again. Obito was waiting for him just outside the door, but his eyes searched their surroundings; he also sensed the strain in the room. For some reason, Daisuke's mind wandered back to what Aunt Kiko had told them about resentful energy not long ago, and an idea stirred in his mind.

Brows furrowed, his head tilted when he looked at his friend again. "Can you help me try something?"

Obito was wary, which he felt was justified whenever his partner asked that question, but his own curiosity was often his undoing in these situations. "What do you have in mind?"

"I doubt a woman who was murdered by one of the hitokiri was given proper funeral rites. Let's give that symbol your aunt talked to us about a try—if it works, maybe it'll help us later on with the Shadow Priestess or Zandaka's Servant."

"Did you hit your head earlier?" Obito sighed. Although he was tempted to berate himself for giving it even a second of consideration, after everything else he'd witnessed between the High Priestess and the Priestess of Shadows, and hearing about several of his friend's dreams which had become reality, anything seemed possible. "I'm sure there's some ink and brushes in the Senator's office. Let me check."

Daisuke chuckled to himself when he heard drawers being opened across the hall, followed by a few curses muttered by his friend as he rifled through parchment, then finally the hollow wooden noises of brushes being knocked together. Several moments later, Obito returned with a prepared inkstone and a decent brush. The ink had a strange smell to it, but when it sloshed around a bit in the stone and revealed an orange tint under the sunlight, he realized Obito had to use the emulsified snowberries to mix the inksticks he'd found. A commendable improvisation for someone with a sensitive sense of smell.

"I didn't think I'd ever find a desk less organized than yours," Obito grumbled as he came to Daisuke's side, who snickered at the commentary, though their amusement soon vanished. They somberly looked at the open floor between them. "What do you think? Here?"

"Can't hurt to try. I left the actual book under your bed with my journal, so I'm not sure what else needs to be done."

Obito opened his mouth to comment on the information, but ultimately let it go with a shake of his head; he supposed if he was so deeply opposed to Daisuke's antics, he could just as easily tell him to stop. Rather than wonder why he hadn't, he knelt to the ground and dipped the brush into the ink. His hand hovered over the wooden floorboards just as he was about to begin—gods, he'd never felt so ridiculous in his life. He looked to his left when the floor softly creaked as Daisuke knelt beside him. They held one another's gaze for a long moment, and then Obito wordlessly got to work: three right-facing tomoe—or mitsudomoe—a circle around them, and flames at each cardinal direction of the symbol.

The room remained still with the final brushstroke—no mysterious winds howled, no terrifying lights or clouds, just a disappointing amount of *nothing.* When Daisuke was about to laugh at himself for thinking anything could come of their experiment, Obito dropped the brush, startled by something he'd seen.

They stared in disbelief at a little blue flame floating over the symbol. It circled around it once and swayed near the edge, as if testing to see if it was safe, then slowly lowered itself toward it. It spread itself out and made a sound like a sigh when it touched the ground. The faint, shadowy image of a woman flickered behind the flame, cupping her hands while bowing deeply, then vanishing into thin air and leaving the two onmitsu speechless. They looked at one another in shocked silence, then bowed once in return to the departed spirit before scrambling to their feet and exiting the room.

Interesting...it does *work,* Daisuke thought as they traipsed back through the halls toward the main room, both trying to appear as though nothing of significance had just happened. He wasn't sure how the information might help them yet, but he had a feeling that, between Obito and himself, they'd figure it out quickly enough.

Mika was just finishing organizing his travel pack while Shinta lit the braziers around the main hall to provide the group with some warmth and a place to dry their cloaks and boots. Upon noticing the other four return, however, both immediately stopped and came to greet them at a pillar near the hallway's entrance. Mika smirked at Daisuke, which was a terrible decision on the other boy's behalf. Daisuke's fascination with the undead waned, while frustration and ire at the blackwater situation revived upon seeing him.

"Where were you?" he asked. His smile slipped into a grimace when he eyed his cousin, tone changing accordingly. "Up to no good as usual?"

"Shut up." Daisuke rolled his eyes; unable to stop himself, he added with a grumble, "Better yet, fuck off."

Mika bristled, squaring his shoulders to make himself even bigger than he already was compared to Daisuke. "Who the fuck are you to—"

"Did you miss the point of being told to shut up and fuck off?"

Shinta burst out laughing at the exchange, but a seething glare from his beet-red partner made him go quiet. From the corner of his eye, Obito caught Raku rubbing his face as the three bickered, and wondered if he should try intervening on his behalf; given the predicament Daisuke had suddenly landed in, he wasn't sure he could argue with his friend's anger enough to try.

"Enough," Jido sternly told them as he stepped between the younger onmitsu, silencing everyone with an icy scowl, and sparing Obito from making the decision altogether. Since his partner had already defended himself, it probably wouldn't have been necessary, anyway.

"Thank you, Jido." Raku cleared his throat. "As I was about to say, we've only found a few inconclusive things here, so we're going to Nishinuma after we've rested and dried out for a bit. I'm hoping someone there might have answers for us—all the better if it's the Senator himself giving those answers. That being said, I still feel like we're likely to encounter Yin in Nishinuma. Whatever he's up to, he's dangerous, so I want everyone to be on high alert until we've handed him off to Imperial guards in the Capital."

"We'll use the night to our advantage." Everyone looked at Jido when he spoke. "It'll be harder for him to see us coming as it gets darker."

Raku nodded. "We'll send Daisuke and Obito to talk with Yin first—Obito's well enough trained with the kyoketsu-shoge by now that he should be able to react with it, if need be, and Daisuke can try negotiating with Yin while the rest of us get into positions to capture him."

"Negotiate?" Daisuke couldn't help his sputtered laughter.

"Provoke, same difference sometimes," Raku amended, thankfully in good humor.

"Wait, wait. So, they get all the credit when we report back to Master Yujin?" Mika argued.

"Are you stupid? That's not what he said at all." Shinta pinched the skin between his brows. "You find any reason to complain, I swear."

Raku ignored Mika's words and their spat. "Well-rested or not, you're expected to be ready when it's time. Leave your things except for any weapons you want to bring along—all things considered, I don't think Senator Ming will mind our intrusion."

The four younger onmitsu responded in varied, half-hearted ways as everyone removed their wet outer layers. Once Jido and Raku exited the main hall again, Daisuke nudged Obito and shot a quick look in Mika's direction, then took off toward the Senator's office where the snowberries were found. He gave it a second before following his friend's gesture and glancing at the other two; while Shinta seemed predictably oblivious to anything beyond the obvious, his cousin's expression was incredibly nervous, as if some great secret was about to be exposed. Hiding the suspicion his own face no doubt reflected, Obito disappeared down the same corridor his friend had taken.

When the group finally departed for Nishinuma later that afternoon, Obito couldn't keep himself from watching Mika at every turn.

ANOTHER ROUND OF COLD rainfall began when the group started toward Nishinuma, further melting the tops of high snowbanks and frost from cattails in the more distant parts of the swamps. The road sloped upward again as they neared the village, bringing them into the dense coverage of elms and tamaracks still covered in orange needles. Daisuke eyed the underbrush as they passed; he bit his lip and burrowed into his cloak when he recognized the three-pointed leaves on snowberry bushes, all of which seemed to have been picked clean. Although he hoped it'd been done by animals, deep in his gut, he knew better.

Even with a plan in place, Raku and Jido remained wary of what they might find upon arriving, and gave multiple terse warnings to their charges to obey every order. Their tense postures when they thought no one was looking were impossible for Daisuke or Obito to ignore. Shinta also seemed to notice, as he shot several furtive glances at the two bringing up the back of the formation. The expression in his eyes grew more desperate as the skies dimmed with the encroaching evening. His anxious demeanor was no doubt amplified by the hunched, borderline terrified manner with which Mika carried himself as the group walked—Raku and Jido hadn't noticed from where they led the way, but the other three couldn't dismiss it. Shinta, especially, didn't have the option. Whenever he tried to engage with his partner, the other boy snappily silenced him or didn't respond at all. Mika's moodiness was nothing new, but he rarely took it out on Shinta as much as he had so far this trip. Daisuke turned to Obito after the third instance of it, but he merely shook his head, urging him not to get involved.

Daisuke sullenly huffed, earning a slight smile in return.

"You'll live."

"Fine, I guess. Who wants to get between whatever the hell those two have going on, anyway?"

"I know I don't—you're more than welcome to when we're done here. For now, though..." Although Obito trailed off, both their minds reverted to their conversation in Fukainuma. They had to keep an eye on Mika. Perhaps his behavior really was due to nerves over the situation, and he had nothing to do with what was happening beyond handing off the blackwater recipe, but neither could shake the feeling he'd disappear at any given moment.

No one else spoke until they reached Nishinuma's outer edges, which was also when Jido ordered everyone to huddle together near a half-rotted stump covered in wide mushrooms. The smell of woodsmoke drifted through the forest, making the damp air seem even colder than it already felt.

Raku tugged at the strap on his eyepatch a few times until Jido couldn't stand it anymore; he let his partner gently take his hand away from it. "The rain should provide us with additional cover, and if we're lucky, it'll fog over soon. Give us some time to get word out to the villagers and hopefully locate Senator Ming. When we come back, we'll put our plan into motion. I don't want *any* civilian casualties—is that clear?"

A unified confirmation rose into the air, and the seniors descended the slope into the village undetected.

Not a single noise passed between the four younger onmitsu for a long while as they waited under the reaches of an elm's bare branches, hidden by the evergreen shrubs beneath it. Unable to take much more of the agonizing quiet, Daisuke spotted an opening in the underbrush and got down on his belly, cringing when he felt the wet, thawing ground saturate his clothes. He did his best to ignore it and the urgent whispers from Shinta to return to his post, wriggling through the brambles until he could peer down at the village from the hillcrest. Lanterns and a few low fires protected by tarps lit the darkening ravine Nishinuma slept in; he couldn't locate the hitokiri or either senior onmitsu. Yin likely wasn't letting the townspeople too far out of his sight, which wouldn't take much. During their break earlier, Obito had theorized earlier that a village like this wouldn't need many shows of force from an outsider to comply with his demands. These people were primarily rice farmers, not soldiers or fighters.

There wasn't much visible from his vantage point, but Daisuke still felt as though he'd seen plenty. Dirty, huddled villagers around their small fires, or elbow-deep in tubs likely meant for washing the snowberries others still were picking from nearly bare bushes that were likely overrun with them beforehand. He was once again brought back to the conversation with his partner, in which they'd agreed the villagers' compliance came from the awareness—and possibly a demonstration—that they were at the mercy of an Imperial assassin. After all, the reputation of the hitokiri and their brutality reached beyond Perena; not even Grandmaster Norio was arrogant enough to provoke the Emperor's wrath and earn a visit from one. Finally, he shimmied back to flatter ground where he could stand properly beside the other three, intending to report what he'd seen.

"Where are they?" Mika hugged himself, shoulders tense. "They shouldn't be taking this long. Should they? When do we worry?"

Obito rolled his eyes.

Thankfully, Mika didn't notice; instead, he turned to his partner and Daisuke. "This place is giving me the creeps. What's wrong with you two that you're so calm about all this?"

"Shut up, Mika." Shinta looked about ready to keel over from embarrassment.

"All of you shut it, right now," Jido hissed as he and Raku came trotting up the slope leading into the village.

The four younger spies looked at one another anxiously before settling on their seniors again. Jido inclined his head when Raku gave him a wary look, then stepped slightly forward to address his charges.

"This keeps getting stranger. The citizens from both villages are being held captive and forced to harvest snowberries—like the ones we found in Senator Ming's mansion—and crush them. The good news, though, is most everyone seems to be accounted for—cramped in their new living situation and terrified, but mostly safe. Those we were able to reach have been instructed to stay inside for now."

Jido drew his tanto. "We're moving in. Yin is in the big council building on the other hill. Obito, Daisuke, are you ready?"

Daisuke swallowed, but nodded at the same time as Obito in order to appear less anxious. When they started downhill again, Jido broke off with Mika on one flank while Shinta and Raku took the other, leaving the last two to fend for themselves and out in the open. Although they'd be nearby in case anything went wrong at this stage, and he and Obito were armed, Daisuke couldn't keep his mind off how uncomfortably exposed he felt as they moved through the village. If Obito thought the same, he did a significantly better job at hiding it.

While they made their way down Nishinuma's main road, Obito picked up part of their fractured conversation they hadn't yet covered. "We know Yin is in this for the money, and since he's not bright, he'll probably do us the favor of telling us as much. He might even drop his benefactor's name to confirm our suspicions. But, what do *you* think the benefactor wants with blackwater?"

"Encouraging me to talk while we work? Obito, I'm surprised."

"I wish I could say the same about you deciding to be annoying."

"Harsh." Daisuke laughed. "I should make you pay for that one when we get back tonight."

"Are you going to answer?"

"Fine." Daisuke paused to peer up into a tree, pretending he didn't notice their companions moving through the background; their additional teammates were likely the reason Obito refrained from saying Giichi's name aloud, though they were both thinking it. Even this level of discussion came with some risk, so he lowered his voice further, barely audible over the crunch of the path beneath their boots. "At best, personal revenge. But going with the sheer volume of things, here, it's larger scale than that. You said this patron had contact with Zandaka's Servant, right?"

Obito nodded. "Granted, I don't know how direct that contact is. Not the point, though, is it? Either the Servant put them up to this, or the patron is acting independently—maybe to impress or sabotage the Servant, but I know which I think is more likely."

"Personally, I'm circling back to the theory that I'm fucked."

They came to a stop just downhill from a building which was much bigger than any of the other homes in the village, though it was still smaller than Senator Ming's house in Fukainuma. At a different time, one might've said it had a pleasant view of the town. This was likely where the Senator came to address his citizens or where the rice they harvested was stored until their merchants moved it elsewhere. Obito's eyes narrowed when he saw a black horse with a white-speckled muzzle hitched to a cart under the building's lean-to. It was impossible to make out clearly in the slowly fading sunlight, but a shifting shadow and the faintest rustle of cloth indicated someone might be moving around near the cart, as did the horse's twitching ears and restless hoof stamping. Daisuke followed his gaze, then looked at him, and they wordlessly agreed to investigate later if they could—Raku needed them to stick to the plan.

The doors were wide open to welcome in the chilly fresh air, and when they ascended the building's steps, they found Yin lounging amid a pile of cushions as he drank from an overly full jug of wine; one that was already empty sat toppled near his left side, a drop of deep red dangling from its spout. A few candles were all that illuminated his spot. Daisuke thought that, although it'd been a few years since their last encounter, he looked every bit as scraggly as he had upon their first meeting.

The assassin spoke when Daisuke glanced at his partner for further direction.

"I was wondering how long it'd be until the Palace sent its snakes after me." Yin set aside his wine and sat forward to look at them properly. He chuckled, a smirk still tugging at the corner of his mouth when he recognized them. "Well, well, if it isn't my favorite pair of little sneaks. Not so little nowadays, though, are you?"

As with before, Obito was the first to step closer to Yin and speak, not giving him a chance to distract them. "Quite the operation you have here. Care to explain it?"

The assassin grinned as if he'd been asked by a good friend. "Why not? For old time's sake. You see, I was asked to harvest the snowberries that grow here and make a new, interesting poison—unfortunately, I haven't tested it yet. Anyway, I decided there was no way in all of Kuro's Hells or the Four Realms I'd be doing this by myself, so I...convinced, I suppose, Senator Ming to lend me a hand."

"Where *is* Senator Ming?" Daisuke asked as the man took another drink.

"Is he all you came here for?" Yin's cold black eyes went to him as wine dribbled down his chin, and his crooked grin intensified, looking off somehow; it made Daisuke nauseous. "He ought to be around here somewhere—I'm nearly out of wine. By the way, I heard from some of the masters at Kurushima that they've got one of you they just can't seem to kill off. Any relation by chance?"

"But you've never been one to do someone else's bidding, have you? How does that explain any of this?" Obito quickly intervened when he saw Daisuke's hands curl into trembling fists at his sides—of course, Yin had no way of knowing he was right, but they couldn't afford to let him see he'd struck a sensitive nerve.

The hitokiri shrugged, thankfully remaining oblivious and more interested in conversation. "It's pretty simple, boys—money. I was offered more coin than I could make in a *year*."

"Who could've paid you enough for that?" Daisuke asked, forcing himself to move on from what felt like a kick to the stomach, though his temper still threatened to overtake him. Between the jab about his brother and the very real possibility the blackwater would be uncovered while they were here, he was losing control over himself. "Your honesty now could help you later with Master Yujin."

Yin was at least a little smarter than he looked—and entirely too overconfident he had the upper hand this time. He shook his head at the shorter boy as if he'd told a terrible joke. "I don't believe that for a second."

"You won't tell us?"

"Not a chance."

"Then you're a fucking idiot," Daisuke snapped, held back by Obito grabbing him by the belt; he was released again when he showed the restraint to stop himself. "All this for a little extra money, and now you're going to die."

"Am I?" The assassin raised his eyebrows. His head jerked to his left when a board softly creaked in the shadows, face wrinkling into a snarl as he turned back to the two onmitsu before him. "I see. You brought reinforcements this time. Coincidentally, there's something I didn't get a chance to tell you two yet: I have no intention of going along—they won't behead me in front of the masses."

"You think you still get a say in it?" Obito reached behind himself to grip the handle of the kyoketsu-shoge tucked into the back of his belt; Daisuke stepped aside to give his partner more room to use it if needed.

Yin stood—he still towered over both boys. "I'd rather take my chances with you lot."

He lurched forward to attack Daisuke, which was swiftly cut off by the ball-weight of Obito's weapon landing in his right eye. He stumbled backward, clutching his face, though he still had time to dodge when the metallic rattle of another chain sailed through the air toward him. Daisuke followed up with a swipe of his tanto at the man's throat, but he barely missed. He couldn't help but stare in shock. The hitokiri were trained to withstand immense physical pain, but he didn't think *this* was possible—drunk as he was, *someone* should've been able to land a hit. Wryly, he wondered if the alcohol had helped dull the sensation as the other four onmitsu stepped out from the shadows.

The group of onmitsu outnumbered Yin, but a moment of hesitation on Daisuke's behalf—accompanied by plenty of cursing—was all he needed to punch Obito in the ribs and push past the two guarding the door. He fled down the hill at top speed. However, it wasn't long before the group caught up to Yin and spread out around him, outflanking him. He pushed himself hard at full speed, but was quickly overwhelmed by the younger men. The chain of Raku's kyoketsu-shoge wrapped around his ankle, sending him face-first into the ground with a *crunch* that could only be a broken nose—Obito's mind briefly flooded with the memory of when his partner tackled Haruto days after they first met the assassin currently crumpled on the ground before them. Yin writhed and cursed, but knowing he was surrounded and caught, all he did was roll onto his back and bury his face in his hands as the onmitsu got into formation around him. Red rivulets which looked black in the twilight trickled between his bony fingers.

Yin cried out in pain when Raku knelt on his abdomen to further prevent an escape; more blood appeared at the corners of his mouth. Raku held his blade to the man's throat while Jido and Obito stood nearby with their weapons at the ready, though Obito felt his presence wasn't necessary—Raku, normally so soft-spoken and gentle, looked plenty threatening on his own.

Raku ordered through gritted teeth, "Talk, damn it."

Yin's eyes crazily darted around to the other five faces looming over him, each with another blade prepared to strike should he make the slightest mistake. Everyone tensed when he slowly raised one of his hands away from his face, revealing how badly that side of his nose had suffered from the impact of hitting the partially frozen dirt path. Faster than anyone could react, he grasped Raku's hands and forced them into a different, awkward angle, turning the dagger end of his weapon onto himself. Before Raku could try wrestling control of it back, Yin plunged the dagger into his own throat and twisted, creating a deep, jagged puncture. Everyone stared in stunned silence as he gasped and gurgled bloody froth in his mouth; it was a slow, brutal way to go, but his precision prevented any sort of intervention. Even if they'd been able to control the bleeding and stop it, Yin likely wouldn't have survived.

Raku slowly peeled himself off the hitokiri and looked at his blood-soaked dagger, letting it dangle from its chain in the breeze. "Shinta, Mika, can you bring him off to the side of the road? I...I need a minute to think."

Daisuke swallowed the bile in his throat, but barely. "I'll be right back, too. That bush looks like a good one to vomit in."

"Daisuke!" Jido tried to call him back, though he immediately gave up on the idea when the sound of retching reached everyone's ears. He turned to Obito, as if he expected him to do something about it, but he pretended he didn't notice. After a few moments, Daisuke was at his side again, looking paler than usual. A little while longer, and Shinta was retracing the trail of Yin's blood he and Mika had left behind.

He looked at Raku and Jido. "So, what ne—"

Shinta stared at them with wide, horrified eyes, then lurched several steps forward, as if he couldn't keep his balance. Obito shielded Daisuke from a wildly flailing arm as their companion struggled toward their seniors.

Raku and Jido rushed forward. "Shinta!"

"S-som-something—" Shinta gasped, holding the right side of his neck as if he'd received a blow to it. "Something h-hit me!"

He coughed and tried to take in gulps of air as his eyes widened, wearing the same look a person gets when purple and green blotches dance in front of their eyes after being struck. His legs wobbled, but Raku caught him before he collapsed and carefully guided him to the ground.

"Stay down," Jido told him, already scanning the area around them.

Soon after, Shinta's eyes rolled back and he fell unconscious. Daisuke crept forward and tilted his friend's head to one side, revealing a thin, barely visible needle lodged into his neck, nearly swallowed by the puffy red ring of skin surrounding it. A faint orange trickle seeped from the wound—the deepening dusk nearly covered it up entirely.

"Poison," he whispered, drawing everyone's attention. He furrowed his brows. "Mika, do you—"

He'd meant to ask if he knew anything about poison-dipped needles; Mika wasn't proficient in the onmitsu's most infamous art form, but he could ramble for hours about various types of weaponry. However, when Daisuke turned to question him, the other boy was still nowhere to be found, as if he'd vanished. His gaze flicked between the remaining three onmitsu standing near him, who were either helplessly staring back at him or copying Jido's earlier action of searching their surroundings, this time in the hopes of finding their missing companion.

"We'll head for the council house to regroup," Raku eventually declared. "We should interview the citizens and prepare to move Fukainuma's people home, anyway. If we're being honest, I'm not sure I trust the Senator to give us the whole story just yet."

Daisuke brushed the tip of his nose, a signal to Obito, before delicately removing the needle from Shinta's neck. "We'll be right there—we might be able to identify this."

"Be quick." Raku inclined his head and scooped Shinta into his arms, displaying a surprising and impressive amount of strength by lifting the boy's dead weight.

With Jido close to his side, neither Obito nor Daisuke thought to worry about either senior as they began making their way toward the building atop the hill. Once they were a fair distance away, Daisuke pulled his friend to the side of the street where Shinta had been struck down and held up the needle, now wet with blood and the sticky substance that was previously on it.

"Recognize that?"

"Barely—it's almost dark. Is it *your* poison?" Obito squinted at the needle when Daisuke handed it to him for closer inspection. However, no answer was expected or needed, as neither knew of another compound with the distinct orange color made by blackwater, plenty visible even in this light.

"Unfortunately. But...does this needle say what we think it does?"

"We know it does."

Daisuke groaned at the headache he'd somehow created for himself. He looked up at Obito helplessly, but just when he opened his mouth to speak again, screams erupted from the direction of the council house, as did the violent clatter of wood and axles, along with pounding hoofbeats. Stunned, Daisuke didn't fully register the oncoming cart, but Obito just barely pulled him out of the way before it ran them over. They landed in the bushes along the roadside an awkward tangle. Once they convinced themselves to disengage from one each other—which probably took longer than it should have—and reoriented themselves, Daisuke stepped forward as if to follow.

"Stay there," Obito said firmly. He felt a bit guilty for how his tone shocked Daisuke into stillness, but he didn't have time to explain why it'd be better if he pursued the driver. When he was sure his partner would obey, he took off into the trees.

He wasn't as fast or agile as Daisuke, but he *had* seen a suspicious trail leading out of Nishinuma's northern side earlier while waiting for Raku and Jido to complete their perimeter inspection. Although it was dark now, his eyes had adjusted enough to the change; he at least knew where he was going better than he could describe to anyone else, and hoped to cut off the cart and its driver before they disappeared into the forested parts of the wetlands.

Obito slid the kyoketsu-shoge from the back of his belt when he reached a thick patch of underbrush beside the nearly invisible path, carefully untangling the chain and counterweight from how he'd tucked them away again after Yin killed himself. In the back of his mind, he realized how deeply he dreaded dealing with Mika now that his training with the weapon was exposed. As the other boy's most-loathed cousin, he wouldn't let it go easily. Not that anyone—not even Mika himself—could possibly know why, or what he planned to do with his ill intent.

Obito's heartrate spiked when he heard the distinct clatter of wagon wheels slogging through wet ground and he quickly ducked out of sight behind the gnarled trunk of an elm.

Focus. He forced himself to calm down, then cautiously peered out from his hiding place. He stepped back again when lantern light from a post on the front of the cart cast its glow over the area, barely cutting through the encroaching fog.

Pushing through the trembling in his hand, Obito tightened the grip on the dagger end of his weapon as he crouched low into the underbrush. He'd have a clear shot at the cart's hooded driver with the counterweight if he timed it right. He positioned himself for the attack he'd have to make as the person rounded the bend, but stopped when another figure appeared from the opposite side of the path, planting himself in the center. Obito froze when Mika waved for the crazed person and their frazzled horse to stop. They didn't speak to one another as his cousin climbed up, and when they did begin conversing, it was far too low for Obito to hear. He couldn't see Mika's face well, nor could he make out the cowled figure sitting beside him. However, when the driver removed a riding glove, he caught the glint of two ruby rings under the lantern. Obito's anger surged. Against his better judgement, he inched forward, freezing when a twig snapped under his boot.

"Someone's here!" Mika alerted the driver as he leapt from the spot beside him. "Run!"

Fuck! Obito cursed his impatience.

The horse whinnied when the reins harshly snapped against its flanks; without giving Obito a chance to throw the weighted end of his weapon, the driver and Mika fled in opposite directions. With no one else to watch his back and ensure he wasn't being lured out, he pinned himself to the tree trunk again, though it seemed his cousin made at least *one* smart move by heading directly for Nishinuma.

"Fucking hell." He rested the back of his head against the tree, looking up at the dark sky. Frustration bubbling over, he turned and viciously stabbed the dagger's blade into a particularly thick patch of moss. "What the *fuck,* Mika?"

Now certain he was alone, Obito dislodged his kyoketsu-shoge and decided he should do the same as his cousin. He stepped onto the path where Mika previously stood to follow it back into town, but paused when he accidentally kicked something in the muddy trail. He finished putting his weapon away and crouched, searching by touch more than sight for whatever the object had been. He swallowed when he felt cool glass against his knuckles.

"Where the hell were you?" Daisuke rushed over to Obito as soon as he spotted him from the hilltop building's veranda, where he'd been monitoring Shinta's condition while playing with a little girl and doing his best to ignore Mika's existence. He lowered his voice when he saw the distress in his friend's eyes. "What happened?"

"Later," he replied shortly, gaze flicking over to his cousin.

The cold deadpan in his voice was all Daisuke needed to understand; it chilled him to the bone. His stomach sank like a rock as he watched Obito stalk toward Raku and Jido, who were doing their best to calm a hysterical Senator Ming and several others. *Most* of Nishinuma's residents along with those from Fukainuma were gathered here; while Daisuke couldn't imagine Obito would do anything with this many people nearby, anger was an unpredictable beast. Since the unconscious boy seemed stable, and his playmate had since gone back to her mother, he abandoned Shinta to follow on his friend's heels.

He grabbed Obito's sleeve and tugged hard, bringing them both to a halt. Fortunately, no one seemed to notice them, and Obito's anger gave way to confusion.

Daisuke got up on his toes to whisper, "We're heading back to Fukainuma soon. Tell me about it over a cigarette."

Obito looked at Raku and Jido, then back at Mika, now cheerfully talking with an elderly woman as if he wasn't part of the reason she'd been held hostage by Yin. He deftly maneuvered the bottle of blackwater he'd recovered from the trail into Daisuke's free hand. "Then what are we doing with this?"

"I...I'll keep it for now."

FOR AS COLD AND wet as their walk to Nishinuma had been, guiding Fukainuma's villagers home with no more than one lantern for each on-mitsu as they walked with the group was even more of a slog in the darkness. The rain had at least let up by the time the spies returned with everyone, but they were cold, drenched, dirty, and exhausted. Fortunately, Senator Ming all but begged them to stay for a few extra days—both as a chance to recuperate, and with the hope it'd keep anyone like Yin away from the swamplands for some time. Since there was little staff and even less time to prepare, although it was unsightly, the Senator agreed to let them unfurl their bedrolls in the main hall of his home. He allowed Raku and Jido a private place to discuss their mission in his office—after discarding the basket of rotted snowberries they'd forgotten to remove earlier—and showed Mika and Shinta to the bathhouse in town. With the rest of their group and host distracted, Daisuke and Obito begrudgingly agreed to wait until after they smoked and bathed to change into dry clothing, not wanting to miss the narrow window of opportunity for their own discussion.

They found refuge on the town's wall, high above everything else and amid the thick fog now engulfing the swamps. For a while, neither spoke as they passed a roll of white leaf between one another and smoked a couple of cigarettes each, vaguely aware they'd need to convince someone to visit the commissary for them when they got back to the Capital. Obito couldn't repress a small smile when Daisuke leaned on his shoulder.

"How hard did Yin hit you earlier?"

"Barely—it surprised me more than anything." Obito had nearly forgotten about it altogether.

Daisuke gazed through the fog as he blew smoke from his mouth, voice low when he finally asked, "What did you see in there, anyway?"

"Wild conspiracy."

"That so? Do tell."

Obito hesitated, trying to sort through his thoughts for the best phrasing; he suspected Daisuke already understood he was being used as a scapegoat with the use of a poison that could be traced back to him, but he didn't want to be careless or callous in how he delivered the confirmation. When he spoke again, his voice also dropped an octave. "The wealthy connection between Mika and Yin."

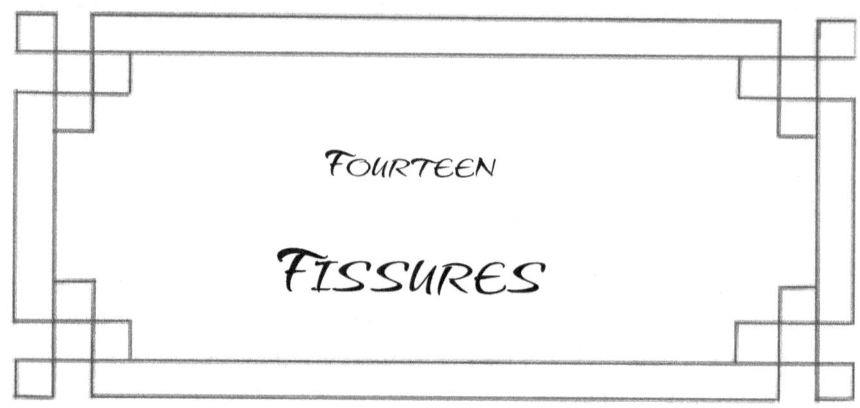

Fourteen

Fissures

MASTER YUJIN DRUMMED HIS fingers on his desk as he weighed what he'd been told by the eldest pair of onmitsu standing before him. His concerned frown deepened, though it was barely noticeable when he swatted away the cloud of incense smoke that wafted in front of his face. "What a debacle."

"With all due respect, Master Yujin, there's no need to pretend it could've gone much better." Jido sighed, still exhausted from the mission even though they'd taken a slower pace home, including a second stop at the inn they'd visited along the way. "Despite what you said during the briefing, I think we all knew Yin's death was the most likely outcome."

Master Yujin might not have *liked* this answer, but accepted it after a moment of deliberation—His Highness wasn't interested in how the assassin met his end, so he also saw no reason to be picky. "I suppose I'll read more about this once you and Raku finish writing up your reports. You know what I expect."

The two older onmitsu nodded curtly and dismissed themselves from the Intelligence Master's presence with a slight bend which could barely be considered a bow—Yujin pretended he didn't notice. Propriety was the last thing on his mind at present, anyway. Besides, he knew the four remaining operatives didn't dare do the same without more explicit permission.

"Is there anything you four wanted to report directly? Something Raku or Jido might not have noticed?" Master Yujin asked.

Daisuke stepped forward, taking advantage of the opening he'd been given. Although he sensed how anxious everyone else was to leave, he wasn't through yet, and he needed them to participate just a little longer. Obito would never let him live it down if he missed this opportunity to perform a bit of stress testing on the group. "Well, sir, there is something I still don't understand,"

"Big surprise."

Obito rolled his eyes. "Shut up, Shinta."

He said it so calmly yet so unexpectedly that Shinta couldn't help but fold under the unimpressed glance Obito shot at him. Daisuke had to force himself to hold back a grin when the other boy shrank back a little—how unfair. To keep from instigating further, he pulled out the small vial of orange blackwater Obito had rescued from the trail just outside of Nishinuma, holding it out so Master Yujin could see it. Almost no other vegetation growing in the swamps could create a compound with its color, so he was confident it'd be easily identified by the Intelligence Master. Despite how he initially hesitated, the vial eventually went to his superior when the man stretched out his hand.

"Curious," Master Yujin commented, eyes narrowing as he tried to discern its meaning.

"Yin was safeguarding a stockpile of those," Daisuke explained. He discreetly eyed Mika, who refused to look at anyone else as he slouched and hugged himself—he was scared out of his wits. Likely for the better, too, as this display was probably what kept Obito from putting his head on a pike. The thought warmed Daisuke's heart. "Bastard killed himself before we could make him tell us who put him up to it, but it doesn't make any sense to have one in the first place."

Shinta must've found his bravery again, as he straightened to address the room once more. "There was also that unidentified man with the cart you all told me about. Did anyone get a good look at him? Obito and Mika both said they tried chasing him down, but...there's some conflicting versions of events from there."

"You were out for most of it, anyway," Mika grumbled, a snarl wrinkling his nose despite the way his arms defensively tightened around himself; his nails dug into his sleeves.

Master Yujin gave the cousins a stern glare. "You'll both be interrogated once I've read your reports."

"Yes, sir," they sighed in unison, refusing to look at one another.

"I have many other questions, but I'll see how many of them remain once I've read your reports. For now, all of you are dismissed." The Intelligence Master rubbed his temples as his subordinates each gave him a bow at the waist before two of them hurriedly left his office.

Obito also turned to leave, but stopped when he noticed that his partner, suddenly lost in thought, hadn't budged. "Daisuke?"

It would've been easy enough to dismiss all of Mika's strange actions as simple cowardice—*if* he wasn't the one responsible for Yin having the blackwater recipe. Daisuke held no doubts about his involvement at this point; to even know about the poison, someone would've needed access to his journal—something Obito alone had but never asked for. He wasn't the only friend who knew about it, either. Mika didn't seem to think Daisuke had noticed, but he'd been acting dodgy whenever he was around, well before any of them were recruited to go into the swamplands, which was what put him at the top of the suspect list months ago. Even if Yin was oblivious to what was ultimately planned for the poison, the person who paid him was not. Of course, Mika's knowledge of further plans was also dubious, and he had no amount of money he could personally offer the assassin, but he *was* desperate to please his father—someone with much deeper pockets. Giichi served another entity for his own personal gain, and Mika had allowed him to place the responsibility for any fallout squarely on Daisuke's shoulders. Not only was it cowardly, it was unforgiveable.

However, there still wasn't solid proof. Without it, everything would be treated as speculation at best—he'd never be taken seriously. He *could* save Obito a little face in the matter before his cousin had a chance to slander his part in it, though. With how swiftly he always came to Daisuke's defense, he felt it was the bare minimum he could do. Besides, if he chose honesty now, he might be able to save himself, too.

Concerned by his prolonged silence, Master Yujin tilted his head. "Akahana?"

He sighed and looked at Obito, then the vial as their superior placed it on his desk before glancing back at his partner, who solemnly nodded. Rather than leaving him to handle Master Yujin alone, he adjusted his stance to remain at Daisuke's side. His chest flooded with another wave of indescribable warmth.

"You're going to yell at me." He laughed, though all signs of humor quickly faded. "But I can tell you more about what's in that vial."

Master Yujin's countenance darkened when Daisuke announced he knew what was in the vial, where it'd come from, and what he and his partner believed had transpired behind the scenes in the swamps, though he refrained from naming anyone directly. The Intelligence Master didn't interrupt his subordinate once. Daisuke thought the man showed an impressive amount of self-control when he merely pinched the skin between his brows and let out a long, heaving sigh at the end. Still, he inched closer to Obito and nervously gripped his arm, as if doing so would somehow protect him. Finally, Master Yujin rolled his shoulders and straightened his spine, shaking his head at the pair as if they were a lost cause.

Maybe we are, Daisuke thought from his half-shielded position. *Well, at least one of us might be.*

"First and foremost, it is considered a highly taboo thing to experiment with our known poisons, as it sows distrust among our ranks. I daresay you knew as much before this misadventure," Master Yujin stated, no doubt using every bit of internal strength he possessed to restrain his fury. "So, not only are you admitting to breaking important protocol, but you're *also* saying someone might be planning to use one of those experiments against the Empire."

Daisuke's eyes lowered to the floor.

Master Yujin's gaze went to the window in his office, his expression somehow giving the sense that he was debating whether he'd be better off to throw himself out of it. After a moment, he dug through his drawers and produced a scroll and brush. As if quizzing him about any other poison in class, he sternly asked, "Side-effects?"

"Well, when it hit Shinta, he gagged and coughed a bit before dropping unconscious—it's hard to say if that's an overall thing, or because it went directly into his bloodstream rather than being swallowed, or mixed with food or alcohol."

"No swollen tongue or throat, no fever or muscle stiffness, just groggy when he woke up again a few hours later," Obito added for good measure.

Master Yujin listened carefully as he recorded their answers, then stared at them once more when finished. He glanced at the orange liquid near his hand. "Realistically, I should make this *your* responsibility, but His Highness would have your head and mine if he found out, so under the pretense of authorized experimentation, I'll have Raku and Jido run some tests to give us a better understanding of the poison's full scope. Meanwhile, *you'll* stay far away from a single ingredient in this. You're sure it can't kill anyone?"

"It didn't kill Shinta," Daisuke muttered, flinching as soon as the words left his mouth; he could've sworn he saw Obito do the same. Gods, he was his own worst enemy at times. Still, he forged ahead. "Sorry, sir. But, I promise, 'blackwater' has that name just because I thought it sounded good—it's intentionally misleading...and probably stupid. None of its components point to it being any deadlier than fangroot, and that hasn't killed anyone yet."

"And while...interesting, all the work in Daisuke's journal is theoretical," Obito cut in, successfully redirecting Master Yujin's attention and saving his partner from himself. "Most of the entries aren't detailed enough to be considered complete by someone who knows what they're doing. The ones that *are* finished mainly list common substitutions for elements in the poisons we already use."

Daisuke sighed in relief; while Obito's bluntness made all the hard work he'd put into those journal entries seem half-mad, it also highlighted the innocence behind his intent. Out of all the ways simple curiosity had gotten him into trouble so far throughout life, he thought this might be one of the worst. If something came of the poison's mass production, which he felt was an inevitability at this point, he'd never recover once its origins were traced back to him—the person who stole it would ensure it to protect himself. Nothing, not even Master Yujin, could help him when Emperor Akuwara learned of it. The Intelligence Master knew it, too; he wasn't exaggerating when he said he would also suffer dire consequences. His fingers subconsciously touched his throat when he thought of how the Emperor would be all too willing to torment and execute him for treason. It'd been painful to accept, and he wasn't keen on admitting it, but the brains behind this operation really had found the perfect scapegoat. Daisuke still couldn't decide whether it being by design or by accident was worse when it came to intent.

"Is there an antidote?" Master Yujin's voice broke into his thoughts.

Daisuke considered it, then carefully stepped out from behind Obito. "The effects are only meant to last for a few hours at most, so I never thought about it. I can *try* making one, but..."

Frankly, it seemed pointless—he wasn't about to tell Master Yujin as much, though.

The Intelligence Master arched his brows as if he'd read Daisuke's mind. "You *will* try. As I'm sure you remember from lessons, some non-lethal poisons can still kill when delivered in high enough concentrations, over time, or some combination of both. We *must* be prepared to handle any situation that could arise from this."

Daisuke grimaced. He hadn't thought that far ahead, either. He didn't know what prolonged exposure to any of his experiments, even something as relatively harmless as this, might do to a person. He swallowed a thick lump at the back of his throat, clinging to his friend for support once again.

"I will see your reports from Fukainuma and Nishinuma in two days along with everyone else's. I expect everything you've told me about the poison to be in there as well." Master Yujin paused. "You're clearly holding back on names for now. If that is due to a lack of evidence, I understand, but I expect to see your suspects listed in writing. In the meantime, do *not* breathe a word of what we've discussed to the other four."

Implicating Mika in whatever plot was unfolding when he likely didn't have the entire story behind it seemed cruel, as his father was a notoriously manipulative bastard. However, he'd had ample time to come forward, confess, warn Master Yujin—do *anything* besides sling insults and be evasive. Mika knew his actions were wrong, which was why he fought back against even the mildest suggestion he'd done something he shouldn't, but Daisuke struggled to see him as more than a puppet in the whole operation. Unfortunately, anecdotal evidence wasn't nearly enough to spur an investigation into Giichi, either. Within a space of seconds, the troubled glance Daisuke and Obito traded said they at least agreed on that point. He was certain Obito felt the same about it all—including how they'd come to regret not saying anything when they had the chance. It could be the only opportunity he'd have to defend himself, and the look in Obito's eyes warned him not to squander it.

This isn't the petty revenge I'd hoped for when this whole journal thing started. Daisuke bit his lip.

"That reminds me," Master Yujin continued, his tone softening slightly from before. "As well as the antidote, I still expect your team to return to investigating the group you encountered in Zhu—since I'm feeling generous, you'll be given a bit more time with these new developments out of Nishinuma. For the love of all the gods or whatever you two consider holy, do *not* make me regret my leniency."

"Told you I was fucked," Daisuke muttered under his breath. Obito elbowed him to keep him quiet, and they bowed to their superior.

Once they left the Intelligence Master's office, Daisuke stood with his hands on his hips as he scowled at the torchlit stones under his feet, yet again lost in thought. Suddenly, he snapped his fingers and was on the move again, already tugging on Obito's wrist when he jolted forward.

"Red poppies," he announced absentmindedly, urging him to hurry.

Obito could've chosen not to budge, but as always, a sense of morbid curiosity had him following his partner as if pulled by a string. "What are you talking about?"

"The antidote. Since I was just fucking around anyway when I made the first vial of blackwater, I tried to add opium to see what would happen—it separated the snowberry pulp from the other ingredients like oil and water."

"What does that have to do with the red—"

"I won't put regular strains of opium in any of my antidotes," Daisuke said fiercely. He blushed when he realized his tone and the way his friend's gaze had fallen on him. "I-it's the principle, isn't it? Red poppy opium has better medicinal qualities than other varieties. That's part of why Northern Nomads value it so much."

Obito didn't fully believe his explanation, but didn't think it was worth pressing him for a different answer just yet—he worried that distracting his friend with pointless questions would be detrimental to his thought process. It was easier than one might expect. "Aunt Kiko should be home if you want to visit her. She *did* say you could have a spot in her garden for the poppies."

Daisuke sighed with relief, then gave him a small smile. It would still be some time before the flowers could grow outside, but a skilled gardener such Aunt Kiko should have a few extra pots laying around, and he wanted to plant the seeds as soon as possible. From the sounds of it, more than just his career depended on it.

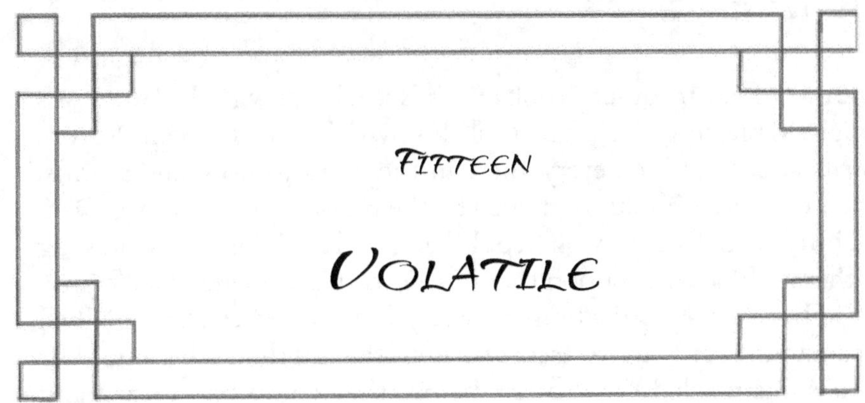

DEMONS, DAISUKE THOUGHT, PLACING a hand over his racing heart. *Kanashimi and Saigai are demons. The Shadow Priestess called the names of two ancient demons, and that stupid fucking box we got from Rin and Gero responded to her. What the fuck is going on, here?*

Feeling as though the passage he'd just read hit him with the force of an ox cart, he swallowed and set the book down on the bedroll before anxiously glancing around where he sat inside one of the signature red tents of the acrobat camp. Admittedly, he'd been spending too much time here ever since he turned fifteen a couple of weeks ago, and not all of it was as motivated by furthering his training as he'd originally intended, though it had given him some extra space to read Aunt Kiko's occult book—for better or worse, it seemed. It was an incredibly weak excuse for his behavior, but Daisuke knew that fewer opportunities to interact with Mika guaranteed his silence about the blackwater incident, and not being around the onmitsu dormitories helped immensely.

Granted, *some* of his time should've been spent training or studying with Obito. He'd been neglecting those things quite a bit lately, much to his friend's silent frustration. He didn't think Obito was outright angry with him, but Daisuke still hoped he might be forgiven if he could shed some light on new information concerning the Shadow Priestess, and soon. Besides, it was a perfect way to ignore his brewing anxieties over making blackwater's antidote; he'd only just planted the poppy seeds.

With these things driving his motivation, he took a deep breath and decided to brave the passage he'd read once more, simultaneously wishing he'd vastly misunderstood it while knowing he was confirming things.

"Because the Raven God did not insist upon ruling within the same domain as Hikari and Kuro, the universe's Balance was kept when he went to cultivate lands in the West, so Zandaka remained silent.

The god of nature quietly took Hikari's teachings with the Goddess's delighted blessing and left to apply his own theories to them. Nature spirits already existed everywhere in the winds, waves, and storms. Their energies were strengthened by the praises and love of the Okami, but ages before the wolf people had ever lifted their voices in song to them, Hikari drew upon that power to create life in all its forms.

"However, Hikari's humans were complicated creatures. When it came time for Kuro to escort them to the afterlife, it became clear their souls needed time to rest before they could be purified and given back to Hikari to continue the cycle of life, and so the Between Realm was created. Zandaka presided there, believing it was only fitting if he watched over one realm of the afterlife while Hikari and Kuro tended to the others. He created his demons to help him, comfort the newly dead, and guide the souls which could be purified toward ascension. Some of the deeply fractured ones with purer qualities remained in the Between Realm as permanent residents, or became a weaker disciple of the Demon King.

"Kanashimi, Tatakai, Jihuang, Hinkon, Wenyi, and Saigai were created by Zandaka himself to be his strongest disciples; each attracted the souls who had died due to what they were named after. The Demon King often called upon their help to greet and calm souls, complete the rituals for ascension, or for sentencing to eternal condemnation with Kuro in the underworld—as a rule of the universe's Balance, some souls were simply too black or broken to cleanse. After time in hell, some rotted into devils and beasts beyond recognition, and grew to worship Kuro as an emperor of the underworld and afterlife.

"All three realms of the afterlife existed in perfect harmony until the Mother Goddess decided to create a balance of her own. Zandaka and his demons were forced to take action by—"

Daisuke jumped at the sharp snap of fabric in the warm spring wind.

He held back a groan when Shinchi's slender figure came through the flap, confronting him with the real reason he'd been hanging about Retsuko's camp too much. At seventeen, Shinchi was already one of the acrobat matron's most prominent performers, and had taken it upon himself to work with Daisuke earlier in the spring. The young Perenin wasn't nearly as pretty or intelligent as Obito, but he was a good teacher, and easy enough to get along with, so Daisuke thought it natural when Shinchi suggested their relationship go a step further.

However, any excitement he'd felt about a budding romance had been relatively short-lived, as it became clearer by the day how the older boy was only interested in sex. Daisuke's curiosity and—frankly—physical urges had gotten him through the first few times, but Shinchi's ever-present pestering for it hadn't tapered off as he'd expected. Now, he spent more time than not wondering how to peel away. It was more difficult than he'd expected. Something he probably shouldn't admit to, especially at his age, was that he *liked* the act; far more than the person he was doing it *with*, too. Put simply, it was an escape, and he was quite aware of it. Who didn't want to occasionally abandon all thought and get tangled in different emotions, no matter how temporary? Wasn't this a better way to cope than his usual methods?

"Time's up, bookworm," Shinchi greeted, bringing the present back into focus.

Daisuke opened his mouth to argue, but couldn't stop the laugh that came out instead when the older boy took the book from his hands and tossed it over his shoulder. The pages desperately fluttered as if the poor thing was trying to fly rather than land with an ungraceful *thud* on the tent's tatami mat flooring. Concentration thoroughly shattered, he leaned into Shinchi's arms—he figured he deserved a *little* time to relax now that he'd found another piece of the Shadow Priestess's puzzle, even if his partner didn't know how selfishly he was using the embrace.

"Fine, fine. What *did* you want to do today?"

The Perenin boy flashed him a devilish grin and pressed himself close, pushing Daisuke back onto his elbows as he tried to make room on the cot. Although his nerves bundled into a messy knot in his stomach, Daisuke's mind went fuzzy when they kissed.

"Don't act like you don't know," Shinchi said huskily once they broke apart, brushing his cheek before placing the same hand on his inner thigh.

Daisuke's heart sank at the touch, and the weight in his stomach grew heavier as his partner started kissing his neck. Before he could stop himself, he asked, "Why is this always the answer?"

Shinchi froze and drew back to look at him, clearly taken by surprise. "Isn't this what you want?"

"I-I mean, not...not *today*. I'm still sore from last time. What if we—"

"Then I think you should go home."

Stunned, Daisuke blankly stared at the other side of the tent as Shinchi stood up, retrieved the book, and placed it in his hands once more; he wasn't sure if he even registered the movements. He barely felt the volume in his grasp when his fingers reflexively curled around it.

The daze gradually cleared from his mind the further he marched away from the acrobat camp—even if he'd wanted to, he couldn't ignore the weight of what just happened, and decided he'd speak with Retsuko privately about a different person to work with the next time he showed his face. It'd be a while before he dared, anyway. He might've been the one hurt, but the camp and troupe were Shinchi's home and family; a guest like him had little room to complain. Besides, his feelings would wear off soon enough—the pain was already beginning to subside. If he were honest, it was a massive relief more than anything.

Daisuke breathed easily and the ghost of a smile touched his lips. It had rained during the late morning hours; the smell of cherry blossoms, a chilly late spring evening, and petrichor kissed his nose as he blissfully walked along. An impulse of whimsy had him swishing his feet through a low, thin fog clinging to the street, until he noticed he was beside the tall white plaster wall guarding the nobility quarter. Without understanding why, he looked over his shoulder, toward the rest of the Capital city, as if expecting to find someone there.

THE EVENING SUNLIGHT BATHED the city in deceptively warm orange and golden hues. A light rain from earlier made the streets wet, but not so muddy that walking through while on patrol was miserable.

Then again, Obito thought any patrol without Daisuke constantly talking at him, taking them on detours, or stopping to chat with others, was insufferably boring. Master Yujin hadn't lightened their extra patrol load over the last few weeks despite the other work he'd assigned them, so when Obito was dragged into this one and his partner was nowhere to be found—yet again—he was left feeling equally frustrated and disappointed as he got ready to head out with the soldiers earlier that afternoon.

He let the ranked soldier he was with lead the way throughout their path, which took them through a small district in the city's center. Save for the occasional greeting called out to the officer, who was often assigned this route and knew most of the locals by name, there wasn't much to pay attention to; Obito couldn't decide if it was better that way or not. The soldier talked plenty, though the subjects weren't nearly as interesting as what usually came out of his partner's mouth, and he was in the unfortunate position of not being able to point out any errors in his logic or stories like he could with Daisuke.

Obito paused when they eventually came to the entrance of an alley. He'd let his mind wander, and got lost in thought over an ethical question one of his classmates posed earlier that day while looking at his feet more than his surroundings, so the suspicious blotch of red and faint drag marks the rain hadn't washed away easily grabbed his notice. Following where they led, he turned toward the alley and was greeted by the unmistakable smell of death.

"Fuck," he muttered, unsure if it was more of a complaint or an exclamation. Already feeling suffocated by the overpowering scent, he ventured toward it. Half-lying in shadow, he found a man slumped against a wall.

Obito's muscles complained when he crouched in front of the man, whose eyes had been left open, but any discomfort left over from training was swept away by another wave of curiosity. The man hadn't been dead for long, perhaps a few hours at most; judging by his thin frame and tattered clothes, he'd likely lived on the streets. While it should've brought up the question of how he'd died in broad daylight and no one noticed, he wasn't sure if he could've expected people to care—how often had *he* unintentionally ignored someone in this situation? He sighed and closed the man's eyes.

"Nakamura?" He turned and stood when the soldier called out to him. Seconds later, the man's face appeared at the alley's entrance, and he came toward his charge once he realized his younger counterpart wasn't simply lagging or shirking his patrol responsibilities. The officer clicked his tongue when he saw what kept him, sounding frustrated and disheartened at the same time. "Looks like someone got ta 'nother drifter this week. Don't worry 'bout it too much. I'll let the night crew know where 'e is so they can move 'im."

"Another?"

"A vagrant here 'nd there shouldn't shake ya that badly, boy." The soldier chuckled. "Y'sneaks in th' onmitsu are always lookin' for somethin' that ain't there. Help me finish this las' round 'nd I'll let ya off for th' night."

Obito opened his mouth to retort, but quickly changed his mind; not only was the man a ranking officer who wouldn't want to hear whatever he had to say, but he wasn't sure he should bring too much attention to the half-dried gash across the man's throat. Instead, he nodded curtly and let the soldier continue on with the patrol route they'd been walking together, then crouched in front of the dead man again and tilted his head to the side.

This looks like a shallow right-handed slash; whoever did this to him either panicked or just didn't have enough experience to finish him off. He probably died slowly, Obito mused as he examined the wound. Sunlight caught the silvery gleam of something in his neck, sticking out of a secondary puncture not far from the gash that killed him. Brows furrowed, he carefully pulled the needle out, wincing when the man's body moved with him, then slumped over once he had it in his grasp.

Fuck.

Blood mixed with a tint of orange liquid tinged the tip of the needle formerly embedded in the man's skin, where a small dribble of the same color leaked from the tiny puncture mark. He pensively rolled the needle back and forth in his palm a few times, then tossed it further down the alley, where it'd likely never be discovered. Giichi—or someone working for him—was testing the blackwater before moving on to the next phase of their harebrained scheme, whatever it entailed. Predictable, but no less frustrating.

If they're moving it to Zandaka's Servant or the Shadow Priestess, though, they likely won't try too many other times, or on higher profile targets here in the Capital—even Giichi isn't that stupid. A cold comfort, for certain, but one Obito had to tell himself to keep from acting irrationally. Thanks to Raku and Jido, Master Yujin had been able to confirm blackwater wasn't lethal, which Giichi also no doubt knew by now. However, just six onmitsu in total could identify it, and two of them were connected to the Tanaka family. Giichi would be better off moving the poison out of the Capital soon.

He quickly drew the sealing symbol in the dirt beside the man's body, got to his feet once more, and bowed. Just as he turned to catch up with the officer before the older man could wonder what happened, a faint blue light appeared in his periphery; it put his heart a little more at ease as he left the alley.

Being allowed to retreat to a place of calm quiet was more than welcomed after discovering the man's body. Rather than trying unsuccessfully to search for a sense of peace in the Royal Library, Obito found himself seated beside the pond where he'd first met Daisuke, in the ravine near the back road between the Palace grounds and the nobility quarter. He didn't have much time before he had to report to Raku for evening training, something that had become quite regular while his partner was off with the acrobats, and concluded if the officer he'd been with was going to report the dead man, he could let it be from there. Maybe it wasn't *right*, but it wasn't his place to speak on it unless asked, anyway.

His back stiffened when he heard the soft shuffle of feet in the grass behind him, interrupting the peaceful hum of frog song he'd been listening to while he smoked. Round bruises from the kyoketsu-shoge's counterweight littered his arms, thighs, and ribs, so the unexpected movement was far from a pleasant experience, which already made him irritable with whoever thought they needed to intrude on this moment of rest.

"Can I sit here?"

Obito's annoyance evaporated at the sound of Daisuke's question. He turned to look at his friend faster than he expected as the little pest settled into the grass beside him.

"Telling you 'no' hasn't made a difference yet, has it?"

A faint smile touched Daisuke's lips. "I'm still waiting for you to tell me 'no.'"

He took the cigarette Obito offered him. They sat in silence for a long time as he smoked, barely moving, both blankly staring at the lily pads floating on the still pond waters before them. Although they hadn't fought, they hadn't seen much of each other in recent weeks; awkward as it felt, it seemed like they both needed time to ease back in and adjust to one another once more. Obito found it especially odd; there wasn't a single other person he coexisted with so effortlessly as he did with Daisuke. However, when the other boy's uncharacteristic reticence persisted, and he caught a hint of sadness lingering like a shadow in those expressive eyes, he couldn't pretend he didn't notice.

"Where were you earlier?"

"Somewhere I didn't really belong." Daisuke sighed, smoke coming from his mouth in a massive cloud before he drew his knees up to his chest. "But, now it's over, and that's what matters."

"I'm sorry."

"Don't be—I'm fine."

"Are you sure?"

"...*We're* fine, right?" Daisuke's brows furrowed. His gaze locked onto Obito after he snuffed out his cigarette on the damp grass; when Obito nodded, he cautiously leaned on his shoulder. "Then, I'm sure. I'd feel *way* worse if I let someone else fuck up our friendship somehow."

Obito hadn't given his own feelings toward Daisuke's relationship with Shinchi much thought—rather, he *forced* himself not to think on it too often. Although he'd been annoyed with how frequently his partner skipped study sessions or just wasn't available to discuss the things they needed to figure out, despite Master Yujin's growing impatience, he was certain his opinion wouldn't matter. Moreover, he didn't believe it was any of his business; naturally, Daisuke was free to do whatever with whoever. When he was around and willing to talk, Obito would simply listen, all the while worrying about how his friend was being treated, a concern which had increased over the last couple of weeks.

Finally, he said, "There's better than Shinchi, anyway."

"Right? Next time, I'll rope in a charismatic court noble at *minimum*. Don't worry, I'd split his money with you." Daisuke chuckled, relief rising into the air around them as the odd bout of tension at last released its hold.

"Don't forget to blackmail him, first."

The little pest's snickering continued. "Ruthless—I like it. We'll go with your plan, then."

Obito smiled a bit, begrudgingly shrugging Daisuke off his shoulder before he stood. "Raku's waiting. Did you want to come with me?"

"What? And get my ass handed to me by a kyoketsu-shoge? Not happening."

"You can't blame the weapon..." Obito rolled his eyes, trying and failing to not let a small chuckle escape him. "I think you'd be better at it than you want to admit."

"Please. We know me, and I see those bruises on your arms—I'll pass. But...do you want to meet me in the library tomorrow morning?" Daisuke's heart fluttered and a wide grin plastered itself onto his face when Obito wordlessly agreed.

"Daisuke?"

Startled from his inner world, he looked up from the cover of his book and glanced around until he fully realized who called for him. His jaw set when his eyes landed on Mika, standing near one of the desks in the empty commons area. Of course. Since Obito wasn't around, Mika thought it was safe to approach him. Daisuke's grip on his book tightened, determined to not let whatever he wanted ruin how the conversation with his partner had helped his emotions rebound.

"What?" he asked, more harshly than he meant to sound; he cleared his throat as heat rose to his face, but couldn't bring himself to apologize for it.

"I'm just...surprised to see you, I guess. You're usually out with that acrobat lately."

"Well...don't be, that's over." Daisuke blinked. "Wait, how the hell did you know about him, anyway?"

"People talk."

Patience thinning rapidly, he rolled his eyes; someone overheard him talking to Obito and thought it was good gossip. Couldn't he get any peace? "I don't see how I spend my free time is anyone else's business—*you* sure as hell aren't entitled to it."

"Fuck off with that. How is it not?"

Mika straightened. Daisuke's heart hammered against his ribcage at the sudden change in his demeanor and the shift in the air—this wasn't his normal, inexplicable jealousy talking. This was pure resentment. Mika advanced on him until he was pinned to the wall near the commons area window, interrogating as he went.

"Do you know how much it hurts to watch you run around with someone else? How many times have you rejected *me*, now?"

"Rejected you? What—?"

"It's bad enough that you make me sit by and watch when you flirt with my fucking *cousin*, of all fucking people, but to hear you're fucking someone on top of it? It's like you have no shame, no pride, no fucking empathy at all."

Daisuke swallowed as humiliation welled in his chest. He clutched the book, as if he hoped it could shield him from the barrage. "Mika, this is getting—"

"Shut up."

Daisuke blinked again. He opened his mouth to say...something, *anything*, but froze when Mika leaned closer and grabbed his shoulders. His heart pounded when Mika's lips connected with his. He tried to push him off, but Mika's grip became firmer, holding him in place with a frighteningly possessive force until he found a chance to turn his head away.

The other boy drew back, still visibly angry. "So, him, but not me?"

"I—"

"Why am I not good enough? Why *not* me?" Mika's voice cracked.

All this after betraying me the way you did? Why would *I want you?* Of course, he couldn't say it aloud. Mounting accusations aside, Daisuke had never seen Mika like this; he probably should've tried deescalating the situation. However, his own anger was rising in his throat like bile and burning in his veins. Who the fuck was Mika to talk to him like this? Why *should* he tolerate being pushed around?

"What the hell are you on about? It's not like you...you don't..." Daisuke trailed off, brought up short once more at the fury blazing in the other boy's hazel eyes.

He barely had time to raise his hand in an attempt to defend himself before Mika's firm grasp on his shoulders became the leverage needed to push him hard. Daisuke smacked into the wall, barely keeping the back of his head from hitting it as he kept his eyes pinned on the other onmitsu—he'd never seen him look so furious. Since he'd been released, he quickly slipped around him for an escape.

"I don't, what?" Mika prompted.

"You don't own me." Unable to bring himself to watch more of those strange emotions flicker across the other boy's face, Daisuke lowered his eyes, stiffly retracted his hand, then turned away without another word. Shocked, Mika let him go without resistance.

"Daisuke, wait," Mika called after he'd taken a few steps, voice breaking again.

With his heart heavy and mind desperately trying to wrap around how quickly this night had deteriorated, he faltered at the sound of his name by instinct. He instantly regretted being so distracted when he paused. He didn't dare face Mika, nor did he know how long he remained there, gazing into the darkness of the corridor's far end, hoping it would stretch forth to swallow him whole as the silence persisted.

"You really won't look at me?"

Daisuke firmly told himself not to answer—he didn't trust what he might come out of his mouth this time. He'd already said more than Mika deserved to hear, and was keeping far too much information from the other boy that he couldn't afford to unleash all because his temper got away from him. He pushed it down further.

"Not talking now, either?" Ragged breaths rose into the air. "Fucking gods—*fine*! Fuck you, too, *silk-spinner*. Not like you're any good to me anymore, anyway."

The last part was the unspoken half of what Shinchi had said earlier, but *silk-spinner*? That word, uttered with so much hate, cut through Daisuke like a blade; he barely heard anything else Mika said over the pounding of his heart against his eardrums. His eyes widened as he sucked in a sharp breath and whirled around, but Mika was already gone. Eyes burning around the rims as his vision blurred with hot tears, he swallowed a few times, then stretched a trembling hand toward the nearest wall. His legs wobbled and felt weak, so he sank to the ground with his back against the cold stone and drew his knees up to his chest.

What the fuck did I do to deserve this? He dug the heels of his palms into his eyes, but each time he tried to control his emotions, a new wave of bitter rage and anguish rolled over him until he couldn't bear the pressure of it against his heart.

Something snapped.

A dark urge beckoned him, sweetly lying about how it would take everything away and let him stop feeling. He rose to his feet again. This time, it wasn't only Honda's voice reminding him—Mika's tumbled over it, as well, as did Junpei's, Emperor Akuwara's, Senator Hajime's...and his own.

"Silk-spinner." He repeated to himself as he stormed back to his room; a dismal cloud of self-loathing descended upon his crumbling rationality. *Silk-spinner, silk-spinner, silk-spinner! Fucking gods! Tell the truth, lie, dare to speak up, dare to set a boundary, and they'll always remind you how fucking worthless they think you are. Every fucking time—*

Daisuke's internal rant became even more incoherent as he burst through his door, threw the book aside, and went for the top desk drawer, searching for the scalpel with fevered urgency. The force of his actions sent the talisman, which he'd been steadily cleaning and scraping grime from, sailing across the room. Being so possessed by his thoughts, he was barely aware of how quickly he pulled the scalpel out and removed his shirts. His clammy, sweating palm closed around the instrument; his entire hand shook with anticipation and shame.

"Fuck," he swore at the sting from the first cut as he dragged the blade across his skin. It hurt, but it wasn't enough to quell his storming emotions, so a second followed, this time loaded with his anger.

Six fresh cuts decorated his shoulders, all much deeper than initially intended. The rag he usually cleaned himself up with was blotted with wet bloodstains by the time he finished, chest still heaving with the occasional, exhausted sob as he tossed it and the scalpel back in the drawer for now. His puffy eyes burned, and he could barely keep them open; he stumbled toward his bed with a hazy cloud looming in his mind. Sleep enveloped him as soon as his head hit the pillow.

The slab of smooth, dark rock materialized under Daisuke's feet again, illuminated around the ridges by a softly glowing green outline that revealed the same speckled pattern of glistening, extraterrestrial swirls he'd seen the first time his dreams brought him here. He still didn't know where that may be, but expected he'd never get a satisfying answer. The galaxy lay noiselessly pulsating beneath him, while above and around remained shrouded in a vast shadow. He wondered what became of those who stared into the void long enough; did they succumb to madness? A sudden—or maybe even slow—death? Did they plummet into endless despair?

Daisuke didn't have a chance to speculate beyond those possibilities. He jumped as a thin white line of light began crawling across the slab's outer edge, connecting two points and then moving onto another. He turned, following the creeping luminescence with his eyes as it joined to a third spot near his side, continuing until it barricaded him in the center of a shimmering hexagonal shape.

He drew in a shaking breath; this was just a dream. Nothing could hurt him here.

An unexpected flash of green from under his feet caught his attention again, and frightened, he scrambled backward, though the surrounding beams weren't about to let him escape. Circles formed at each of the hexagon's points. Terror jolted his heart when he realized the one at the top right looked familiar—it was the talisman he'd kept a secret for all these years, and the other points were beginning to adopt similar appearances, though the names on each were different.

Kanashimi, Tatakai, Jihuang, Hinkon, Wenyi, Saigai... He mentally read them off as his head swiveled around, wide eyes desperate to absorb what little information this strange realm was willing to give. Daisuke remembered the light below, and slowly drew his gaze toward it, heart pounding in his ears as he added yet another name to the list. *Zandaka.*

Lines of glowing jade used to form the name melted away from one another, stretched and flexed, then converged into the long, spindly shape of a massive dragon. Daisuke yelped when the rumbling ground knocked him off balance seconds before the very same beast split open the obsidian like glass, sending the glittering speckles on the surface into the air in a colorful, misting spray. The dragon rose high and bathed the darkness in its otherworldly color, hovering midair with red eyes, long claws, and dangerous fangs fixated on him as he pulled himself back up to one knee.

"Zandaka," Daisuke heard himself say, voice barely above a whisper.

The dragon surged forward with a roar, causing winds to gust with the force of a powerful storm. Daisuke ducked his head in a futile attempt to shield himself, worried yet surrendering to the idea that he'd been wrong, and this might somehow kill him after all. A raven's caw echoed through the chamber like the bellow of a gong, along with the chilling howl of a wolf's song, until the resonation became a high-pitched ring.

Everything turned white.

DAISUKE'S ROOM SPUN INTO view the second his back hit the floor; he barely managed to save his skull from taking a similar blow, while his muscles tightened and recoiled at the collision. He tiredly rubbed his face and groaned once he fully realized he was no longer dreaming, though the sting of fresh cuts on his shoulders made him drop his arms soon after. His head still ached from the tidal wave of emotion that had drowned out his better sense the night before—as always, he found himself cursing how horribly he'd misplaced his anger.

I'll take it out on Mika twice the next time I see him, Daisuke silently vowed. He glared at the ceiling as his fists gradually clenched the more his fury revived itself. When he noticed what was happening, he sighed deeply and flexed his fingers to release it, then declared to whichever dust particles were listening, "One stupid word out of his stupid mouth, and I'll break his fucking teeth in."

A strange, uneasy sense that he wasn't alone suddenly prickled under his skin and made every hair on his body stand on end—it felt like he was being watched. His eyes instinctively went to his desk, where a horrific sight greeted him. The top drawer was slightly ajar, and his towel, speckled with the dark red splotches of last night's blood, had tumbled halfway out. It ominously held the scalpel in a tight knot above the ground, like a hanged criminal left swaying in a noose. Daisuke's entire body ran cold, but once he clambered to his feet, he realized that wasn't the worst of it.

The talisman, supposedly housing the spirit of an ancient demon, sat beside him on the floor; he'd gotten blood on it somehow. A black aura flared around it like fire, an image he'd seen so many times in his dreams. Bright red lettering and the crimson image of a dragon crawled across its surface.

"Tatakai," Daisuke whispered when the demon's name came into full view.

He instinctively shielded his eyes when a bright green flash of light surged from the talisman. The floor rumbled beneath him, and from between his fingers, he watched a black miasma spread throughout the room. When he dared to look up again, he stood before a jade green dragon which barely seemed to fit in the space between the floor and ceiling. Long, snow-white hair swirled around the creature, who stared at him with harsh yellow eyes that sat against black sclera. Under each eye, three black dots appeared one-by-one, as did great horns that scraped against the ceiling with delicate golden chains strung between them. Above flowing white brows, a bar of gold shimmered into existence, forming a headpiece with a hexagonal-shaped center, decorated by six blood red rubies at each point. A necklace of deep purple beads and chunks of rose quartz appeared at its neck.

The dragon snarled and flicked the sleeves of its black outer robe. It leaned toward Daisuke, eyes narrowing as if studying him. "You must possess a great will to stand in this venerable one's presence without fear."

"A-actually, I-I'm terrified."

Wisps of smoke trailed from the dragon-like creature's nostrils. "Yet, your curiosity appears to outweigh your cowardice—I am rarely impressed by the tenacity of humans. Seems I should make an exception this time. If you have questions, you may ask them. I have several for you, as well."

"Really?" Daisuke mentally kicked himself for sounding so stupid, though whatever the being was currently standing in front of him merely lifted a long eyebrow. He swallowed. "Are...are you Tatakai? Zandaka's disciple?"

"I am," the creature answered, bringing back the images of the six names he'd read aloud in the dream. He craned a long neck forward until Daisuke could feel heat radiating off his scales. His voice was deep, commanding, yet he spoke with a slow and relaxed cadence, as if he were inquiring about the weather. "How do you know of the Demon King? And where did you find the talisman sealing me?"

Daisuke's eyes went to where it had rolled under his desk after Tatakai's glowing form broke through the surface—no wonder the thing hadn't brought him an ounce of luck over the last three years. "I read about Zandaka—Demon King? Seriously?—in a book, and your talisman...was sort of given to me, I guess."

"Curious," Tatakai murmured, seeming perturbed by the information. He gestured with a clawed hand for Daisuke to ask more.

"Did my blood summon you?"

"It did." Tatakai tilted his head, gold chain links delicately *clinking* with the motion. "The scent of it has slowly shaken me from slumber for a while, now. But you clearly did not intend to summon me, which means you likely do not desire my powers, nor do you possess my siblings' talismans. However, most disturbingly...I sense them."

Daisuke mutely shook his head, trying to ignore the shudder passing through him when the demon's words conjured the image of the other names he'd seen in his dream— particularly, those of Kanashimi and Saigai.

"I have made a decision, human."

Daisuke swallowed, his mind for once empty of a response.

"Your tithe has created a connection between us. As we now share that blood-bond, we will search for my siblings together. However, I have been half-awake for many years, and these first summons are quite exhausting, so, for now, I shall retreat into my talisman." Tatakai raised his long white eyebrows, somehow affecting a smug expression despite his stern features. "Do not fret, as I am not an omnipresent demon. I quite enjoy sleep, and the daily life of a human adolescent holds no interest for me. There is but a small chance I will answer the next time you summon me—I hardly plan on giving my loyalty to you."

"I figured." Daisuke rolled his eyes, earning a cloud of smoke to the face. He realized he had one more question once he fanned it out of his face. "Where do you go?"

Thicker plumes of smoke erupted from his mouth when Tatakai sighed, similar to the exasperation General Aki or Master Yujin would show if Daisuke asked one too many questions. "I will return to my home in the Between Realm where I've been chained and see what damages must be repaired. When I go back inside the talisman, I will change its shape before resting once more."

"You can do that?"

"Yes...something about tenacity and adaptability in His Highness's curse to seal Hikari's strength. Though, it has been centuries. I cannot recall his words in full."

"W-wait, what do you mean, 'sealing Hikari's strength?'"

"It was a punishment from the universe. When the Goddess incurred the wrath of the universe, we disciples of Zandaka absorbed her sinful traits to diminish her powers and seal her. Afterward, *we* were sealed to prevent the way those sins poisoned us from manifesting in the mortal realm. Now, then, leave me be—I have little strength for a lengthy explanation." The dragon's flowing brows furrowed as he brought a clawed hand to his snout, as if in thought, then he used his tail to sweep the talisman from under the desk behind him until it was at Daisuke's feet. "It's a strange existence, human, for a spiritual being to be locked away like this. We are asleep, but awake; alive, but dead. I am—mostly—under the command of whoever possesses my talisman until the Demon King's powers are restored, so long as fresh blood has been offered to give the command. The spiritual energy from your soul and these tithes will strengthen me. Use this information wisely."

A rush of wind hit Daisuke before he could ask anything else of the ancient being. When he could see again, Tatakai had vanished, but a second black, resin bracelet now adorned his right wrist. He stared at it in amazement—it looked identical to the original, like they'd been a set all this time. No one would even think twice about it. He carefully pulled it off his wrist and furrowed his brows as he stared at it, waiting for something to happen. Just when he was about to give up, it jerked in his hand, and the talisman sat in its place, looking as if a drop of blood had never touched it. Amazed, he repeated the action several more times, but doing so seemed to thoroughly test the limits of the demon's patience. When the talisman burned his palm, Daisuke decided he'd played around enough.

Somewhere down the hall, a door slammed shut, which alerted him to the rest of his surroundings once more. He had no way of knowing what time it was or for how long he'd been awake, but at the sound of other human activity, he finally peeled away from his inner world. Unfortunately, that came with the stinging, burning reminder of the cuts on his shoulders. Swearing, he found his clothes and opted for heading to the infirmary for the medicine Obito had once mentioned.

Thinking of his friend made his heart sink—he should've been in the library already to discuss his findings from the book, but it wasn't the only thing haunting him. He touched his lips, disgusted with what Mika had done, but also with himself; he couldn't believe he hadn't been able to get away somehow before the kiss happened. He was normally so quick on his feet that it should've been entirely preventable. *Fucking hell. This makes* three *things I don't know how to tell him about.*

The knock on his door that came once he was dressed was both dreaded and expected. He bolstered his courage, then opened it for Obito. Although he gave his friend a grin and prepared some nonsense about oversleeping, he knew by the worry on his face, it would have fallen flat. Instead, he looked toward his feet and waited for his partner to say something first.

Obito's gaze also dropped. "I've been waiting for you in the library. I...I thought you just overslept."

Daisuke laughed weakly—usually, it'd be a fair assumption, but he also knew Obito could tell when he had a night like the one from last night. Without thinking, he let himself collapse in his friend's arms; Mika's words viciously swarmed in his head at the action, but dissipated like a wisp of incense smoke when Obito held him. Relief flooded him, and he tightened his grip—he'd be able to talk about that part, at least, though he still wasn't sure he had words for this morning.

"I'm sorry."

"Don't be." After a moment, Obito spoke again. "Come on, I'll take you to the infirmary."

Daisuke opened his mouth to argue, as he didn't want him to see the fresh cuts or scars, but all he responded with was a soft-spoken agreement and a nod.

THE DUSTY STORAGE ROOM at the back of the house had always been suffocating, poorly lit, and held a general sense of dread, which had only increased since the door was painted to blend in better with the wall. Now, it remained locked at all times, and decorative, gauzy red curtains covered it—no one had reason to think of them as more than a questionably tasteful splash of color in an otherwise monotone home.

Of course, Mika wasn't about to mention any of his complaints to his father. Instead, he watched as the man rifled through one of many crates filled to the brim with the blackwater poison. Although a couple of low-risk tests on vagrants had revealed it wasn't lethal, Giichi was confident it would cause the mass chaos he wanted; Mika was still contending with whether he was truly prepared to point the blame toward Daisuke when it was inevitably discovered as the cause for such terror. Master Yujin already knew it existed, but he doubted the Intelligence Master knew where it came from. A person who lied as swiftly as Daisuke—and someone as under-handed as Obito—surely wouldn't implicate themselves in the debacle.

Mika knew what his father expected of him, but couldn't easily reconcile everything in his head. On the one hand, of course it was wrong to even consider using Daisuke as a scapegoat; on the other, Mika hadn't gotten over being so soundly rejected a couple of weeks ago, not to mention repeatedly, and wanted something to relieve his need for vengeance at how he'd been treated. The way Daisuke ignored him now, accompanied by hateful glares he received from Obito—indicating he knew about their disaster of a kiss—whenever he looked their way, justified a darkness steadily manifesting inside him.

"Lost in thought, son?" Giichi dispassionately asked, wrestling him away from his muddled mind.

Mika rubbed his face and leaned against the wall. "Just tired, I think."

Giichi wordlessly studied him for a moment, then went back to stuffing a vial of blackwater in his satchel before loading it into another bag he intended to take up the mountains with him. Mika knew he shouldn't have anticipated sympathetic words or anything similar, but his chest still grew heavy when they never came.

"What should I do with the rest of this while you're gone, Father?" He hoped he didn't sound as mopey as he felt. While Giichi wouldn't pry, Mika didn't know if he could honestly answer that he was heart-broken over another boy if asked; not even his uncle, the Nakamura patriarch, tolerated such things.

"Watch over the place and the stockpile—I can't go running back to Nishinuma for more snowberries, now. It would draw far too much at-tention, and I can hardly expect the same of you without the Intelligence Master's prodding." Giichi fastened the straps on his bag. "If anyone tries to enter or comes snooping around, I want you to stop them. Use force if necessary—hell, at this point, I wouldn't care if you killed them and left the body here so it wouldn't be found. Your tanto's sharp, isn't it?"

Mika nodded, trying to hide how nervous the idea made him—at this point, anyone who came here to poke around would be one of his fellow onmitsu. He crossed his arms to hide his shaking hands. "And my contingency measures?"

"My boy, I know you're smart enough to understand *why* we have a scapegoat. Use him—that's an order from your father, not a request."

Mika's blood ran cold even as his face burned with shame. Despite his doubts, he already knew he'd capitulate.

SAIGAI'S FLUTE LET OUT a halting note when Kanashimi's claws closed around the purplish-black orb they'd summoned with their fan. He watched as they squeezed the orb until it popped like a bubble, leaving behind a wispy trail of shadow which slowly dissipated from the fresh, early summer mountain twilight. Laughter and chatter from the Shadow Priestess's followers could be heard on the far side of the complex, away from where the two demons were hidden near the ancient shrine. While he still wasn't thrilled about being bound to a human by a blood ritual, he quite enjoyed the area surrounding the ancient hot springs. In the lost times before becoming sealed within his talisman, he could've played his flute for hours undisturbed in a place like this, cultivating his spiritual energy and watching the souls he cleansed dance to the pleasure of music.

"Solstice soon," the dragon demon quietly stated. When his sibling made no move to respond, he asked, "What is it?"

Kanashimi's eyes settled on the ground. "Tatakai is awake."

"That lazy garden snake?" Saigai rumbled, a cloud of smoke obscuring his face when he snorted. "Curb your optimism. He likely went back to sleep after rolling over in his nest."

"Your disdain for our brother aside, we should summon him. It seems he's been aware for a little while, now."

"You know I am not powerful enough for these things yet. Besides, two of us doing the summoning by ourselves would surely result in failure—or unknown consequences. You've sat in meditation for days trying to sense a wisp of Tatakai or any of the others. That alone should be evidence enough that we aren't capable without our siblings."

"It's how I found you. Besides, the Shadow Priestess is an excellent student and devoted to her manuals. It will be easy if we work together with her."

"What will be?" Kagura called from the other side of the small pond. Kanashimi turned to her, excitement alighting their eyes, until they noticed the other mortal happily clinging to the woman's arm. Kanashimi's expression turned into sadistic delight when they noticed the second falter slightly at the sight of the two demons.

Saigai rolled his eyes and settled on a large boulder near the little shrine, where his talisman lay upon a gleaming, sturdy mahogany altar. He leaned against the roof in a continued demonstration of defiance by refusing to further scale himself down as Kanashimi did. His other siblings would likely make a good show of being in charge whenever they arrived, though he knew it was pointless. That annoying blood-bond meant they could only do so much without direct permission from their summoner—like him, they'd be resigned to this fate. Although this Priestess of Shadows had thus far respected the boundary he'd set months ago when he first awakened here, something would not allow him to trust her as easily as Kanashimi did. Perhaps it was for the best—he sensed his sibling's flaring jealousy every time she came around with the other woman. Saigai was content to give the younger one space, and even more willing to keep himself away from the one called Kagura, or Lady Shadow, or whatever she chose to be on a particular day.

"One of our other siblings has awakened," Kanashimi explained. "Tatakai, to be exact."

Lady Shadow's dark eyes widened at the news. "That must mean General Aki has finally accepted our offer—we should go to the Capital at once to collect him and Tatakai."

"I've never been to the Capital before," Natsumi, the other woman, said dreamily, though the wistful look on her face soon faded when Kanashimi's stern gaze turned to her, and she shrank behind Lady Shadow once more. The Priestess either genuinely didn't notice or intentionally ignored the interaction, causing Saigai to tilt his head with mild interest.

"We may not need to leave at all," Kanashimi continued, ignoring their brother's scoff and focusing instead on Kagura's intrigued expression, feeling entirely smug that they alone held the Priestess's attention. "There is an ancient ritual we can use to call him here instead, though it takes quite a bit of blood and spiritual energy."

Natsumi traded a concerned look with Lady Shadow, which prompted Kanashimi into proceeding with their thoughts.

"We could use the old woman with the white eyes."

"You will not," Saigai quickly warned with a growl. "She's one of the few tolerable humans here—she likes listening to my flute. I play for her while she does the washing."

"The poor thing is nearly as ancient as we are by human standards," Kanashimi argued. Sensing their brother would stand firm, however, they merely sighed and put a clawed hand to their snout in exasperation. "I forgot you could be like this. Fine. Does my venerable brother have another suggestion, then?"

Saigai looked a bit indignant. "As I stated, we should avoid this ritual. I am not strong enough to help you, no matter what you believe, and it is better to do this sort of summoning with more of us—gentle as she is, Jihuang alone would be far more help than only myself."

Lady Shadow opened her mouth to speak, but anything she might've added was cut off by the call of her name piercing through the evening air. She turned toward the person who needed her, then in a panic quietly ushered the demons toward their talismans to keep them concealed. She had plans for when she would reveal them to her followers, but such a moment was not tonight. Once the dragons were gone, she shook Natsumi off her arm to hurriedly shut the shrine's double doors, just in time to face a young woman who was carrying a mass of black fabric in her arms. The matron's normally straight shoulders slumped when she recognized the bundle as the heavy robes she and other members wore when conducting official business, as to disguise their true identities.

"My lady," Emi bowed, though it was a little awkward with the robes in her grasp—Natsumi took them from her. "I apologize for interrupting, but someone is here to see you. Rather, he's here to see Zandaka's Servant."

Lady Shadow slowly breathed through her nose to keep calm, then silently bared her throat so Emi could use her Healing powers to change her smooth, rich voice into a rough, gravelly sounding one beyond recognition. Haruki had taught the two other Healers living amongst them how to perform this technique, but her skills remained unmatched.

"Thank you, Emi." Despite a grimace at her voice, she returned the bow, making the younger woman flush. "Please, make sure our guest is comfortable and tell him I'll be along shortly. Natsumi?"

Natsumi looked nervous at first, then straightened her shoulders and held out the robes, intending to help Lady Shadow into them, as well as attend this meeting with her; it was her first time directly involving herself with her lady's affairs. No one anticipated this person, but since only so many messengers could die along this mountain trail without raising suspicions, sudden visits from the nobles Kagura dealt with weren't too uncommon. Though she would've much preferred working with their wives, the men never brought them along. A lamentation for another time.

"Are you ready, my Lady?" Natsumi asked once all the layers and sashes were properly secured.

"As I'll ever be, I suppose." Kagura pulled up her hood and gently took Natsumi's arm. "Do yourself a favor, my love, and don't speak to this obnoxious pig directly."

LADY SHADOW STILL WASN'T sure what part of her thought it was ideal to entertain these long-winded men who prattled on about themselves with few breaks. This one, unfortunately, was the most insufferable of the lot, but also her best source of information. She lost track of how many minutes she'd never get back while he droned on. He must've thoroughly enjoyed the sound of his own voice—if only she felt the same. A scowl wrinkled her brow when Natsumi poured more wine in his glass, and he didn't pause for even half a breath to thank her. While he wasn't known for benevolence toward anyone he deemed lesser, something must've emboldened him further, as he was never *quite* this rude toward her "staff."

The nobleman dug into his robes and pulled out a vial of orange liquid, which he placed on the table beside the wine decanter; she barely spared it a glance. Appearing quite proud, he reclined against the pile of cushions behind his back. "I do, however, have a brilliant plan for your next move."

"Giichi," Lady Shadow seethed from under her disguise in the rasping voice she hated, resisting the urge to clutch Kanashimi's talisman, which hung at her throat again. Saigai's had gone into a safe pocket in her sleeve. "You are aware I have not interacted with the outside world in *years*. As such, I followed your advice in the past—much to my detriment. It was *you* who said that bumbling fool Hideo could reliably pass on Tatakai's talisman to General Aki, yet we've lost sight of it since. *You* convinced me a lowly traitor might need Saigai's power for protection when they brought you Tatakai's talisman to give Hideo. We almost lost his talisman as well. *And*, it was *you* who begged for time to search for it in case it'd been lost, starting far away at Nakamura estates. You were nearly caught by Lord Nakamura in the process."

Giichi's indignant posture had stiffened with each mistake she listed off, but now he looked as though he'd finally begun to consider his blunders; Kagura internally bemoaned how she'd never be taken this seriously if he knew she was a woman. Misame had scouted this fool from a tavern in the Wen Valley, while specifically targeting embittered gentry who could provide enthusiasm and funds to their cause. Lady Shadow never fully trusted his competence, or sudden loyalty to Demon King Zandaka, but also had few other options at the time. His hatred toward his in-laws, and frustration over what he believed was rightfully his, made him an easy and willing first recruit. Manipulating him with the nonsensical patriotic talk over what was happening with the Giahatian throne was an easy path into his mind. The succession drama was a useful cudgel and didn't matter much to Lady Shadow—they'd all perish, anyway.

Lady Shadow pressed, "Why should I trust another of your half-witted schemes?"

"P-please, let me explain." Giichi straightened when he realized he was cowering—he was supposed to *be* the authority, not the one *bending* to it. His hand still trembled slightly when he took a slow sip of his wine; gods, he'd already had so much—how much more could he possibly drink? "If *this* plan succeeds, you could gain control of the Wen Valley."

"Don't toy with me."

"A-and if it doesn't, we already have someone else to blame it all on—a slaveborn, to be exact, who has no right being in Imperial intelligence and has already earned plenty of Akuwara's scorn. I have everything needed to make the boy seem responsible, starting with my own son. Once I return to the Capital, I'll have Mika set out and start poisoning the wells in key Wen Valley cities."

Lady Shadow paused, this time giving the vial a proper look. Giichi didn't know she'd gone to Zhu last autumn—she saw no reason to tell him—so he wasn't aware that she'd already come across the boy in question. If he was still alive and wandering around the Capital, then either Haruki hadn't tracked the right team of onmitsu, or...the alternative was unthinkable. Surely, the girl she'd so generously saved from the elements and starvation wouldn't betray her just for a few fancy things in the Palace.

She dismissed her concerns and coaxed him further, "What makes you think you'd get away with it? And so flawlessly, at that."

The slight sway in the nobleman's bearing hinted that the amount of wine he'd consumed was finally too much for him to fight against. He flexed his right hand; the red glint of two ruby rings caught in the candlelight. "I managed to get away with what I did to my youngest nephew a few years back."

Natsumi stiffened at Lady Shadow's side, though she would never speak directly to Giichi. The matron also felt a heavy ball forming in the pit of her stomach, as if she already knew what he meant without asking. Nonetheless, as Giichi was a lucrative benefactor, she had to ensure she understood. Plus, perhaps a softer part of her that still existed, buried somewhere deep, desperately wanted her instincts to be wrong.

"I'm afraid I don't understand."

"I wanted to get back at Takato for the way he's treated me over the years, and for denying me what's rightfully mine. So, I took what I could from him—his sense of safety and security, his arrogance, his self-righteous posturing. It was so busy at the wedding, no one noticed when my nephew didn't return when he should've."

"Lord Tanaka, did you murder this boy?"

"Not quite." The nobleman paused to hiccup; his words had taken on a particular drawl throughout his previous statements. "Hitting him never seemed to make a difference—I can't imagine killing him would've been terribly satisfying. Now, he and his bastard father must live with this hideous humiliation."

Natsumi sucked in a breath, disgust and outrage overriding her fear of the man. "You violated the boy."

"And you should see the shame and vulnerability it's brought upon the Nakamuras. It's been nearly five years, and they still haven't fully recovered within the family structure. There're gaps everywhere to exploit."

Unable to take it any longer, Kagura feigned clumsiness and knocked over the decanter between them, spilling the remaining wine down the front of her robes. "Wretched—forgive me, my Lord. I'll have the head matron come clean this up. Natsumi, please keep Lord Tanaka in good company for a few moments, will you?"

The young woman swallowed, then dipped her head. "O-of course...Servant."

"Is everything to my Lord's liking?" Kagura asked as she delicately waved her fan. Training as an actress in her youth made it easy to switch between the gruff persona of Zandaka's Servant and the sultry façade of the inn's head matron, but it could never be enough to completely suppress the bile rising in her throat. With a graceful sweep of her kimono sleeve, she covered her mouth so her lips could quickly slip into a malevolent frown before resuming her act. At least Emi had also stayed nearby to change her voice back to normal.

"For the most part."

Lady Shadow frowned, this time genuinely confused. "Is there something you find unsatisfactory, my Lord?"

"For one thing, I sure as hell wouldn't mind seeing some proof that these talismans have been recovered," the nobleman indignantly huffed.

"You will, in time, and with patience. The Servant is planning a grand ritual soon on the solstice—all are invited to attend."

"A ritual?" Giichi's nose wrinkled in dissatisfaction. "We don't have time for parlor tricks and nonsense."

"I believe you misunderstand." She used the fan to disguise her malicious smile. "However, if you insist."

Lady Shadow calmly knelt across from him, where she'd cleaned up the spilled wine only moments ago, and placed the talismans of Saigai and Kanashimi on the table between them, beside the ominous orange poison in the vial. The drunk man's unfocused gaze watched her as intently as possible. While changing clothes, she had discussed the nobleman's words with the dragon demons, and they agreed something should be done about him. Although Saigai's apparent empathy for some humans was not what she'd initially expected of the Demon of Disaster and Wrath, in this case, it was quite useful. Upon hearing the recount of Giichi's confession, had he been allowed to set fire to the man then and there, nothing could have restrained him. Lady Shadow may have abandoned most of her qualms about killing, but to do something as heinous to a child as what Giichi admitted was beyond unforgiveable.

"Kanashimi, Saigai," Lady Shadow said as she gently, soundlessly closed the fan and set it on the table, reveling in the way Giichi's eyes never left hers, locked in awe and terror. She took the knife from her obi and pricked the pad of her forefinger, smearing blood across the two talismans. "Perhaps you would like to introduce yourselves to his Lordship, that way we can show him the power of the ritual."

"*Still* nothing?" Daisuke griped as he held a clay pot up to his face, squinting at the tiny, frail shoots weakly trying to poke through the soil. He groaned and slumped on the ground beside Aunt Kiko's brown tabby cat, who barely acknowledged him. Despite hours of patient nurturing, the red poppy seeds Daisuke had obtained from Retsuko failed to thrive. Abysmally. He'd been excited when they first showed signs of life in the safety of their pot in Aunt Kiko's garden, but now that several days passed without progress, he couldn't remember the last time he'd wanted to scream so badly out of sheer frustration.

What am I doing wrong?

So few Northern Nomads lived in the Capital that he felt he couldn't show up unexpectedly and pester them for advice. Frankly, he wasn't even sure where to find them outside of the nobility quarter, and was too afraid of a repeat from Zhu to try seeking them. Not to mention, even among his people, not everyone could make the red poppies grow, and no one exactly *owed* him their time. In theory, he could've *forced* them to talk, but the idea of throwing his weight around as Imperial Intelligence didn't sit right; at least, not in that scenario. Those people had enough to worry about without his empty threats.

The sealing book he and Obito exhaustively read from confirmed the names of Tatakai's siblings, but had no substantial amount of Nomadic lore despite several mentions of the Raven God. A search of the library turned up a few forgotten volumes of wildly insulting, factually inaccurate pieces about his people, which Daisuke then removed and burned in a fit of fury. Undeniably piqued by the whole premise and amused by his reasoning, Obito happily handed him the matches.

Daisuke's grandmother and the women she toiled alongside had always been his primary source for learning about Northern Nomadic culture. He couldn't remember *much* about her anymore, but she often encouraged everyone to join in the Northern Nomadic meditation prayer performed on solstices and equinoxes. According to her, more people meant higher amounts of spiritual energy, which made it more effective, though Daisuke had his doubts. After all, everyone who participated was still enslaved on Grandmaster Norio's plantation. His cynicism aside, entertaining the idea made him feel ridiculously silly, as he doubted the Raven God or any of the worshipped deities existed as they did in their stories. Little more than legends further exaggerated for human comfort.

Today's the summer solstice...

Another sweeping glance at the dying poppy sprouts led him to another conclusion: he was desperate, and willing to try anything to nurse them into healthy flowers.

He absentmindedly stroked the cat's chin before he sighed and pushed himself to his feet again, grumbling to the disinterested brown tabby, "Here goes my self-respect."

It purred, then mewed at him with a slow blink, which was far more encouraging than he expected. It also got up and stretched before trotting away to join its sleek black playmate on the other side of the garden. Daisuke laughed when the other cat instantly pounced on it.

He found Obito in one of the Palace courtyards, hiding from the late morning sun under the shaded terrace while facing an enviably healthy rose garden, watching in silence as court nobles and servants alike milled back and forth across the way. When it became apparent that his partner hadn't noticed him, a mischievous plan to sneak up on him and give him a good scare formulated in Daisuke's mind. He disappeared behind one of the pillars and slowly padded toward Obito in the same manner, peeking out intermittently to ensure he hadn't been seen. Stealth was something he prided himself on, but his partner rarely reacted when he tried practicing it. Unable to help it, a snicker escaped him when he noticed a steady plume of white smoke hovering around the area, giving away his position.

"Daisuke, knock it off."

"Caught you. So much for trying not to smoke," he teased as he finally gave up and slinked toward his friend.

Obito glanced at him when he reached his side. "I thought I'd lost you to the poisons room again today."

"You could only be so lucky." Daisuke followed his gaze across the courtyard, though he was certain his friend wasn't focused on anything specific—he'd recognized the subtle, slightly distressed look in Obito's eyes. "What are you doing out here, anyway?"

"Lost in thought."

"Vague answer. Care to explain?"

"You know I don't."

"That thing's creeping up on you again, isn't it?"

"It always does eventually." Obito handed him a cigarette of his own—halfway to make a polite offer, but also a wordless plea to shut up and, perhaps more importantly, drop the subject before he had to discuss it. Although he'd rather see his friend unburdened by his past, Daisuke accepted. He didn't quite understand how or why, but letting Obito light the smoke for him made a ridiculous yet familiar butterfly sensation dance in his belly again. He blankly watched when two thin trails of translucent white curled around the rose garden's thorny brambles.

It took the entire cigarette and a drawn pause afterwards for him to figure out how to broach the reason he'd originally sought out his teammate. He'd decided on honesty, but fortunately, Obito broke the silence first.

"You said this morning you were going to check on the poppies before doing anything else. Are they growing?"

"I fucking wish. Don't laugh, but I'm so fucking desperate that going to perform a traditional Nomadic ceremony today to see if it does anything for them. I...I think I need your help with it."

Obito didn't bother hiding how much the request had taken him aback—he didn't think he would've been able to, anyway. Daisuke knew better. "Why would you need me? I've killed more plants than I care to admit."

Distraught, Daisuke subconsciously twisted the lower stud in his left ear before gripping a fistful of hair near his temple. "Because the solstice ritual works better with more participants, and you're the one person I know who won't call me crazy for trying. I told you, I'm desperate—I *need* those sprouts to grow."

"Still not taking suggestions for blue or yellow poppies?"

"No chance," he firmly refuted.

Sensing this wasn't the time to prod about why his partner refused an easier solution, Obito relented. "Fine. What do you need?"

THE LITTLE POND WHERE they'd first found each other had since become a favorite place for the pair to meet, second to the library and sometimes far more private, especially with the fact that they still hadn't figured out who among the Healer consort was eavesdropping on them; granted, neither could say they'd put much effort into it yet. Since she hadn't made another appearance, they didn't consider her a priority—she'd either changed her mind or decided to back down for now, which was best for all three of them at present. Lush greens all around and pastel wildflowers gave the ravine an unmatched serenity, shaded by the cedars and thin birches surrounding it as the low buzz of honeybees droned. A warm early summer breeze wound its way through Obito's hair, reminding him to breathe.

He'd arrived early, both out of habit, and due to an anxious nagging in his mind he couldn't calm. The peaceful scenery helped a little bit, but his nerves remained on edge toward whatever it was they were about to do. Even so, he couldn't deny that any doubt or skepticism he'd previously held toward the idea had already given way to curiosity. Besides, it wasn't common to see his friend agitated in the way he'd been earlier; since Obito didn't have the same proficiency in poisons or their antidotes, lending a hand in any way possible seemed like the least he could do to help Daisuke chase down all his options.

Which wasn't to say he believed gods existed, especially as they did in the minds of people, nor that they deserved worship—he knew he wasn't the only one of the pair who held such beliefs. However, it seemed there *was* another plane of existence, as evidenced by their study of souls and sealing rites over the last few months. It opened endless possibilities to analyze, but Obito thought any amount of trepidation was both normal and healthy—he found Daisuke's apparent fearlessness about it admirable and, frankly, worrying.

The first trill of frogs hiding among the long grasses surrounding the pond marked the time Daisuke had designated to meet, as did the orange glow slowly overtaking the skies. Just as it wasn't surprising for Obito to be early, he reined in a trace of mild annoyance when Daisuke was late—he'd come to expect as much over the last few years. When he finally heard the little pest's crashing steps break through the underbrush leading down to the pond, he already had a sarcastic remark on the tip of his tongue, though it quickly vanished when he saw his partner's slightly reddened complexion along with the small basket clutched to his chest.

"Did you run all the way here?" he teased as he took it from Daisuke's grasp.

"I got sidetracked. Shinta wanted to talk about some stupid sonnet he didn't understand—like *I'd* know any better—"

"—You would—"

"—And it took *forever* to shake him off. *Then,* on top of that, Yuki and Masaki wanted to *follow* me around like the little pests they are—"

"—They like you—"

"—And they had *so* many questions, and—" Daisuke huffed, then composed himself before he began digging around in the basket. "Never mind. Sorry I'm late."

"Somehow, that makes this less unnerving," Obito dryly commented as he shifted his grip on the basket's handles to keep it steady.

Daisuke removed a sable raven feather that took on a bluish shine when the sunlight touched it, a single stick of incense infused with the scent of sandalwood, and the pot of poppy sprouts. Obito was shocked when he saw how they looked to be on the verge of death. In stark contrast with his own botanical capabilities, Daisuke rarely lost a plant. He hadn't devoted the time to it this year, but last summer, he'd had a few thriving potted ones lined up against the window in the commons area of the onmitsu dormitories; Shinta had taken over their care when the two left for Zhu. These poppies should've been safe and happy in Aunt Kiko's garden, as she'd insisted, so seeing all the effort his friend had put into them amount to such a sight was, well...more depressing than Obito expected.

He mentally shook himself from his thoughts as Daisuke traded the objects he was holding for the basket, set it down, and then took the incense from him again.

Obito watched as he stuck it in the ground and lit it—choosing not to think about how or when he'd swiped the matches from him—before he asked, "What exactly is your plan, here?"

"Don't laugh, but...we're going to pray." Daisuke winced a little before checking his friend's reaction; Obito's brows furrowed dubiously, but he didn't dismiss the idea or argue with it. He uneasily continued, "M-more accurately, we're going to meditate so we can connect with the spiritual realm. Or...hang on. It's something like that, I think—gods, I wish I remembered better. My grandma was the one who always talked about this stuff, not my parents, and she died when I was eight."

"She sounds like someone Aunt Kiko would've liked."

Daisuke laughed, which released some of the tension dammed in his chest as he eased himself onto the ground and crossed his legs. "Probably. They could've talked about their old lady magic together."

Obito joined him on the ground, careful with the feather and pot of fragile sprouts, then placed each item between them. "Before you do this...why the red poppies? Why do they matter so much?"

"What? Are we writing an essay on the terrible things I've seen?" Daisuke swallowed and briefly looked elsewhere when Obito raised an eyebrow, clearly unimpressed by his poor attempt at making light of it. "Look, it's not pleasant, but...it's because of my mom. She was an entertainer—Grandmaster Norio hated the word 'prostitute,' even though it's the same fucking thing. Anyway, to make them compliant, overseers or other slaves served them tea laced with opium. That forced addiction aside, Mom genuinely loved the stuff—she never resisted a craving for it. She was so desperate to escape, she did anything for more. I can only remember a handful of times when she wasn't high."

Daisuke sucked in a sharp breath, hoping to hide the unexpected break in his voice, and hugged himself. He couldn't face Obito's unreadable expression anymore.

"Red poppy opium *does* have better medicinal properties, but it also isn't addictive. I just *can't* knowingly give someone something if it could make them turn out like my mom. I know I've made deadlier things than this, but if I use regular opium in blackwater's antidote...it just won't feel like I've actually made things better. It'd be one thing if I wanted to *kill* the person, but..."

He trailed off, and Obito didn't pursue it further—there wasn't a reason to, anyway. He'd said more than enough. The depths of his friend's empathy never failed to surprise him, but now and then, it hit him a little more squarely than he was prepared for. After a moment, he wordlessly offered Daisuke his hands, a gesture common in Giahatian group meditations, which he readily accepted.

"Just focus on your intentions, then, and I'll do the same."

"Intentions," Daisuke repeated quietly, then sighed and directed his focus on the poppy sprouts. *What am I doing? Trying to make an antidote to help people I might indirectly harm. It doesn't matter who was wrong—accountability comes later—because now, it's up to me to make things right. I need these poppies to grow strong and healthy for the sake of others.*

He swallowed the tightness in his throat as his gaze flicked to Obito's, though the calm reassurance in his friend's eyes banished the flood of anxiety ready to swell inside him. Even if he wasn't entirely confident in following this theory, he wasn't alone, and someone trusted him enough to help him try. An irreplaceable faith he wasn't sure he deserved from anyone. Daisuke straightened his back, then closed his eyes, slowly drawing in a deep breath. Encouraged by the steady, calming strength of his partner's hands, he took in the scent of the sprouts and their soil, the sandalwood incense burning nearby, warm sun on his skin, and an easy summer breeze winding through his hair.

"I'm ready," he whispered, tightening his grip on Obito. If this was more than myth, their connected energies should reach the Raven God with greater ease than if he attempted the prayer on his own. He stole one more glance at his tiny sprouts, then measured his breathing and prepared to sink into a meditative state, letting the weight of his hands rest in Obito's palms as he closed his eyes.

The summer solstice was a prime choice for one's first journey into meditation to seek the Raven God's blessings. In traditional Nomadic societies, solstice and equinox days represented openings to one's own spirituality and to the realm occupied by their god, the figure who "blessed" them with life, the ability to read their own futures in dreams, and with their high tolerance for the freezing temperatures of the Nomadic Isle. Daisuke had never intentionally sought anything related to his own spirituality before, and was still ready to dismiss it as nonsense, but he quickly banished those thoughts. Instead, he took Obito's advice of focusing on his intentions, the red poppies, and the raven feather between them.

There was an order to what one prayed for: blessings for one's friends, their family, and finally, themselves, often including a special wish within the last one. These prayers also signified the change in seasons; spring and summer blessings were for spiritual and physical growth, while autumn and winter blessings were for maintained health and the safekeeping of what one loved. Love, in some sense, seemed to be a central theme of the Raven God, his blessings, and the prayers sent to him. Daisuke hadn't known much about it in his early life, but what he'd experienced since then meant the world to him—most notably, was the fondness he'd fostered toward the one currently holding him in place over this whole mess.

"Keep my friends in health and abundance, protect Kulako and Obito from evils that may wish to harm them, and, please, let these poppies grow healthy and strong so I may help others."

"Quite the wish," the familiar, warm voice of a woman replied.

Daisuke opened his eyes. He wasn't met by the sight of Obito sitting across from him and looking at him as though he had three heads. Instead, he found himself deep within a warm, sunlit forest he didn't know, sitting in a thicket several feet away from the white wolf's ethereal figure. Overjoyed, he jumped to his feet and rushed toward the center of the clearing; trees bowed and swayed in the breeze, their leaves dappling his skin in shadow and an orange evening light.

"Haven't seen *you* in a while," he teased the wolf spirit with a grin. He wasn't sure how he knew, but it seemed as though she gave him the same look in return as she trotted toward him.

"Bold as ever, I see." She hesitated, then bumped the bracelets on his right wrist with her nose as soon as she came up to him—his body went rigid until he realized nothing would happen, and she calmly sat down. *"This one is relaxed enough to not create a barrier, but I should still keep my distance when able—the demons of the Between Realm aren't always fond of forest spirits because of what happened to them."*

"Is that what you are, then?"

"It's slightly more complicated, but in a broad sense, yes. Being a nature spirit himself, the Raven God grants my people sanctity in the spiritual realms, where we can watch over our living loved ones. Wolves and ravens are quite intertwined, after all."

Daisuke blinked. "You were Okami."

"Very astute." The white wolf's tail swished in approval, but before he could barrage her with more questions, she had one of her own. *"It is the time of the solstice, is it not? Does this mean you've come for the Raven God's blessing?"*

The familiar way she addressed him was a soft comfort, like what he often imagined a mother's embrace should be; since she'd never proven herself as anything other than a kindhearted spirit, he *wanted* to tell her. "I'm trying to right a wrong, but since I'm on Perena, the red poppies I need won't grow. I'm running out of time...and, well, hope."

"Did you ask for them to be blessed upon planting?" she asked. When Daisuke mutely shook his head, her ears twitched as if in amusement as her tail wagged a bit behind her. *"When conducting a ritual, you* must *complete all steps properly. For your red poppies, asking the Raven God to bless them once their seeds are buried in soil is part of theirs."*

Embarrassed, Daisuke grumbled, "How was I supposed to know? I didn't even think there *was* a planting ritual."

Ignoring him, she gently continued, *"As you are a descendant of the flowering region, the Raven God will be happy to bless your red poppies. The raven feather and this meditation will carry your wishes to him."*

He sighed with relief. The wolf appeared as though she wanted to tell him more, but inexplicably froze. Hackles raised, her snout wrinkled as a deep growl rumbled in her throat and she bared long, sharp fangs. It was the most vicious Daisuke had seen her since the night she'd rescued him from Grandmaster Norio's hounds. Without warning, the Okami spirit leapt to all fours and darted toward the dense woodlands, her figure dissipating into nothingness before she reached the thicket's edge.

"Wait!" Daisuke called after her, though no one responded—creepy silence filled the air, and he remembered what she said about demons not always taking kindly to nature spirits. Perhaps Tatakai had scared her off after all.

He took a deep breath and tried to release himself from the vision, but no matter how many attempts he made in bringing himself back to reality, the meditation wouldn't end. A chill slithered down his spine when he sensed his surroundings had somehow changed. When he turned around again, the forest had turned from full and living to gnarled, decaying trees which were parted to reveal a dark, foreboding path. The sunlight had vanished along with the wolf spirit.

As if startled awake, searing heat flared against Daisuke's wrist, and seconds later came a flicker of green light. He stared up at Tatakai's massive form helplessly as the dragon floated above him in the air, long white hair billowing behind him as oppressive gray clouds passed by.

"H-how are you here? This is supposed to be a Northern Nomadic ritual."

A large, curved claw drew a circle over his head, but when he gave the dragon demon an inquisitive look, smoke blew into his face. Daisuke coughed and waved it away as Tatakai replied, "Your kind naturally have high spiritual energy, and the Raven God's realm is a paper-thin one between life and spirits, as proven by your dreams and his Oracles. And all souls share the Between Realm. As such, you and your friend—whose energy is far steadier than yours—accidentally made a bridge, and broke into this place of much darker energy. You can sense it, can't you?"

Daisuke mutely nodded—how could he not? Without the white wolf to suppress it, the energy surrounding him had rapidly become overwhelming, heavy, and ominous.

Tatakai retreated toward the black bracelets once more, his form shrinking until he was like a tiny ghost clinging onto them with his tail. If the situation were any different, Daisuke might've laughed at how hilarious the proud, powerful demon looked now.

"You shouldn't be detected, but proceed with caution," the demon sternly warned in a way that seemed oddly concerned. "Two of my siblings are close, and I sense immense resentment in both—it must be the blood-bond they've been sworn to."

Daisuke had been staring down at the trail, but, alarmed, whipped his head in Tatakai's direction at the announcement. However, when he looked, the demon had already disappeared into the bracelets again, leaving him alone to face the trail's pitch-black maw once again. He took a slow, deep breath to steady himself, then crept toward the waiting forest.

The moment he stepped onto the path, his surroundings shifted once more. He was standing on what appeared to be an old stone square of sorts, and everything was dark, as if it were taking place in the shadow of a towering structure. His heartrate and breathing quickened, but still, Daisuke tried not to make a sound. A strange pattern he couldn't quite make out was drawn on the ground, and from all around, cloaked figures lurked on its edges, forming an unbreakable barrier and trapping him inside the circle. It was as if he were completely transparent. No one seemed to notice him as their voices droned in a hypnotic, indistinct chant accompanied by the even beats of unseen drums.

Hysterical screams suddenly tore through the deepening twilight, broken only by the man's begging and pleading, chilling Daisuke to the bone.

He jumped when a hand gripped his shoulder, but when he worked up the courage to see who'd joined him, he found Obito. His wide eyes were fixed on the scene unfolding before them, nearly unblinking with shock; if one looked close, they'd notice the quiver in his fingers as they tightened on his partner. Relieved he wasn't about to be dragged into whatever disturbing ritual this was, Daisuke shrank against his friend, and they held each other as well as their breath, as if bracing for the down-burst of a violent storm before it passed.

The cries abruptly ended with a sickening, strangled yelp, but the chanting continued as if nothing happened. Petrified, Daisuke and Obito helplessly watched as blood pooled on the stones.

A woman's rich voice confidently called out over the clangor, "Kanashimi, Saigai, beloved Demons of the Between Realm, the Shadow Priestess summons thee."

Two bright jade green lights appeared on each side of Daisuke's periphery, but he didn't dare look, as the call of both names sent an icy shiver through his entire body. A flute began to play, and shadows arose from the circle like a thick miasma. Purple lightning crackled underneath. The cloaked figures standing around him took a slight step back with one foot, but piercing flute notes kept playing, unceasing like the drums and chants.

"Now, Shadow Priestess!" another called. Heart in his throat, Daisuke buried his face in Obito's chest rather than search for the voice's owner. When he felt brave enough, he peeked at the center of the circle, where only the silhouette of a human form was visible.

"Tatakai, Demon of War!" the woman shouted to the heavens. "Kanashimi and Saigai summon thee!"

A tremor rumbled beneath Daisuke's feet; he pressed himself closer to Obito. The shadows swarming the ground were pulled toward the middle, then surged outward in a violent wave of black dust and violet lightning, scattering across the land in every possible direction. Everything went dark.

Daisuke gasped as his eyes flew wide open to reality once more, then locked onto Obito's, whose slightly ashen face mirrored his shocked expression—without a doubt, he'd also seen everything. After a moment, they looked away from one another, mainly at the blades of grass swaying near their knees, both unsure if and how they should comment on what they'd just witnessed. Clammy with a cold sweat, Daisuke searched for anything he could use to ground himself, and eventually found his red poppy sprouts.

Another, softer gasp escaped him.

"Obito," he said quietly, worried he'd scare them into shriveling up again if he spoke too loudly, and that his voice would betray his confused emotions. Gods, it was all he could do not to cry. "Look."

Obito's eyes fell on the pot, then quickly went back to Daisuke's face, clearly in disbelief. Within the meditation's time, the small, sickly shoots had become healthy, sturdy stems sporting buds, ready to bloom.

A few days later, the poppies miraculously flowered in abundance. Daisuke quickly set to work with Obito, sneaking into the poisons room late at night to avoid classmates while harvesting seeds and to milk opium from the poppies' ovaries in peace. Tension hung in the air between them, as it had since the meditation prayer closed, not helped by the characteristic silence his partner had lapsed into. Usually, it meant he needed time to think something through, whether it was a problem or an emotion, but Daisuke's patience could be difficult to wrangle whenever Obito acted like this. Currently, he found it damn near impossible.

I guess I'm not being fair, am I? Although Daisuke was plenty accustomed to strange visions due to the nature of his dreams, he knew Obito was not, and the real-world implications of what they'd seen made it much more terrifying than anything he'd encountered before. It was one thing to be *told* they were dealing with demons—observing what it meant firsthand was a different experience altogether. Never mind the frightening power of the woman who had invoked the spell. He likely needed space to make sense of it all.

What little of it there is, Daisuke mentally added. He sure as hell didn't understand what they'd witnessed on solstice night. Unfortunately, this hadn't made any attempts to talk to his friend about Tatakai easier. He'd hoped that telling Obito about Mika's unwanted kiss would've lent courage to this situation, or a somewhat natural way to lead into it, but his voice lodged in his throat every time he tried to mention the dragon demon sleeping in the new bracelet on his right wrist.

It didn't help that the race to complete an antidote for Master Yujin had since taken immense precedence to everything else, as their superior's patience clearly thinned each time he'd called them in for report at the end of every week. He likely couldn't keep the new poison a secret from Emperor Akuwara much longer. So, most of their time had become dedicated to reading whatever they could find relating to botanicals, medicines, or providing them with a potential substitute outside of the opium family. Daisuke could've laughed if it didn't make him want to cuss out the heavens themselves. So much misdirected effort, just for a bit of meditation to be the answer.

They'd been working for hours in total quiet, save for the scraping of metal tools and delicate *clink* of glass vials. Upon realizing how confusing the whole situation was, and just how much it must've taken for Obito to abandon logic to help him in the first place, Daisuke set down the scalpel in his left hand and wiped his forehead with his right. He leaned forward on his elbows and sighed into his hands. Should his partner have chosen to walk away from the project—or worse, him—he would've understood entirely, even if it hurt.

Obito paused and glanced at the diagram Daisuke had propped up in front of them on the worktable, which was thankfully taken from a book rather than drawn by his friend's hand. He understood this was a delicate operation, and had been following his instructions with extreme care to avoid wasting a single drop of the precious red poppy opium. "Did I do something wrong?"

"No, not even close." Daisuke bit his lip, then turned to his partner. Unable to maintain eye contact, he instead settled for looking at the numerous vials they'd already filled with blackwater's antidote. "I don't think I properly thanked you for helping me the other day...or for trusting me through any of this. I made a huge fucking mess, and you haven't said a word against me this whole time."

"Why would I?" Obito's brows furrowed, and he also set his tools aside so he could face him better. "It's not your fault Mika took your journal. He knows better. Besides, you're my friend—I won't speak against you unless you *actually* deserve it."

Daisuke laughed, and, giving into impulse, tightly wrapped his arms around him. "Thank you."

Obito rolled his eyes. As much as he might try to resist acknowledging it, he recognized the flutter in his chest as fondness, though he didn't think he'd ever be ready to confront the seemingly boundless depth behind it. Nothing would ever be the same if he did.

"Enough. Let's get these ready for Master Yujin to store somewhere."

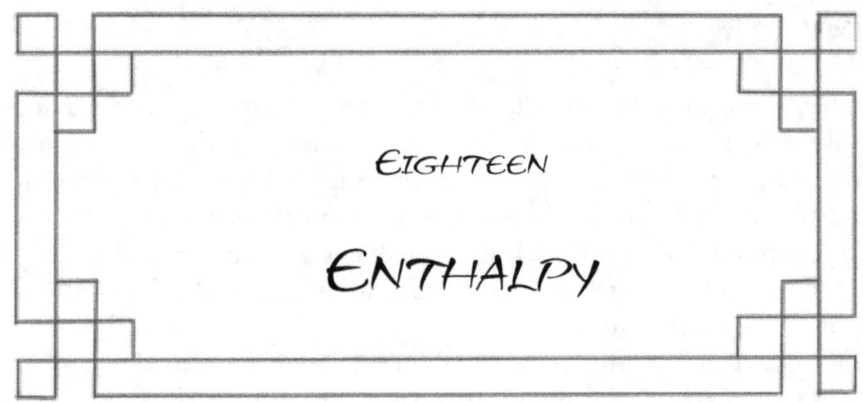

TATAKAI GREW INCREASINGLY RESTLESS in the days following the solstice prayer, frequently alerting Daisuke with small burns to the inner wrist that left no mark as he and Obito continued working on the blackwater antidote. His dreams—during the few opportunities for sleep he could get—didn't help, as those were becoming inundated with the demon's image, to the point where anxiety weighed on his chest as soon as that ominous green glow appeared. There was something urgent happening. What, Daisuke couldn't say, and it seemed Tatakai couldn't properly communicate it without being summoned. If the Demon of War was worried, it had to be important, but he didn't want to meet with the dragon again until his partner could join the conversation. He just had to find the right time.

Fortunately, such an opportunity came once they'd produced as much of the blackwater antidote as they could make from the red poppies—Daisuke had also, by some miracle, remembered Retsuko's request for some red poppy ointment, and had enough left over to make a little for her and himself. After dinner, on the same evening they'd corked the last vial of antidote and stored the crate away in Obito's room, Daisuke turned to his friend with a half-hearted version of his usual devious grin. They'd just enjoyed discussing a few outlandish scenarios conjured by their equally sleep-deprived minds, so he figured one more couldn't hurt before they had a chance to make their way upstairs.

"While we're on the subject of wild things, you wouldn't happen to know somewhere we'll be left alone, do you?"

"I do." Obito shot him a—rightfully—suspicious glance. "But why?"

Daisuke bit his lip and fiddled with the second bracelet on his right wrist, intentionally ignoring the one where Tatakai slept, silent as he struggled to find the best words. "I have something to show you."

They stopped in the middle of the corridor. Obito's eyes searched Daisuke's face, not in a way indicative of mistrust or doubt, but in a manner which conveyed a deep concern through the usual sternness that settled into his expression by default. Most couldn't look past the first layer to see his underlying emotions, but Daisuke knew Obito better than they did. After a moment of this wordless exchange, Obito nodded and waved for Daisuke to follow him.

Obito had once—quite cleverly, in Daisuke's opinion—made a map of several secret passages or tunnels burrowed within the Palace walls. He'd lost it a couple of years back, and though he'd yet to make a new one like he'd wanted, he had several of these pathways memorized; he could navigate them with ease. After a while of crawling or walking through the seemingly endless network of tunnels, he eventually brought them through one that led to a long-abandoned office which was locked from the inside. The desk was in ill repair, and the lone source of light came from a tiny, dust and cobweb covered window, but a small fireplace still held old coals. After taking a minute to observe their surroundings, Daisuke grabbed one and placed it in Obito's hand.

"Do you think you can draw the sealing circle in here? I know I've probably been acting distracted lately—"

"—I hadn't noticed."

"Liar," Daisuke laughed. "But I think this is the easiest way to clear a few things up. Do you remember the good luck charm I showed you? The one you said looked like a talisman?"

Wary, Obito nodded.

"And you trust me?"

"...You know I do." Obito sighed, still looking skeptical, then cleared dust off a patch on the stone floor and got to work. The last time he'd drawn the circle was for the dead body he'd found while on patrol; since the infantry hadn't reported the death as suspicious, he still hadn't mentioned it to anyone, especially not his partner. Even so, the symbol's markings were distinct, and he pictured it more frequently than he cared to admit. Although this was only his third time, he could draw it with ease.

He set the chunk of coal aside when he was satisfied with his work and glanced over his shoulder at his friend. Daisuke hesitated, then knelt beside him at the edge of the completed circle before he removed the first bracelet from his wrist. He paused again, then haltingly set it inside the symbol's center. Obito inhaled sharply and drew back when it emitted a jade green glow before it started to change shape, but his eyes were soon drawn to more movement from Daisuke, who was leaning over the circle with the tip of his tanto pointed at his right hand.

"What the hell are you doing?" Obito worriedly grabbed his wrist, sending the dagger to the ground; fortunately, it didn't interfere with the charcoal markings when it landed.

Daisuke instinctively jerked in his grasp, but didn't pull his arm away. "This ritual needs my blood to work. You'll understand in a second, I promise!"

"...You *hate* the sight of blood—look at how much you're shaking." Obito slowly eased his grip when he realized he was still holding onto his friend, then finally released him. He sighed, unsure which part of the situation it was intended for. "Does it need to be *your* blood?"

"As far as I know."

Obito went quiet for a moment, then carefully retrieved his friend's dagger when he realized how determined Daisuke was to go through with this. Clearly, he had his reasons; the energy emanating from the talisman was palpable, now, as if anticipating the offering about to be made. "You'll cut your fingers off at this rate. Hold out your hand and look away. I'll be as gentle as I can."

Daisuke blushed—the offer was an incredibly, if not oddly, sweet gesture that he probably shouldn't have found as endearing as he did. He trusted Obito as implicitly as the inverse, so doing as he was instructed came without a second thought or worry. He did them both a favor by closing his eyes tight; he didn't want to think about how close the knifepoint was to his skin or panic at the last second. He hissed at a sharp poke into the pad of his right index finger, but didn't open his eyes again until he felt Obito pull his arm toward the center of the circle. Obito gave him another uncertain look before he squeezed Daisuke's fingertip to let the little bulb of blood drip onto the talisman's surface. As before, the letters of Tatakai's name and a long, winding dragon appeared in red.

"Lazy fucking garden snake," Daisuke swore when nothing else happened. "Wait, he didn't come out the first time until after I said his name...really? You need me to be formal with you? Fine. Tatakai, *Demon of War* who wields Hikari's tenacity, I summon thee."

"Name-calling and being sarcastic with an ancient deity somehow sounds like a bad plan, Daisuke," Obito said under his breath, hoping it'd disguise his nerves.

Anything else he might've said was cut off by a flash of bright green light and a plume of smoke that choked the air and consumed the scant lighting. When he looked again, he scrambled to his feet as fear invaded his chest. A dragon with flowing white hair and golden eyes stared at them from the inside of the circle, robes billowing around it. His partner more slowly got to his feet and joined him as the dragon demon shook its massive head, as if it'd just rolled out of bed.

"The other side of the bridge," Tatakai sleepily rumbled as he peered at Obito, who barely remembered to back away when the demon leaned in for a better look. His serpentine eyes narrowed, suddenly sharp and alert. "And a soul I recognize."

"I heard the bridge part during the meditation prayer, but what does the 'soul you recognize' thing mean?" Daisuke's genuine curiosity sliced through the tension, causing both his partner and the dragon demon to turn their gazes on him; Obito never looked so relieved over him causing a distraction.

Tatakai shook his massive head. "An explanation for another time. You may be surprised to hear it, but I am happy you summoned me, as I must tell you something urgent. The ritual you witnessed during your prayer to the Raven God was an attempt to summon me, as you surely noticed, but it also means someone *is* intentionally gathering my siblings, likely for some sort of personal gain. That ritual failed because I am already bound to you, and because there were not enough of us present to perform it, but even so, I believe my two siblings who were already awakened *have* sensed me. To make things worse, one of my other siblings *was* roused by the ritual. Toward the north, in a place you humans named 'Baohu' in ancient times."

Daisuke and Obito looked at each other sharply.

"I see the name has not changed."

"What do you mean, 'another' of your siblings?" Obito asked, voice barely staying steady as his eyes darted between Daisuke and Tatakai.

"There's six of these talismans. One for each of the demons we read about," Daisuke explained; Obito hadn't gotten as much time with the book as originally planned, but he *had* been pointed toward the passage mentioning the demons as the Between Realm's caretakers. "The Shadow Priestess has two—the ones holding Kanashimi and Saigai, which was the whole reason she attacked us in Zhu. Turns out, Tatakai was in the one I got from General Aki."

"Which is the same one *Hideo* delivered to General Aki, but the Shadow Priestess clearly wants all six of the talismans for herself. She—or the Servant—must've been using Hideo to get General Aki on her side for whatever reason, and planned to take this one back as soon as she had him going along with her."

"*Why*, though?"

"We'll have to track down Hideo to ask—we both know my uncle won't be any help."

A loud rumble came from within the sealing circle, causing both boys to jump as they remembered the glowing green dragon curled inside of it. Tatakai's eyes were pinned to them as they went back and forth, miffed about how easily they'd forgotten him—not that Daisuke blamed him. He imagined he'd also be quite annoyed if, as an immortal spirit, he was so easily ignored by two mortal teenagers. Obito froze once more when the dragon leaned toward them again.

"If you're quite through," Tatakai said. "I'd advise haste in getting to Baohu. If one of us has slept there all this time and was—rudely, I might add—awakened by a failed ritual, there's no telling what sort of damage has been done. My sibling must be sealed once more and then summoned properly, if they're to be called upon at all. It'd be wiser to let us sleep, though such a request doesn't appear to be something your adversaries are willing to entertain."

Daisuke had leaned over the circle with his hand hovering over one of the tomoe, but froze at the word "adversary." Enemy. They hadn't experienced anything as direct as the encounter in Zhu, so he'd struggled to view the Shadow Priestess as an active threat, but a glance at Obito told him his partner had likely, quietly, harbored the same sentiment as the dragon demon for a while. Perhaps this was the confirmation they'd both needed to realize they were, yet again, entirely fucked.

"Does this mean you won't help us?" Daisuke asked.

"Since I have not been awake for long and my power is still quite weak, I would rather not, as I cannot predict what might happen if I call upon my abilities. But, it seems I may not have a choice. That being said, you two will need to do most of the work." Tatakai kept his gaze on them for a few minutes, then sighed, plumes of smoke puffing from each nostril. "Please, release the summons. This is exhausting, and I will need the rest if I'm to do anything. Your path becomes more dangerous from here."

"Thank you, Tatakai."

Daisuke obediently ran his hand through the markings, dispelling the summoning as he'd been asked, and allowing the demon to leave. It happened so fast that the pair barely noticed, but a transparent image of the great dragon cupping his clawed hands and bowing appeared before he was gone. Once Tatakai retreated, Obito wordlessly stared at the talisman until Daisuke scraped it off the floor and it returned to the form of his other bracelet, which finally shook him from his daze. Daisuke started messing more of the charcoal lines he'd drawn, but stopped when he noticed his partner silently walking toward the entrance to the passage they'd taken.

"Wait, where are you going?" he called after him.

"Drinking." Obito turned with a scowl when Daisuke rushed toward him. "*Without* you."

"Like hell!" Daisuke cackled and latched onto his arm.

LADY SHADOW LOOKED UP at a pensive Kanashimi as they lounged beside the pond together, enjoying the warm summer air and a quiet evening filled with crickets and frogs singing to the moon and stars. It'd been a while—too long, perhaps—since she'd enjoyed time with her favorite companion in such a manner, but something about the demon's silence loomed heavily over an otherwise perfect setting. Kanashimi hadn't said a word the entire time; they only watched the moon's reflection as it rippled now and then in the light breeze.

While Saigai, Kanashimi, and even Natsumi had agreed that murdering Giichi was their best course of action—they couldn't let someone who did such things to children be around the few youngsters in the cult—and thought he should've had plenty of blood to sacrifice for the summoning ritual, they'd yet to see signs of Tatakai. Somewhere in her heart, Lady Shadow knew this to be what bothered her companion so deeply.

"The ritual failed, didn't it?" she softly inquired.

Kanashimi nodded slowly. "Saigai is correct when he calls Tatakai lazy, but not even his vast stubbornness could have helped him fight the compulsion a successful ritual should have created. I worry for my brother—whose hands he may have fallen into. But, I shouldn't despair, as there might be some good news to come from this. It seems as though our ceremony may have reached another one of my siblings—I sense someone near Baohu, though I'm not sure who. If it is Wenyi or Hinkon, it will be an immense advantage, as they are usually near one another. If we have one, we will find the other soon."

Lady Shadow carefully weighed their options. "We'll still carry out Giichi's plan—it should create a distraction and buy us some time to reach Baohu unnoticed. His youngest son is enlisted with intelligence. We can use him to distribute the poison, as Giichi planned, and to figure out if the two onmitsu we encountered are still around since I haven't heard from Haruki, either."

"You killed the nobleman over his actions toward one of those boys, yet are quite set on ensuring their deaths."

"They're nearly men at this point," Lady Shadow flippantly countered. Still, she knew it was a weak argument even as she pushed aside the guilt Kanashimi's point brought up, as well as the mental image of a woman's beautiful face with clever, forest green eyes, which ought to have stayed deeply buried in her past. She cleared her throat. "B-besides, it's as I said to Haruki months ago. If the Intelligence Master believes them even for a second, our goals are in danger."

"Is that so?" Kanashimi's serpentine eyes narrowed, as if conflicting, unexpected emotions had arisen within them. However, whatever those misgivings might've been remained unspoken, as they humbly bowed their head after a moment. "Then, I am once more at your service, Priestess."

A FEW SHORT WEEKS ago, Obito never would've imagined he'd follow the instructions of a demon—he still wasn't quite sure he could wrap his head around it. However, there was little sense in denying what he'd witnessed with his own eyes over the last several days between the meditation vision and coming face-to-face with a deity of the Between Realm. When coupled with the shadow magic that had separated him and Daisuke in Zhu, this seemed like the most natural course for things to take. Part of him resented such thinking, but ultimately, he surrendered to it and had since taken a more practical approach to drawing the summoning symbol. Art wasn't his strongest skill, but *one* of them had to do it as easily as writing their names. Daisuke's sketches were hilariously awful, which he immensely enjoyed pointing out to his friend, but they weren't intentionally done that way—pitiful as they looked, he really did try.

With that, and an experimental method for using the design in mind, he'd begun constructing several paper talismans with the symbol drawn on them. If he was right, meditating over the papers would help them gain the spiritual energy needed to be useful, and would be much more efficient than trying to find room to draw it every time, especially if they found themselves in a situation lacking the space for it. Moreover, it allowed them to do what they needed without leaving anything behind.

Obito rolled his eyes when the page he'd been working on flapped in the wind yet again.

"Daisuke, stop that."

"What? The fan doesn't feel good?"

"Just—it keeps moving the page on me."

"Come on, you've been at it long enough."

"And I'm almost done, now back up. It's hot."

Deciding not to provoke his friend further, Daisuke did as he was asked and settled for using the purple folding fan on himself instead. They'd retreated into the shade provided by the wall guarding the Palace grounds to escape responsibilities and the summer heat, surrounded by the earthy scent of long grasses and dandelions; thankfully, the last traces of the wine they'd drank the night before were already gone by the time he awoke in the late morning, slightly lessening his misery at the weather. Dozing off together in the fresh air until they'd roused again not long ago likely helped, too.

"Are you just grumpy because I finally got you to drink with me, then passed out on you last night?" he teased, cackling when he received the deadliest of glares he thought he'd ever seen from his partner. Whether Obito was flushing from the heat or something else, Daisuke didn't think he'd ever know.

Obito cleared his throat and put his things away in the leather satchel Daisuke had brought along, signaling how desperately he wanted to change the subject. "When Master Yujin wants the update about Zhu, we should tell him about Baohu."

"What luck," an unfamiliar voice commented menacingly, drawing their attention to a young man with a pockmarked face standing only a few yards away with Yuki and Masaki behind him. He sneered. "Nakamura and Akahana?"

"Present," Daisuke quipped.

Unamused, the newcomer scowled at him, though Daisuke easily recognized the type of disgust also lining his features; yet another fuck who didn't think he belonged here. "I've been searching for at least an hour—it should *never* be so difficult to locate a team of operatives when the Intelligence Master could require your presence at a moment's notice."

"We're off-duty today," Obito interjected, bringing the focus of the interloper's disdainful, hate-filled expression onto himself as he handed Daisuke the satchel and got to his feet. He took a moment to harshly size up the other young man dressed in a black onmitsu uniform with golden-yellow accents in his shitagi and belt. "Besides, I don't believe we've met."

"My name is Ewah, Master Yujin's chosen apprentice."

Daisuke and Obito stole a glance at one another when he also stood. "Wouldn't that make you—"

"Future Master of Intelligence, correct. You will address me as Second Master from now on." Ewah's countenance somehow became even more grim as he studied the skeptical and unimpressed faces they wore at the announcement. "If you're through wasting my time, Master Yujin needs you. He says it's time to turn in *all* of your work—whatever that means."

Cheerful bastard, aren't you? Daisuke barely managed to keep the remark to himself.

Much to his partner's confusion, Yuki was too afraid of Obito to ever look at him directly, but he cowered behind his teammate more than usual and didn't seem as if he dared to speak. Usually, he could muster the bravery to say at least a few words. Daisuke's eyes raked over to Masaki. Though he was normally the more enthusiastic of the pair, even he seemed quite downtrodden from following Ewah around; it was depressing to see two young onmitsu looking so glum. In his opinion, he already knew everything he needed about this future Master of Intelligence, and the type of leadership he would bring to the position. He didn't like any of it.

Ewah insisted on acting as an escort while they retrieved the crate filled with blackwater antidote from where it'd been stored on the desk in Obito's room, which clearly whittled away at Obito's patience with the whole situation. Daisuke watched his friend's expression carefully the entire time; not a single word passed between the group, but none were necessary. He thought it'd be wise if Ewah learned—quickly, ideally—how easily acting like an ass would get him on his partner's bad side. It was a place *he* sure as hell never hoped to find himself; despite their differences in rank and power, Obito undoubtedly had his own ways of making Ewah's life as Intelligence Master miserable.

These thoughts relentlessly swarmed in his mind, but Daisuke managed to behave and keep his mouth shut all the way to Master Yujin's office—he'd annoy Obito into praising him for it later.

All that calm and decorum fled his body when they crossed into Master Yujin's office.

"General Aki!" Daisuke called out excitedly, forgetting himself and rushing over to the older man. He hadn't seen the General since his transfer to onmitsu from infantry, but when he realized how dire a situation must be to have an unexpected reunion in Master Yujin's study, he remembered to step back and keep his composure.

Even so, the General greeted him with a fond smile and inclined his head slightly. "It's good to see you, too, lad. You're looking well. I have to say, though, I thought you would've grown more by now."

"Actually, sir, you should know I'm getting *very* tall for a Northern Nomad."

At nearly five-and-a-half feet in height, it was true, but that didn't stop Obito—who was getting closer to six feet tall every day—from laughing at his argument. He looked away as soon as Daisuke rounded on him with a glare. They both froze when Ewah firmly nudged Daisuke with his shoulder as he passed, which made a dangerous expression flash through Obito's eyes as he watched the oldest of the three.

"Daisuke, Obito," Master Yujin said in warning from behind his desk, though his gaze was also on his apprentice, who pointedly pretended he didn't know it also applied to him. "By the look of things, I trust you have a suitable antidote?"

Frustrated, Daisuke flushed and turned to the Intelligence Master.

"Yes, sir. Turns out, red poppy opium is a bit thicker than normal opium, so the conversion was a little tricky, but it worked even better in the antidote than the other stuff." He passed a vial of foggy red liquid to Master Yujin while Obito set the crate filled with the others on his desk. Up until their reprieve the previous night, the pair had spent the last few days working constantly to make an acceptable amount of the blackwater antidote with a couple hours of sleep here and there on the benches in the poisons room.

"By the skin of your teeth, Daisuke," Master Yujin murmured as he rolled the vial in his palm. "But it's hard to argue with results—I hope you wrote this down."

He flinched, but Obito was quick to place a sheet of parchment in front of their superior.

"I did. He was busy."

Master Yujin looked over the sheet, hummed, and placed it on top of the vials in the crate. Daisuke sighed with relief—making an official record of the antidote had been the last thing on his mind while they were busy with it. After things had calmed down, whenever he thought of how easily the poison recipe had been stolen from under his nose, he couldn't force himself to make a single brushstroke as shame and rage consumed him all over again. Seeing Obito cover this for him made something frighteningly close to affection wriggle in his chest.

"Now, then," the Intelligence Master called his attention once more. "You've had some time to think while pulling this together. Have your convictions changed?"

"I—" Daisuke swallowed and helplessly glanced at Obito, who nodded his silent encouragement to proceed. "I know I don't have solid proof, sir, but I still believe it was Mika."

Master Yujin's eyes widened, though not out of surprise; shattered hope quickly passed through his expression just before he schooled it. Now composed, he sternly told his student, "That's an extremely serious accusation."

"It is, sir, but as we reported, Mika acted suspiciously the whole time we were in Nishinuma, and he's always copying my notes, even when they don't make sense. Aside from that, though, he and Obito are the only two who previously knew about my journal. It just makes too much sense."

"We're also firm in our belief that his father might be involved in something tied to the magic we encountered in Zhu." Obito usually refused to offer an opinion during any discussion involving his uncle or cousin; although he was uncomfortable adding one now as he'd be any other time, he wouldn't let Daisuke defend his stance alone. "We don't have solid proof of that, either, but it would provide a motive for why Mika stole the journal. What my cousin and I both lack in poison-making, Daisuke more than makes up for."

"So, you believe Giichi Tanaka, a considerably well-off nobleman with no previous suspicious activity, joined with some unknown entity, asked his son to provide him with a poison, and then had it mass-produced in Nishinuma?" Master Yujin rubbed his temples.

"Anyone can make it sound like a conspiracy when they say it that way," Daisuke muttered. Obito reflexively placed a hand over his partner's mouth to keep him from digging their graves any deeper. He caught the rising contempt in Ewah's face, but pretended the future Master of Intelligence wasn't looking at them.

Master Yujin rose from his seat and slowly strode toward his office window, hands behind his back as his brows furrowed over his dark eyes. He didn't speak for a long while; neither subordinate was brave enough to move from where they'd become anchored to the floor as they watched him tensely. Finally, his chest heaved with a slow, deep sigh, and he looked at them from over his shoulder.

"There is another matter at hand," he said quietly as he crossed the room once more.

Daisuke nervously scanned the room once Ewah joined Master Yujin at his side. Although the Intelligence Master returned to his desk, he didn't take a seat. With his most direct subordinate standing at perfect attention, and on the other end of his desk, General Aki also waiting with his hands behind his back, and two younger onmitsu effectively guarding the door, he couldn't help but feel they were on trial. He glanced at his partner, desperate for reassurance; when their eyes met, Obito breathed slowly, a sign for Daisuke to do the same.

Sensing the mounting tension he'd accidentally created, Master Yujin looked at each man in the room, then finally addressed his two older pupils. "General Aki agreed to stay for this meeting in case the infantry needs to be mobilized. But, as I've given you several months, I need an update on what happened to the artifact in Zhu."

Obito cleared his throat, uneasy about their provable findings and relying on a conversation with a demon, of all things. "We've determined the missing artifact isn't of Okami origin—it's likely a religious object from Perena's ancient times. Our research on it has brought us to Baohu."

The Intelligence Master's eyes narrowed. "What aren't you boys telling me?"

"Nothing we don't know for certain," Daisuke intervened, evidently too quickly for Ewah's liking, as his scarred upper lip curled into a sneer before the room descended into an unsettling quiet. Nervous, he glanced at Obito again, then forged ahead. "But we need to investigate some old grounds in Baohu if we want to get any further with this. With your permission, sir, we'd like to leave as soon as possible."

Although pensive, General Aki was the first to break the second wave of heavy silence which followed. "Daisuke, does this have anything to do with that odd good luck charm you found while you were still in the infantry?"

"Yes, sir." Daisuke was relieved; the General might not know about the demons of the Between Realm, but he sure as hell knew to suspect anything Hideo did.

"I see. We've recently lost contact with the infantry outpost in Baohu, which was originally what I came here to report before I agreed to stay." The General paused, then grinned at Master Yujin. "This settles it in my mind. If you boys were under my command, you'd be leaving immediately."

Master Yujin pinched the bridge of his nose. "Very well, then. If this is all you can really tell me for now, I dismiss you and grant your request to travel. But because it's such short notice, you'll be on your own financially. We can discuss reimbursement when you come back."

"'If,'" Obito muttered, rolling his eyes.

"Master," Ewah began coldly. "Are you sure this is wise?"

"As future Intelligence Master, you need to learn as early as possible that you must trust your subordinates to know what they're doing without constantly peering over their shoulders. Whether you admit it to yourself or not, sometimes, their failures will also be yours." Master Yujin pointedly looked at the two standing before him. "Let this be an example of that. General Aki, do you have anything else to add?"

"Baohu is a key city for northbound shipments of goods—I'd advise you to make use of infantry aid should you need it rather than pestering Senator Yumio. He's a good man, but extremely busy." General Aki paused thoughtfully. "One of my soldiers should be somewhere along Yingxiong Pass to deliver supplies to Baohu's barracks. If you see him, tell him to give you a ride."

"How about a game instead?"

"Forget it." Obito rolled his eyes and kept going along the trail. Although the hot and humid weather wasn't nearly as oppressive this far into the mountains, it was still enough to make both of them miserable; neither seemed to fare well after a certain temperature. He knew a firm rejection would stun Daisuke into silence, but wasn't sure how long it'd take for his partner to realize they'd already begun playing. Either way, a period of quiet was a hard-won but brief victory, so he decided to enjoy it while it lasted—he could already hear the little pest jogging to catch up with him.

"W-wait! I'll let you pick which one!" Daisuke all but begged.

There it is, Obito thought as an exasperated, if not fond, smile touched his lips. He slowed his gait to keep in stride with Daisuke and turned to him. "It really does kill you to keep quiet, doesn't it?"

"Please?"

Obito opened his mouth to object, but he understood that any argument he made would only convince Daisuke to keep grinding away at his willpower. Even though he knew better, he caved. "Fine. One game, but *only* if you promise to be quiet until we get to Kyoshu."

"And the others think you're no fun." Daisuke's impish grin unabashedly filled with smug pride as he turned to start walking backwards, impressed with Obito's ability to refrain from shoving him into the juniper shrubs lining Yingxiong Pass. "Here, I have a copper in my pocket. If it lands on blossoms, you can dare me to do something. If I refuse, I have to tell you the truth."

"What if I dare you to stop talking?"

"Against the rules."

"That hardly seems fair."

Daisuke cackled. "Fine, fine. To be honest, I was hoping I could trick you into telling me who you're interested in."

"Did you just *admit* to being annoying?" Obito glanced at him, then quickly looked away again when he realized how warm his face felt and how relentlessly his heart thundered against his ribs. "What makes you think I'm interested in anyone?"

"Obito, we're fifteen."

"And? We both know that doesn't mean anything."

"Please?"

"No." Obito sighed in defeat, mumbling after a pause, "You know them."

"That's all I get?!" Daisuke burst into laughter again, despite a poor attempt at sounding outraged.

Obito was about to say something else, but the familiar, almost frantic sounding clatter of wagon wheels and pounding of horse hooves rose into the air from behind him. He turned when Daisuke stopped in his tracks and squinted at the path behind them, eyes going wide when he saw that he barely had time to get out of the way. Obito grabbed Daisuke by the sleeve and pulled them both off to the side of the trail as a foul-tempered horse and its panicking owner, desperately calling for it to stop, heed, *something* to slow down, came over the hill. The wagon finally slowed as the two onmitsu cautiously stepped onto the road again. The horse snorted and tossed its head as the driver uttered a few calming phrases; the animal didn't seem convinced by his words in the slightest, but it didn't take off again. As the young man holding the reins had seen them as he came over the hill, he already had an apology on his tongue when he could turn to look at them.

"My deepest—wait, I know you two!" the driver exclaimed, then yanked on the startled horse's reins.

Daisuke peered up at the young man and threw his head back with a groan. "Junpei?! Why?!"

"General Aki *did* say he had someone along this road," Obito quietly reminded him, earning a scowl.

"What are you doing up this way?" Junpei leaned over as much as he could without falling from the driver's seat.

"Demon hunting."

"Daisuke." Obito rolled his eyes.

"What? It's honest."

Junpei's brows furrowed in an unconvinced expression; it seemed as if he halfway believed Daisuke, but didn't *want* to, let alone say as much.

Before the two onmitsu could note his pause, he settled on giving them a nervous laugh.

Obito decided to further intervene, preventing Daisuke or Junpei from antagonizing each other. "We could ask you the same. Aren't you stationed in Zhu?"

Junpei winced. "Bit of a story, there. Meet me up ahead at the Guang-shu Inn in Kyoshu and I'll explain over a drink."

With that, the young man snapped his horse's reins again, and after much protest, the animal and the cart lurched forward once more.

Daisuke and Obito looked up at the towering building, shaded by even taller pines and cedars stretching over its highest roof. Kyoshu was one of the largest and wealthiest towns along the well-populated Yingxiong Pass, but neither onmitsu expected to find an elaborate structure such as the Guangshu Inn; few inns within the Capital were constructed with the pride and elegance of this place's exterior. Going in suddenly became more intimidating when they shifted their gazes to the cotton curtain hanging from the door frame, swaying easily in the summer breeze that made its cherry blossom pattern dance in the wind.

Daisuke grimaced. "Leave it to Junpei to pick a place like this—I can hear the condescending nobles and merchants from here."

"We already agreed to meet him." Obito sighed; it wasn't as if his opinion on the soldier differed that much. Finally, he started toward the entrance, and Daisuke was on his heels within half a heartbeat.

"Did we, though?" he countered.

"I think even *you* aren't so stubborn to argue with a ride to Baohu at this point."

"And *I* thought *you* knew better than to challenge me like that."

"Remind me how your feet feel, Daisuke." Obito gave him a knowing smirk; if *his* feet ached, his partner's also had to be throbbing from all the rough terrain they'd covered—and slept on—over the last few days during this part of their journey. The Yingxiong Pass was well-maintained and equally well-traveled, but it cut through a mountain, a fact no amount of grooming or upkeep on the road could change. Some parts of the pass were still steep and rocky.

Daisuke looked as if he was ready to retort, but after a moment, he settled for rolling his eyes and shot his partner a final, grumpy scowl before pulling the soft white curtain aside so they could enter.

Guangshu Inn was as pleasant on the inside as it'd been from the main path. Their boots didn't stick to an unknown substance on the floor, the front room was clean, open, and the smell lingering in the air came from sandalwood incense in burners hanging from the ceiling by thin chains. Low conversation from several groups of fellow travelers, punctuated by the occasional round of laughter, filled the room. Despite all his fire, Daisuke moved closer to Obito and shrank in on himself a little—it wasn't always easy to shake the sense that he didn't belong in certain public spaces, especially when they were unfamiliar.

"He's not here," he said quickly. "Let's go."

"We just got through the door."

"So? Obito, did you forget that Junpei hates me? Or that you had to *bully* him into helping you in Zhu? What makes you so sure it'll be any different now?"

Obito didn't think Daisuke's deduction was entirely right, or that simple coercion was the sole reason Junpei had gone along with him all those months ago, but he also didn't have the energy or desire to argue with him about it—for all he knew, he *was* being naive. After a moment, he wordlessly nodded; his stance further crumbled when he noticed the flood of relief in his partner's eyes. Just as they were about to leave, however, Obito caught movement from the corner of his eye and turned toward it. Daisuke swore under his breath when they found Junpei flagging them down from a table in the far corner.

Sullen as he'd been about the idea of spending time with the soldier, Daisuke's stomach betrayed him when they made it to the table. Three bowls each piled high with freshly cooked rice awaited, while steamed vegetables sat in a heap on another plate beside a mountain of grilled fish which was bright red from whatever hot spice it'd been prepared with. A green bottle of alcohol sat by a trio of small, overturned glasses near Junpei's right hand.

"Sit, sit," he invited, waving them to the empty seats across from him before setting up the cups properly. "They feed you well here. We might as well eat while we talk—it's not good to drink on an empty stomach, anyway."

Unable to help it, Daisuke's eyes narrowed as he knelt on one of the soft cushions. He blurted, "Did you poison the food or something? You're being awfully nice for someone who called me 'silk-spinner' every chance he got."

Junpei flinched as if he'd touched something scalding hot; his eyes flicked to Obito in a desperate plea for help. When none came, and Obito instead settled in beside his partner with an expectant look on his face, Junpei sighed as his gaze dropped to his lap. He remained silent until he at last summoned the courage to look at Daisuke again.

"Look, I was raised...*differently*, I guess, but it was also wrong. *I* was wrong...about everything. Who you are, the way I treated you—dead fucking wrong, and I'm sorry. Can we—can *I*—try again?"

It felt like everything came to a screeching halt, like all sound and life had been sucked from the air when Daisuke's eyes landed on him in shock. He'd been feigning disinterest by examining the few chips in the black polish on his nails, but never in a thousand reincarnation cycles did he expect to hear an apology from Junpei Ikimori, of all the people. Worse yet, it sounded *sincere*. Junpei was proud, but so was he, which meant he understood how hard it was to utter those words. Setting aside pride, it didn't make sense to fake it—the soldier had nothing to win or lose by associating with them. Daisuke sighed in defeat.

"Fine. But if you fuck up, I *will* make sure you suffer in the most humiliating way possible." Surprisingly, the relief in Junpei's face didn't go away with the threat—Daisuke wasn't even sure how much he'd meant it, anyway. "Now, come on, you said you had things wanted to tell us."

"I guess it's not really that long of a story. I've been reassigned." Junpei opened the bottle of liquor and tilted it toward the rim of a glass, but paused when Obito held up a hand, eyes darting between both onmitsu.

"You're older," Obito explained.

"You're onmitsu. You outrank me." Junpei shrugged, then poured equal amounts of the clear liquid into each glass before distributing them, first to Daisuke and Obito. They downed the alcohol, and he poured more before he continued speaking. "Anyway, once that other onmitsu—Hayate, I think—started going through what happened with Senator Hajime, my name inevitably came up for helping you. Naturally, the captains were *furious*, so they stripped me of my training captain title and sent me back to the Capital to face General Aki. And probably a dishonorable discharge. Don't get me wrong, I was pissed at first, but…well, the walk to the Capital from Zhu is *long* when you're by yourself, so I had plenty of time to think. After the General heard my side of things, we worked something else out. I didn't want to be assigned to a new command all that badly, and General Aki also thought it might not be for the best yet. So now, I deliver supplies to the different barracks as needed. Sure, my old man would be *livid* about it, but…I don't think he needs to know."

Obito and Daisuke were no strangers to dismissing the approval of their fathers, or families in general, so they both paused before bringing the ginger-flavored liquor to their lips and glanced at one another. A subtle, begrudging sense of solidarity passed over them. Obito had and would continue to fall short of Takato's expectations, just as Daisuke never could've earned Honda's affection or gentleness, and it sounded as though their new companion was beginning to make peace with something similar.

"He doesn't. You don't need his praise, anyway." Daisuke finally said before taking his drink and placing a few cuts of the fish atop his rice, which was apparently enough of a cue for the other two to do the same. His senses lit up with delight when the tender texture and first taste of heat touched his tongue.

As they ate and talked more, Junpei revealed he was also going to Baohu to deliver soybeans and rice to the barracks there, and before either could ask, he offered them the ride General Aki said they should request from him. Whether it was the alcohol or illusion of being in good company, no matter how much Daisuke mentally kicked and fought, he found it impossible to continue being as defensive toward the soldier as he wanted. He had an infectious laugh he'd never noticed before, and *loved* conversing with Obito; even if the enthusiasm wasn't reciprocated, Daisuke certainly couldn't fault Junpei for that—he knew how enjoyable it could be. Soon, he found himself leaning forward on his elbow, unable to resist staring at the way warm golden light from hanging lanterns glimmered against Obito's forest green eyes.

A small, absentminded smile tugged at the corners of his mouth. It would've been a far more enjoyable sight without Junpei's voice in the background, but—

Wait, what the hell was that? Daisuke jerked upright again and shook his head. He forced himself to look away as embarrassment turned his cheeks unbearably warm and took another swallow of the soju the group had been sharing—they were on their third bottle. His heart pounded when his fingers brushed Obito's hand as he reached for his cup. *Gods, I'm in trouble if I can't shake this.*

"Daisuke?" Obito was looking at him as though he had three heads. "What's wrong?"

"N-nothing, nothing. I was just thinking, since we're getting acquainted, we should...play a drinking game." He winced at how terrible of an excuse he'd made, but at least now Obito looked as though he deeply regretted asking. The idea must've had him wishing Hikari would strike him down on the spot, but since his partner could never have such good luck, he instead became an unwilling participant. Daisuke couldn't help the teasing grin working its way onto his lips.

"Fine by me. But, I've already yapped a lot, so I think it's your turn." Junpei's eyes swept across the main room to ensure no one was listening before he asked, "So, this demon hunting thing you mentioned on the road. It's just for fun, right?"

"'Fun?'" Obito shot back before Daisuke had the chance. "Do you honestly think Master Yujin would let us go this far for a hobby?"

"W-well, I mean, you get leave, don't you?"

"Not to go chasing around ancient stories," Daisuke grumbled into his cup.

The soldier looked helplessly between them. "Then...that means the demon is real?"

"As far as we know." Daisuke shrugged. He tilted his head when he realized Junpei seemed torn, but not entirely deterred, leaving both onmitsu to wonder what was wrong with their new companion.

After a while, Junpei's questions became a lot simpler to answer, which was probably for the best, as it was getting late and they'd all had quite a bit to drink. He downed one last shot, then asked Obito, "If you were in the onmitsu for that long before Daisuke was reassigned, how did you two even meet? And shouldn't he have a different teammate?"

"The pond behind the nobility district," Obito answered dismissively—naturally, he wasn't about to tell a stranger how his original partner died, so he acted as if a good portion of the question hadn't been asked.

Perhaps it was wishful thinking, but he seemed even less impressed by the idea of spending time with Junpei than Daisuke originally had. Of course, he still didn't have the whole story of how they'd come to work together in Zhu when he was captured by Senator Hajime, but Obito was acting icier than he normally would around someone else. Although Daisuke had yet to see him treat Junpei terribly, barely restrained by a sense of deeply ingrained decorum, he could tell the alcohol had watered it down ever so slightly. Wildly amused by it, he had to see how far his friend's bluntness would go.

"Actually, we met one time before then," Daisuke said slyly before taking his last drink, grinning when Obito rolled his eyes. "Come on, I know you remember that night at the festival. Music, fireworks, a valiant rescue from a group of bullies."

"Surprise," Junpei muttered.

Obito looked at him, puzzled. "Weren't you one of them?"

Daisuke burst into laughter at the embarrassment on their companion's face, but his gaze quickly went back to his partner as mischief swam through his hazy mind again. "You know, you should thank me for keeping this all a secret. Imagine how hard I'd have to fight for your attention if any girls knew you had such a heroic streak."

"Do you ever stop talking?"

"I think I've had too much to drink for that."

Junpei chuckled. "Then let's turn in for the night. Besides, if we want to make it to Baohu in good time, we should leave early."

"Fine by me." Daisuke stood. He put a hand on the table for balance when he wobbled a little, then turned to Obito, batting his eyelashes—it took every ounce of his waning willpower to resist leaning into him. "Carry me?"

"What?!" Junpei spluttered when Obito only sighed and let Daisuke climb into his arms.

MIKA GLANCED OVER HIS shoulder every few feet as he made his way through the nobility district. His relief at Daisuke and Obito leaving town for whatever mission they'd been sent on was short-lived, as it seemed like Raku and Jido were keeping their watchful eyes on him ever since. While he doubted the older onmitsu knew what was going on, something deep in his gut told him the first two had figured something out. For all his bluster and the insults he threw out, he knew Daisuke wasn't an idiot, and had to begrudgingly admit the same about his cousin.

He tilted his face toward the warm summer breeze gliding against his skin and forced himself to breathe slowly, trying to soothe the unease picking at his nerves. He didn't *feel* like he was being watched at the moment, and even if Raku and Jido *did* follow him, what would they possibly uncover? The back room where the vials of blackwater were stored couldn't be accessed by outsiders.

Mika's hand subconsciously touched the hilt of the tanto at the back of his belt. His combat skills weren't to be underestimated, but he didn't think he could take on two experienced onmitsu simultaneously, let alone permanently silence them. Though he'd had time to weigh his options, he still didn't think he was prepared to take any of the actions his father wanted him to—but how could he not do what was expected?

He swallowed as he nervously opened the house's front door. Although it was as empty as he should've anticipated, he couldn't shake the feeling there was something else awaiting him. After locking the door behind himself and doing a cursory search of the main floor, he decided his paranoia was just that, and with a grunt, pushed aside the part of the wall in the kitchen to open the storage room. A lantern hung from a hook on the wall near the entrance, which he lit before advancing further. His hand trembled a bit when he held it out to check the gleaming bottles, winking back at him under the flame's illumination, then crossed the room to pull back the curtain from the window and let in some natural light.

Wind swept by his ankles, sending a chill throughout his entire body. His heart dropped into his stomach when he heard shuffling on the floor behind him. Slowly, he turned toward the source of the sound, praying he'd find his bravery somewhere along the way.

Mika's soul nearly ascended to the heavens when he saw a silhouette on the far side of the room; it took everything in him not to drop the lantern and accidentally set everything ablaze. His other hand flew over his mouth to stifle a yelp when the heavily cloaked figure rose from their makeshift seat on an overturned bucket, only able to stare with wide eyes as the person reached for the cowl covering their face. Every hair stood on end as he tried not to imagine what the hood kept hidden.

"Y-you aren't s-supposed to be here!" he finally forced out, giving the interloper pause. "Th-this is Lord Tanaka's private property!"

The hood came down, revealing a woman with long, loose black hair and equally dark eyes. Her painted lips ticked upward into a smile that seemed slightly vicious just beneath the surface; he shivered. "Dear boy, who do you think sent me?"

Mika squinted at the woman; he didn't recognize her, but he knew who would've scolded him for treating her with anything less than hospitality. As she casually perused a crate of blackwater, running her slender fingers over each vial, he realized his father would be irate if he fell for a lie so easily. He had to test her.

"Who are you? And why did my father send you?"

He jumped when another figure appeared beside the woman. Its shape seemed off, somehow; a mass of blackness with no distinct features and a fuzzy outline, like dancing and roiling shadows. He subconsciously took a step back, prepared to run as fast as he could for the nearest soldier or patrolman, but the woman clutched the front of his uniform. His eyes widened with terror when she showed no signs of loosening her grasp, no matter how he resisted.

"You can call me Lady Shadow," she finally introduced herself once he surrendered just enough for her to talk. "And what should I call you, young Lord Tanaka?"

His hazel eyes swept across the room once more—the mysterious dark mass still wasn't moving. "M-Mika."

"A lovely name," Lady Shadow said as she stroked his cheek. "It's best if I make this visit brief, though, so I see no need to waste your time or mine. Your father has a brilliant plan that he's entrusted me to put into motion, but I won't be able to pull it off without your help."

Lady Shadow pressed two pieces of cool metal into his palm. When he looked down, he found his father's set of twin ruby rings with gold bands—irrefutable proof that he'd had contact with her.

Mika swallowed as his fingers clenched around them. His throat tight around his voice at first, his eyes darted toward the vials, then the strange figure which had remained unmoving near where Lady Shadow had emerged from the darkness. He reminded himself of his promise to his father, and to be brave. "W-what do you need me to do?"

"You promise to be loyal?"

"Of course."

Lady Shadow smiled at him; behind her, a clawed, glowing green hand appeared from the mass. "You, my dear, clever boy, are going to distribute those across the Wen Valley. But, first, I'll need bit of a...a tithe, if you will. A drop of your blood, and I'll be able to protect you from afar."

OBITO AWOKE THE NEXT morning with a throbbing headache, damp hair sticking to his forehead, and the rest of his skin coated in a sheen of sweat. It didn't take long to figure out why, as his heart nearly stopped when he realized Daisuke was lying on top of him, still sleeping soundly, locks of loose, silky black hair loose fanned out in every direction. Panic, embarrassment, and at least half a dozen other emotions rushed through Obito's veins when he looked over and saw their shirts in a pile on the floor.

He couldn't fully remember what happened once they'd entered the room, where the room even *was*, or how much they'd had to drink, but he had the vague mental image of an argument involving the need for sleep toward the end of the night. He'd flopped onto his bed, and Daisuke, being a menace, sprawled across him like an over-sized cat because he wanted to keep talking. They must've fallen asleep from there. It wasn't much of a relief, but it'd put his mind somewhat at ease; Daisuke was a shameless flirt sober, and even more so when drinking, which was something Obito didn't trust his inebriated self to handle very well if it turned onto him. It was a large part of why he generally refused any offers his friend made about drinking together—he couldn't live with himself if he somehow made a fool out of Daisuke.

Obito was about to shove his friend off when Daisuke shifted again, making him freeze instead when he curled against him more. Just as Obito regained his sanity—if it still existed at this point—he caught sight of the newer scarring on Daisuke's left shoulder; his heart sank when he found the rest on his right. Thankfully, the marks indirectly inflicted by Mika and Shinchi weren't accompanied by anything more recent, but he still felt guilty whenever he saw them. For all his fire, Daisuke rarely got into physical altercations with anyone else, and took that negativity out on himself instead.

After a moment, he carefully pulled himself out from under Daisuke.

"Fucking hell," he cursed how stiff his back was when he got to his feet and reached for his shitagi. He shot Daisuke an irritated scowl when he heard him mumble in his sleep, but his eyes lingered on the way the bright red petals of his higanbana tattoo elegantly curled around the muscles on his upper arm. This gradually turned into admiring the deceptively soft lines that made up his body, before finding faint defensive wounds near his wrist from sparring, barely visible unless seen from the right angle and under certain lighting. He shook himself out of his embarrassingly improper stupor when the folding screen softly scraped against the tatami floor. The movement exacerbated the pounding in his head, but at least his focus had returned.

He turned to Junpei, who cautiously peeked around the screen, as if he expected to find something he didn't want to see. Obito's memory was suddenly flooded with the soldier's offer to split the room the previous night, saying there was plenty of space and an extra bed he didn't intend to use; he'd pulled out the screen to give himself privacy to change while Daisuke continued with whatever ridiculous argument he'd picked with Obito for fun, but never came back. Despite how Daisuke laughed at Junpei's snoring, all three were soon passed out, drunk and exhausted from the heat and their travels. Obito was relieved—his concerns from earlier were likely unfounded.

Junpei yawned and swung his arms wide for a stretch, though panic overwhelmed his features when he accidentally smacked the folding screen in the process. Thankfully, he caught it right before it could topple onto Daisuke, who slept on in undisturbed bliss.

Now visibly self-conscious, the soldier cleared his throat as he righted it again. "I thought I heard movement. I wanted to let you know we should leave soon, but...what about him?"

"Don't bother yet." Obito rolled his eyes and shrugged into his shitagi. "He's hard enough to get out of bed without drinking, and I don't have the energy to argue with him right now."

Junpei grinned. "Late night?"

For all his stupidity, he at least had the sense to make himself scarce again when Obito gave him an irritated scowl from over his shoulder. Once Junpei was out of sight, he shook his head as lightly as he could manage and sighed, then retrieved his outer gi from under Daisuke's in the pile they'd made.

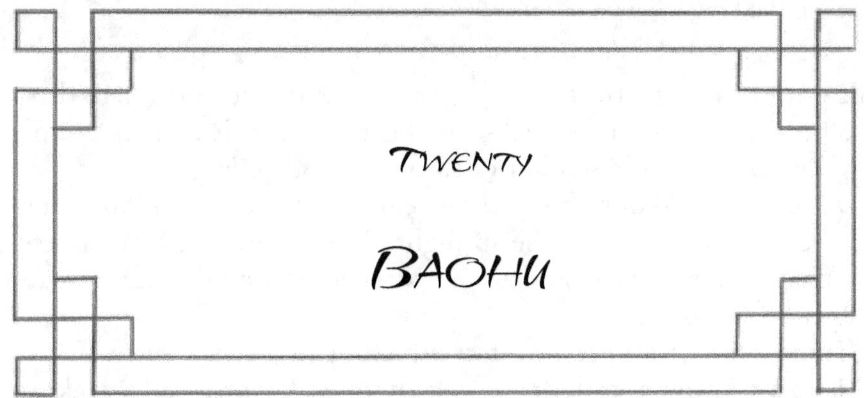

THE CERULEAN SKIES ABOVE were deceptively cheery if one didn't look to the west, where dark storm clouds slowly encroached on the region. The air was thick with the sort of humidity that made breathing difficult, even though it was barely past midmorning; a bead of sweat uncomfortably slipped down Daisuke's neck as the cart rocked closer to Baohu. A storm like the one about to descend on the city later would more or less signal the end of summer, but he hoped it wouldn't interfere too much with their plans once they arrived.

As he watched the foothills disappear behind the horizon, he couldn't help the bout of mixed emotions suddenly swirling around one another in his mind. It was only a short year ago when he and Obito had disembarked for Zhu, a city he couldn't get away from fast enough; because of what happened there, now it seemed like their mission in Bahou was something no one else could do. Perhaps the feeling stemmed from a naïve sense of self-importance. However, since Master Yujin had sent them on their way without too many questions, it meant he believed they could handle whatever came their way—and that he thought they were right. With the Intelligence Master's implicit trust backing them, was he really expected to feel anything else?

There was a slight shift in weight beside where he'd been lounging against a sack of dried soybeans in the back of the cart.

"Daisuke, were you listening?"

He nearly jumped out of his skin at Obito's voice, warmth not from the hot day rolling into his cheeks when he noticed how close his friend was to him now. He must've been further off in his daydream than he realized. "I-I guess not."

"Don't worry. It was just Junpei talking, anyway."

"I heard that," Junpei groused, glancing at them from over his shoulder. "As I was saying, we should be in Baohu soon. Are you two *sure* you don't want to stop by the Senator's place first? It'd be nothing to drop you off on the way to the barracks, and he might be able to help. I don't know *how*, but he could send priests, soldiers—*something*."

Daisuke flopped onto his back once more and stretched long, closing his eyes and basking in the sunlight. "We're on 'official' business. It's usually better to lay low until we're desperate or need something we can't get on our own."

"Is that about the time you start punching innocent soldiers?"

"I don't know about the innocent ones," Obito said, making Daisuke cackle. "But aside from all that, you already said you'd help us out, which should be plenty. Unless you're too afraid."

Junpei spluttered. "Afraid? Me? No—hell, no. Absolutely not. If anything, I should be worried about *you* two running out on *me*. Besides, you said back in the foothills that you don't even know if there's really a demon here. 'Just checking,' I think, is the exact wording you used."

Daisuke cracked open an eyelid to share an amused smirk with Obito. Since poor Junpei had put up with more than his fair share of teasing from them ever since the trio took off from Kyoshu together, they decided to let him off easy—*this* time. He might've been a susceptible target when it came to Obito's dry sarcasm and Daisuke's wicked humor, but neither wanted to push him too far. After all, he *had* agreed to stick with them through whatever mess they were riding into, and if nothing else, he could provide a reliable report to Master Yujin. Whether it was to corroborate their own or inform the Intelligence Master about how they'd died remained to be seen. Plus, Daisuke thought, he seemed to be following through on his promise to do better than he had in the past—making an effort had to be worth something at some point.

They stopped not long after to rest the horse and stretch their legs. As much as it was preferred to walking, the cart still became incredibly uncomfortable after a while of riding in it. Not far from the creek where Junpei led the horse for a drink, a patch of tall wild plants growing in abundance caught Daisuke's attention. He wandered toward the field and crouched beside the hemlock swaying in the breeze. He wasn't fond of the smell emanating from the white umbrella-like blooms, as he found it too grassy and pungent all at once, but as far as poisons went, he thought it wise to gather as many of them as he could carry. From what he'd read, it seemed to grow anywhere *besides* areas around the Capital, where it was incredibly expensive—having something this toxic in his pouch, for *free,* no less, was too good of an opportunity to pass up.

"Daisuke, come on. We don't have time for this," Junpei called from the roadside, exasperated. "It's already getting late."

The soldier's overworked horse snorted at her handler in a way that could only be described as annoyance, and Daisuke couldn't contain a crooked, wry grin. Deciding he could process the plants properly while riding in the wagon later, he uprooted several of them, just to realize he had nothing to store them in when he got to his feet. He sighed in disappointment, prepared to leave his bounty where he'd found it, when he heard Obito clear his throat behind him. When he turned around, his friend held out a small satchel. A second look revealed it was the same pouch he used for storing the tools and other supplies he needed when making his concoctions—he didn't think he'd remembered it.

Daisuke gave Obito a small smile as he packed the toxic flowers into the pouch, trying to ignore the furious blush he could feel scorching his cheeks. When they turned to rejoin Junpei, he was giving the pair an odd look, as if he wanted to comment on something he hadn't fully figured out yet. Then again, it seemed like he'd been making that face at them a lot throughout the trip.

Daisuke shyly glanced at Obito again before calling out to Junpei, "Let me wash my hands off, then we'll go."

Junpei's jaw went slack. "You're just picking flowers!"

"Idiot, it's poison hemlock. You *want* me to clean up before I touch anything else."

"I think we can make time for that," Obito casually intervened as he started toward the cart once more, bag in hand.

The strange expression reappeared on Junpei's face, but again, neither of his companions knew what it was meant for; perhaps he didn't, either. Instead, he settled for rolling his eyes and slumping against the cart, shooting a scowl at the horse, who nickered as if in approval to the prolonged break as she grazed on the grass nearby.

Baohu's entrance was marked by a beautiful red gate towering over the roadway like a beacon, visible for miles. One of the city's other, and perhaps more well-known defining features, was a canal which split the city into eastern and western halves, with several bridges connecting both sides. This canal did more than control the flow of the river they'd followed since the foothills; it was also what made Baohu so integral in shipping goods to and from the mountains, as General Aki had previously mentioned.

After they arrived in town around midday, Junpei left Daisuke and Obito outside of a shop that sold candles and incense. He wanted to let his poor, exhausted horse rest, and drop his order of rations and supplies at the barracks before reconvening with them at an inn on the city's eastern side he'd recommended. Junpei had heard good things about it during his travels before they'd met up, and since neither Obito nor Daisuke knew much about Baohu's layout, they figured it couldn't hurt to follow his advice at least once. Being this far north, they didn't need to worry about any uncomfortable run-ins with the slave trade like they'd had in Zhu, which allowed Daisuke to breathe easily once they'd secured their purchases and began making their way toward their destination. However, this ease was short-lived upon a quick scan of his surroundings.

Baohu's wide cobblestone streets were lined with well-maintained homes, shops, and market stalls, with occasional patches of grass and greenery shaded by maple or fruit trees. It was a peaceful, clean city, but something was undeniably off. Daisuke halted in the center of a bridge, which made Obito do the same a few feet ahead of him. By now, he'd also no doubt realized the apparent absence of human life in the streets. Although people were still milling about indoors, a city like this ought to be bustling with activity in all corners, even on an oppressively hot summer day, but it felt nearly as abandoned as Fukainuma had when they'd first arrived there a few months ago. The only time someone came outside was to rush to their next destination after several furtive glances at their surroundings; one man had paused to look at them suspiciously, but never approached and went on his way. It hadn't helped the perturbed feeling planting roots under Daisuke's skin.

He swallowed, then took the few steps to close the gap between himself and his partner, grabbing hold of his sleeve before he fully realized it. "Something's way off about this place. I don't think the weather has everyone in hiding."

Obito looked down at the boats tied below them. The vessels also seemed to be devoid of life, and the only noise coming up from the river was the hollow sound of water lapping against the hulls. He faced Daisuke after an enormous koi fish swam for the bridge's shade. "There were plenty of people inside the shops. Maybe someone can tell us something when we get to the inn—if anyone's there."

The footpath leading to the inn's front entrance was shaded by a large oak and marked on each side by a short half-wall made of gray stones, seemingly for decoration and to prop up the establishment's sign more than anything else. A gentle, warm breeze rustled through blades of grass in the yard where wild daisies swayed in the wind. Daisuke subconsciously smiled at them as he passed by; lately, the sight of happy plants made him feel the same, at least for a moment, though he always missed how his change in expression was reflected in Obito's.

They were met by a similar sight as to what they'd experienced when first arriving in Guangshu Inn—a clean, tidy front room where people quietly conversed as they ate or drank. A few groups briefly stopped to look at the pair as they made their way toward the innkeeper, but unlike when they were in Zhu, Daisuke felt no reason to fear this temporary change in demeanor. Given everything else they'd seen thus far, it seemed like a reasonable, wary reaction—now that he thought about it, they hadn't seen anyone else on the road leaving Baohu, either. Something strange was happening in this city, and he had a sinking feeling Tatakai's suspicious were behind it. A woman's enthusiastic greeting pulled him out of his thoughts.

"It's a good thing you arrived before nightfall," the woman said once they reached her counter. "I know I shouldn't say this, but if the infantry-men were worth their salt and still patrolling, they would've kept you from entering altogether."

"Why?" Obito asked after the pair traded a worried look.

"Haven't you heard?" She blinked. "Senator Yumio enacted a curfew just a couple of weeks ago to try keeping the deaths down—there's always a few who try defying the order, and at first the soldiers helped enforce it, but now..."

"What deaths?" Daisuke pressed, eyes wide as he leaned forward on his elbows. The young woman blushed at how close he was, to which Obito rolled his eyes, knowing full well his partner planned on taking advantage of it as soon as he noticed. As if on cue, he batted his eyelashes at her in a way that also got under Obito's skin with infuriating ease. "Maybe we can help if you give us the whole story."

"How could you possibly?"

"We…we…" Daisuke glanced at Obito, who couldn't help but wonder the same thing. "practice the ancient arts. We've been traveling the countryside looking for chances to test our skills."

"That doesn't sound like a real job," she criticized, forcing Obito to stifle a snicker at his friend's soured expression; they quickly schooled their features. "But we *are* desperate here. You're sure you won't think it's too outlandish?"

"You wouldn't lie to this pretty face, right?"

The young woman giggled, and her brown eyes softened as the last vestiges of hesitation melted away. "Baohu usually has a pretty active nightlife, but sometime after the solstice, people started disappearing or turning up dead when they went out after dark. At first, everyone thought it was a murderer, so Senator Yumio ordered General Yuta to increase nighttime patrols. But…then one of the soldiers saw something. He said a creature came out of the darkness by an old path into the forest and attacked a fellow soldier. It sucked him dry of any blood and then carried him off into the dark."

Obito raised an eyebrow. "Is there a way for us to speak with the one who saw all this?"

She shook her head. "He killed himself after, and then the curfew was put into place. People still went out at first, thinking the Senator was being paranoid, but folks kept dying—namely the infantrymen on patrol."

"Was the Capital informed?" Daisuke's brows furrowed when she shook her head; he'd hoped the question would help him determine why General Aki had lost contact with General Yuta and his soldiers stationed here. "Why not?"

"I'm afraid you're asking the wrong lady." She laughed a little. "If I were in charge, it would've happened already."

"I've no doubt."

"If only." She sighed wistfully before offering them another smile, then placed a key on the countertop. "Will you need anything else before I show you to your room?"

"Actually, I'm afraid I must trouble you for an extra set of bedding later—we have a companion joining us. And, even though I've already asked for too much, do you have a couple of incense burners we could borrow?"

Daisuke smiled at her sweetly. He caught Obito rolling his eyes for a second time, which made keeping up with his act incredibly difficult—he wanted to tease his friend even more now. "They don't need to be fancy. Anything you have will be perfect."

She made a note about the bedding before glancing over her shoulder, searching for the burners. "I should have a few over here—the mistress usually keeps a few spares on hand. Just a moment."

Once she turned away to dig for them, Daisuke and Obito looked at one another again, silently agreeing they should prepare to head out as soon as they could when night fell. Riding with Junpei had given them plenty of opportunities for research that they wouldn't have had if they'd been exhausted from traveling on foot all day. During this time, Daisuke came across a ceremony he thought would be best for "blessing" the paper talismans, as they'd originally thought to do, but neither were sure if it'd be effective.

The woman brought them to a room that was surprisingly spacious; it was already prepared with two folded futon beds spaced a few feet apart, a small table with cushions, and a folding screen sitting in the corner. When Obito wasn't paying attention, Daisuke hastily scooted his bedding closer, barely escaping notice when the rustling fabrics made his friend look up from digging things out of his travel pack. Namely, the book they'd taken all their information from thus far. Hoping to further distract him from what he'd done, Daisuke pulled out the incense they'd purchased and passed one of the several long sticks in the bushel to his partner.

"What do you make of her story?" Obito asked, eyes on the incense as he twirled it between his fingers.

"I hate to say it, but it sounds like Tatakai might've been right. Good thing you insisted on bringing those paper talismans you made."

"You never did say if you thought they would work for anything, though, or if 'blessing' them would help." Obito moved the table out from the center of the floor in preparation for the ritual they were about to perform. "And given what we just heard, I don't see how we can save them all for sealing the demon again, so that changes our plan a bit."

Daisuke absentmindedly twisted the lower earring in his left ear, then sat where the table had originally been, soon joined by his partner. "Theoretically, they should, but you're right—I thought we'd use them to set up a barrier of sorts and catch Tatakai's sibling, but we need to make sure the resentful energy of their victims doesn't linger. I have a feeling it'd only help the demon fight us off."

"The most annoying part about all of this, is that the priesthood at Baohu's temple should've already taken care of the demon before so many people died."

"Come on, we both know you can't rely on the Temple for anything—I mean, the High Priestess kicked us out just for asking questions without giving us a single answer. But, we're here now, and the paper talismans are just convenient versions of the sealing symbol. We know it works from our time in Fukainuma."

Obito gave it some thought, and Daisuke got swept up in watching his face, jumping a little when his friend spoke again. "I made a dozen. Let's keep at least one for the demon."

"G-good idea."

Obito flipped open the book and thumbed through it before producing the ream of paper talismans he'd made prior to leaving the Capital. He checked them over for mistakes or smudges, then handed the stack to Daisuke, who carefully laid them out between them in two rows of six. They each placed a long stick of incense in the simple burners they'd received from the woman out front; once lit, they looked at one another for a long moment, dozens of unspoken questions and worries passing between them.

"This is probably going to get...well, fucking bizarre," Daisuke warned with a half-hearted chuckle.

Obito's eyes briefly went to the talismans before his gaze went back to Daisuke's. A wry smile touched his lips. "What part of us knowing each other hasn't been?"

"Rude, but fair." Daisuke couldn't help the stupid smile that worked its way onto his face at that; at least Obito wasn't about to request a reassignment the second they returned to the Capital. He took a deep breath to center himself again. "So, basically, the book says to focus our energy into a ball, and then roll that ball onto the talismans. Ready?"

"About as ready as I will be."

As with the solstice prayer, they sat across from one another and joined hands. With their goal in mind, they closed their eyes to meditate, and soon, Daisuke felt a sphere of energy beginning to form in his core. Warm at first, and pleasant, but it changed rather quickly. It burned. The shock of the sensation forced his eyes open—Obito was already looking back at him with the same surprise etched into his features. Color flashed in Daisuke's periphery, and they both looked to find strange, misty tendrils surrounding them.

Daisuke tightened his grip on Obito when the sparkling threads of energy began dancing about them in a circle and twirling around one another; red to ward off evil, green for harmony, purple for divinity, and blue for growth. He clenched his teeth as the energies twisted like a cyclone into the center, hovering above the talismans, but a steady squeeze on his fingers from Obito kept him grounded, focused, as if he'd sensed his partner's temporary lapse of both. Their concentrated spiritual energy lowered the spinning threads, forcing them down until they were absorbed into the papers, which fluttered as if in the wind. Yellow light burst from the talismans' surfaces, and everything was still once more.

Obito slowly worked one hand free from Daisuke's grasp, then cautiously picked up one of the finished sealing tags. Disbelief colored his features. "It's heavy."

"You mean...we did it? Seriously?" Unthinking and overcome with excitement, Daisuke tightly interlaced their fingers on the hands still joined as he took the paper from his friend with the other to examine it for himself. "That wasn't quite what I expected, but, hell, if it works, it works."

Obito was about to wonder aloud why the energies had interacted in such a way, but of course, that *had* to be when Junpei's voice and an insistent knock sounded from the other side of the door. Daisuke's shoulders slumped, and he shot Obito an annoyed look, which was mirrored back to him.

Together, they let out an exasperated, "Come in."

"That's one hell of a way to greet someone," Junpei muttered as he opened the door, though he could hardly say he hadn't expected it—by now, it was the most common of all the interactions he'd had with them. The soldier opened his mouth again, likely to complain further, which was also when he finally seemed to notice the ritual materials spread out on the floor. "Am I—*did* I interrupt something?"

Obito shook his head, which was also when he finally remembered he had a hold of Daisuke's hand and released it, missing the deflated look on his partner's face. "No, we're done here."

Junpei scratched his head, then shrugged before letting himself into the room and flopping down on a cushion beside the table they'd pushed out of the way. Apparently still not convinced, he took a little more time to study the two onmitsu, then slowly began with, "Seems like there actually might be something dark going on around here."

Curious, Daisuke titled his head, a wordless prompt to continue.

"I went to deliver those supplies to the barracks, right? Well, when I got there, I found out there were only about a dozen soldiers in the whole building. I brought rations for thirty. When I tried to ask what happened to the others, no one would say anything except 'the monster,' and 'won't go out.' So, I thought I'd go to General Yuta, but...he's in self-seclusion right now."

Obito shared an uneasy, yet curious look with Daisuke before he asked, "No one would give you *any* details?"

"Well, not there, at least." Junpei fidgeted in his seat, clearly not proud of whatever confession he was about to make. "Because it was all so strange, I...might've broken protocol a bit, and went to Senator Yumio's place since it's right next door. He was a lot more willing to talk—*desperate* to, actually, which worked out well for me. He said General Yuta's in seclusion because he's ashamed of how many soldiers he's lost. I'm not sure how much I believe it, but I guess some monster's been picking them and civilians off basically every night since the solstice."

"Unfortunately, all of that sounds like it lines up with what the lady out front said," Daisuke told Obito before turning back to Junpei to explain, "It's why Senator Yumio insisted on a sunset curfew for civilians."

"Think it's your demon, then?"

"I don't really want to say yes without seeing it for myself, but I'm not sure what else it could be."

The two onmitsu lapsed into silence again. Neither looked at one another nor their companion until the hot ash from one of the incense sticks hissed as it fell into the burner tray. Obito's eyes abruptly went to Daisuke, then Junpei, making both jump a little at the suddenness of it.

"Your bed should be here soon. Let's make our plan, then get some rest. It's going to be a long night."

THICK BLACK CLOUDS MOVED against a gold, purple, and deep blue backdrop, making the twilight skies appear even more menacing than they had earlier. The wind had picked up a bit, and the scent of impending rain clung to the humid air. Occasional lightning flashed in the clouds as they drew closer, but from the looks of it, Daisuke thought he and Obito still had a little time to start their investigation before the storm began; they'd yet to hear a rumble of thunder. He breathed deeply, slowly, then made his way outside, where they decided to meet once they were both ready.

For now, Junpei had gone back to the barracks—armed with one of the sealing tags for protection—to try spurring the few remaining soldiers into action. Already sensing his mission was pointless, he'd also agreed to inform Senator Yumio that a pair of travelers he'd met along the way to Baohu were investigating this so-called monster. Although this would leave the two onmitsu isolated from help, Daisuke knew it was best to keep others away—as he'd thought earlier, only he and Obito could do anything for Baohu in this situation. If they were going to go against the Shadow Priestess at some point, he believed they should expect similar scenarios in the future.

Grim as things felt, his mood still instantly improved when Obito turned to him as he hopped onto the half-wall at the end of the footpath, then took a seat. He didn't think it was the appropriate time to consider why that look made his heart skip a beat, but maybe if they came out of this alive...

He swallowed dryly, trying in vain to dismiss a dreadfully familiar and increasingly frequent wave of a feeling so frighteningly close to affection.

Fortunately, Obito didn't seem burdened by the same experience—another reason to keep his mouth shut for now. "Cigarette first?"

"And a fat roll of white leaf when we're done." Daisuke grinned as he accepted the offering.

"Your roll, then."

"Deal."

By the time they'd finished two cigarettes each, a bell rang into the night from Hikari's Temple on the western side of Baohu, answered by the pounding of gongs in other parts of the city, meaning Senator Yumio's curfew was now in effect. For the first time since they'd left the Capital, true fear settled in Daisuke's stomach like a heavy rock. He glanced at Obito as he slid down from his perch, hoping to find something in his friend's face that might provide reassurance—the calmness with which he watched the storm brewing above in the sky helped immensely.

"Let's hurry," Obito said, pausing when thunder rolled in the distance. "It could rain any moment, now, and those sealing tags won't be worth anything if they get wet."

The plan was simple; spread out several talismans to attract any lingering spirits and reduce the amount of resentment in the air. When the suspected demon came prowling for its next victim, Daisuke and Obito would follow it back to wherever it slept—likely somewhere in the woods near Baohu's west half—once it found nothing and gave up the hunt. Once they had it cornered, they'd seal it with the last paper talisman. Meanwhile, Junpei would use his authority as an infantryman to ensure the streets stayed clear, mostly as a contingency in case someone decided to try their luck against the creature. Once the two onmitsu were in pursuit, he would also retreat into whatever nearby shelter was available until dawn. Obito hoped the impending storm would make the soldier's job easier, but humans, for better or worse, were often unpredictable in the face of danger. Daisuke looked over his shoulder once as they left the perceived safety of the lit braziers near the wall, then hurried to ensure he was within the ring of light provided by the lantern his partner carried.

The rain held off a little longer than expected. Daisuke and Obito managed to cover quite a bit of ground in just a couple of hours. They'd divided the city into sections on a map they'd borrowed from the inn, then went through with a paper talisman raised—in nearly every area, as soon as either Obito or Daisuke lifted the talisman from where they were kept in their belts, several, if not dozens, of blue flames rushed toward the sanctity of the sealing symbol. Once all the souls in the vicinity had gravitated toward them, the paper would burn up in their hands and disintegrate. Whether the souls were all deaths from Tatakai's sibling or other causes didn't matter, but giving these spirits a chance to rest did, and a hint of warmth tugged at Daisuke's heart.

The first warm droplet finally fell on the tip of his nose as a talisman burned up in Obito's hand, marking the completion of the first half of their mission, and drawing his eyes skyward. Lightning danced across the clouds as another bulbous raindrop hit his forehead. Wordlessly, they agreed to head toward the woods.

Obito's arm protectively and instinctively shot out in front of Daisuke's chest to stop them both in their tracks when a blood-curdling scream rose into the pitch-black night. They searched for the source of the sound; when another pierced the air, Daisuke motioned toward the western part of town. They hurried across the nearest bridge as the downpour began, water splashing under their boots and creating a commotion against roof tiles. Although they sensed they were too late to save the person's life, it didn't slow their haste to catch the culprit. Breathing heavily, Obito halted when a little blue light floating just above the ground caught his attention, its ethereal glimmer rippling in the puddles beneath it. He grabbed Daisuke's sleeve to stop him from going on without him.

The glow belonged to a lone blue flame, which appeared to be confusedly wandering around in a circle as it illuminated a large part of the street. The faint smell of iron still lingered in the air. Curious, Daisuke tilted his head and leaned in closer, the blaze of the flame bathing his skin in the same hue; it wasn't hot, nor did it seem malicious. A soul of the departed, just as he suspected they'd find once they arrived on the scene. While it was unusual for one to come forward without the beckoning of the seal, the circumstances with this one were a bit different; they'd never met one belonging to someone so recently deceased. The little flame sputtered, then vanished, leaving them with only their lantern for light once again.

"Let's seal it," Daisuke told Obito, who mutely nodded as he reached for their last available talisman. "Whatever killed this person is probably somewhere nearby."

"Then stay close to me."

Daisuke's gaze went to the ground as he shielded the talisman Obito held from the weather. There was something barely concealed against the darkness, just beyond the glowing ring of their lantern. Every hair on his body stood on end when he realized he was standing in human blood, but before he could mention it to his partner, came the sickening crunch of bone not far from where they worked. Obito evidently hadn't missed it, either, as the paper rustled with the tremble of his hand.

A low growl arose from the dark, followed by what must've been rapid clawing. It sounded like an agonizing grind of metal against stone and set Daisuke's teeth on edge. Silence descended once more when the clawing stopped as suddenly as it'd begun; the thud of his heartbeat pounded in his ears when an inhuman screech pierced through the night. He clenched his jaw as if it'd help keep his fears firmly under control while he tried tracking the source of these noises, but they faded away soon after. The overpowering sense that something heavy loomed over them finally lifted as well—whatever this thing was, they'd been dangerously close to an encounter. Perhaps the presence of the paper talisman had driven it away and spared them this time. A violent tremor rattled Daisuke's body as he turned back to Obito.

"Y-you heard all that, too, right?"

"Could you trace it?" Obito quietly asked when the talisman finally disappeared in a puff of smoke, a sound like a sigh of relief coming from the air near his hand as the spirit began its journey to the Between Realm.

Daisuke nodded, eyes darting to every inch of their surroundings that he could see when Obito held out the light. "What do you think 'it' even was?"

"If I had to guess, it's the reason for this." The lantern's flame shuddered as Obito moved it slightly to gesture toward the pool of blood at their feet; the constant rainfall was already washing it away.

"I was afraid you were going to say that."

Daisuke took the lantern from Obito and held it out to show him more flecks of blood left on the orange-bathed street, though it was also becoming smeared and running in rivulets with the deluge. They looked at each other, then nodded once they recognized the wordless agreement written on one another's faces; this was the trail they needed to follow, and with a heap of luck, they'd put an end to this terror.

A cold shiver danced along Daisuke's spine and rattled his bones when they finally came to the last few, tiny flecks of blood. Obito also showed no signs of wanting to move further as they stared down the mouth of a dark, forested trail. Staked in the ground to their right was an old wooden sign, far too weathered to properly read, which gave them more reason for pause. Wherever the creature had taken up residence was likely abandoned, isolated, and had been for years; once they started down this path, there was a chance they'd never be seen again.

"Did you find something?!"

Junpei's abrupt question had Daisuke whirling on his heel, tanto drawn, and Obito just as prepared to defend them. Upon realizing who it was, however, the pair sighed—relief laced with an undeniable amount of irritation. The bouncing lantern light revealed the other boy's sheepish smile through sheets of rain as he realized how badly he'd startled them.

"Sorry," he muttered. "Did...did you find anything?"

"We have reason to believe the demon killed someone tonight," Obito reported once he had his fill of glaring at their companion. "But we were able to follow it here, which means it's probably hiding somewhere down the trail. Know anything about it?"

Junpei was surprised he'd been asked, yet proud to be included. "I don't know a whole lot about the area. But, before the curfew bells, what I *did* overhear *was* a group of men in the tavern by the Senator's talking about an abandoned farmstead between here and Nansui. They *also* thought it was hiding there—this must be the way."

"Listen to you. A bit of time on the road with two onmitsu and you're practically one of us." Daisuke grinned when Junpei gave him a dirty look.

"Never mind that. More importantly, Baohu's citizens are getting restless. The lack of military presence in the streets now hasn't helped ease their feelings at all—they seem to think the Empire's abandoning them to this mess. We should get this taken care of before someone does something stupid, so *I've* been thinking—"

"Shocking."

"Shut up, Daisuke."

"Stop, both of you." Obito pinched the bridge of his nose.

Junpei glared. "*Anyway*, staying back like you two asked seems...well, cowardly. I'm not afraid of this thing."

"But you already promised us you *would*," Obito reminded him, brows arching when the soldier's mouth opened in protest. "We need you back here more than we'll need you to help us with this next part."

Junpei sighed. "I just..."

Daisuke begrudgingly intervened, "Obito's right, naturally—beauty and brains with this one. The point is, we can't have anyone following us, so we need you here to keep civilians in line and safe while we take care of things. If nothing else, guard this trailhead until the storm gets too bad for you to stay out in it."

Junpei's black eyes helplessly darted between them. The lanternlight skewed his expression slightly as another gust of wind threatened the flames within, but his discomfort at both of those possibilities was clear as day. Thankfully, his unwillingness to let more innocent people die was more prominent—Daisuke smirked a little, though the emotion behind it was hardly his usual snarky or vicious flare. This must be the mindset separating Junpei from his peers in places like Zhu nowadays; wanting to learn and improve, and trying to do what he could to keep everyone safe.

"Man your post, soldier. That's a direct order from the onmitsu." Daisuke smiled half-heartedly.

"...Fine," he finally conceded with a sigh. "I'll get the horse in a bit in case either of you idiots get stupid and hurt yourselves fighting this thing."

"You still have the talisman we gave you, so you'll be the last barrier between the demon and the city if we fail," Obito said as thunder and lightning danced together in the sky, illuminating the intensity in his dark eyes. "Keep yourself safe, too."

Junpei nodded, showing his willingness to cooperate by moving aside to stand under the shelter of a tree nearest to the weathered old sign. When Daisuke looked to see if his partner was ready to proceed, he was met with a half-teasing smirk on Obito's face which he dismissed with a roll of his eyes. They hesitated a moment longer, then started down the trail with rain noisily pelting the canopy of leaves above them.

The storm worsened considerably by the time they reached the end of the trail, twenty slow-moving minutes later. Their path was incredibly slick with mud and dangerous to try navigating any faster in the dark and inclement weather. From the hillcrest, they peered down at a dilapidated barn, which looked like it was barely holding itself together in the howling winds; its wooden sides groaned and creaked louder than the trees at every gust. Thunder raged against the heavens as lightning crackled in blue-white streaks across the sky, but their little lantern bravely persevered through it all as they strayed from the trailhead and crouched low behind a grassy mound near the barn's entrance. The doors had been left partially open, meaning the creature hadn't yet returned or couldn't close them all the way by itself. Daisuke wasn't sure which option chilled him more, but when a blast of wind interrupted this internal debate and blew one of them off like it was made of flimsy paper, he nearly jumped behind Obito for protection.

Obito tried to at least appear less shaken by creeping closer instead; he could see a beam of light on the ground amid the sheets of driving rain, as if every lamp or lantern inside was lit. Besides, he told himself that whether their ritual materials or marital skills were required, it'd be pointless to try anything while they were soaked and exposed to the elements like this. He waved to get Daisuke's attention and then gestured to the remaining door. When his partner nodded in confirmation, he blew out their lantern flame and started forward.

The rain muffled any noise from their boots as they inched toward the entrance.

However, instead of stepping into a barn lit by dozens of lanterns, all they found in the center of the hay-strewn floor was a strange tree. The wood on its trunk was pitch black and looked as though a large beast had used it to sharpen its claws; maple-like leaves hung from thin, sickly-looking branches, all the same shade of deep red. Even more odd, the tree seemed to be the source of the light. Moving in step with one another, they approached it as quietly as possible, water still dripping from their hair and clothes. When they were near enough, Daisuke's hand trembled as he reached out to touch the blackened trunk, feeling as if he wasn't in total control of the action. He flinched when he felt a warm and wet droplet on his shoulder, but couldn't take his gaze off the crimson liquid ebbing under his palm. Obito tried tugging his friend's arm away so they could find a place to hide before the creature found them out in the open like this, but his eyes widened when he also felt something wet drip onto him. He slowly looked upward; the leaves had turned an even deeper shade of red as blood fell from them like raindrops.

"Daisuke," he urged, now forcefully pulling on his partner, which made him stumble backward into his grasp. "We need to get away from this thing."

Daisuke numbly nodded, leaned into him for a second to ground himself, then looked toward some barrels hidden beneath a tattered canvas tarp, coated in a thick layer of dust and cobwebs. "There, behind those."

As soon as they ducked into their hiding place, Daisuke realized his mind felt much clearer, as if he'd been shaken from a daze. He listened to the storm battering the outside of the barn, finding solace in the raging thunder, wind, and rain—*anything* was more soothing than the captivating fright he'd felt racing through his veins at the sight of the ominous tree. He swallowed, then looked at Obito. Curiously, there was no sign of the bloody rain that had fallen on them only seconds prior. Just as he was about to open his mouth, undeniable dread leaked into the air, and they dared to poke their heads over the barrels again. The light surrounding the tree dimmed, and its shape morphed until it transformed into something much more terrifying.

It stood at least ten feet tall with long, skinny arms ending in three curved claws, and its misshapen body looked as if it'd been slathered in a thick layer of pitch. The smell of rotted flesh, stale blood, and death wafted through the air whenever it moved, and to their horror, a half-eaten man hung from its jaws. The creature's noises sounded almost like purring as it finished devouring the poor soul, tearing through flesh and snapping bones. Sensing the cry lodged in his throat at the sight, Obito clamped a shaky hand over Daisuke's mouth to keep him silent, though neither could look away from the blood dribbling down its jowls.

"That thing's massive," Obito said, barely audible. He turned and glared at Daisuke when he heard the little pest trying—and failing—to suppress a fit of giggles, wishing he didn't understand what had set him off. "Really? *Now?*"

Daisuke put one of his hands over Obito's and pressed them both down, as if he thought the reinforcement would help to keep himself quiet. Obito rolled his eyes and pinched the bridge of his nose with his free hand.

"You idiot," he muttered, which seemed to make Daisuke's efforts even more useless. Despite his initial annoyance, he had to shake his head to keep himself from also laughing, which would've surely blown their cover. Frankly, he wasn't sure how it hadn't happened already. He wriggled his hand free and busied himself with a survey of their surroundings.

Once he'd finally collected himself, Daisuke joined Obito in taking another peek over the barrels. He quietly swore under his breath after a second, more objective appraisal of the creature. "This is going to be tough. What's our plan now?"

"I doubt we can hit it like normal." Obito stretched up just enough again to squint at the back of the creature's neck, then quickly knelt by Daisuke once more. "But there's a symbol of some kind there. Do you see it?"

"I think so. I'll get our last sealing tag ready."

Obito dug around in the leather pack until he found it. After a nearly imperceptible second of hesitation, he handed it over. He didn't think he'd ever been so nervous to give anything to Daisuke; if this went wrong—if *he* was wrong—his friend could die. When Daisuke reached out to take it, he placed his other hand on Obito's, a silent reassurance reinforced by the determination in his eyes.

"How good are you with your kyoketsu-shoge now?"

"Much better than the last time we talked about it."

"Good enough to get our friend over there around the neck?"

Obito looked at the beast again. "The chain won't be strong enough to hold if it resists, but...it *might* buy us some time as a distraction. I don't like it, but I think that's all we'll have."

Obito was stronger, but Daisuke was the faster of the pair. Thanks to his additional training sessions with the acrobats when he could find time, his speed, flexibility, and reactions had all improved greatly. He was hardly the helpless boy he'd been upon arriving in the Capital, but this wasn't normal combat sparring with Obito or another of the onmitsu at the Palace; if he made one wrong move or—somehow—made the mistake of underestimating the monster's prowess, it could be fatal. The consequences from there were unthinkable.

Daisuke's eyes found Obito's again and his lips parted before he knew what he wanted to say.

"I can always try summoning Tatakai," he told his partner, though he knew it was far from what was originally on the tip of his tongue. "I don't know if he'll answer, but..."

"Either way, you need to find a safe spot to wait, like up in the loft." Obito pulled his kyoketsu-shoge from his belt and went back to watching their target as it lumbered around the barn, sluggishly dragging its tail as glowing red eyes mindlessly roved everywhere.

Until they locked onto him. Its narrow, slitted pupils gradually rounded out to look more human, and an intense glow emitted from the creature's irises, casting a faint light over the blood staining its slick skin. Obito couldn't look away, no matter how he tried.

A low, resonating ring like that of a heavy bell thrummed through the air, rendering him immobile. He winced when the sound turned into an unbearable pressure against his ears, but when he shook his head to face the creature again, his surroundings had shifted. Rather than being crouched behind the barrels in the barn, he now stood at the end of a long, eerily familiar hallway. He could hear muffled chatter and laughter, as if a large gathering were taking place only a few rooms away, but what kept his eyes glued to the corridor was the single, half-open door letting a sliver of golden light pour onto the floor's dark wooden planks. Obito jumped when a hand curled around the door and brusquely shoved it open further; two ruby rings caught in the light.

The scent of plums suddenly infiltrated the air. When he looked at his feet, which were now much smaller, and adorned with clean, formal-looking boots rather than the scuffed, muddy ones he'd been wearing, delicate white blossom petals littered the ground.

He brought his gaze to the corridor again. *This isn't real. I haven't been here in years.*

"Obito!" Daisuke's voice was distant, as if his head were plunged underwater, but the sound of him calling struck the illusion like a heavy stone against glass. Rain from a slot in the barn's rotted roofing dripped onto his forehead, shattering the memory and viciously pulling him back down to reality.

When Obito looked to his left, Daisuke was still beside him, eyes wide with worry. He breathed deeply, taking control of his frenzied breathing and emotions once again.

"What happened?" Daisuke whispered.

"I'm not sure," he admitted. He shook his head, willing it away. "An illusion, a memory—maybe both. I'm fine, so focus."

Obito's eyes settled on his partner in a way that didn't leave room for questions or further prodding; no matter how heavily those things sat on Daisuke's tongue, he begrudgingly agreed to drop the subject—for now.

"It looked right at you like it wanted to attack, but it's just sitting there, now. See?" Daisuke bit his lip. After a little more silent observation, he looked at Obito again. "Let's move in."

When Daisuke had barely taken two steps toward his position, a horrible, mangled sound came from the creature's throat, freezing him in place.

Is it...crying? He swallowed his fears and forced himself to keep advancing toward a ladder leading to the barn's loft. Luckily, he'd still gone unnoticed by the time he put his hands on the highest rungs he could reach. The monster kept wailing, unable to hear their soft movements over its own noise. When he looked over his shoulder to check Obito's position, he saw his partner weave between the shadows as he carefully brought himself closer to their target.

Obito drew the kyoketsu-shoge when he was only several paces away from the creature's back, which should've been Daisuke's cue to climb the ladder as fast as possible, but instinct froze him to the spot. His eyes stayed on his partner. Obito wrapped the chain nearest to the weapon's dagger end around his left wrist and carefully lowered the ball weight to keep the links from rattling too loudly, but all his caution seemed to be a waste, as one particularly noisy *jangle* made everything go still. The monster's massive form turned toward Obito and it stood in one surprisingly fluid motion; his eyes went wide, but he didn't waver and started spinning the weapon even when the creature made a confused screeching noise.

Fuck! It sees him! Daisuke's heart stuttered in panic as he released the ladder.

Obito couldn't easily get himself out of the way with all the momentum his weapon built up, nor did it look like he planned to; they couldn't afford for him to back away. Daisuke could only think of one thing to help. He wriggled the first bracelet off his wrist and slathered it with the blood he'd already drawn for the sealing tag before it had time to change into its talisman shape. He sprinted toward them.

"Tatakai, demon of war, I—!"

The creature swiveled at the sound of his voice and swiped at Daisuke before he finished, slashing his stomach with a cold, iron-hard claw. It happened so quickly, he didn't process it until his back hit the ground. He rebounded once before sliding across the barn floor. The realization of what happened barely had time to dance in his mind before his vision went black.

WHEN DAISUKE OPENED HIS eyes again, he was standing on a mountain trail with harsh winter winds lashing at his face. The squall carried tiny, cutting pellets of ice and snow in massive drifts, groaning like a wandering ghost as they rolled through the air. He looked left and right, but it was impossible to know which way he should go; he pivoted several times as he tried to choose a direction, then finally decided to take a cautious step forward. When he moved, the storm abruptly dissipated into nothing more than a few stray snowflakes and a lingering, thin fog in the icy air. Daisuke looked toward the sun, sitting high and small above him in the sky, then at the sheer rockface before him. The mountain stood silent and still, as did everything else.

The air grew so cold it hurt to breathe in, though it soon became the least of his concerns when veins of ice crawled up the rock formation in front of him. They stretched and spider-webbed toward each other until they formed a thick wall. Once the last few feet at the top were also covered, an echoing boom sounded across the mountainside as the ice settled, leaving the howl of wind in its wake. Daisuke couldn't feel the beat of his heart or hear the heave of his breath even though small puffs formed and rose in front of his face in rapid succession. The cold stung at his face, to the point that his skin felt as if it were burning, a sensation he'd never experienced before. The horrible cold spread throughout his body as if the frozen air and ice coursed through his veins.

He felt heavy and weak, so he instinctively reached for the wall, desperate to find support before he collapsed onto the frozen ground—it looked like snowflakes were emerging under his skin as it took on a slightly purple hue. When his palm met the frigid ice, it felt like his hand melded to it; he tried to pull away, but all he could muster was a tired shrug of his shoulder, which wasted even more of his rapidly depleting energy.

Am I...freezing to death? he wondered, mind nearly as numb and leaden as his body. He shook his head, then defiantly glared at his feet. *No, that can't be it*—this *can't even be real. It's more like one of my dreams, isn't it? This must be what happened to Obito...how do I get back to him, though?*

Crunch. The sound of a footstep in the snow forced him to turn around faster than he thought he'd be capable of doing—he barely noticed when his hand came free. His jaw dropped in shock when his eyes landed on a figure in the creeping shadows behind him. The long blade of a katana flashed in the fading light, and when the wind picked up, strands of long red hair flowed in the breeze. Daisuke yelped in terror. Rather, he *would* have, but no sound came out despite the strain on his throat. Panic seized his lungs.

Fuck, fuck fuck! Release the fucking illusion—something! Get me out of here!

As if whatever controlled this strange realm heard his thoughts, the image of a plum blossom began to carve itself into the ice, and seconds later it shattered with a faint green glow threaded with purple and black flecks of light, startling him. He stood in a small orchard of plum trees; their blossoms fell around him like snowfall. The illusion melted away into blinding white as a high-pitched ring overwhelmed his senses.

Daisuke sucked in a huge gulp of air when the real world came into view once more and the ringing subsided. He moaned and slowly raised his left hand to examine it through bleary eyes, grateful to find his skin its normal texture and color. He nearly let himself sink against the ground where he lay, but an earth-shaking, bellowing roar made his head jerk toward the source. Ignoring the intense pain in his abdomen, he was on his feet again in an instant, unsteady and vision blurred, though both righted themselves soon enough.

Obito held the enraged creature at bay with the impossibly strong chain of a kyoketsu-shoge Daisuke had never seen before. A pulsation slammed against his ears like a gong and rippled through the barn as the black metal links grew thicker; they were wound around both of Obito's forearms to give him what little leverage he could gain. The monster pulled on its restraints, sending the dripping, inky pitch texture of its skin everywhere, but he didn't give it an inch. His feet sank further into the earth as the dagger end of his weapon, glowing a jade green, swung near his leg.

Tatakai had come through after all. Daisuke couldn't believe it.

Although his entire body shook from the sight before him, the vision, and searing pain throbbing in his wound, he removed the prepared sealing tag from his shirt with a trembling hand and stepped forward. Whether or not this was their demon, Obito couldn't hold whatever the beast was in place for much longer. When it let out another furious roar and pulled again, the heavy beat pounded in his ears once more, and Daisuke rushed toward his partner. Once they'd exchanged a glance to quickly assess one another's state, they turned their focus on the creature.

"Hold it steady for me," Daisuke told him as he sized up the chain, barely wider than an acrobat's balance beam.

Obito followed his gaze, then tightened his grip as the thing tried to surge forward, which sent any reasonable arguments out the window. "You're fucking insane."

"Maybe," he agreed as he jumped onto it, wincing at the movement. The chain slacked a little under his weight at first, but Obito and Tatakai wasted no time adjusting as he carefully found his footing. "But you trust me, right?"

"You know I do."

Daisuke felt a small, involuntary smile tug at his lips. "Then that's all I need."

He cautiously made his way up the chain, which seemed to continually adjust under his feet in order to keep him balanced; he had no idea how much sentience Tatakai possessed in this state, especially when he'd barely managed summoning him, but it seemed the demon was willing to help. Though the creature snarled and roared, pulled and fought against Obito's hold on it, the chain didn't budge—clearly, *something* drove the proud dragon's will to help them stop this monster.

I wonder, then... Daisuke paused when he finally reached the end of the chain, nearest to the symbol Obito had previously pointed out on the back of the creature's neck. He had to use his hands and feet to keep himself upright, and as the monster was still thrashing, he couldn't get a good look at first. Thankfully, all it took was a second of the beast staying still, and he could finally read it. A small gasp escaped him. "This is—you really *are* Jihuang."

Now he understood the urgency with which he had to act, and why Tatakai had been so determined to assist them, despite the reluctance he'd demonstrated prior to leaving the Capital. Daisuke steadied himself the best he could as he got into a wobbly, half-crouched position, then leapt from the chain onto the demon's shoulder, just barely managing to stick the sealing tag over the characters for the name before it tried throwing him. He grimaced at the feeling of sticky pitch on his skin and clothes.

"Obito!" Daisuke called from over his shoulder as he clung to the monster's massive neck. He felt as flimsy as a paper doll—were the situation any different, this might've looked almost comical. "Make a blood offering with the dagger, then throw it to hit the paper seal!"

"You're making this up as you go, aren't you?!"

"Sorry!"

Obito had to pull hard on the chain again to make sure the beast wouldn't toss his partner across the barn like a ragdoll. "How the fuck—"

The glowing dagger made an unexpected move, as if it were obeying Daisuke's command. It slipped further away from where it dangled in Obito's grasp, slacked its chain by itself, and swung toward him. Because of how things were unfolding on the other end, he didn't have a chance to so much as flinch away from it. The dagger grazed Obito's cheek, then circled again until he could grab the chain near its hilt. This was the duality of the kyoketsu-shoge—entrap on one end, then use the other to attack with precision. Fighting through the sting of a fresh cut and the sensation of warm blood beginning to trickle down his face, he started swinging the weapon forward until it moved in a blurry, fast-spinning circle at his side. He had only a narrow window to hit his mark. As soon as he felt he'd make it, he let the bloodied dagger loose and sent it sailing through the air, praying to gods he didn't even believe in that it wouldn't accidentally strike Daisuke.

He tensely watched the glowing blade arc toward the monster, holding his breath until he saw the tip of the tanto pierce into the paper seal. The chains around his forearms disappeared into a plume of smoke as Daisuke's grip finally failed when the creature thrashed around again, and Obito ran forward to meet him. He—somehow—gracefully landed on his feet like a mischievous black cat. Daisuke tried to shoot him a grin, but he winced and hunched over to clutch his stomach instead.

The monster roared again, making them turn toward it as it lurched forward several steps, its back still to them, and they watched in fascinated horror as the impenetrable skin seemed to liquefy as it fell away from its form. Piece by piece, it melted off and revealed a jade green light, which blazed like an angry flame and gave way to the massive form of a dragon hovering feet off the ground.

Daisuke reached behind himself, catching Obito by the front of his uniform before pulling himself into his partner, who instinctively put his arms around him while they braced for what was coming.

As if distraught, the dragon demon wailed and began swaying from one side to the other, smashing down the barn's walls as it did so. The forgotten dagger, half-buried in dirt and hay, suddenly came to life again. It jumped off the ground and was replaced by Tatakai's regal form, his eyes glowing pure yellow as his snout lifted toward the other demon in the room. Though the second dragon still seemed hazy and unfocused, it made for the ceiling as soon as it sensed Tatakai.

"Jihuang!" the Demon of War bellowed as he slithered through the air at lightning speed. "Don't you run from me, little sister!"

"No, no, no! Stay away, stay away!" the other dragon cried, breaking through the beams and tiles barely holding the roof together while the two onmitsu ran for whatever cover they could find. "Leave me alone!"

Tatakai's body shielded Daisuke and Obito from some of the falling debris as he chased Jihuang higher and higher, swirling into the sky like a beacon of light until he caught up to her. A screech erupted from the other dragon, a horrible, garbled sound Daisuke couldn't place the emotion behind.

Twin columns of glowing jade green raced downward from the heavens, wildly twisting and dancing around each other as they careened toward the ground. As they neared the earth, Tatakai appeared to coil tightly around Jihuang before the two unexpectedly split apart, as if one demon had viciously thrown the other. Two flat, circular rocks resembling Tatakai's talisman appeared out of nowhere, waiting to catch each dragon. The shrieking demon hit one stone talisman's surface, expelling a plume of black shadow seconds before a bright light blinded Obito and Daisuke, and the subsequent shockwave knocked them both off their feet. Daisuke smacked into one of the barn's walls and braced himself against a gust of violent wind, though he was quickly shielded by something else. A daring peek showed his partner had come to the rescue yet again, using their difference in height to hunch over him and block both of their heads and faces until everything settled. Once Obito was certain nothing else would happen, he carefully pushed himself away, stifling the pained noise rising in his throat when he put pressure on his arms.

Dead silence filled the air once the dragons crashed into their respective talismans, interrupted only by Daisuke's ragged breathing. He stepped around his partner, toward where Tatakai's had settled beside Jihuang's amid scattered dirt, debris, and straw, but a signal from Obito kept him from going further, as if he instinctively knew not to approach. Another flare of green light erupted from the new talisman's face, and the second black resin bracelet wrapped around Daisuke's right wrist again.

Daisuke collapsed against what little remained of the barn's wall as he closed his eyes, sighing with relief, though it didn't last longer than the time it took to light a cigarette before another thought occurred to him. "Fuck. Obito, we need to do a sealing ritual."

Obito stiffly went over to the remaining talisman and picked it up before returning to Daisuke, which was when he noticed the deep, angry chain link indentations littering his forearms. The chains had so deeply imprinted into his skin that Daisuke wasn't sure how his arms hadn't been crushed. Ignoring it, Obito simply dropped Jihuang's talisman into his outstretched palm.

"No," he firmly answered; his face looked slightly ashen, and while he spoke as if nothing was wrong, his next words revealed that he wasn't doing much better than his partner. "We need to find a Healer before we can do anything else."

"Fine," Daisuke groaned as he pushed himself off the wall. "But you're carrying me back."

Knowing full well his partner couldn't support his weight, he'd meant it as an artless joke, and a way of trying to brush off the fact they'd nearly died just now, but he stumbled when he stepped forward and fell against Obito's shoulder. Startled, neither of them moved; somewhere between a flurry of emotion and the fog of exhaustion, Daisuke caught himself thinking this was a nice place to rest. He decided he'd stay there until Obito couldn't stand it anymore, and closed his eyes again to let the first signs of morning light staining the sky ease his mind. It wasn't until now that he'd realized the storm had subsided, and yet another layer of relief laced its way into a slow sigh.

The faint yet familiar clatter of wagon wheels sounded in the distance as daybreak touched the horizon. Since Junpei was the only one who would think to look here, they could only assume it was him approaching, and fast—his poor horse. Daisuke wanted to be furious he wasn't still guarding the trailhead as he'd agreed to earlier, but couldn't summon the energy for it; really, he was thrilled the soldier was on his way, likely driven into action by whatever he might've seen or heard from his post.

Obito's body jerked a bit when he also heard the cart coming. He cleared his throat. "We should probably…"

"R-right," Daisuke agreed, hoping it was still too dark for the flush in his cheeks to show. When they shifted to separate, he felt something warm on his abdomen and glanced down at the seeping wound. Black blotches dotted his vision as he swayed a little. "Is…that's my blood dripping everywhere, isn't it?"

"Don't look." Thankfully, Obito's hands were quick to grip his shoulders, keeping him upright—he didn't even know how he could move his arms with the condition they were in, but Daisuke was grateful. Just as grateful as he was for the crescendo of noise from Junpei's cart.

BARELY ABLE TO CLING to consciousness, exhaustion forced Daisuke to drift off while he and Obito rode in the cart as Junpei rushed them back into the heart of Baohu under a pink and gold sunrise. His grip on reality slipped through his fingers several times, and he believed himself to have fallen into a full-blown illusion once again by the time he felt someone lift his body through a thin moment of awareness.

Muffled voices came, and soon after, he felt as though he'd been caught in a tangle of shadowy tendrils. Fear spiked his heart rate when something wet touched his lower lip, then slid down his throat; he squeezed his eyes shut to hold his stomach together at the pungent aftertaste. Worried he'd fallen victim to another use of shadow magic, he fought against everything trying to pull him down. The voices grew louder, urgent, but he still couldn't make out their words, or even if they belonged to men or women. Several blurred faces came into view as warmth spread across his abdomen, looming like crows circling a field mouse, and he gasped when he thought he saw a claw coming toward him from the corner of his eye.

Without warning, strong hands clamped down on Daisuke's wrists and pinned him to something much softer than he expected—a bed. He tried to resist the hold, but every time he pushed up, he was held firmly in place, and he soon felt gentler restraints on his legs. A flash of clarity showed him the very real sight of deep markings against dark skin; he frantically searched his hazy surroundings.

"Daisuke, look at me," Obito said firmly, and his frenzied stare instantly went to him, finally breaking through the fevered hallucination. "Breathe. Again, deeper this time."

With a second, more measured breath in, Daisuke's fists gradually relaxed, and in turn, so did Obito's grip on his wrists. They repeated the exercise until Daisuke's thundering heart slowed, and his eyelids grew heavy; a sense of calm washed over his senses when he closed his eyes.

While still hovering on the edge of lucidity, he heard Obito say, "Let them help you."

Daisuke didn't move again until his eyes fluttered open hours later. Everything was quiet, and the soft glow from a single candle flickered somewhere in his periphery, casting a warm light into an otherwise darkened room. Since someone had kindly dressed him in sleep clothes, removed his boots, and untied his hair, he was quite content under the blanket placed over him; he thought a few more minutes of rest couldn't hurt. However, before he could drift off again, he heard quiet humming on his right. His body jerked when he tried to sit upright. Although it didn't respond in the way he'd hoped, the sudden movement caused a dull ache to thrum across his abdomen, eliciting an involuntary moan. He winced, then settled for simply turning his head to search for the source of the humming.

A woman dressed in blue and white robes with an ivory ribbon holding back her silvery hair stood near his bedside, bent over a small table as she set a basin upon it. Apparently sensing his eyes on her, she looked his way, then smiled gently when she saw him trying to blink the exhaustion out of his mind.

"You're awake," the Healer said; her voice was calm and steady. "You may be sore for a bit yet, so try to avoid quick movements when you can. You should be right in a few days."

"What happened?" His throat was dry. "Where am I?"

She began washing her hands. "You're in a room at Senator Yumio's estate. I'm not surprised you don't remember—you were quite out of it when those other young men brought you to us. Luckily, Senator Yumio had the foresight to bring my Healing consort to his home before the storm started last night. He wanted us to be ready to work with all three of you should it be necessary."

Daisuke's eyelids drooped as he settled into the comfortable bedding once more, soothed as he listened to the elderly woman's explanation.

"One of your friends was quite adamant that we shouldn't give you opium to sedate you, which was...problematic. Turns out, you're quite the fighter, so putting you to sleep while we worked was necessary." She paused, and Daisuke thought he could hear the way she'd grinned while doing so. "In any case, because of your frenzied state, I also worried about using our Healing energies to *make* you sleep, so we went with a different medicine instead. Thankfully, the alternative worked and kept you out for a while. Once we began healing your...mysterious wound, we encountered an even stranger energy. Drawing it out and sealing it properly was tedious work, even with how well it responded to me—it *wanted* to go, but couldn't. I had to have one of my girls drag a priest over here by the ear to help."

Daisuke's eyes flew open again, snapping back to her as she dried her hands.

"I'm afraid that's all I know. Your companions are being quite tight-lipped about the whole situation."

"Sister," he weakly began. The title was no longer in common use, but a Healer of this woman's age should still expect to be addressed as such—it was proper, and more than deserved for the one who helped him. "Our work isn't over yet. We need to seal the monster away for good, and as soon as possible. Is there anywhere we can perform a ritual?"

She took a moment to study him carefully—judging by the sudden, subtle flash of realization in her eyes under the candlelight, she knew he wouldn't be allowed in the Temple. He didn't particularly mind having the option eliminated; something in his gut told him not to trust the priests with Jihuang's spirit, which was why he called her a monster rather than trying to explain. The Healer clicked her tongue; somehow, he knew the derisive noise wasn't directed at him.

"I suppose you *do* have Northern Nomadic blood, don't you? Half, I'm guessing?"

"Twice more than half." Daisuke chuckled; it was cut short with a wince and a jab of pain. For once, though, he was thankful for the clergy's idiocy when it came to "heathens" like himself—it was probably how the priest had justified leaving without further questions as soon as the residual demonic energy was sealed.

"I'm sure I speak for all in Baohu when I say I'd rather you take that thing far from here, but you won't be up for travel for a few days. Let me see...that's right. There's an abandoned temple near the main east bridge. Perhaps you can take it there; you shouldn't be bothered and have plenty of space."

"Thank you, Sister. Please, apologize to your consort for me."

"Rest a while longer," the elderly Healer told him as she came to his side, then pulled the covers under his chin again. "I'll let your friends know we spoke—they've been worried about you."

Daisuke fell back into a deep slumber before she finished speaking.

He awoke again sometime later. He wasn't sure how long it'd been since he drifted off, but judging by the light and scent of fresh air, someone had recently opened the window and parted the curtains to invite in the evening sun and a pleasantly cool breeze. Windchimes faintly sounded from somewhere just outside. He gently pressed down on his abdomen, relieved to find it was now only a little tender compared to earlier, and felt confident enough to pull himself upright. Even after he was cleared for travel, he likely wouldn't be up for sparring or any other training for a bit longer, but he didn't necessarily mind. He looked forward to any excuse he could find to avoid practicing with Junpei, and the three had spent plenty of evenings on the way to Baohu engaged in it.

He was unsteady at first when his bare feet touched down on the wooden floor, but it didn't take long for him to find his balance. A screen had been erected just on the other side of the small table where the Healer had washed her hands earlier; replacing her basin, a clean set of his clothes were folded neatly with the blue tie he liked to use in his hair curled atop them. He figured he'd be fine in the white linen shirt and trousers for a few more minutes. He wanted to bask in the sunbeams and clean air for a little while before getting dressed, then setting out to find his partner and their companion.

However, his plan quickly changed when he stepped out from behind the screen. In the corner near the window, where long cotton curtains easily swayed in the breeze, Obito slept soundly. Likely for the first time all day. Daisuke let himself get caught up in the sight, admiring the way late afternoon sun cast a warm glow on his brown skin, how the wind gently tousled his dark hair, and the peaceful expression resting on his face while he dozed. Daisuke smiled to himself, unable to suppress the surge of affection blooming in his chest. He didn't think he would've been able to even if he'd tried.

"How long have you been here?" he whispered as he crouched in front of Obito. Driven by impulse, he brushed stray hair away from his eyes; long eyelashes fluttered, but he didn't stir. He smiled again, letting himself stare a little longer. "Well, I'm somehow on my feet again, so I guess I'll get dressed and find out how hard *you* are to wake up for a change."

Daisuke drew back slightly to get up, but paused when his gaze subconsciously fell on Obito's arms, and his fingers followed, hovering over where the chain's deep indents once were. Resisting the urge to touch his cheek and risk waking him, he saw the cut from the kyoketsu-shoge was also gone. He sighed in relief, then went behind the folding screen where someone had neatly set aside his regular clothing earlier.

Not long after pulling on his gi, rustling and a light creak on the wooden floorboards alerted him to movement from the screen's other side. Another smile crossed his lips; a softer version of his usual devious grin.

"Did you wake up just to see me half-naked?" he playfully chided over his shoulder.

Obito stopped on the other side, clearly exasperated when he said, "You're obviously feeling better."

Daisuke continued with his teasing as if he hadn't heard his partner. "You know I'm not shy—if you wanted to look, you only had to ask."

Obito sighed. "Hikari's sake. Daisuke—"

"Are you rolling your eyes at me?" Daisuke snickered as he finished rolling back the sleeves on his gi and shitagi; his grin widened when he heard Obito swear at him under his breath. "I was injured. Can't you be nice and feel bad for poor little me?"

"Not when you act like this—if anything, I should see if the Healers left that medicine around."

"The gods let me live another day. Don't you think it'd be a waste if I didn't make them and everyone else regret it?" Unable to keep up with his own nonsense, Daisuke's act fell apart with another laugh, which was also cut short when his body reminded him of how sore it still was; getting dressed hadn't exactly been a speedy process for a reason. He subconsciously shook the bracelets on his right wrist, hoping his recovery wouldn't somehow interfere with the sealing ritual.

He blinked, suddenly realizing he hadn't seen Jihuang's talisman since he and Obito were still standing amid the broken debris of the barn.

"Where's the talisman, anyway?" Daisuke asked as he finished tying his belt, then poked his head out from around the screen before pushing it back to let the light from the window into the rest of the room.

Obito shook himself, quickly recovering from how unexpectedly close his friend's face had been to his own. "Junpei has it. We put it in an iron box for safekeeping, and I told him I'd kill him if he lost it, so he's been protective over it. It hasn't caused any problems yet."

"Not surprised—he always listens to you for some reason. And, I guess, if nothing else, he *is* a good soldier." Daisuke sat on the bed and sighed with relief. Yet another nightmare confronted, and now it was nearly finished. He was sure the people of Baohu were ready to rest easy once more.

After a moment, he gestured for his friend to join him, and they listened to the streets below in comfortable silence.

DEMON'S SEAL

SENATOR YUMIO REFUSED TO take "no" for an answer when he offered to have them take up lodgings at his residence for the rest of their stay in Baohu. Daisuke and Obito watched with immense discomfort as one of the Senator's servants brought their things—as well as Junpei's—from the inn to new rooms at his estate, but neither could scrape together the energy to protest it. Besides, the poor man looked so exhausted from everything that had transpired lately, even Daisuke's contrarian nature became muted when speaking with him, which Obito found nothing short of impressive. Not even a stern lecture from Master Yujin could accomplish such a feat most days.

"Whether or not I approve or feel it's too soon, it seems the townsfolk are insisting upon a celebration tonight," Senator Yumio told them as the servant bowed and disappeared down the hall. "Please, feel free to join the festivities. I believe you've earned it as much as they have."

Along with his apparently boundless generosity, Senator Yumio had a quiet demeanor, soft smile, and kind eyes, which made it annoyingly difficult to dislike him on the principle of class difference alone. Arguably, he was nothing like Senator Hajime or other nobility—Daisuke had little choice but to change his opinion of the man, which he hadn't been fully aware of forming in the first place. A gentle nudge to his shoulder from Obito snapped him from his thoughts, and they bowed together.

"Thank you, Senator."

After the ordeal they'd just endured, any amount of celebration sounded like far too much excitement, even for Daisuke, but he couldn't deny the rumble in his empty stomach. He blushed at the noise it made, then sheepishly looked at his partner. A hint of an amused smirk played at the corner of Obito's mouth.

"Guess I'm hungry."

"Good—that makes two of us."

Once they'd walked around a bit and ate their fill of a shared order of spicy gyoza, Daisuke decided he'd already had more than he could take of merriment and revelry. It was noisy, crowded, and the smells of ale and wine and various fried street foods were giving him a headache. Finally, he looked at Obito, who also seemed desperate to escape to somewhere less central to all the excitement, though it was less of a surprise from the quieter of the two.

"Do you think we could go somewhere to talk about what happened last night?"

Relieved for an excuse to escape, Obito answered quickly, "I think we should. Besides, if I remember right, *you* promised a 'fat roll of white leaf' earlier."

Daisuke grinned. Around half an hour later, they'd found their way back to Senator Yumio's mansion and climbed onto one of the lower roofs of the Senator's home, where they had a decent view of the city and an even better look at the continuing celebration in the square. Since Obito insisted on not letting Daisuke have the matches—admittedly, a wise decision on his part—he handed over the white leaf he'd promised for his friend to light.

"How did you do this?" Obito muttered to himself as he fixed Daisuke's hack job at rolling the substance into a paper, then directed his next question at his friend. "Haven't you learned by now?"

"Please, I'm too pretty to worry about that. Some warm soul always shows up to help."

"Is that right? Sounds like I should make you do this yourself next time."

"You're so mean to me, just like those boys who pull on girls' braids."

Obito rolled his eyes and handed over the finished product, but he hadn't argued with Daisuke at any point. Neither of them knew how to feel about that when they silently acknowledged it, so they settled for passing the roll back and forth in peaceful quiet until it was nothing more than a smoldering nub which Obito snuffed out on a nearby roof tile.

Now plenty high and in a much chattier mood, Daisuke eventually figured out how to ask, "Did you hear the way Jihuang screamed when Tatakai took her down? I thought it was pure rage, but now, that doesn't seem right. I don't think pain fits, either. What was it?"

Obito's gaze went to the street below, blankly watching those still enjoying the festivities. "Fear."

"I wonder, then..." Daisuke wiggled the first bracelet off his wrist and with a shimmer of green light, it shifted into the stone talisman. "Is she *afraid* of Tatakai? For being the demon of war, he's not exactly scary, but if they have some sort of hierarchy...no, they refer to each other as siblings. Siblings don't have a hierarchy beyond the typical younger-older dynamics, do they?"

"They do in noble families, even the ones who don't follow traditions as closely. Youngest sons like me have a lower social status than their younger sisters."

"They're usually treated like family servants if they aren't conscripted, too, right?"

"Right."

After a moment, Daisuke laughed helplessly. "Fuck me. Blame it on the white leaf, but...where was I going with this?"

"What Jihuang fears." Obito chuckled at the confused look on Daisuke's face, but his thoughts drifted to the names of the six talisman demons as he'd read them in the book.

Jihuang's name meant "famine," but this particular demon had absorbed Hikari's fears when Zandaka—the supposed Demon King—sealed the goddess's heavenly abilities. In the Between Realm as one of the Demon King's disciples, Jihuang was responsible for the gentle, calm healing of souls who came to her and her siblings, just as Tatakai oversaw the souls of soldiers and those who faced other insurmountable difficulties in life. As far as anyone knew, she didn't have the power to directly impact the yield of crops, but cared for those who had died under those circumstances.

Obito was deeply familiar with the ways fear could make a person lash out; perhaps these demons weren't so different. "We know from the book that Jihuang won't cause a famine anytime soon, but she's clearly afraid of something. Maybe the ritual used to summon her made being awake feel more like a nightmare, or something even simpler, like being afraid of living humans—she probably isn't used to them. As for why she hunted them, she might not even know; it could go back to the ritual again. In any case, if Jihuang *is* afraid, sealing her won't be easy without some extra steps."

Daisuke snapped his fingers and touched the talisman to his wrist to make it transform again. "Right. We need to make sure she feels calm and secure before we can seal her."

"What are you thinking?"

"I *can't* think anymore. I'm too tired." Daisuke sighed and leaned against Obito's shoulder; a sense of quiet contentment, coupled with a slight twinge of embarrassment, warmed a spot in his chest when he once again thought of how nice it felt to rest there. Comfortable, safe...he swallowed. *Dear gods, I'm in so much trouble.*

Obito may have reflexively stiffened at first, but it didn't take long for the worry to ease itself—only Daisuke could get away with this, and even though he felt like he could never vocalize it, he didn't mind the touch. After a brief silence, he asked, "Do you want to go inside?"

"Not yet. Let's stay here for a bit."

Somehow, Daisuke was up and dressed before his two companions the following morning, not long after the first hints of light touched the sky. Obito almost didn't believe it. He even blinked several times out of surprise to ensure he wasn't still half-asleep when he discovered him, sitting cross-legged beside a table in one of Senator Yumio's tea rooms across the hallway from the accommodations they'd been provided. The little pest stayed quiet, flipping through the pages of the occult book, looking more studious than Obito could recall from recent memory.

Daisuke turned to him with a smile already on his lips when Obito settled in next to him, placing the candle he'd carried beside the one his partner was using to read.

"The Head Healer told me yesterday there's an abandoned temple we could use to properly seal Jihuang again," Daisuke explained when his friend joined him, absentmindedly twisting his earrings as he spoke. "We'll have to get the directions from Senator Yumio, but it being former sacred grounds should help a lot. Am I reading this right? The seal we've been using should work fine?"

Obito took the journal from his hands. He studied the page Daisuke had indicated for a minute, then nodded. "That's how it reads to me, too, but we'll need to follow some extra steps."

"We were ready for that, anyway."

"What's going on?" Junpei sleepily mumbled from the doorway. Hair a mess and clothing disheveled, he slumped into a spot near the corner of the table as they turned to look at him. He rubbed his face a few times, trying to force himself into a more awake state. He'd been out late carousing and drinking, as he'd announced when he returned and interrupted his companions' sleep. It took every ounce of Daisuke's willpower not to laugh at his sorry-looking condition now.

"We're going to the abandoned temple here to make sure the demon is properly sealed before we head home," Obito explained as if it were the most ordinary thing he could've said.

Rudely shaken from his half-awake state and now on high alert, Junpei nearly leapt out of his skin. He stared at them, mouth hanging open until he found his outrage again. "Are you two insane?! You can't go into an abandoned temple! Those things are haunted!"

Obito traded a sidelong glance with Daisuke, noting how Junpei's nerves grew visibly rattled when they grinned at each other. He cleared his throat; it was never too early for easy entertainment. "Daisuke, does the ritual require *willing* participants?"

"Not many do when dealing with demons and ghosts. Really, as long as there's another warm body on the sealing circle, we can still manage if he doesn't scream or thrash around too much." Daisuke barely held in his laughter, then added, "We might want to gag him just in case, though."

"Good thing he keeps plenty of extra rope in his cart."

"Won't this be a fun story to tell everyone when we get home? Why—"

"Fine!" Junpei interrupted, slamming his hands down on the table and making the candle flames dance—just as Obito assumed, no soldier could stand the idea of losing face to the onmitsu. Looking slightly pale, he said in a much smaller voice, "Fine. I'll go."

The abandoned temple certainly lived up to its name. From where they stood at the base of the stairs, rot, loose boards, and broken tiles were clear indicators that no one had worshipped here in decades. Overgrown shrubs nearly blocked the way up, and ivy crawled everywhere along the temple's outside. Obito had procured the directions from Senator Yumio and still almost missed it due to the trees and long grasses surrounding it. Thankfully, the steps leading up to the balcony were made of stone and hadn't suffered nearly as much weathering in the unknown years since the temple's last use. According to what Obito knew about temple structure, the inside should be similar to the one on the Palace's grounds. Those who lived in temples had quarters in the lower levels, while the upper worship hall was meant for the public to come and pay respects to a statue of Hikari, meditate, and to speak with the priests for guidance or divination. Many of the boards making up the veranda and railing on this one were either rotted or dangerously sunken and soft, so they had to watch their step as they approached old double-doors, where braziers filled with water and debris stood on each side.

Junpei frowned at Daisuke when he took two cigarettes out of his leather satchel and handed one off to Obito. "You two aren't seriously taking a smoke break first."

"Are we in a hurry?" Daisuke tilted his head. "You're more than welcome to stay out here with us if you're afraid to go in there alone."

It'd been a few days since Junpei had a chance to give them one of those strange looks he seemed to reserve just for them—truthfully, Daisuke was beginning to miss it—but Obito ignored it as he lit both cigarettes. Their companion eventually gave up on trying to articulate whatever he was thinking and stepped toward the door; to no one's surprise, it gave away with ease.

Junpei stared into the darkness for a moment, then finally turned to them and said, "You know, on second thought, take your time. Someone should do a preliminary sweep, anyway."

Obito furrowed his brows once the soldier disappeared indoors with a lantern and a pack of matches he'd brought along. "Why is he like this?"

"Because he likes you." Daisuke shot a smug little smirk Obito's way when he noticed his friend covering his face with one hand. Choosing to lean into how one might mistake his action for irritation rather than exasperation, he added, "Don't hate me just because I'm right."

"I'm not sure how to tell you this, but I don't think he likes either of us very much." Obito rolled his eyes. "And you know I don't hate you."

For some stupid reason, Daisuke's heart skipped a beat. "C-come on, you know that's not what I meant. It's more like hating me in the moment, like when I won't stop annoying you or saying things that get under your skin just to get a reaction out of you."

"I knew that." Obito glanced at him, a hint of amusement playing on his lips. "But I didn't think it'd be that easy to make you confess to your terrible ways."

Daisuke flushed. He couldn't take it; flustering and teasing was *his* job. How the *hell* did it flip around on him? He watched Obito for a long moment, wondering when he'd picked up on his devious plan and decided to use it for his own devices, while also trying to resist feeling so impressed by it. Still, he had to try regaining control over the situation at least one more time for the game to keep going, and needed to strike while the iron—and his blood—was hot.

"Pulling my braids again." Daisuke gave him the most devilish grin he could muster, crossing his arms as he casually leaned against the wall after he put his cigarette out and Obito did the same. "You don't need to be like that—we both know you'd kiss me if I let you."

Those forest green eyes locked onto Daisuke in such an inexplicably forceful way that it made his heart race and his body go still.

Obito didn't know what came over him. After enduring Daisuke's teasing for so long and playing back with shows of annoyance or quick comebacks, his self-control suddenly evaporated into nothing. Deciding it was time to meet the little pest on his level, and mercilessly, he closed the gap between them before bending toward Daisuke's ear; their cheeks were so close to brushing, his skin prickled with warmth.

"What if I would?" he asked, voice low, all but daring his partner to give him another smart-ass answer.

Daisuke felt like he'd been struck dizzy, certain his face was literally on fire as a rush of indescribable, almost unbearable heat surged through his veins. By the time he floated back down to reality, he realized his mouth was hanging open, and he forced it closed. He also saw Obito had already broken away and was entering the building without him, as if the exchange never occurred. He caught his breath and clutched at his pounding heart.

That wasn't even close to fair! Daisuke internally griped, scowling at the ground when he finally forced his unsteady legs into motion so he could follow. *When the hell did he get so good at this game?! Did I get worse at it? What...what the hell just happened?!*

He bit his lip. Perhaps worse, despite all his private complaints, he'd thoroughly enjoyed it.

It didn't matter for much longer, though, since the dim light cast by Junpei's lantern showed how much work needed to be done before they could use the space in the temple's main room. Fortunately for him, his companions didn't share his mindset of hating physical work when it came to something like this. Junpei eventually found brooms, cloths, and a bucket in a cobweb-filled closet down the rickety stairs where old living quarters existed.

The three busied themselves with sweeping, dusting, wiping the floors by hand, and lighting the other braziers and lanterns in the temple's main worship hall. Junpei took extra care when cleaning off the small, heavily eroded statue of Hikari toward the front. Noting the worried crease in his brow as he did so, Daisuke sensed the ritual wouldn't be easy for their poor soldier. Even so, he helped make sure the floor was clear for when Obito began drawing the sealing circle in charcoal.

"What does it all mean?" Junpei nervously asked when he was about halfway done, looking away yet again from watching Daisuke place candles and incense in whichever good spots he could find around the room.

Obito sighed in annoyance, as this was a much larger seal than he usually had to draw, but still explained as he kept making the proper markings. "The mitsudomoe represent the three spirit realms, a thick circle around them symbolizes the barrier between spirits and the living, and flames in each of the cardinal directions call upon the elements of nature."

"I didn't think *you*, of all the people I've met, would believe in this stuff."

Obito made a noncommittal noise, but didn't put much effort into a more intelligent response—he didn't want to admit how much he felt the same some days. Daisuke had to stifle a cackle at the pair.

"So, if this creepy thing's ready to go," Junpei began when Obito put the charcoal away; he looked as if he were about to be sick, but Daisuke had to commend him for his willingness to cooperate and listen...even if he *had* been bullied into it a bit. "What's next?"

Daisuke tried not to snicker at the soldier's expression as he lit the candles, then calmly said, "We each need to make a blood offering on the circle."

"...Seriously?"

"We're not messing with you this time. It's a small amount, anyway." Obito unsheathed his tanto, took Daisuke's hand, and gently pressed the tip into the pad of his ring finger; the shorter boy's face became sallow the second a tiny bulb of crimson appeared.

Junpei wiped his face, then took out his own knife after watching Obito prick his own finger. "I'm never going to recover from doing this mission with you two—I can't believe I signed myself up for it."

"Neither can we." Daisuke grinned when the soldier gave him a dirty look.

Once they'd each left a streak of blood near one of the three right-facing tomoe, on the circle surrounding the swirls, Daisuke caught Junpei's expression from his periphery while he stood by, tensely gazing down at the symbol as he awaited the next steps. There wasn't a single doubt he was absolutely frightened. He reminded himself of how Obito had reacted after they witnessed the summoning ritual during the solstice prayer, and thought he shouldn't let Junpei suffer the same if he could prevent it.

"Junpei," he softly called out; their companion's eyes instantly went to him. "Obito told you about everything that happened while I was out of it yesterday, right?"

Fists clenched, he mutely nodded. His gaze briefly flicked toward Obito as he came to stand at Daisuke's side, as if it'd somehow confirm he wasn't losing his sanity with every passing word of this conversation. Amusing as it was, neither blamed him for it.

Daisuke continued, "We talked more last night during the celebration. Jihuang *is* a demon, there's no argument against that, but she isn't an evil entity—she's just afraid, and really wants to go home. We all need you to stay calm and centered so we can help her."

"*She's* afraid?" Junpei didn't seem to notice the light, coaxing tone in Daisuke's voice. He swallowed, then narrowed his eyes as he pushed his shoulders back. "And just where the hell is 'home' for a creature like this?"

"We don't know yet," Obito answered; a half-truth, but Junpei clearly wasn't ready for all of it. "But I assume we'd all rather have her there than here."

Daisuke handed Junpei a little silver bell attached to a purple tassel and one of the incense sticks he'd brought along. "We'll let you decide when to begin. Once we've all started meditating, ring the bell to open the way for us to reach the demon, and keep an eye on this incense. When it burns down, you'll ring the bell again to close the meditation and the window to the spirit realm—the *most* important part, though, is for you to stay calm."

"Fine," Junpei agreed after a moment of squinting at the bell, though he still looked skeptical. "Let's just get this over with."

"That's the way."

They each stood near their respective blood offerings on the circle, and Junpei, trying his best not to shake, lit the incense. Everyone gave each other one last cursory look—a final chance to back out—before Daisuke and Obito closed their eyes. Junpei hesitated, then did the same, unsure if he *wanted* to open them again to keep watch.

The space of a deep breath later, the bell gently rang.

Daisuke opened his eyes again in a familiar place—the mountaintop where snow swirled around him without touching him, as if an invisible dome protected him from the elements, his pure white surroundings starkly contrasted by the black trunk of a completely bare tree. When he looked to his left, Obito was at his side, looking just as bewildered as he'd felt the first time he'd visited wherever this sacred place might be. Perhaps it didn't even exist outside of the spiritual domains.

Daisuke sighed in relief when he saw the white wolf waiting for them near the red rope barrier protecting a cave that let no light inside. "We're safe here."

Obito examined the area anxiously, as if he couldn't see her. "If you insist."

He gave his friend a soft, encouraging smile and linked their arms before they stepped forward together. The white wolf vanished in a flurry of snowflakes as soon as they came near, but Daisuke remembered what she said about the demons of the Between Realm often harboring resentment toward forest spirits. Obito lifted the rope so Daisuke could pass under, then followed, and they went forward at one another's side until they reached the bottom chamber of the cave. A galaxy of glowing, multicolored speckles illuminated the normally solid black floor. The seven dragon statues stood on their pedestals at the far side, surrounded by a gentle, warm light. A gold orb sat like an inlaid jewel upon the foreheads of four, while two remained without, and the one in the center had deep cracks all throughout its winding body which made it look as though it should've shattered by now.

Obito couldn't help but think of the little dragon figurines he'd once found in Zhao while he waited for Itsuki to deliver a message from Master Yujin to the Magistrate who presided there. Before his memory could venture further into that night, the soft, ethereal light surrounding the dragon statues gradually flared until it filled the room in a jade green glow.

"Fucking gods," Daisuke whispered in shock as he subconsciously latched onto Obito's arm again, his hushed exclamation echoing throughout the chamber. "I've seen this place in my dreams so many times, but it's never looked this lively."

"Which could be good *or* bad," Obito pointed out, though he was also undeniably fascinated by the otherworldly beauty surrounding them. For all the nights they'd spent stargazing, whether on the way to Baohu or while at home in the Capital, he'd never seen anything this stunning.

Two long, jade green dragons arose like spirits from the second and third statues that stood on the left from the center. Tatakai was easily recognizable by now, but the one beside him had softer, smoother features and looked far more delicate, more like a glass figure rather than a protector of the Between Realm. In an unagitated state, Jihuang seemed as serene as the meditation they'd used to begin the sealing process; her robes, like Tatakai's, billowed all around her, as did a mane of white hair that was decorated with a delicate hairpin and threaded with braids here and there. A purple glass plum blossom dangled from one of the plaits hanging over her shoulder. Her golden eyes settled on the pair of onmitsu before her, and she tilted her head toward her brother.

"These are the ones?" she asked quietly. A single streak of black came down from her lower eyelids as serpentine slits formed her pupils. She wore the same golden headpiece as Tatakai, and like his, six rubies twinkled at each point.

The Demon of War wordlessly nodded and patted his sister's arm with a clawed hand in a surprisingly gentle motion, then gestured toward them.

The second dragon demon lifted herself high above her statue before she smoothly drifted toward them. Her long body trailed behind her as she circled a few times, before coming to rest in front of Daisuke and Obito, expression soft as she shifted from appearing transparent to solid, much like the two boys in front of her.

"Don't you two make an unlikely pair?" she mused with a light chuckle. A massive, curved claw gently stroked Obito's face first, then Daisuke's. "I must apologize for causing you such trouble, young ones. I was not myself when you faced me—whoever tried to summon me did so with an odd ritual, and before I knew it, my slumber turned into a nightmare. It seems you were both healed, though; trust that I am grateful to Hikari's Healers for looking after your wellbeing."

"What can you remember?" Obito asked, unable to understand *why* he'd opened his mouth.

Jihuang's expression turned pensive and sorrowful. Slowly, she answered, "Hunger. Aching, inescapable hunger. And the humans I tried to satiate myself with. It...they...nothing was enough. If His Highness learned of my actions..."

"You didn't have control over yourself," he reminded her. "And it's over, now."

"And, like my venerable self, you are in the care of *these* humans, not the ones who dared disturb you." Tatakai floated to her side and playfully blew a plume of smoke at their faces before addressing them. "These things said, your sealing ceremony has done wonders, but we both need time to recover in the Between Realm after such events, and to discuss the ritual she was summoned with. I expect you won't be bothering us unnecessarily."

"Big mean lizard," Daisuke teased, nearly making Obito's heart fail.

Tatakai laughed as more smoke came from between his jaws and Jihuang shook her massive head. As a final gesture of goodwill, she touched the tip of a claw to each of their foreheads, then sailed back to her statue with Tatakai in tow. Both dragon demons cupped their hands and leaned forward in what looked like a deep bow, then disappeared into their jade statues once more. Silence filled the chamber until the light jingle of a bell abruptly pulled them back into reality.

ABOUT A WEEK AFTER Jihuang had been allowed to rest once more, Junpei opined it was beyond time to return to the Capital—something neither Obito nor Daisuke could argue against. They'd only stayed in Baohu as long as they had to ensure the seal would hold, cleanse the destroyed barn's grounds to the best of their abilities, and help Senator Yumio with whatever he might need to clean up from the disaster Jihuang's awakening had brought. General Yuta was still too ashamed to show his face, but Junpei persuaded him into attending to his soldiers and their grief, rather than keeping his barracks cold and closed off; eventually, he even found the bravery to write a detailed report to General Aki, which he gladly entrusted to the younger soldier.

The morning of their departure brought a light rain and delightfully cooler temperatures, but didn't deter their decision to leave Baohu. Summer was beginning to wane, which meant these sprinkling showers could come and go at any moment—it'd be against their best interest to try waiting for it to pass. Any further delays could lead to a dangerous situation in the mountains once the first rounds of snowfall arrived.

Junpei said his farewells to Senator Yumio and went to prepare his horse for the journey home. Daisuke and Obito had packed their bags already, and were now left alone with the Senator to continue their conversation, respectfully kneeling in his main office as they waited for him to speak again.

Senator Yumio faced the window, hands behind his back as he examined the drizzling sky. He was silent for a few moments before he rounded on them once more. "I won't deny what happened—I *can't*. My citizens went through hell, and doing so would dishonor those who were lost and their surviving loved ones."

"I don't think I understand the problem, then," Daisuke confessed after exchanging an equally confused glance with Obito.

The Senator pursed his lips, as if choosing his words carefully. "It's that pesky rumor mill. Once word gets out, I'll have fellow politicians calling me all manner of nasty things and insist on unseating me on the grounds I'm mentally unfit. And then there's the people who will inevitably come poking around about the incident. What am I meant to say in either situation?"

"Nothing. There's no need to say anything. We'll report everything to the Capital, which means the other politicians get to complain to higher-ups all they want and get nowhere with it, and you can let the locals take care of the stories. It'll draw more people in that way." Daisuke chuckled at the man's concerned expression. "You're too honest for your own good, Senator. Play your cards right, and this will be something positive for Baohu. Trust me."

Obito nodded. "If you have more people coming around to see things for themselves, you can take the extra tax revenue from the increase in tourism and use it to pay reparations to the families most heavily affected."

Senator Yumio smiled softly as he entertained their ideas for a bit, then gave them a sincere bow. "Worrying for nothing as usual, I suppose. In any case, Baohu owes you two its deepest gratitude. Please, don't hesitate to call on us if you ever need anything in the future. We will answer."

"I DON'T KNOW ABOUT you two, but I can't wait to get back to the Capital," Junpei announced as he jumped down from the driver's seat and stretched.

Although they'd tried to politely decline, Senator Yumio had insisted on funding at least part of their journey home. Since he'd given them the money as a "gift," returning or more firmly refusing it would've been extremely rude, so they'd begrudgingly accepted while the man's eyes held a subtle, victorious gleam. He was surprisingly forceful for being such a gentle person. Even with the unexpected bump in their budget, the three remained careful with the extra coins and camped more often than not. The early autumn nights weren't so cold to be considered unbearable yet. However, now that they were miles from Baohu and a few days away from the Capital, the group had agreed to an overnight stay in a small village on the south end of Yingxiong Pass. From here, they'd only encounter a few widely scattered estates and farms, until they reached Kai'yei. While they didn't have much further to travel, they did need supplies for what remained of their time on the road. One night of comfortable beds and not needing to sleep in shifts to keep watch couldn't hurt.

Quite tired of either being jostled by the cart or walking until his feet ached, Daisuke rubbed his lower back after he also got down from the cart. He sighed as he gave Junpei a sidelong glance. "If I never go back over the mountains again, I'll be a happy man."

"You know, it's the funniest thing," Junpei said as he went to check on his horse. "Obito never complains half as much as you do. Really, I don't think I've heard him complain at all this whole time."

"That's because he does enough of it for both of us," Obito commented from the back of the cart, where he was hauling their bags toward the edge to make them easier to grab.

Daisuke *wanted* to argue, but a mischievous little snicker was all that ended up coming out of him when he tried. Instead, he refocused his troublemaking efforts toward their companion, and sidled up next to Junpei, who stroked the horse's muzzle while Obito made sure they had everything they'd need for the night. Because he had to board the horse, Junpei had already volunteered to reserve their rooms at the inn a friendly merchant had pointed them toward; since they weren't planning on getting their supplies until morning, that left the two onmitsu with plenty of time to wander about the village until he caught up with them again. After that, they'd search for a decent place to eat, drink, then stumble back to their beds. They hadn't indulged in such antics since one of their last few nights in Baohu.

"*You* know," Daisuke said to Junpei, voice low so he wouldn't be overheard; he *had* to get in one more opportunity to tease him before the group parted. "Instead of flirting with Obito, you *could* just tell him you're interested."

Junpei spluttered, nearly losing the leather strap currently in his grasp and making the horse snort at him. "I don't think so. No offense to either of you, but you're both a little too...*male* for my tastes...and mean. Besides, I already have a girl back in the Capital. Maybe you should take your own advice, though."

Daisuke blinked, confused. He glanced over to where Obito slid off the cart once more, then back to Junpei, trying to ignore the way a surge of something like hope had wildly fluttered in his chest. Genuinely baffled by the look on his companion's face, the soldier huffed and rolled his eyes, then tugged on the horse's reins to urge her into motion again.

"You're hopeless," he groaned as he started walking away. "Both of you."

"What's his problem now?" Obito tilted his head as he watched Junpei stalk toward the inn with the cart and horse in tow. Daisuke nearly jumped when he realized how close they were to one another, but the tiny crackle of panic went unnoticed. "Rather, what did you say to him this time?"

Desperate to further hide his jittery nerves, Daisuke laughed the exchange off, but he was still failing miserably at trying to put the soldier's words out of his mind. "Come on, it's hardly fair to blame *me* when you know how he gets. He might be nicer now, but he still hates every other word out of my mouth."

"You *do* pick on him a lot."

"I'm pretty sure I pick on you even more." Daisuke grinned as they started aimlessly down the village's main street, burrowed into the warm cloaks Junpei had taken from Baohu's infantry outpost before the trio's departure—apparently, one of the captains was quite insistent on it, for which all three had been grateful. It was still summer when they'd left the Capital, and they'd greatly underestimated how long it'd take to travel, even with Junpei's cart. "Besides, you said that like he *doesn't* deserve it."

"I did not." Obito rolled his eyes, the action somehow fonder than anyone might've guessed it could be. "We both know he does."

They came to the main square, where all sorts of stalls and vendors were calling out to passersby. Endless streams of chatter and intermittent laughter engulfed the area. The pair went by a man selling bamboo figures, another offering delicious-smelling peppered flank steak skewers, and eventually paused near a display of ink paintings to examine the artist's wares. They stood behind a group of women who had stopped to do the same, barely listening to the people in front of them or the various conversations at the nearby stall as it all turned into a monotonous hum. Crickets and frogs sang in the woods behind them as the chilly twilight descended. Slowly, the street became bathed in the warm glow of lantern light; somewhere close by, a flute and guqin duet rose into the air. Daisuke couldn't resist a small smile—it was a lovely evening.

Despite how thrilled he'd been earlier when the group decided to stop for the night, and the soothing atmosphere, he felt oddly restless; he kicked a rock near his foot and fidgeted with his earrings, but his body still thrummed with an implacable energy the longer they waited for Junpei. He couldn't figure out why the weight of a thousand words seemed to be on the tip of his tongue, but every time he glanced at Obito—who was responsibly keeping an eye out for their companion—his face burned and the thought of saying anything evaporated.

He suddenly remembered the promise he'd made before they'd gone to confront Jihuang—a promise to be honest with himself and his friend, although he already knew his own terrifying answer to a question he didn't know how to ask. Junpei's statement from before made more sense. However, even if the soldier's words carried some weight behind them, it was equally hilarious and ridiculous to assume his feelings would be reciprocated; it was a large part of why he'd tried to resist letting them take root for so long. Daisuke subconsciously touched his lips. If nothing, he supposed a little stress-testing never hurt, and at best, he could finally get over his nonsense and give Obito some peace.

Some, Daisuke mentally emphasized with a small smirk, though it faded incredibly fast when his stomach swiftly tied itself into a knot. He'd already lost his nerve at the very *idea* of being rejected—unbelievable. *How pathetic!*

He took a deep breath to summon all his courage. His heart thundered against his ribs; before he could stop himself, Daisuke's fingers had clamped around Obito's wrist to keep him from moving, even though he hadn't shown any signs of going anywhere. He froze when those intense forest green eyes settled on him.

"C-can we talk?" he asked, heart in his throat.

Obito was clearly curious, and perhaps a bit concerned, so he agreed without uttering a syllable of protest. Daisuke moved them away from the ink paintings and off to the side a little, under the protection of a maple tree; the leaves were already beginning to turn bright red, much like his face.

Impulse took over, not giving Daisuke a chance to pick intelligent, clever, or even halfway pretty words. "I...I know we were just messing with each other at the time, but, a-about what we said back at the temple. Would you really kiss me if I let you?"

Obito swore his heart stopped—it certainly felt like his ability to think did. Of course, there was always the possibility Daisuke was messing with him, now, too, but judging by the shade of red coloring his cheeks and the determined look in his eyes, that didn't seem right. Although disbelief coated his words, eventually, he convinced his mind and tongue to cooperate long enough to ask, "Would you actually let me?"

"Yes! I-I mean, I would if you—I-I mean, I-I really want you to, but if you don't—" Daisuke couldn't stop stumbling over his words or his nervous babbling until another shock of impulsiveness jolted through his veins; he really couldn't take it anymore. "Fuck it."

His hand trembled slightly as it released Obito's wrist, then worked its way up to grip the front of his cloak. Even though Obito was already bent toward him, Daisuke still got onto his toes for better reach, and when their lips finally met, it was as if his heart exploded with insurmountable delight that threatened to sweep him off his feet. No resistance, becoming gentler and more familiar as they surrendered to the moment, to each other, and neither gave it a second thought when they briefly parted for a breath and kissed again. Obito's head spun even as he slowly regained his senses. His arm had found its way around Daisuke's waist, and they were pressed close together; he realized he wasn't about to let go, either. Daisuke unclenched his fist, but was too dazed to move otherwise. They stared at one another for a long moment, flushed and lost in one another's eyes, until an interruption made them both jump.

"Finally!" Junpei's voice cried from somewhere in the twilight.

Daisuke and Obito broke their embrace just enough to flip him off.

Kai'yei was a smaller city than Baohu—perhaps about half the size—that rested along the banks of the river which went by the same name. After crossing a weathered red bridge, the Capital was just an hour or so away. They were tantalizingly close to home.

When the exhausted trio entered Kai'yei from a northwest road in the late afternoon, its bustling streets felt like their first brush with humanity in the three days since they turned off the mountain paths. Naturally, they'd encountered the odd fellow traveler here and there, but it was hardly comparable.

Junpei was the only one of the three who could say he was familiar with the city, so he navigated the streets while Daisuke and Obito followed him; they hadn't taken this way to Yingxiong Pass when they first left, and had instead used a different road from the Capital. Obito hadn't passed through Kai'yei since he first came to the Capital to enlist with the onmitsu. Daisuke only ever stood on the other side of the Kai'yei Bridge, where he and his partner met Lord Giichi Tanaka there for an escort a couple years back. He'd never cared for his friend's uncle, and made a point of hoping the man was doing horribly whenever he crossed his mind. This time was no exception.

While it wasn't uncommon to see familiar faces in cities like Kai'yei or Zhao—both the closest neighbors to the Capital—there were certain people Daisuke expected less than others. He squinted in the direction of where he found a young man who looked a lot like Shinta, glasses and all, then nudged Obito and pointed him out to his friend. Junpei, who had been walking with the horse rather than trying to guide it from the cart, noticed the whispers which had ensued in trying to confirm the young man's identity.

He raised an eyebrow. "What are you two doing now?"

"Trying to decide if that's one of our classmates or not," Daisuke answered, using Obito's shoulder for support as he stretched onto his toes, trying to see over the crowd. "That *really* does look like Shinta, though."

"You're going about this all wrong." Junpei rolled his eyes, then cupped his hands around his mouth to yell out, "Shinta!"

For as mortified and ready to murder him as Obito looked, the call got Shinta's attention straightaway. Junpei grinned with satisfaction at his companions when the third onmitsu began to make his way over to them through the crowd. His abrupt intervention hadn't given them time to explain this was not someone they'd normally call out to, and just as he was about to scold their companion and tell him as much, Daisuke realized that list included a surprising number of their classmates. With that thought, he decided it was better to drop it altogether and let the grumpy-looking spy continue toward them.

Shinta huffed when he finally made it. "I'm in the middle of some extremely important and time-sensitive business. What do you want?"

Junpei also hadn't realized they had no *reason* to call out to Shinta, so Daisuke quickly changed the subject. "If it's important business, what are you doing in Kai'yei by yourself? Shouldn't Mika be with you?"

Shinta's eyes raked across the travel-weary group, settling on each of them individually to take them in, and his expression almost imperceptibly softened. Try as he might to hide it, there was a gentleness in his personality he couldn't seem to escape.

He adjusted his glasses and sighed, pretending to sound agitated, though there was a subtle slump to his shoulders and the corner of his mouth twitched down in a frown. Daisuke and Obito looked at one another to confirm they'd seen it, but the third onmitsu kept them from analyzing it too closely when he started speaking again.

"It's a bit much to explain in passing, but there's a decent teahouse over that way. Why don't we talk there instead of being in everyone's way like this? You lot look like you could use a break, anyway."

After weeks of travel, yet another stop when they were so close to home was the last thing anyone wanted. However, Shinta and Raku were quite similar in their pragmatism and thoroughness—the suggestion he needed time and space to explain himself was plenty to make Daisuke and Obito agree. Junpei, who didn't want to report on Baohu's events without them, had little choice once they started following their classmate; on top of that, he worried they'd track him down and bully him relentlessly for leaving without them if he tried. Resigned, he clicked his tongue and tugged on the tired horse's reins to lead it toward the teahouse mentioned.

They chose two benches and spread their things out between them to keep other patrons from sitting too close, but no one said much of anything until the tea and rice balls they'd ordered arrived. The early autumn sun and breeze were comfortable against Daisuke's skin; this moment of peace was soon ruined when a cold shiver ran through him. Shinta was staring at him as if he suspected him of a most heinous crime—he could only helplessly stare back and wonder what the hell he'd done wrong this time.

I'm sure it can't be good. Might as well get it out of the way. He mentally swore at himself, then asked aloud, "I've hardly said two words since we sat down. Why—*how*—are you already pissed at me?"

"Daisuke," he heard Obito and Junpei groan in unison.

"What?"

Shinta shook his head and sighed. "I'm not angry with you anymore, but it's taken a bit—I'll get to that, don't worry. First, though, is what's going on in the Wen Valley. In the last two weeks, Master Yujin's been flooded with reports from villages and towns all over the Wen Valley, saying people are succumbing to some sort of sleeping illness."

"A sleeping illness?" Junpei cocked his head in disbelief.

"You heard me right." Shinta nodded gravely. He took off his glasses, cleaned them on his belt, then set them on the bridge of his nose again before he went on; Daisuke's heart was in his throat the whole time as a horrendous, knowing feeling formed in his gut. "But it hasn't spread to nearby areas like a normal disease would. The messengers from these places aren't passing it on, and no one's died from it yet despite entire towns being affected. The Palace medics were stumped by the list of symptoms for days before admitting they didn't know what was going on, especially because it's resistant to other medications. Fortunately, Master Yujin had a solution, but no damn clue if it'll work. Which brings me to *you*."

Daisuke grimaced when those dark eyes fixed on him again. He knew this would eventually come back to haunt him—with how long it'd been since the last development, he'd foolishly hoped it'd just be further scolding from Master Yujin rather than something this big.

"Told you I was fucked," he grumbled to Obito, who elbowed him lightly.

"Given the symptoms and patterns described," Shinta continued, "Master Yujin determined it had to be the work of poison."

Junpei tilted his head. "Wouldn't the Master of Intelligence recognize most—well, actually—*all* of them, though?"

"Normally, yes, but it seems someone among our ranks thinks these are things to play around with. No surprise who." Shinta's glare intensified. "*Your* stupid little experiment is the reason this is all happening in the first place. Blackwater? Isn't that what you named it?"

"It's a working title," Daisuke sullenly murmured before raising his voice again. "Don't say it like I *planned* on any of this happening—*you* even called it an experiment just now."

"But how could you even let it get away from you?"

"My journal was stolen out of my room when Obito and I went to Zhu last year. That's hardly my fault."

"It was irresponsible to make it in the first place!"

"I—!"

"*Nobody* would be dealing with this if you *hadn't*!"

"Fuck off, my hands are clean! You should be blaming the thief who started this, not me!"

"Does that mean Master Yujin's already sent out teams of onmitsu to the affected areas in the Wen Valley?" Obito's question halted their argument; Junpei sighed in relief, and Shinta nodded after taking a moment to collect himself. "Do you know which ones? Or were you only told about where you're going?"

Shinta blinked, then dug through the pack resting on the ground next to his feet until he pulled out a map. He handed it over, and Obito opened it so Daisuke could also check the bright red markings painted over at least a dozen towns in the Wen Valley. Daisuke's stomach flipped at the sight of them. Whoever or whatever was responsible must've worked with incredible speed to poison so many places in such a short amount of time, meaning it was either something inhuman like the talisman demons, or a large group of people. A small, subconscious whine came from the back of his throat as guilt gripped his insides; so many people, their livelihoods, and even their senses of safety were directly impacted by his naivety. Shinta's instinctive anger toward him wasn't out of line—*his* family might have fallen victim, too, and he wouldn't know until he got word from his hometown. Using their search of the map as an excuse, he gripped Obito's arm tightly for support, which made his partner glance at him. The lack of reproach in his eyes intercepted the self-loathing threatening to pounce on him.

"You haven't answered their original question yet," Junpei suddenly spoke up, likely unable to handle the heaviness looming over his travel companions. They all turned to him, noticeably confused; he shrank a bit. "Daisuke asked what you were doing here alone—you sneaks always work in pairs, don't you?"

Shinta gave everyone a miserable look, though this time, it wasn't directed at any of them. "...My partner was *supposed* to be with me, but I haven't seen Mika in...well, a while, now. He still hasn't returned from the leave he took not long after you two left for Baohu. Master Yujin held off on sending me by myself for as long as he could, but in the end, he had no choice."

Interesting timing on Mika's part...I wonder what he's hiding from, Daisuke thought, brows furrowed. He glanced at his partner; the subtle change in his expression as he handed back the map said enough.

"Where is he sending you?" Obito asked as if neither of them held suspicion toward his cousin.

"The Twin Mills and Kyuumura—Kinumura's the only one of the silk cities that hasn't been affected yet. Since the Mills are smaller, if Mika were with me, I'd have us each take one so we could deal with them at the same time, meet in Kinumura to check things out together there and in Kyuumura, then head home."

"Does that mean you have extra antidote?" Obito waited for Shinta to nod. "We'll take Kyuumura, then."

"By all means. I'd still like to meet in Kinumura before heading back to the Capital together."

"We'll be there, anyway."

Daisuke's eyes widened a little further at each pass of this exchange as he listened—Kyuumura was Mika's hometown and a place Obito liked even less than Kinumura. Even if it was the right thing to do, shouldn't he have volunteered them for the Twin Mills instead?

Since it hardly felt appropriate to complain, he decided he'd wait until later to ask Obito what he was thinking.

Shinta once more expressed his deep aggravation with how awry Daisuke's rather innocent experiment had gone, but his griping didn't last long. Not only did a dirty look from Obito finally shut him up about it, but the four agreed it was better to focus on plans instead. The three onmitsu would meet again in the northwestern Wen Valley, while Junpei would return home, report to General Aki, and request reinforcements for the commanding officer in Baohu. Once everything was sorted, food was finally more important. With the air cleared, a much easier atmosphere settled among them, and even Shinta seemed to be in a much better mood by the time he stood and announced he was ready to depart and continue his journey north.

Daisuke and Obito waved him off while Junpei went to check on his horse and the contents of his cart around the corner of the teahouse, though he was still well within earshot. Once Shinta disappeared among Kai'yei's traffic, the remaining onmitsu returned to the benches where Obito placed their vials of crimson-colored antidote carefully in his pack before kneeling in front of where they'd sat. He pulled out some writing materials, and quickly began drafting a letter, content to ignore Daisuke reading from over his shoulder as he wrote. He either didn't notice or equally didn't mind the light touch Daisuke placed on him while leaning over for a better view.

"We're going to check on Kinumura first, aren't we?" Daisuke asked when it looked as though he'd finished, fanning a hand over the parchment to help the ink dry faster.

Obito didn't respond for a long while, then slowly nodded as if he didn't want to admit it.

"Worried about your family?"

"I shouldn't be." Obito sighed as he got to his feet again. "Shinta's map showed places where the noble and merchant families are generally in good standing with the Emperor—I don't know if that's ever applied to my family. But if the blackwater is being distributed by who we think..."

"Then there's no reason to assume it—or maybe even worse—*won't* find its way to Kinumura. Right." Daisuke bit his lip and twisted the lower stud in his left ear. "But if we're meeting Shinta there, anyway, why not just send *him* to Kyuumura?"

"He's from the Twin Mills. You...didn't know?"

"I..." Daisuke cleared his throat, embarrassed. "I guess I never asked."

Obito decided not to dwell on it; he wasn't sure if he should've expected his partner to know, anyway. "I'm sure he's worried about his family, too, and there's a slightly faster route that splits off from Han'ei Road, which is basically the only way to Kinumura and Kyuumura from here."

Daisuke took a moment to absorb the information, then turned to their remaining companion; there was no way he hadn't overheard everything. "Junpei?"

He looked away from tending to his horse, a smug little smile on his face. "Sounds like you need me to run a message to Master Yujin for you."

"If you don't mind. It's better if we can leave for the Wen Valley as soon as possible," Obito explained as he rolled up the parchment. "Going back to the Palace means we could be held up for a few days, if not longer."

"Well, I *suppose* I could do this one for free, but *only* this time, since I'm already playing messenger boy for General Yuta." Junpei snickered when he took the letter from Obito's outstretched hand. His laughter was cut short when he noticed the two onmitsu were bowed at the waist.

Daisuke smiled at him in earnest as the two straightened again. "We couldn't have done this without you. Thanks for everything."

Since Shinta's journey had just begun, he was determined to use what remained of the evening sunlight to his advantage and make it as far as he could on Han'ei Road, the Wen Valley's most popular travel route, until it became too dark to go further. Daisuke had no idea where it split into the other road Obito had mentioned, but he hoped their classmate could make it at least that far before he had to stop. Junpei was eager for a well-deserved rest in a soft bed at the end of his long, unexpected adventure, so once he had his marching orders from the two onmitsu, he let them have what was left of the supplies and chose to leave for the Capital straightaway.

Before long, Daisuke and Obito were by themselves in Kai'yei for the night as the sunset turned the skies violet and pink; with how late it was, and how much they'd already walked that day, neither could convince the other to head north again just yet. There didn't seem to be a good argument against the idea of a comfortable night's sleep before two more weeks of camping on the roadside while they went toward Kinumura. Besides, although Obito might've been worried, he wasn't particularly anxious to go home.

Exhausted as they were, while they walked the alley between one of Kai'yei's communal bathhouses and their inn—a shortcut verified by the innkeeper—Daisuke's heart pounded with nervous anticipation and giddy excitement. They were alone, now. When they got back to their room, they'd be sleeping in the same bed. Only this time, unlike with the hundreds of other times before, nothing would separate them—they'd be directly beside one another. It was so simple, but meant more than it ever had before.

At least, Daisuke assumed it did; he'd spent most nights out of the last year in Obito's room without a second thought, so perhaps he was overthinking things. However, he'd noticed something different since their kiss a few days ago. There was a new, intense, and entirely inexplicable sense thrumming softly in their shared energy, but maybe this was only a deeper version of the comfort and security they'd always found in each other.

He stopped in his tracks; the absence of footsteps behind him made Obito do the same, and Daisuke's breath hitched when his partner's eyes settled on him.

"What's wrong?"

"Nothing." Daisuke shook his head, the few remaining droplets from the bath going everywhere as he did. Swallowing his nerves, he took two long, confident strides to close the gap between them and grinned. "Just thinking."

Obito's expression flashed between suspicion and amusement. "About?"

"How much I want you to kiss me again."

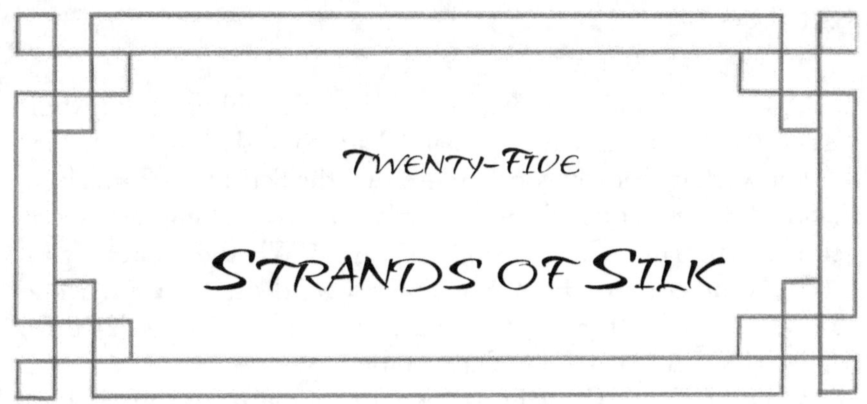

STRANDS OF SILK

DAISUKE BEING LOATHE TO wake early was nothing new, a quirk Obito had grown quite accustomed to, and one he'd often contend with in a no-nonsense manner. The inevitable whining he'd listen to afterward was an unfortunate side-effect of it, but it rarely lasted more than an hour; he could even tune it out entirely some days. However, given how long it'd been since they'd had room to breathe, he chose to let his partner sleep while he prepared them for their journey to the Wen Valley. He didn't mind having a bit of time alone to think about it, anyway; in a sense, the idea of returning to Kinumura felt like going back on his principles. He needed the space to talk himself out of thinking in such a way as he packed their things, or else he'd talk himself out of going.

That, he decided, was an even more unacceptable betrayal of his beliefs. It didn't matter that he'd been told to never show his face there again—the poisoner only wanted to sow discord, whether or not the people targeted deserved it. He couldn't allow it.

He went to the window in their room, which looked out over a thick fog blanketing Kai'yei; orange sunlight warmed the cold, hazy ground in color, and droplets from an overnight rain still clung to the clouded glass pane. Dogs barked in the distance. In the peaceful stillness of it all, Obito let his mind wander toward...everything, really, that had transpired lately.

Considering the information Shinta had provided, Obito had to assume Mika's disappearance was directly linked to the distribution of blackwater in the Wen Valley; judging by the look Daisuke had given him upon hearing their classmate's story, he knew his partner believed the same thing. Naturally, Obito suspected his uncle had originally designed the plot to steal a poison from the onmitsu, and paid to have it mass-produced, though he doubted either Giichi or Mika had the ability to assess the blackwater tincture was experimental from the outset. Either way, he also had every reason to believe that Mika's involvement stemmed from his insatiable need to please his father, unable to see nothing he did would ever be enough. Giichi, on the other hand, had reduced himself to being a useful idiot working for someone else—either the Servant of Zandaka or the Shadow Priestess, and had willingly enlisted his son alongside himself. Consequences be damned, Mika wouldn't say no. Whether poisoning the noble houses and citizens of the Wen Valley was a distraction, a warning, or a test, Obito couldn't say, but he had a feeling it was a bit of all three. It'd be up to him and Daisuke to find out for sure.

He rested his forehead against the cool windowpane. Stupidity was one thing to deal with; malicious stupidity was an entirely separate beast to handle, especially when obstinance led the way. If Mika *had* gotten himself this far into trouble on his father's behalf, there was little chance of talking him out of it. If all his suspicions were confirmed, his cousin was now a deserter and a traitor. Were it not for the written reports and verbal statements Master Yujin already had from him, the Nakamuras might've been implicated in all this, as well; hopefully, the Emperor's judgement wouldn't also fall upon the Tanakas still living in Kyuumura. With how shattered those bonds were, there was no reason to suspect anyone other than Mika or Giichi was involved, but he didn't think either of them had considered—or cared—about their other family members beforehand.

A twinge of guilt squirmed in Obito's chest, but he didn't have much time to weigh why—Daisuke was stirring, and he didn't have the words to explain his thoughts just yet. Besides, at this rate, it would take until nearly noon to convince him to leave for the Wen Valley.

Han'ei Road might've been aptly named after prosperity, as both the lands and people of the Wen Valley generally experienced their lives in such a way, but Obito felt deeply uneasy more than anything else when they at last set foot on the northbound path toward his hometown. At the very least, listening to his partner's endless stream of excited chatter as they left Kai'yei was soothing in a sense. While he initially thought Daisuke would've been less than thrilled to head out again rather than returning home, he seemed to view their extended time on the road as another adventure, a chance to explore more of Perena's vast lands. The more he talked, the more Obito began to feel the same.

However, not long after they started walking, Daisuke yelped and swore as if something were causing him pain. Before Obito could ask what was wrong, a thick plume of black shadow erupted from the first bracelet on his partner's wrist. The force of it knocked the shorter boy into him.

Daisuke grinned, content for a convenient excuse to stay there, until he realized the cloud of blackness hadn't dissipated. Begrudgingly, he pushed himself off to confront things.

"What the hell was that all about?!" he yelled at Tatakai as the dragon demon emerged from the shadows with Jihuang. Obito's soul nearly left his body at the fearlessness—or, rather, the sheer audacity.

"Always so much noise with this one," Tatakai commented dismissively as he eyed Obito, who sighed in exasperated agreement. The dragon tapped a claw against Daisuke's forehead. "Silence, little human. My esteemed sister has something she would like to say."

Jihuang, who so far seemed to be much demurer in personality than Tatakai or Daisuke, gracefully floated in front of her brother and settled like a coiled snake on the path before them. She dipped her head in a bow—and glared at Tatakai when he snorted at the action—then swept the talisman that had fallen from Daisuke's pocket toward Obito.

"As I said before, I was summoned by an odd ritual. An old one, which failed miserably," Jihuang said. "Such a ritual would have required a massive sacrifice of blood and spiritual energy—it would take the essence of an entire human. A putrid soul was used for my summoning, which may also give reason to why I awoke in the state I did. Please, be cautious. Whoever woke me truly called for Tatakai, and my esteemed brother tells me they already have Kanashimi and Saigai. Despite this misstep, I fear this person knows what they are doing should they find all of us."

"Summoning the Demon King," Daisuke supplied, looking between the two for confirmation. He swore under his breath when they each nodded.

"Because of this," Tatakai started, flicking his hair and straightening his posture. "we have agreed to lend you our strength when you call upon us. However, allowing a creature of the Between Realm to feed off your energy when summoned is quite a burden on a single human's soul. I already have your blood, Daisuke, and I will not accept another tithe."

Both dragons looked at Obito, who froze in place, then rubbed his face when he realized what they meant. His mind went back to the night they'd confronted her; Jihuang had already received a small offering from him, when the dagger that had grazed his cheek pierced the sealing tag, effectively forming their blood-bond.

"When you are ready," Jihuang told him gently. "Since Tatakai has already been awakened and bonded well with Daisuke, if you have no need to call upon me while you are traveling, then I agree to be wise and let me sleep. Being summoned is quite an exhausting affair. If you ever wish to use my power, it will be better for both of us if I am at full strength, and if you are ready for the weight of it."

"Let us get this thing taken care of, first," Daisuke answered for him, much to his relief. "And if we find out anything before we get back to the Capital, we'll let you know about it."

Tatakai dipped his head. "In the meantime, I suggest you two meditate together when possible. You'll want to bolster your spiritual energy if you're to find our last two siblings or, perhaps worse, confront the Shadow Priestess you mentioned. You'll need the strength if she has Kanashimi and Saigai bound to her."

"I knew you'd give us more work," Daisuke quipped, laughing when Tatakai blew a plume of smoke into his face. Obito shook his head, unsure how his partner could mouth off to an ethereal being, of all the things—then again, he wasn't sure he *should* be terribly surprised by it.

The dragons both cupped their clawed hands in front of themselves and bowed before another cloud of smoke consumed their glowing figures. Obito took a deep breath, then bent to retrieve Jihuang's talisman and store it in an extra pocket inside his uniform—he'd had a bad feeling this might happen when he first picked it up in Baohu, but at the same time, wasn't entirely sure he minded.

Never mind what this says about my sanity. He sighed, then glanced fondly at his partner, who stood behind him, before he started walking again. *Not that I've ever had much of it, anyway.*

"Obito," Daisuke began, waiting until his partner turned around to say, "...thank you."

Obito blinked. "For what?"

"I mean, well...this entire year's been absolutely *insane*, hasn't it?" He chuckled, but there wasn't much humor behind it. He ran a hand through his hair and scrubbed his face. "Like, nonstop bullshit since we got to Zhu, and we *just* talked to two fucking *demons* for the second time in a month. It's like we've been in constant trouble with the Emperor and Master Yujin. Between all of that, my brother, the blackwater, I...I honestly don't know if I would've made it without you."

After trying to find the best words he could respond with and coming up empty, Obito simply extended his hand to his partner. Daisuke eagerly ran underneath his arm, curling against him when he enfolded him in the embrace, and he happily leaned further into it when Obito pressed his lips to his temple.

SAIGAI LOWERED HIS FLUTE when Lady Shadow coughed, frozen as a small amount of blood appeared in the corner of her mouth. His serpentine eyes urgently flicked to Kanashimi, who caught the Shadow Priestess gently in their claws before lowering her to a fallen log on the ground, where she slumped and hugged herself as she gasped for air. Her dark hair fell from its loose style and a couple of strands tumbled in front of her face.

"You overexerted yourself," Kanashimi tenderly chided; their gaze went to their brother from over their shoulder, silently blaming him for not giving her enough of his power. The Demon of Disaster bristled, but said nothing, and instead allowed a short burst of smoke to indignantly shoot from his nostrils.

The Priestess of Shadow wiped her lips on her sleeve as she steadied herself. Kanashimi offered their hand once more as she rose from the dirt. "But Jihuang *was* here, was she not, Saigai?"

Saigai's eyes roamed the moonlit remains of the farmstead, littered with splintered bits of wood and rusted old equipment; if one didn't know better, they might've assumed him responsible for this mess. With his flute and Kanashimi's help, he'd tracked the faint traces the wretched nobleman—Giichi, he believed the Shadow Priestess called him—and his equally putrid soul left here when the failed summoning ritual cast its haphazard net. Using the music from his flute as a conduit of sorts, he and the Shadow Priestess had been examining the area for all traces of spiritual energy, but doing so in tandem with what Kanashimi needed to help the Priestess's other plans move forward had placed a heavy toll on their human summoner. He didn't particularly care for the woman, but he could sense the tiny fissures forming in her soul—despite his moniker, his compassion toward the human souls that entered the Between Realm due to traumatizing deaths was what had made him one of Zandaka's most trusted disciples. In truth, his sense of mercy extended to most of the souls he came across in the afterlife, and remained the source of his strength rather than his anger.

Finally, Saigai reluctantly nodded. "I would recognize Jihuang's spiritual signature anywhere."

"Disappointing—she was always so weak compared to Wenyi or Hinkon," Kanashimi murmured absentmindedly.

"You continue underestimating our sister at your own risk." Unimpressed, Saigai turned back to Lady Shadow. "As you no doubt realized, Shadow Priestess, Tatakai was also here, along with three humans—it seems they tried to cover their tracks with cleansing ceremonies, too."

"Tatakai?" One of Kanashimi's long eyebrows bounced in the breeze as they raised it in disbelief—they hadn't sensed him at all. "Are you certain?"

"You doubt me? That useless lizard is just as recognizable as our sister."

"Who could have possibly summoned him?"

"One of the three humans, I would surmise."

"Must you be like this?"

"Such a temper—I merely answered your question."

Lady Shadow groaned as she lowered herself onto a half-rotted stump, cutting off the dragon demons' argument—if she'd been in a better state, she might've found it rather amusing. However, her mind was already spinning to work through the same query Kanashimi had made. She rested her elbows on her knees and tented her fingers, then rubbed her face after some thought. "Of course. It was those onmitsu rats we've been worried about. As I should've expected would happen, General Aki never accepted Lord Hideo's offer, so he turned Tatakai's talisman over to Imperial Intelligence for investigation. But if *they* have it, Haruki has either betrayed me or been caught—frankly, I'm not sure which is worse."

Baohu's locals were still chattering about a monster which had allegedly arisen from the shadows just after the solstice; there were several small altars set up around the city where they and tourists alike left offerings to honor those killed by it, so it wasn't hard to find someone willing to talk to an outsider. This farmstead was where the monster had supposedly set up its lair. The city's citizenry also excitedly went on about how they'd overcome such a formidable beast—with the help of three young men, whom one local inn worker insisted she'd personally met. Despite the Senator's attempts to keep them as anonymous as possible, some people had pieced a few things together, and the stories ran wild from there. Presumably, they were same three whose signatures were left alongside those of Jihuang and Tatakai. Although Lady Shadow rarely trusted rumors, one particular detail stood out among the rest.

Of those three young men, one was a Northern Nomad.

A slow smirk spread across Lady Shadow's dark purple-painted lips as the facts of the situation started lining up. She rose and started toward the trail into town again, waving her companions along as she spoke from over her shoulder. "Do you remember those two onmitsu we dealt with in Zhu, Kanashimi? The ones I've asked Haruki to eliminate should she find them in the Capital? As I've told you, I thought back then, the Giahatian boy in that pair was also a Nakamura—he looks so much like Shizune, after all."

Saigai arched an eyebrow, the distrust in his face dimming his vibrant green glow.

"Shizune was a dear friend of mine at one point in time, but we lost contact after her marriage to Lord Takato Nakamura. Wouldn't you agree it's a touch tragic, how I've never met any of her children? Why, they'd practically be my nieces and nephews, if only we'd remained close. I can't help but wonder, with our newest operative moving about the Wen Valley, if I might finally have a chance to meet my youngest nephew."

Kanashimi gave her a worried look—they understood where she was going with this, and still didn't approve, though their reproach for the situation went ignored as usual.

Lady Shadow paused to gently run her hands over the trunk of a maple, its branches heavy with bright red leaves from the shifting seasons. "Rest well tonight, my beloved demons. Once my energy has recovered in a few days, we will need to leave for Kinumura."

Saigai floated toward Kanashimi once Lady Shadow had disappeared up the trail a little way—she wouldn't recall them to their talismans before they were ready. A grim expression had already settled into his yellow eyes when he looked at his sibling. Kanashimi glanced back briefly before their gaze went to the forest floor in shame. He watched as they removed a glass hair ornament from their robes, delicately crafted with purple blossoms. Saigai jumped when Kanashimi's fist closed over it, and their eyes fiercely went to the Shadow Priestess's back once more.

Neither would say it aloud, but both knew they would have to ensure this human stayed in control, one way or another. However, something told Saigai that Kanashimi's goals were much more ambitious than giving the woman whatever power she desired. Demons of the Between Realm weren't supposed to have such agendas; whatever was going through his sibling's mind, he hoped he could talk them out of it soon.

FALLEN GOLDEN-YELLOW LEAVES LINED each side of the road leading to the crumbled remains of an ancient wall at Kinumura's entrance. The mulberry trees standing above the piles of colorful leaves creaked softly under a heavily overcast sky as the cool autumn breeze wove through them. It was a familiar sight, but Obito couldn't place the emotions passing through him, along with too many memories to count as he and Daisuke ducked behind an oak to change into their formal black uniforms and have a smoke before heading into town.

Han'ei Road split at Kinumura; Kyuumura lay three miles up the fork's left path, home to Tanaka estates and a winery which made wine from plentiful mulberries after silkworms had their fill of leaves and both were harvested from the trees. To the slight southeast on the fork's other path, was the northern road leading to two closely neighboring cities named the Twin Mills where silk was processed, dyed, and sold to merchants. As part of the economic deal between the four towns, which were sometimes grouped together as "the silk cities" or "Silk Valley," some of the processed silk also came back to Kinumura and Kyuumura for trade.

In addition to helping around the house, in the mulberry tree orchard behind his family's estate, and looking after his two younger sisters, Obito had spent most of his first ten summers walking the path to Kyuumura with his brothers and cousins. Other times, they'd drag him into their games in the fields between the two roads, where he'd also often find his sisters if he went too long without paying attention to where they'd gone.

This view of Kinumura was also the last he'd seen of the town on the day his father sent him off to the Capital, days after he'd finally worked up the courage and broke the news to his parents about what his uncle had done months prior. He'd had plenty of arguments with his father before, but none like what had transpired then; Takato couldn't bear to have such a scandal in his family, nor could he stand the idea of circulating rumors that might besmirch the family name. Shizune, though furious with her husband, couldn't publicly go against his decisions; not even his eldest brother could have been expected to do such a thing.

Ultimately, Obito was alone back then.

After spending a long while staring at a similar scene in the early summer, he'd turned his back on his hometown, and assumed he'd never need to return. He'd been perfectly happy with the idea of fulfilling his father's request to never show his face again. Although returning now was of his own volition, it didn't hold off the tidal wave of anxiety ready to pull him under; no matter the circumstance, this was still one of the last places he wanted to be.

Daisuke cautiously brushed his fingers along Obito's, startling him from his thoughts as the last of his cigarette burned up. "You still remember everything, don't you?"

Obito slowly nodded.

"We don't have to go."

"...Yes, we do."

"I guess I get it, but...I *also* understand what you've told me about your old man." Daisuke took a deep breath and put his hands behind his back, squaring his shoulders in what was probably one of his best attempts yet to appear dignified. "Look, I know this whole thing between us is pretty new—like, brand new—so, if you don't want to stir up more trouble for yourself...I'll go along with it."

"Why would I do that?" Obito's eyes found Daisuke's again; they'd gone wide with surprise. "I think it's long past time for me to stop feeling ashamed of myself for someone else's sake. My father won't accept it either way, so why pretend?"

Overwhelmed, Daisuke took a moment to respond, barely managing to squeak out, "You're sure?"

"Of course. Just..." Obito sighed, as if he instinctively knew better than to utter the words he was about to use. "Behave? Mind your tongue? Do either of those mean anything to you?"

Daisuke gave him a cheeky grin. "If you insist, but you should know I'm quite good with my tongue."

Obito stared back at him expressionlessly as an inexplicable heatwave passed through his body. When he finally mustered up the ability, he stiffly walked away from the cackling little demon, who was all too aware of what he'd done.

Evil little menace, he grumbled to himself as he began to plot how he'd make him pay. Even so, a smile crossed his face and warmth bloomed in his chest when he felt Daisuke's arm wrap around his. Obito's heart was surprisingly light as they continued toward Kinumura together.

RED PAINT SPATTERED ACROSS the vanity as the hollow *bang* of a fallen paintbrush echoed throughout the High Priestess's personal chambers. She couldn't bring herself to retrieve the brush from the vanity's surface, and helplessly stared at what her reflection showed her as a violent, persistent tremble wracked her body.

After the first two gems on her headpiece became corrupted from their brilliant ruby red into the marbled black and green, she'd taken to painting over the jewels to hide them from the priests, His Highness, and other visitors to the Palace Temple. Those two young spies who had visited her made the importance of doing so exceedingly clear. She'd gotten quite good at keeping the paint within the jewels' inlays, but had apparently become too confident that she would only need to worry about the couple that had already changed.

Just as she'd finished completing this routine, she noticed something off about the jewels at the second and third points of the hexagon. She'd watched in horror as they began to turn black in the mirror. None of her cleansing rituals and no amount of meditation had been able to fortify her spirit against this. Perhaps more terrifying, her worse fears were being realized, one-by-one. Before, she thought these were accidents from some blundering human who had happened across the talismans, but this was far worse. Now, she couldn't deny what the universe was all but screaming at her.

One of the awakened Demons of the Between Realm sought revenge, revived with a forceful resentment so dark and deep, it rippled across the land.

And Hikari, the Goddess of Light and Life, was powerless to stop it.

THIS STORY CONTINUES IN
ACT III: DUELS OF BLOOD

The Keeper Trilogy
Keeper of the Fallen
Keeper of the Broken
Keeper of the Vengeance

Poison and Opium
Dance of Demons
Talismans of Sin
Duels of Blood (TBA)
Realm of Shadows (TBA)
Empire of Lies (TBA)

Maybe we as writers aren't supposed to be super honest in this section, but I'd like to be. Anyone who follows me on social media has probably heard (seen?) me say that this book and I *wrestled* each other from start to finish. But, in the end, we pulled through, and I'm so proud to bring you this story.

Getting this far wouldn't have been possible without Kira, who kept me grounded so I wouldn't nuke the whole thing yet another time. She's one of my most valued friends in writing and publishing, and I'm so lucky to have her (and a double-special shout-out to her for providing the kanji/hanzi on the front cover. Mine is terrible and I even had two dragons mixed up. It was a mess until she stepped in). I'm also lucky to have friends just as supportive and wonderful as her everywhere in the writing community. To anyone who kept me laughing at myself and the boys—looking at you, especially, V.C.; humor is part of my process and you didn't let me forget that—talking about this book, and focused, you're amazing, and I hope your pillow is always cool.

And, of course, I'd be nowhere without my lovely readers. I deeply appreciate you all, and hope to see you for the next leg of Daisuke and Obito's adventure.

About the Author

Alyssa Lauseng is a fantasy author living in Michigan's beautiful Upper Peninsula. When not working as a part-time writer or full-time daydreamer, she enjoys drawing, reading, obsessing over weaponry, and spending time with her family.

She can be found picking on her characters and crying over others' on BlueSky and Instagram under 5FeetofRedFury.

www.ingramcontent.com/pod-product-compliance
Lightning Source LLC
Chambersburg PA
CBHW051506150726
47997CB00001B/132